"WHO ARE YOU? SUPERMAN?"

Better make her forget. "Stella," he whispered, and pulled her will to his. This was one strong-minded woman! It took power to enter her thoughts. He glimpsed more anxieties and worries than a woman should bear. He needed to do something about them. *Later.* He skimmed off the memory of his race down the garden and leap over the gate. "Not to worry," he said as he released her mind and she blinked up at him.

The unexpected vulnerability in her eyes undid him. That and the heady scent of her lifeblood racing thorough her veins. Lust rose like a wild force, and without thinking he threw a full-power glamour over her.

LOVE ME FOREVER

ROSEMARY LAUREY

ZEBRA BOOKS
KENSINGTON PUBLISHING CORP.
http://www.kensingtonbooks.com

ZEBRA BOOKS are published by

Kensington Publishing Corp.
119 West 40th Street
New York, NY 10018

All Kensington titles, imprints, and distributed lines are available at special quantity discounts for bulk purchases for sales promotion, premiums, fund-raising, educational, or institutional use.

Special book excerpts or customized printings can also be created to fit specific needs. For details, write or phone the office of the Kensington Special Sales Manager: Attn.: Special Sales Department. Kensington Publishing Corp., 119 West 40th Street, New York, NY 10018. Phone: 1-800-221-2647.

Zebra and the Z logo Reg. U.S. Pat. & TM Off.

ISBN-13: 978-1-4201-1496-6
ISBN-10: 1-4201-1496-4

First Printing: June 2010

10 9 8 7 6 5 4 3 2 1

Printed in the United States of America

*For George, who always believed in me,
even when he had a few doubts about vampires, and
special thanks to Morgan Arce and Patricia Jones,
for helping sort out Stella's life.*

Chapter One

"How long can we stay, Mom?"

Stella Schwartz smiled at her son. Her feet ached and she longed to get home, but she'd promised—and after a childhood of broken promises, she'd long ago vowed to never go back on her word to Sam. "How about fifteen minutes?"

Sam slammed a clenched fist against his free hand. "Right on, Mom! Thanks!" he paused. "And I know, Mom. Just to look, right?"

Heaven help her! She hated not having money to buy him more, but groceries always took more of her paycheck than anticipated. Thank goodness she didn't have to find money for rent. "Next time we'll buy you a book. This time just look, okay?"

Sam seemed more than content. She turned the car up Fifth Street toward the tiny shop on the corner of Jackson. Two large pumpkins sat on either side of the limestone steps and spiderwebs and furry bats decorated the window. They were definitely ready for Halloween. Sam grabbed the knob, pulled open the solid wood door and all but skipped into the Vampire Emporium.

It had to be the name that first attracted him, or maybe just a nine-year-old's fascination with spookiness, but Sam loved this little shop. For Stella, it was a hard reminder of all the things she couldn't afford, but Dixie, the owner, never seemed to mind that they seldom bought anything and she encouraged Sam to read the books.

"I used to be a school librarian," she once told Stella. "I miss the kids."

The shop sold mostly books, everything from paperback children's books to signed first editions and leather-bound collectors' volumes. They also stocked plastic vampire fangs and capes for the tourists that filled German Village at weekends and the place was now crowded with costumes and face paint for Halloween.

"Hi, Dixie!" Sam said as he opened the door and then stopped in his tracks.

Dixie wasn't there. Instead of a young woman with a soft southern accent, the shop was manned by . . . a man. Stella all but gaped. Talk about a hunk! Tall, with chestnut brown hair brushed back from a face that could give Mel Gibson serious competition and dark eyes that seemed to scan her, taking in every detail, but not in a leering way, more like a surgeon evaluating an interesting case. His wide, full mouth smiled at Sam, and her.

"Good afternoon," he said in a smooth, British accent that set Stella's toes curling. "I'm afraid Dixie isn't here. Could I, perhaps, help you?"

He could go on talking all afternoon as far as Stella was concerned. After staring at him a good minute, she made herself reply. "We're just browsing." She found herself smiling back. "Sam likes to look at the kid's books."

"Browse right ahead, Sam," Hunk replied.

"Thanks!" Sam took off to the far corner and curled up on one of the giant pillows with a copy of *Bunnicula*, leaving

Stella the other side of the narrow counter from a fantasy-come-true with a voice like Hugh Grant.

"I'm Justin," Hunk said, "Justin Corvus. I'm a friend of Christopher and Dixie's, just over for a bit of a visit." He held out his hand.

"I'm Stella Schwartz." His palm was smooth and cool against hers, his handshake just strong enough to feel good. He held her hand firmly but without a macho finger crush or a smarmy squeeze, a very, very nice handshake. So nice in fact, she had to remind herself to let go. She took her hand back and half-wished she hadn't. She found herself breathing fast and all but staring into his beautiful dark eyes. This was nonsense! She had to say something to break the silence that seemed to sizzle around them. "You're visiting them and they left you minding the shop . . . literally!"

He even shrugged with style. "Not to worry. They had a problem with the house and I offered to fill in the gap. They're talking to someone about a sump pump. Seems their basement sprung a leak in that storm a couple of days back."

Stella understood. "I think a lot of houses round here took in water then." Heck, she still had a vast puddle in her basement. "It's the price of living in an old house." And keeping a promise to her mother.

"You live in German Village, too?"

When pigs flew. "No," she shook her head. "I live on Lubeck but I work in the Village. Sam goes to a sitter near here and this is his favorite stopping-off place."

"I'm glad you came by." He offered a slow smile. "It's been pretty solitary here. You made it worthwhile staying open."

What was she to make of that? Was he hitting on her? No. He seemed genuinely friendly but didn't appear to realize Lubeck was a world away from these expensively restored houses and neat, tidy streets. "Been a slow day?"

"Pretty much. A couple of people are supposed to pick up costumes. Other than that I'm spending the time sticking stamps on postcards." He paused and reached into the stack beside the register. "Here, if you're a regular customer you've probably got one coming in the post, but until then . . ." He handed her a rectangle of shiny, cream card stock. "They're having a big open house for Halloween. Maybe you and Sam could come? I gather Halloween is quite an event here."

Where had he been living? The moon? "It isn't in Britain?"

"Not the way it once was." He paused, as if thinking back. "In some country parts they still carve turnips for lanterns and make masks and bob for apples and so forth, and in recent years, we seem to have imported some of your American customs of costumes but it's nothing like you have here." He shook his head. His most definitely, very handsome head. "Dixie's been filling me in on local traditions."

"Beggars' Night really is a major, big deal. It was when I was a kid, and still is. I can't imagine not having it." Heck, that sounded a bit rude. "I bet you have other things, right?"

"Yes," he agreed, "we do. But I must admit, I'm rather looking forward to my first, genuine, American Halloween."

"And all the witches and vampires and goblins?"

His dark eyes seemed to gleam as his wide mouth curved at the corners. "Especially the vampires."

"You won't see as many as a couple of years back. Pokemon and the Hulk seem to be the biggies this year." And she still hadn't bought Sam's costume.

"Your son's going to dress up?"

"You bet! I couldn't keep him home."

"Be sure to come by the shop, won't you?"

"Sure." Why had she agreed? She'd need to drive up here. On the other hand, why not? It was a far safer neighborhood than their own. It might make sense to spend the whole evening up here. "See you on Beggars' Night." Ridiculously, she wanted to. There was something about this man that . . . would only complicate her life. "Sam!" she called. He'd reshelved the book and was eyeing a black velvet cape with the same look he used to give his bottle when he was a baby.

"Coming, Mom." He was as good as his word, stepping up to the register with a happy grin on his face. "Excuse me," he said to Justin, "but how much are those capes and do they come in kid's sizes?"

Stella's stomach sank. She didn't need to hear his answer to know the price was way above what she could afford for one.

"We've only got adult sizes, I'm afraid," Justin replied, and Stella all but hugged him with relief. That took care of that, and they'd get the Hulk one this very weekend.

"Could you get a kid's one?" Sam persisted. "I want to be a vampire for Halloween." She was going to have to talk money to Sam on the way home—something she hated to do, but he had to realize how things were.

"Possibly," Justin said, "but those costumes aren't the sort of thing you can buy with pocket money. You might need to talk this over with your mum. Doesn't she have last say in these things?"

For that he did deserve a hug! *Better not!*

"Yes," Sam admitted. "But one of those would be wonderful." Stella's heart tugged at the wistfulness in his voice. She realized Sam was watching her face, when he squeezed her hand. "Never mind, Mom. I don't want one that much." Hell, he was trying to make her feel better for not having money to buy the Halloween costume he wanted. Something was way off here. Time to go home.

"There is one thing," Justin said. Sam's face began to glow and Stella wished she'd dragged Sam out while she had the chance. This man had better not say they had a cape. "I don't know for sure . . ." He paused, casting her a cautious glance before looking right at Sam. "No promise. Understand?"

Sam nodded. Stella bit her lip. "I know Dixie has some old costumes at home, orders that weren't picked up, or didn't fit. Things like that. Why don't I ask her to check and see if there's anything that might be your size?"

Sam's eyes were as big as golf balls. "You really think so?"

"It's possible, that's all," Justin said. "Remember I said no promises. We can't have you carrying on at your mother if one doesn't turn up."

"I won't fuss, Cub's honor." Sam raised two fingers in salute.

Justin chuckled. "I knew I could count on a Cub Scout." He reached under the counter for a tape measure. "Let me just get your size and I'll have word with Dixie."

Sam happily stood still while Justin measured and jotted down figures on a notepad. Stella began to get a bad feeling. If he did find something, how in heaven could she afford it?

"That's it, I think," Justin said. "One last thing, your phone number." Sam bit his lip—he knew as well as Stella did that it had been cut off again.

"Let me give you my work number," Stella said. "They can take a message and I'll call you back. I'm off tomorrow but I'll be there the rest of the week."

Justin looked up and straight at Stella. She felt herself sinking into his dark eyes. "I'll give you a bell when I hear something." She guessed that meant he'd call her and half-hoped he wouldn't. "Don't worry," he said. "We'll work something out." Ridiculously, she believed him and trusted him utterly.

So, it seemed, did Sam. "Yeah, Mom!" He all but skipped. "Thank you," he added, bestowing his best smile on Justin. "Come on." He tugged Stella's hand. "I've got homework to do."

In the car, Stella came to her senses. There was no way in creation she could afford one of those costumes. Even if it was discounted. She'd just have to call back tomorrow and make that clear.

"Justin!" Dixie would have gasped if she still breathed. "You want me to produce a custom-made costume in two days or sooner."

"Is it too much to ask?"

No, it wasn't and he knew it. She owed Justin a bunch, and if he wanted a rush costume job, he'd get one. It was just she couldn't see Justin, Master Vampire with his Saville Row tailored duds, dressed up as a campy Hollywood vampire. "You really plan on going gung-ho for Halloween? Or rather Beggars' Night, as they call it up here."

"It's not for me!" He sounded almost shocked—much more like the Justin she knew. "Let me explain."

He did.

Dixie was silent a good minute as she digested this. "Okay, let me get this straight. You want a kid-sized custom costume but it mustn't look custom-made and you're going to give it away?"

"Heavens no, Dixie! Stella doesn't seem the sort to take anything even whiffing of charity. I thought you could make it with a deliberate mistake." His mouth curved a little. "Make it up with a flaw near the hem. Something like a selvage showing. That would make it unsellable but if she turns up the hem it would do."

"How come you know so much about sewing?" Stitching up people, he was good at. She still had faint marks on her forehead and under her breast, where he'd repaired injuries. Neither scar had faded after her transformation to vampire.

His eyes went distant. "Long before you were born, I knew a seamstress." He looked back at Dixie. "Can you do it?"

"Of course." She could hardly outsource this, the requirements were too odd. "Give me a day or so and I'll see what I can come up with." She smiled at Christopher, her love, her lifemate, who'd been listening intently. "You two going feeding tonight?"

Christopher shook his head. "No. You want to?"

"No." Over a year vampire, and she still wasn't comfortable with live feeding and used blood bags as much as possible. She was slowly getting use to living off blood but definitely missed Lindt chocolate and Starbucks ice cream.

"I thought Justin and I would take a turn round the village. Just to keep an eye on things."

"You're deputizing him, are you?" She had to smile.

"Just letting him see what I do with my spare time." Christopher crossed the room and hugged her. "You worry too much, Dixie."

"Why wouldn't I? You're taking on crooks!"

"Just discouraging petty criminals from targeting the neighborhood."

They never would see it the same. Christopher wasn't invulnerable, even if bullets couldn't hurt him. "Be careful."

"With you to come home to? Of course." His lips were cool and inviting and she'd much rather he took her upstairs than left to wander the streets.

"Make sure you don't come back with a whacking great hole in your shirt!" She'd nearly flipped out the time he did that. Even if the wound had half-healed by the time she saw him, the bloodstains and singed bullet hole in his broadcloth shirt would have given her palpitations—if her heart still beat.

"Don't you think the pair of us can take care of anyone we meet?" Justin asked.

She scowled at Justin. Now there were two of them out to play "stop the bullet" or "trick the thug," or whatever silly macho games male vampires played when no one was watching. "I don't want to think about what the pair of you are likely to get up to!"

Okay, petty crime had dropped since they'd moved into German Village. So what? It didn't ease her mind to know her lover was swooping the streets discouraging would-be burglars. She'd seen herself how closely Christopher skirted injury. "Take care of him, Justin. If I'm making that costume, I won't have time to repair slashed and punctured clothing."

"You know we'll come back, don't you?"

She'd never had much luck arguing with Justin. "Yeah." She kissed Christopher and hugged Justin and watched them disappear around the corner before she shut the door and went up to her attic workroom.

Velvet. Justin's suggestion of a missewn selvage wouldn't work with the nap, but she did have a bolt end she'd put aside, as it had a row of flaws. Five minutes with a tape measure and Sam's measurements and she had it figured out. She'd make the cape three inches too long and put the row of flaws at the hem. Stella could easily turn it up and make it the perfect length. Or better still—Justin could take it around and check the length and deliver it back after she'd fixed it. That way he'd be invited into Stella's house and could reenter at will when he needed sustenance.

Dixie sat bolt upright and stared at the ceiling. Had she really thought of Stella as a food source? Dixie shuddered but slowly calmed. Yes. She had no other choice. She was vampire and fed off blood—when she ran out of blood bags, it had to be animals or mortals. That was the way her world was now ordered. She thought back to the times Christopher had fed off her before her transformation. Stella wouldn't be complaining and Justin would do right by her.

And Justin would soon be back with Christopher, so she'd better get going. There was enough spare velvet to make a pair of pants. She'd leave the bottoms unfinished to add to the "just something I found" myth and Stella could add a tee-shirt or sweater. Busy with scissors and sewing machine, Dixie almost forgot her anxiety about Christopher. She was glad to be working, and particularly pleased to be making something for Sam.

She missed the kids she'd worked with in her librarian days, and Sam was neat. Bright, polite and an avid reader, heck he was the answer to a teacher's prayer, and obviously Stella's pride and joy. And Dixie liked Stella, admired her independence and determination to get the very best for Sam. Interesting really, after asking for the costume as a favor for Sam, Justin's conversation had been ninety percent Stella.

Dixie chuckled. Could ethical, straightlaced Justin be smitten? She shook her head. Hardly likely. He'd been more adamant even than Christopher that mortals and vampires avoid emotional involvement. No, Justin was just being kindly towards a poor kid. Very typical of him. Besides, what chance was there of Justin ever linking with another female while he still carried a torch for Gwyltha? Not that Dixie understood that after all that had happened, but men were hard enough to understand at the best of times and add vampire to that complication. Dixie shook her head and reached for her tailor's shears and started cutting.

"You're not being injudicious over this venture, are you?" Justin asked.

Christopher braced his feet against the gutter and leaned back on the slate tiles of the school roof. "What do you think?" They had a perfect view over the park and the houses on Reinhart, and one house in particular.

Justin kept his sights on the shadows in the park. "That flamboyance has always appealed to you."

"Can't much help it, walking around with an eye patch gets people's attention."

"Walking around is one thing, setting yourself up as the neighborhood vigilante is another."

Christopher replied without taking his eyes off the house on the corner by the alley. "Justin, I discourage young thugs from continuing a life of crime. Hardly vigilante activity."

"But it will get you noticed. You can't take that risk."

"No one is noticing me, except a few juvenile delinquents and some petty thieves. I'm not out to obliterate crime." He paused. "Now *that* would get noticed. I just aim to get the word out that German Village isn't easy pickings."

"Be careful, Christopher."

Satisfied the two dark figures who turned down Jaeger had passed the empty house, Christopher relaxed a little. "Surely you didn't come all this way just to exhort me to discretion."

"No." Justin folded his hands behind his head. "I came out here at Gwyltha's urging."

That almost had Christopher falling off the roof. "I see." It was an outright lie. What was going on? Had Gwyltha finally come to her senses and come back to Justin? If so, what was he doing this side of the Atlantic? And why would she send him here? "And I thought it was just for old times' sake."

"That too. But she convinced me that if my protégés were living in Vlad's territory it behooved me to make peace."

Dropping to the ground in shock got more probable by the minute. "We're hardly in his 'territory.' That's why we picked this part of the Midwest. To stay clear of him."

"Seems the Northwest is overpopulated and vampires are migrating."

That made sense. Too many vampires in an area meant trouble all around. "He's moving in here?" If so, how could he and Dixie oppose him? Damn! They'd just got settled and, hell, he liked it here in German Village. It took him back to the narrow streets of the London of his youth. "What do we do?"

"Nothing right now." Justin stretched, seeming relaxed, but Christopher knew him better. "He's established a colony in Chicago and is looking to spread out. I'm meeting with him there next week."

"And . . ." Surely Justin wasn't going cap in hand to the man who'd taken Gwyltha. They'd up tents and scatter before he let that happen. "Look, you don't have to do this."

"It's no matter," Justin interrupted.

Christopher didn't believe that for one second. "Look here . . ."

"No!" Justin shook his head. "It isn't . . . now. Funny, really. When Gwyltha gave me the ultimatum, I all but went into a snarling fit. On the flight over, I kept telling myself it was inevitable and to get it over with. But now, sitting here looking at the stars, it doesn't seem that hard. I'll meet with him, claim Ohio for my kindred and that will be that. I don't even feel the rancor I have for the last century or so." He gave a dry chuckle. "Must be the invigorating air of the New World changing my outlook . . . or maybe just seeing you and Dixie together tells me Gwyltha and I weren't suited after all."

Christopher forbore pointing out Gwyltha and Justin had been suited, on and off, for fifteen hundred years until Vlad Tepes took advantage of one of their off times. Still, if Justin was at peace at long last . . . "What next?"

"What next is," Justin paused, head angled to listen, "trouble I think." He stood up and crossed the roof, Christopher right behind him. "Thought so."

Justin was right. A van without lights was parked on the school side of Stewart. "Never thought they'd go for the school," Christopher muttered. "Makes sense. Most houses have one TV, one VCR and one computer. A school is full of them." And if the three louts getting out of the van had their way, it would soon be empty of them. "I'll take care of them." He clapped a hand on Justin's shoulder. "Want to join the fun?"

"What exactly do you have in mind?"

Christopher laughed. "Mayhem!"

"And you deny you're flamboyant! Use your sense!"

"I will. And I'll be careful. Dixie will throw a wobbly if I come home again with bullet holes in my shirt."

"You really think petty thieves will be armed?"

"Justin, this is the United States. Pickpockets pack guns. Hell, children take them to school." Christopher ran his hand through his hair. "We're outnumbered. There's bound to be a fourth driving the car. Let's wait until the others get inside. You get Fred there to open the bonnet and then send him bye-bye and I'll take care of the van."

Justin smiled. "I think I get your drift. Nonviolent intervention?"

"What did you expect? I might be an ocean away from the rest of the colony but I'm still part of it. I'd never harm a human. Give them a bit of a scare, you bet. Terrify them into lawfulness, okay. But harm anyone? What do you take me for?" Kit grinned. "Watch me and follow my lead."

They hung over the gutter and watched. These weren't amateurs. In minutes they had disabled the alarm and seconds later all three climbed in through a ground floor window.

"Time, I think," Christopher said and dropped to the ground three stories beneath.

Justin was right behind him. Brushing off his hands, he strolled up to the driver and requested he open the bonnet.

"They call it a hood, here," Christopher whispered and darted to the front of the van.

Justin's reworded request got results. In moments, Christopher had the distributor cap in his hand, and just in case they happened to carry a spare one with them, he yanked out all the spark plugs as well. And, in the unlikely event they had the foresight to bring another set of plugs, he slipped to the back of the car and pulled off his socks and stuffed them up the exhaust pipe.

"Everything all right." he asked Justin, who was gently patting the driver's shoulder.

"He's out for a while and . . ." Justin reached into the open window. "Hell, you were right." He pulled a gun from the driver's jacket pocket. "Nasty things."

"Never mind, we'll get rid of it. Up for a bit of flying?"

Christopher soared, Justin just seconds behind. Minutes later they landed on the riverbank.

"Nice spot," Justin said.

"Jogging path really, but quiet this time of night." As Christopher spoke he tossed the plugs and distributor cap into the water. "Throw the gun, too. I used to dump them in the pond in the park but decided that was too risky, in case they ever drain it."

Pausing just long enough to slip out the clip, Justin tossed the gun one way and the ammo the other. Both made a heavy splash in the night but the sound died fast and they stood in silence watching the widening circles on the surface. "Now we go home?" Justin asked,

"Nah! Not yet. The fun's just beginning. Come with me."

Kit walked this time, a couple of hundred meters to an all-night petrol station. While Justin mentally translated the prices into pounds and decided petrol couldn't be that cheap, Kit went up to a pay phone and punched in 911. "I just drove past Stewart School. Something's going on there. You need to check. Looks like a robbery," he said and hung up.

"That's it?" Justin asked.

"It's enough," Kit replied. "Columbus's finest always come to a call. They haven't let me down yet. We can fly back and beat them there perhaps, or we can stroll by and observe the proceedings like concerned and horrified citizens. I prefer the view from the roof."

They flew back and watched, hanging head-down from the gutter so as not to miss a single detail. Kit had a point, this was well worth watching. The burglars walked out the front door with the first load of computers, just in time to meet the first blue and white car with flashing blue lights. Two others arrived right behind and the getaway was beautifully botched. Nothing like a dead car to slow things down.

Lights came on in the houses opposite. No one could sleep through the sirens and the shouts. The thieves were cuffed and shoved in the back of police cars. Two uniformed policemen wrapped the van in yellow tape, and slowly the excitement died down.

"Seen enough?" Kit asked. "I'd like to get back to Dixie before dawn."

"She still sleeps throughout the day?"

Kit grinned. "Let's say she's livelier at night."

Justin refused to feel the pang at his friend's words. Kit deserved Dixie after what they'd gone through together, but it underscored his own solitary state.

Sitting with an unread book open on his knees after Kit went upstairs to his companion, Justin tried to assess his own feelings and had a darn hard time of it. For decades, he'd mourned the loss of Gwyltha, felt an empty pang whenever he thought of her. Suddenly the pain had faded and all he could summon up were distant good memories.

If Vlad could give Gwyltha what contented her, so be it. Justin could hardly believe his own thoughts, but he meant them. He'd used up all his hurt. He hadn't lied to Kit in saying he was untroubled at meeting Vlad. All that mattered now was that he establish a clear territory for Kit and Dixie, and that Stella accept his disguised "gift."

* * *

"Have you heard what happened last night?" Stella's neighbor, Mrs. Zeibel, stopped her as she got out of the car.

"What happened?" There was always trouble in this neighborhood.

"Young Sid Day got himself arrested."

Stella wondered how they'd slept through it. "When? What happened?" *Might as well know the worst.*

"Over at the Stewart School. Four of them caught taking computers and suchlike." Mrs. Zeibel clucked her tongue and frowned. "Those boys. I don't know. Their poor mother."

Their poor mother was no doubt resigned to having her sons arrested. She had to be to keep going. Between Sid getting arrested again and the younger one, Johnny, always hanging around with the drug dealers . . . Stella sighed. This was no place to raise a child. She only stayed because she'd promised her mother to take care of her house. *Dumb promise.*

No point in worrying about it now. She had plenty to do now that she'd dropped Sam off at school, but when she shut the door behind her, the man in Dixie's store yesterday was foremost in Stella's thoughts. Justin Corvus! She said his name under her breath as she scraped oatmeal off the cereal plates. It suited him. Polished, smooth—but not in a nasty way, good-looking to the point of dangerous, eyes that did strange things to her thought processes and as for that voice . . . He could talk her out of her panties in a heartbeat. *No, he couldn't!* She had too much self-preservation instinct for that!

She laughed aloud as she reached for the drying cloth. Who was she fooling? Men like that dated bankers and lawyers, not dry cleaner clerks—and just as well. The last thing she needed right now was another complication in her life.

Chapter Two

Justin half-wished he still possessed the ability to take slow, relaxing breaths. He hadn't felt this nervous in centuries. Why did it matter so? All he had to do was deliver a box. Delivering was the easy bit. It was what to say afterward that bothered him. "I long to taste your rich-scented blood," would *not* be the thing to say, but he had this awful fear of blurting it out anyway.

Abel, help him! He wasn't a randy youth or an untried fledgling. He was a master vampire. He had more than enough control to converse with a mortal for ten minutes. Didn't he?

"You okay?" Dixie asked as she handed him a slip of paper with a roughly drawn map to Stella's house. "Want me to take it?"

"No!" Hell, he'd all but snapped. "I'll be fine, Dixie. You need to rest. You've been up all night." Sewing for Sam . . . and him.

"So have you!"

"I have the advantage of centuries."

She grinned. "No one would ever guess!"

"No one ever does, Dixie."

She looked up at him, her green eyes alert as if catching his mood. "I can easily deliver it. The sun's not bright and it will only take ten minutes."

"I want to, Dixie." As if he'd have her run his errands. He tucked the map in his pocket and the black-edged box under his arm.

"Take the car." She held out the keys.

"I thought it was close. I'll walk."

"No." She pushed the keys into his hand. "You want to appear mortal, right? Drive." He made to hand them back, but she shook her head. "A few blocks south of Thurman, the neighborhood changes. It's not the sort of area where people go strolling for pleasure. Drive in and drive out is what anyone else would do."

In that case, what in Hades were a single woman and schoolboy doing living there? "Okay." He closed his fist over her car keys and hoisted the black-and-white box closer. "Thanks, Dixie."

"Just be sure to tell her she can pay me whatever she'd have spent on another costume."

"Will do." He curled his hand over the knob and opened the back door. "Bye, and thanks again."

"And remember to stay on the right side of the road!" she shot at him as he stepped out the door.

Justin unlocked Dixie's car, and then realized he'd opened the wrong door. Would he ever get used to this? He placed the box on the passenger seat and walked around the bonnet and unlocked the driver's side. By the time he finished readjusting the seat and fiddling with the rearview mirror, he could have walked there! But Dixie's caution worried him. She was most definitely not a woman to get overly nervous, and if she thought an area risky . . .

He'd soon find out.

Her directions were easy to follow and precise, and her

warnings about the area were spot on. As he turned left onto
Lubeck, he couldn't miss the boarded up, dilapidated house
on one corner. Now that really did look like a place for
Hollywood vampires or ghouls to lurk! The house across the
way wasn't much better, but it was inhabited. Two shaven-
headed young men lurked on the sagging porch.

Justin checked house numbers. At least Stella's was a distance down the road. Two blocks down. Heck, he was thinking in the lingo. He pulled the car into the curb and looked
around. Her house was shabby but tidy-looking. She had no
sagging sofas in the front garden, nor did she have a rusty,
disused water heater decorating her front porch like one of
her neighbors. Stella's front steps were flanked with a pair of
pumpkins, and a cardboard cutout of a green-faced witch
hung on the front door. Obviously a witch didn't mean the
same to her that it did to Kit and Dixie. Stella was fortunate.

He took the steps two at a time and rang the bell. And
waited. And waited. He sensed a heartbeat behind the locked
door. "Who's there?" Stella asked.

"Justin Corvus, Ms. Schwartz." *As if she'd remember!*
"From the Vampire Emporium." Only Dixie could come up
with that name for a shop the size of a shoebox. "Dixie sent
something she thought Sam might use."

He heard a bolt slide back and a lock turn. The door
opened a few inches and Stella peered out before releas-
ing the chain lock. "Come in," she said, opening the door
wide.

At her invitation, he stepped over the threshold into a tidy
but shabby sitting room. He held out the box. "Dixie hopes
this fits Sam."

Stella looked doubtful but took the box. "Thanks."

"Have a look. See what you think."

She slipped the lid off and reached into tissue, putting the
box on a chair, before shaking out the cape. Her lips parted
as she stared at the velvet hanging in rich folds. She should

be wearing velvet like this. Velvet and the finest satin and lace not blue jeans and a worn sweatshirt. "It's beautiful," she said, "but . . ."

Her skin would surely taste like new cream on honey cake. He smiled. "You don't think Sam will like it?"

She laughed. "He'd love it but I really think . . ."

He could feel the tug between her longing and her anxiety. "Look, Stella . . ." She hadn't balked at his use of her given name, so he went on. "See if it fits him. If so, why not keep it?"

"Because it's more than I can afford!" Her face flushed red with mortification at her admission. He could hear the rush of blood to her face. Abel, help him! He had to will his fangs to stay retracted. He hadn't realized how much he needed to feed.

"We haven't even mentioned a price."

She fixed him with an exasperated look. "I know what things cost and this was custom-made."

Yes, custom made for Sam!

She started re-folding the cape. She really was going to refuse! It would be so easy to will her to agree—she was halfway there, all it would take was a little nudge of her mind and she'd agree to what her heart wanted to accept. He resisted the temptation. Somehow it seemed important that she accept freely. "It was a special order." By him. "But there's limited market for children's outfits." That much was true. "Yesterday evening it was sitting up there in Dixie's workroom, no use to anybody." Because it was still on the bolt. "If it fits Sam, at least someone is getting use out of it and it won't go to waste."

That last line was a touch of genius. He bet "thrifty" was her middle name. She nodded. "Thanks." She paused. "I didn't mean to sound ungracious."

"You didn't. Just careful. No one wants to run up obligations they can't meet. Dixie said to pay her whatever you'd have spent on another costume."

He should have stopped when he was winning. Stella looked at him. "That would hardly meet the cost of the fabric."

"No," Justin replied, and watched as she frowned. "But it's more than she'll get with it sitting in a box in her storeroom, and this way someone gets to use it other than the moths." Now he was tempted to push her will just a little. "And if you promise to bring Sam by the shop, it will be a great advertisement for us."

He sensed her acceptance a second before she spoke. "Thanks." She had a smile that could fell a strong man. How any mortal man had ever resisted her, he'd never know. It made this vampire want to . . .

"Would you like a cup of coffee?"

He wanted her blood, rich and warm and flowing over his tongue. He needed her skin against his lips. "Coffee would be brilliant."

She brought the box with her as she led the way into the kitchen, a bright room with a tall bay window. Justin sat in the chair she offered, glanced out of the window at a sandbox and swing and a dilapidated garage at the end of the garden, and then gave his full attention to the object of his lust. A lust he'd better damn well keep reined in.

Stella filled a kettle and put it to boil. She reached for two mugs from a row on hooks under the cabinets. "Instant okay?" she asked as she measured out spoonfuls from a large jar.

"By all means." Fluids would slow his metabolism down, and about time too. *Of course walking out of here would work even better.*

"Cream and sugar?" Stella half-turned his way.

"No, thank you, just black."

She busied herself, bending down to get milk from the

fridge, reaching for sugar from a cabinet and finally taking the boiling kettle from the stove. "Here." She placed the steaming mug in front of him. The aroma rose strong and fresh but masked by the scent of warm-blooded woman. He took a long swig from the mug.

Miscalculation that. She was staring at him. "You must have a throat made of asbestos."

"Hot drinks don't bother me." *Any more than heat or cold or bullets. Fire could be fatal but . . .* "It's good coffee."

"Thanks."

He remembered to drink the rest of it at a more mortal pace. "There's also a pair of trousers in the box," he went on when she'd relaxed a little. "Dixie thought they might do." Stella was giving him her don't-patronize-me look again. "They're an odd size she wasn't able to sell. They're bound to be too big, but Dixie can take them in if you like."

"I'll fix them," Stella replied. "Or I'll end up owing for alterations as well as the costume."

That was her acceptance as well as her bid for independence, and Justin acknowledged it with a smile. "Think they'll fit him?" Dixie had assured him they were far too big, but wearable under the cape, and the mismatched sizes would reinforce their fable of stray garments just hanging around the place.

Stella fetched the box. Putting the cape over the back of a spare chair, she pulled out the trousers. "Yes, they are a bit big," she said holding them up, "but that's soon taken care of. The waist's elastic and I can turn them up." She folded them away and then picked up the cape, her hands stroking the velvet as she folded it carefully. "They really are beautiful," she said. "Sam will be thrilled. Thanks." She smiled.

It was the sort of smile to shatter a man's mind or exalt his soul—or send a vampire's thoughts down forbidden avenues. She was prospective sustenance not solace. "You'll come by the shop on Beggars' Night?"

"You bet!" She glanced at his now-empty mug. "Want another coffee?"

"No, thank you. I . . ." A great crash from outside stopped him.

"What's that?" It sounded like a small explosion but surely not . . .

Stella had jumped up and now frowned out of the window. "It's those no-good Day boys!"

Children were doing this? "What did they do?"

"They're throwing bottles and trash at my garage." She shook her head. "Do it all the time. They . . ." She was interrupted by a great shout from behind her house and another smash.

"Not anymore, they won't!" Justin said, racing out the back door and down the garden. Without pausing to think, he vaulted the sagging chain fence.

He landed just feet from one youth and inches from another.

The shorter one scowled at Justin, the taller, presumably older one drew his arm back, a glass jar clutched in his fist. A mass of broken glass and stones decorated the ground.

"Stop that!" Justin said.

The younger one laughed and bent to pick up a bottle from the bag at his feet. "You gonna stop me, white man?"

"Yes." It was ludicrously easy. Their minds had the substance of sawdust. The older one lowered his arm to let the bottle dangle. The younger stood up and blinked.

They were children. Wreaking havoc. He relaxed his hold on their minds, just a little. "Why aren't you at school?"

The older one shrugged. "Sid got suspended. I ain't gonna go if he ain't there to look out for me."

Familial solidarity was admirable enough but vandalism didn't seem quite the way to nurture it. "I see." It was a lie, he didn't. Any more than he'd ever understood the innumerable acts of vandalism he'd witnessed over the centuries.

He'd never had an answer before and didn't expect one now. He held both boys in his thrall. "You've a free day. Good. You'll spend it picking up every shard of glass here, and when you're finished, clear the rest of the rubbish from the alley."

The both nodded mutely and at his signal, repeated his directions. "When you pick up," Justin went on, "put everything in that bin over there." He directed their attention to a wheelie bin leaning crookedly against the fence. "And you will never bother this house again. Is that understood?"

They nodded. "Yes." The younger one surprised Justin by adding, "sir."

"Good." He left them bending and retrieving what looked like several months' worth of smashed bottles and rusted tin cans and turned back towards the house. Stella was standing halfway down the patch of yellowed grass, staring open-mouthed. He was struck simultaneously by her beauty and his own stupidity. What was wrong with his reasoning? He'd raced out of her house and leapt the fence without thinking. He *never* flaunted his strength before mortals. Well, he had now! "Ms. Schwartz," he called, "don't worry! They won't annoy you anymore."

She looked as if she wanted to believe, but hesitated. "Those boys are nothing but trouble!"

"Not anymore. Do you have any bin liners? They've a lot to pick up."

That distracted her . . . a little. "Bin liners?" Her brows creased. "You mean trash bags?" She went back to the house and returned with a couple of heavy, green plastic bags. "Think this will do?"

They did beautifully, and with Justin giving their sullen brains a nudge, the two miscreants accepted them with thanks and offered abject apologies and assurances they'd never offend again. The youngest even added a hesitant "Ma'am." Perhaps there was hope for him after all.

It was back in the house that Stella turned to Justin. "Who are you? Superman or an Olympic athlete, the way you jumped over that fence."

Better make her forget. "Stella," he whispered and pulled her will to his. This was one strong-minded woman! It took power to enter her thoughts. He glimpsed more anxieties and worries than a woman should bear. He needed to do something about them. *Later.* He skimmed off the memory of his race down the garden and leap over the gate. "Not to worry," he said as he released her mind and she blinked up at him.

The unexpected vulnerability in her eyes undid him. That and the heady scent of her lifeblood racing thorough her veins. Lust rose like a wild force, and without thinking he threw a full power glamour over her.

She was soft, warm and alive and he pulled her compliant body into his arms. He resisted the urge to caress her breasts and the lush warmth of her woman's curves. *Not now! Not ever!* He'd taste her blood and thus slake his need and the raging desire he barely kept in rein. *Taste her—no more!* He brushed her honey-colored hair off her face and lifted her shoulders so her head hung back, offering her soft white throat. He pulled down the neck of her sweatshirt and gently lapped her skin, savoring her living taste. When she was utterly relaxed and let out a little whimper of pleasure, he nipped.

Never in all his born—or dead—days had he tasted such richness. Her sweet thick blood flowed through his lips, warming his mouth and a heart long hurt. He sucked, knowing he should stop soon, but needing the solace and comfort of her warmth and life. It was her nipples hardening under the loose sweatshirt that brought him back to reason. That, and the scent of her arousal.

He forced his lips off her and slowly licked the wound to seal it. The mark was hidden by her sweatshirt and in a few hours would fade completely. He smoothed her hair forward and sat her in a chair. Only then did he remove the glamour.

"Whee!" Stella shook her head and ran her hands through her hair. She looked around, frowning as it registered she was sitting down. "What . . . ?" she began.

"You got a bit woozy," Justin lied, despising himself but knowing the truth was impossible. And she probably *was* woozy after all he'd taken. "The last few minutes were a bit stressful."

"I've never gone giddy over the Day boys before," she said and looked at Justin as if remembering. "I owe you for that."

"You don't owe me anything." Heck, he now owed her! "Want me to make you a cup of coffee? It might make you feel better." And moving might well help him get a hold of himself.

She shook her head. "I'm fine."

He wasn't the only one lying. They were even. *No!* They'd never be. He'd darn well better get out of here while his resolve held. "Hope the costume works for Sam."

"It will."

He nearly ran a massive, hexagonal, red stop sign, and that gave him the jolt he needed. He had to get his mind straight. He parked, making sure he wasn't in one of the complicated parking zones, and strode down to the park. Gathering a handful of pebbles, he sat down by the pond and skimmed them across the water, but stopped when he realized that was no way to stay unobtrusive. The first two skipped several times and embedded themselves deep in the opposite bank.

He dropped the rest of his stones and looked up at the clear October sky. He was burning with need. Feeding should have eased his appetite; instead it woke yearnings. Dangerous yearnings for far more than a taste of her sweet blood. He was a fool! Feeding in daylight! What vampire in his right mind did that? If one of those hobbledehoys in the alley had seen! He'd endangered Kit and Dixie with his mindless lust and taken unpardonable advantage of a defenseless woman.

He had to get himself in hand. Tonight he'd ask Kit to take him hunting. He had to have blood, and plenty of it, before he saw Stella again.

Justin closed his eyes, trying to fathom what had happened. He needed, wanted Stella—had from the minute she walked into that little shop two days ago. *Two days!* He was going bonkers! No other explanation. Maybe his need for native earth was deeper than he anticipated. Maybe the time change played merry hell with his reason. Maybe he needed a woman!

Why not? He'd enjoyed plenty of liaisons over the centuries, exchanging sexual rapture for their blood. He'd always been discreet, careful. Not one of them had ever guessed his true nature. If they ever got close, he ended the affair. But he didn't want a brief fling with Stella. He wanted what Kit and Dixie shared. A union of souls and spirits.

He had rocks for brains as well as balls!

Impossible! To join their blood union, she'd have to die. As if he'd wish that on any mortal. As if he could. Stella was as unobtainable as her namesakes in the night sky and he'd better face facts.

He needed to return to Kit and Dixie's and arrange his meeting with Vlad. Now *that* would yank him back to reality without any trouble. Giving a dry laugh, Justin shot a last stone across the lake with such force it embedded ten inches into the mud on the other side.

"I think you're beating your head against a metaphorical wall," Dixie said, watching Justin with her arms folded on her chest, "and quite unnecessarily, too!"

He glared at her but she just shrugged. "You're not listening." Maybe she didn't understand, she was a woman after all. "I used her!"

"Oh, for heaven's sake, Justin! You fed off her . . . Okay, *tasted*." She'd caught his frown had she? Good. "How many times have you and Christopher exhorted me to feed regularly?"

"Dixie," Kit broke in, "I think you're missing the point." Justin turned to his old friend in relief. At least he understood. "Justin fed in daylight. We don't do that." Kit's smile at his companion caused a knot in Justin's heart. "Remember?"

"Yes, dear."

Justin wanted to shout his frustration to the skies. Kit hadn't understood either! "Kit, that wasn't my worst concern," Justin said. That got their attention. He glanced up at the window moldings as he braced himself for the admission. "I wanted more than blood from her . . . In fact, I doubt if blood will ever be enough."

Kit let out a slow whistle—or the closest a vampire managed with no breath to draw on. Dixie reached over and squeezed Justin's hand. The unexpected and so human gesture shook Justin.

"It'll work out, Justin," she said.

"Dixie, it's not that easy. Stella's mortal, for God's sake!" Kit said in an exasperated voice.

Dixie turned on him. "For crying out loud, Christopher! Do you think I don't know that? I didn't lose my memory when you transformed me." She gave Justin's hand another squeeze. "So you've fallen for her in a big way have you?"

"She's magnificent. I want to take her and build her a palace on a mountaintop and protect her from all harm and dress her in silk and jewels."

"Yes, well. She might have something to say about that. Stella does have a job to hold down and a kid to support."

That reminder struck like a cold iron. "And I used that!"

"Justin, will you please stop maundering!"

He looked up. She was nose to nose with him and frowning. "You don't understand . . ." he began.

"Believe me, I do. I had firsthand experience of your taboos about relationships with mortals."

That he wouldn't deny, or her cavalier attitude towards the same taboos. "They happen to be your taboos, now."

She ignored that reminder. "Justin, listen to me a minute. I'm not suggesting you flout some immutable vampire law. I just think you should stop beating your breast about it. And to be honest, if the earth moved for you when you fed off Stella, do you imagine she just walked away afterwards and got on with the ironing as if nothing had happened?"

That was supposed to make him feel better? "I put a glamour on her!"

Dixie nodded and gave a wry smile. "Yup, I think Christopher tried that a few times with me."

"Look here, Dixie," Kit began.

Dixie neither looked nor paused. "Justin," she went on, "okay, Stella is mortal and taboo as far as a long-term relationship but heck, why not enjoy her company for the three weeks you're here? Most women would give their right arm and their favorite mascara for a man like you. I don't recommend trying to incarcerate her on a mountaintop, but take her out a few times, feed off her when you need, and treat her well. And when you go back to England, we'll look out for her. Christopher can include her street in his nightly sweeps."

As if he wanted anyone—even his get—including his woman in the nightly sweeps! Except Stella wasn't and would never be his. Justin wanted to rear his head back and howl like the wolves that once roamed the dank hills of Britain, but that would bring attention to them all! He settled for gritting his teeth.

Dixie stood up and kissed him on the forehead.

Twice.

Justin stared. First at her and then at Kit. Far from being affronted, Kit was amused.

"It'll work out," Dixie said. "My Gran always used to say, if it was meant to be there will be a way." She gave him a quick hug and walked out.

Kit sat there grinning like an intoxicated hyena. "Do you always smile like that when your woman goes around kissing other men?"

Kit shrugged. "First time she's done it. If it gets to be a habit, I'll say something."

How could Kit be so complacent? *Because he is so sure of Dixie.* Justin shook his head. Hell, if he didn't have to meet Vlad in a couple of days he'd do best to hie back to England. *No.* He wasn't leaving a day before he had to. "You think I've got my brains in a twist, don't you?"

Kit nodded. "I do know what you're going through, you know."

"Things worked out for you and Dixie."

"Yes, but the events in between were a bit off for Dixie."

Justin ran his hands through his hair. How could he wish harm, much less death, to Stella?

"Thought you'd see my point."

"What the hell am I supposed to do?"

"I think you should follow Dixie's suggestion."

He couldn't be hearing this! "What? Just feed off her a few times and toss her aside?"

"Isn't that what you've always preached mortals are for?"

"This is different!"

"I know!"

They were silent for several minutes. "What the hell do I do, Kit?" Justin asked at last.

"For want of a better solution, be a friend to her while you're here and we'll take care of her when you go."

"It's going to be damn hard."

Kit nodded. "Can't deny that, but think of the old adage about half a loaf being better than no bread."

"Then I'd better feed long and deep before I see Stella again," he paused. "Kit, I'm scared I'll hurt her, take too much."

Kit shook his head. "You won't hurt her. Trust me." He clapped him on the shoulder. "Let's get Dixie and go feed."

Justin left Dixie and Kit where they'd landed in the middle of Schiller Park and set off towards Stella's. He pictured Kit and Dixie strolling hand in hand as they walked up City Park Avenue towards their house. It was impossible to envy them and not feel ungracious. Heck, after what they'd both gone through, he didn't begrudge them one iota of their happiness, but it cut him to the core to realize he hadn't a hope of that with Stella.

He shrugged. He hadn't lasted this long by maundering over can't-haves. Dixie was right. Amazing how a vampire barely past fledging could be so wise. He could make things better for Stella, and then leave her and Sam in Kit and Dixie's care.

Justin ran at vampire speed though the night streets, keeping to alleys when he could. As before, the sudden switch from affluence to the rim of poverty shook him. Some houses showed stalwart efforts to keep front gardens neat and porches swept, but others were tending to dilapidated and a few were fast on the straight road to slum. Stella and her son needed to be out of here.

Stella! Just thinking about her sent his mind and body into overdrive. At least he had his hunger under control. He'd fed not an hour ago from a street person down by the river. Justin wanted—no, *needed* to be close to Stella. He set off at a run in the direction of her house and almost plowed into a youth leaning against a corner. After that, Justin slowed but stayed in the shadows. He was just a hundred meters or so from Stella's but the streets seemed unnaturally busy for this hour of the morning. In the block ahead he noticed several cars parked, one drawing away as he watched. The others waited, engines idling. Justin leaped up to the fence to his left and climbed up the side to the house. From the roof, he'd have a better view.

The dilapidated house he'd thought deserted earlier, wasn't. Several men stood by the open front door and from time to time, went inside and then walked down to one of the waiting cars before it drove off. Every so often, someone went into the house and stayed. *Drugs!* It was the most likely possibility, all within hailing distance of where Stella and Sam lived.

Not for much longer!

Could he do this single-handedly?

Unfortunately not and still have strength to face Vlad tomorrow afternoon—although that prospect didn't depress him the way it had a week earlier, before he'd met Stella.

Maybe he couldn't obliterate the drug house yet, but he could cause a little judicious mayhem. Justin climbed down to the ground. Amazing really how many times he'd done this and never been noticed. Mortals rarely looked above eye level.

Characters he'd identified as lookouts manned the three corners that approached the house. Two of them openly carried guns. Justin measured the distance between them, watching the third carefully, and noting he kept his hands in his pockets. Keeping his weapon and hands warm, perhaps.

Not for long.

Silently vaulting the fence to land right behind the first, Justin yanked the gun out of his hands and ran at vampire speed. Before the punk's shocked yell got the others' attention, Justin had the second weapon and was racing to the third man. That one he had to shove to rip off his jacket, but he had all three disarmed and disoriented. Bundling the weapons inside the jacket as he ran, Justin leaped over the first fence and up into a tree that, praise Abel, just waited to hide him.

An almost bare tree gave little cover but it was off the ground and from there it was an easy leap to the nearest rooftop, which gave a grandstand view of the confusion below. In response to the shouts, a good half-dozen mortals poured out of the house and parked cars sped off with tires squealing. If nothing else, he'd disturbed this night's trade.

Once he got back from Chicago he'd shut up their shop permanently.

Meanwhile, he was stuck with three weapons that no doubt could be traced to umpteen crimes. Kit's disposal method seemed in order . . . but then Justin noticed the brick chimney at his elbow and grinned to himself. Remembering a scene from a film years earlier, he took the first gun, snapped off the trigger and an inch or two of the barrel and dropped it in the opening. He jumped from house to house sending a fragment down each chimney. At a good guess most hadn't been used in years and his contributions would join the debris of soot and old birds' nests. The coat he tossed over a telephone line, where it hung like discarded washing. He'd been tempted to donate it to a tramp sleeping in one of the alleys but decided, *No.* Too risky for the recipient. The jacket would be recognized with its logos and badges, gang colors he guessed.

He dropped the last gun fragment three houses down from Stella's. The general confusion hadn't spread this far so he climbed down and crossed the street, opening her gate and walking up her path towards the pumpkins and the cardboard witch. The front door light was still on, so he slipped into the shadows and climbed up the side of the house.

He found a bathroom window ajar.

And he had her invitation to enter.

He was inside in seconds. Listening, all he caught were two heartbeats. Smiling to himself he opened the door and crossed the landing to the faster heartbeat. Sam was fast asleep, the black velvet cape spread across the foot of his bed.

Stella was in the next room. Her head against the pillow, one arm over her head, the other across her chest, her hand resting between her breasts. She wore a blue-and-green-checked flannel nightgown, the sexiest sleepwear he'd seen in his long life. The soft fabric outlined her breasts, which rose and fell with her breathing.

He wouldn't taste. He'd taken more than enough for one day, but he had to touch. He reached out to the soft flesh under the brushed cotton. She was warm and living and he was desperate for her and was condemned to friendship! He ran his fingers over her cheek and down her neck, gently nudging aside the fabric at her neck. His mark had all but faded. By morning it would be gone. And so would he.

But he was coming back.

He bent closer.

Her eyes snapped open.

"Justin!" she said, frowning up at him.

"Hush," he said, passing his hand over her forehead and willing her back to sleep. Her eyes closed but her lips parted as she gave little sigh.

It was her parted lips that undid him.

He bent his head. Her lips were warm and sweet and soft, a million times more tempting than in his wildest dreams. He pressed gently and they opened like a welcome. She responded with a light touch but a certain one, moving her mouth under his as if reaching for more. He sensed her hunger, the need for physical loving and longed to give all she needed, to have all he yearned for.

He contented himself with a kiss.

He lifted back just enough to trace her lips open with his

tongue. Her breath came faster as she lifted her head. He slid his arm under her shoulders, opening his hand to support the back of her head. His fingers burrowed, ruffling her short hair as he lifted her close.

Their mouths fused, joined in their mutual need. As his tongue smoothed the inside of her lips, she pressed her tongue against his, and a wild spate of longing almost obliterated his reason. Almost. He couldn't, wouldn't, let that happen. He had to keep hold of his convictions and satisfy his need to pleasure her.

His hand cupped her breast through the soft cotton. Her response stunned and delighted him. A ripple of desire shot from her hardened nipple to her mouth as her body shuddered with want.

Justin stroked her other breast. At once her nipple sprung hard and her little whimper was swallowed in his kiss. Their tongues met, touching and tasting as if sipping each other's desire. Now his body responded. Hard. Caught up in wild need that all but engulfed him. A need he had to master. He eased his lips off hers, tracing a path of soft kisses down her neck as she muttered need and longing. He licked the site of his earlier tasting, adding to his ache and her pleasure as she arched and sighed in his arms.

If he didn't leave now, he never would.

He settled her back on the pillow and pulled the covers over her.

"Mom?" Abel help him! He'd been so wrapped in desire he'd forgotten Sam. Seeing Stella slept deeply, Justin left her room and crossed to Sam's. He was sitting up in bed, his eyes groggy from sleep but his shoulders shaking. His eyes opened wide at seeing Justin.

Poor child, waking to find a vampire in his room in the middle of the night. "Hush," Justin said, "your mother's asleep. What's the matter?"

"I had a bad dream."

"Never mind. You'll be all right now." He made certain by casting a light glamour so Sam slept, and reaching into his thoughts to skim off the memory of Justin Corvus in his bedroom.

Justin left the house as he'd entered.

The moon had gone by the time he arrived back at Kit and Dixie's. He'd have a few hours of rest and then he was off to face Vlad Tepes. A week earlier, he'd dreaded dealing with the alien vampire who'd stolen Gwyltha's affection. Now it scarcely mattered.

Five hours later, rested, and fortified by his feeding and memories of Stella's embrace, Justin took the plane to Chicago. It wasn't until he landed and was seated in a taxi bound for the rendezvous that he remembered he hadn't removed the memory of his visit from Stella, and if that wasn't bad enough, he'd held and loved her, without casting a glamour.

He was letting hormones fog his reason.

Chapter Three

Typical Vlad showmanship. A Goth bar! Justin looked around at the dark-clad, pasty-faced mortals and wanted to laugh. He didn't. The atmosphere suggested a dearth of amusement. Crossing to the table in the corner where Vlad lounged with a wry smile on his face, Justin sent his senses scanning. That Vlad hadn't come alone was a given. Justin expected a show of power. He sensed two, no three vampires. Clever. Enough to suggest superiority but not enough to intimidate. As always, Vlad was the consummate tactician.

"Welcome." It wasn't quite Bela Lugosi but not a bad try.

"Vlad." Justin paused at the table and nodded.

Neither offered a hand and Vlad remained seated. Dixie would call it a "testosterone power play." He missed her. Kit was one lucky vampire. A Saturday afternoon strolling in Schiller Park, or helping out in the little shop, or better still, sitting at Stella's kitchen table, beat negotiating with Vlad Tepes.

"Be seated."

Justin took the empty chair, angling it away from the wall. "Interesting choice of venue."

"Amusing, don't you think?" A mortal would have missed the eye movement to the left. Justin was long beyond mortal. He sat upright, every sense alerted to the other vampires in the crowded bar. Vlad went on. "Yesterday a young woman offered to bite my neck. Claimed she was a vampire of the clan of Lilith."

"Did you accept?"

The smile reached both sides of his mouth. "I fear my blood would have overpowered her. If the truth had not overwhelmed."

"She was a believer."

Vlad shook his head. "Of a fantasy. These children enjoy their games. We live in the reality."

"Yes, that's what we're here to discuss . . ."

Justin turned to his right as a silent figure approached. The vampire he'd last seen behind the bar stood at his elbow. Without a word he placed two glasses on the table between them, nodded to Vlad and withdrew.

Vlad pushed one glass towards Justin and took the other. "Gwyltha suggested this would please you, domestic, but drinkable. I value your opinion."

The mere mention of Gwyltha's name on Vlad's lips should have seared like acid. It didn't. Gwyltha was a hundred-year-old heartbreak that eased with every passing day. Was it distance or the rejuvenating air of the New World? As he raised his glass, Justin caught the bouquet of a fine, vintage port. "To a satisfactory resolution."

Vlad nodded, lifting his glass in acknowledgement. Justin sipped. Not bad at all. He held the dark liquid in his mouth savoring it on his tongue before swallowing slowly. "Tell Gwyltha I applaud her selection." By Abel! That was easy enough! It was as if he'd asked Vlad to convey a message to a mutual friend, not the woman he'd stolen. Justin tasted again to focus his thoughts on the business at hand. "So." He put the glass down on the marble table with a soft clink.

"Where shall we draw the line? The Mississippi? You take the lands to the west . . ."

"And leave my colony here adrift among your people? Impossible!"

"They'd have nothing to fear." Justin looked Vlad the Impaler straight in the eyes.

"I know that, my friend, but they don't." He lifted his hands, palms up. "These New Worlders . . . insecure, anxious, uncertain, in constant need of reassurance."

Vlad was mixing with the wrong New Worlders! Those were not the adjectives to describe Stella—or Dixie. "What more reassurance would anyone need than the protection of Vlad Tepes?"

"Certainty of secure territory."

"My people need the same."

"Two, one still a fledgling, need very little territory."

"Who knows how many more there may be in time? Better set boundaries that won't need revision in the future."

Vlad raised an eyebrow. "You envisage enlarging your colony."

"I envisage safe and assured boundaries for both our colonies. With all courtesies of passage and cooperation." Let old Tepes chew on that one. Justin sipped his port, his excellent port, he amended to himself and watched Vlad.

"Are boundaries necessary?"

"Yes!"

Vlad nodded. "I agree. As you will, I'm certain, concede my need for greater territory to accommodate my larger numbers."

"We must exclude territory known to be staked by other colonies."

Vlad grimaced. "Not the best choice of words."

Julian grinned. A deliberate choice of words. Still, Vlad had survived his staking. "Forgive me . . . Now to boundaries . . ."

"I suggest you take Ohio and Indiana."

"And Pennsylvania, Kentucky and Illinois." That should give everyone enough stomping ground for centuries.

"Illinois is impossible. I have an established colony here."

"All four of them?" Justin added the vampire he assumed was lurking outside to follow him. "Set aside Chicago as yours and I'll allow them permanent safe passage."

"Impossible."

"Very well, you keep Illinois. We'll go east. Add Virginia and West Virginia." Even better. Access to the sea.

"Agreed."

"Agreed."

Vlad nodded. Justin reached across the table, enjoying the surprise in the other vampire's eyes as he took his hand. When had they last shaken hands?

"Another glass of port?" Vlad asked.

Justin shook his head. "Thank you, but no. As they say, I have a plane to catch." And this place with its pasty-faced, red-lipped mortals gave him the willies.

Vlad rose with him and walked him to the door. "It's been a pleasure doing business. I never imagined the stern Dr. Corvus would be so reasonable."

"I'm not unreasonable, Vlad," he replied. "My thanks for the excellent port. Gwyltha ever had a good nose for a fine vintage."

Vlad smiled. "A pleasant flight and . . ." He paused. "By the way, I have five. Perhaps you missed one of the ghouls."

Shocked, Justin rescanned the room. In addition to the three vampires, there were two ghouls. Both young women, one behind the bar, the other carrying a tray to a table in the corner. Ghouls! Was there no end to the man's depravity?

"Ah!" Vlad all but chuckled. "You disapprove?"

"You know my stand on that!"

"Yes." He smiled. "They are raised from the grave. You raise from the dead. Is there any difference?"

All the difference in the world. Not that he was about to debate ethics with Vlad Tepes. "Give my regards to Gwyltha."

Regards! The word jangled at the fringes of his mind all the way out to O'Hare. Regards! Was that all he felt for the woman who'd once ruled his life and owned his soul? Regards? Yes. Memories of Gwyltha were just that. Joyous, passion-filled, and sore. But the pain of almost a century had faded. Was this the re-energizing atmosphere of the New World? Or the acquaintance of an intriguing New World woman? And now he was returning posthaste to the same woman and, he conceded, to share the good news with his friends. Vlad never went back on his word, Justin had to hand him that. Kit and Dixie were assured enough ground to roam comfortably for a least a couple of hundred years.

"Be a good boy, Sam."

"You know he will!" Lindy Zeibel, Stella's next-door neighbor, ruffled Sam's head. "Won't you, Sam? We're going to bake brownies and then he can take his bike up to the park. I've got a video to watch later, so you take your time. Drive carefully."

"What video?" Sam's eyes glowed with curiosity.

"Secret, you'll see soon enough." She glanced towards the inside of the house. "I've a pack of brownie mix out on the countertop. You go along, read the box and figure out what we need. And watch the oven, it's already on."

Sam hugged Stella. "Bye, Mom."

She watched him disappear inside the house without a backward glance. Staying with Mrs. Zeibel was never a hardship. "Thanks. I'll be back as soon as I can."

"No hurry. Don't speed, now, and tell your mom I say hello." She glanced into the house where noises of fridge-opening and spoons jingling showed Sam was readying to bake. "And tell her she's got one fine grandson there."

"I will."

"You've got to tell him sometime, you know."

Knowing Lindy Zeibel was right didn't help anything. "Not yet. Later. What good would it do right now to know his grandma's in jail?"

Mrs. Zeibel nodded. "He's fine for now. Ain't anyone going to tell him. Except those Day boys, and he'd never believe them."

Thank heaven! Sam was scared of them and she wanted it to stay that way. Mind you, they'd been noticeably quiet since Justin had confronted the younger ones. No matter how he denied it, she did owe him. But . . . "Must get going. Thanks for keeping Sam."

"He's no trouble, dear. It's nice to have a kid in the house. Drive carefully, now."

Stella drove carefully. Cars were passing her and disappearing in the distance but what did she have to hurry for? She hated making this drive every two weeks to see her mother. Hated the checks and double checks, the questions, the searches and the locked doors. And at the end of it, she had to face Mom's complaints and recriminations. Stella always told herself Mom was under stress, depressed—heck, she was in jail, she was entitled to moan a bit—and it was a daughter's obligation to visit her mother. But it would be nice, just once in a while, to be greeted with a smile or be thanked for coming.

Trying hard to squelch her undaughterly thoughts, Stella parked and went through the motions of the system, the questions, the cursory search of her purse. On her first few visits, she noticed the almost incoherent boredom in other visitors' eyes as they went through the process. Now she suspected her eyes looked the same. It was a means to let the humiliation slide off her soul.

"You're late."

"Sorry. There were road works on thirty-three. They fixed

the stretch on the way back but now they're working on the other direction." It was all too obvious Mom wasn't interested in repairs to roads she'd not be traveling along for years. "Sam's doing real well in school." Mom seemed only a little less bored over Sam's progress. "Did you get the school picture I mailed you?"

"Yeah, I got it. Nice looking boy, you got there."

Stella felt herself warm inside over even that crumb of approval. "Yes, Mom, and he's growing like a weed."

"When are you bringing him to see me, then?" The silence that followed was heightened by her mother's smirk.

"Mom, you know how I feel about that. This is not the place to bring a kid."

"Other inmates have their kids and grandkids visit. I suppose you're just too ashamed to tell your son his grandma's in jail?"

Since Mom put it so bluntly . . . "It's not something he needs to know right now."

"I knew it!" Mom's narrow eyes gleamed. "Ashamed of me, aren't you?"

Stella choked back the truthful response. "Mom, it's not that." She looked straight into her mother's skeptical eyes as she went on. "I'm not ashamed of you, you're my mother. But I'm doing my darnedest to raise Sam to be law-abiding, and I just don't think now is the time to tell him his grandma is doing time for bank robbery."

Mom gave her the full benefit of her hurt expression. "I see." Her mouth became a narrow, tight line. "That's how it is. I suppose next thing, you'll decide you're too proud to come and see me."

"No, Mom!" The accusation hurt. "I've always come and I always will. Didn't I promise?"

Mom waved a careless hand. "Yeah, yeah, you promised. I know you'll come. It just gets me down being here. You don't know what it's like."

True enough. The little Stella had seen was grim—but not grim enough, it seemed, to discourage Mom's repeat visits. "No, Mom, I don't, but I come as often as I can."

"You could come every week."

"Yeah, I could, but then I'd never have time to take care of the house."

That changed the subject fast, as Stella had hoped. "How is the house?"

"Fine. I had to replaced the toilet in the bathroom. Other than that the house is okay." If you ignored the house being two blocks from a drug dealer's Mecca and having felonious neighbors.

"Good, you take care of my house, girl. I'm looking forward to going back there when I done my time." And Stella looked forward to moving away. If only she hadn't promised . . . "That house is special to me, you see."

"Yes, Mom." That was a lie; she never could see why her mother was so attached to that house. It was paid for, yes, but that alone mystified Stella, she never could fathom, or perhaps didn't want to know, how Mom had come up with the cash to buy it. A year or so back, Stella had suggested selling it and moving to a safer neighborhood, not into the yuppie part of German Village, that she could never afford, but she found a nice house up near St. Leo's. Mom had gone ballistic. Caused a real sensation, that had. Stella shivered at the memory.

"Are you cold?" Mom asked.

The unexpected concern touched Stella. "No, not really. Must have been someone walking over my grave."

"Huh! You've got years yet, Stella. Not like me. I sometimes wonder if I'll die in here."

If Mom continued her felonious lifestyle it was more than probable. Stella stayed another half-hour and by the time she left felt thoroughly depressed, torn between annoyance at Mother's moans and complaints and guilt at her irritation. It

was always like this. From the "You're late!" greeting to
Mom's parting, "I suppose you're glad to be going, aren't
you?" visits always followed the same pattern. She should be
used to it by now. Truth was, Stella *was* glad to be going, to
leave behind the locked doors and the stale air and walk
away. Something Mom couldn't do.

As Stella headed south, she tried to turn her thoughts
from Mom to Sam. Beggars' Night was coming and with it
the problem of paying for the costume. It had to be beyond
her pocketbook, whatever Justin might say.

Now there was a man to fill a few idle daydreams—and
get her heart broken, she didn't doubt. Good looking, sexy
as all get-out, and enough charm to lure the birds out of the
trees. For a few miles, she let herself indulge in the fantasy
of Justin asking her out on a date. It would be nice to spend
the evening with a cultured, educated grown-up. Just a few
hours listening to Justin speak would be better than a week's
R & R. *Right!* Talking wasn't what a man like him had in
mind! As if he'd want her for her wit and polish! Stella
chuckled. *More likely, a little diversion to liven up his vacation!* Once upon a time she'd have been right there with him.
Now she had more important things in her life, or rather one
very important person.

Back in town, Stella decided to drop by the Vampire
Emporium and settle up with Dixie. If there was any difficulty, she didn't want Sam knowing. Better sort it all out herself and if Justin was there . . .

He wasn't. Neither was Dixie.

"She won't be in until later, but I'm Kit, her partner. Can
I help you?"

Did every man she met these days have a smooth, British
accent?

Stella looked across the counter at the dark-haired man
wearing a leather eye patch and hoped she wasn't staring. "I
wanted to settle up with her," she said. The man was slender,

but looked stronger than the oak counter between them. "I owe her for a vampire costume."

"You're Stella Schwartz."

"Yes." Why be surprised he knew her? They were partners, weren't they?

"Does the costume fit your boy? Think it will do? Dixie was afraid it might be too big."

"It's perfect—other than needing shortening so Sam doesn't trip on the hem and a taking in of the waist. In fact, that's why I came in. I need to pay for it." She paused. "Justin wasn't sure how much . . ."

"Yes, now . . . right . . ." Kit shuffled through a stack of papers in a file folder. "Dixie left a note somewhere." He handed Stella an invoice. "Here you are."

She stared at the figures. It couldn't be this cheap. "Isn't this a mistake?" Like a decimal point in the wrong place.

Kit shook his head. "I don't think so. Dixie doesn't make mistakes."

"But surely it cost more than this." She knew what a yard of cloth cost and this was velvet!

He nodded. "Yes, it probably did originally, but it's useless now. The original order was canceled and not many people want pint-sized capes."

"It's not just the cape. There were the pants as well."

He stared a minute. "Oh! The trousers!" He shrugged. "Sorry, have to do instant translations a lot." He gave Stella a searching look. "To be honest, you're doing me a favor taking it out of the house. I've been telling Dixie for ages we need to have a clearance sale. We've got three bedrooms and two are chock-full with old stock."

Justin slept in one of those bedrooms. Did he climb over trunks and boxes to get into bed at night? Did she care? She counted out the money and pocketed the receipt. "Thank your friend Justin for dropping it by."

"I'll be sure to pass your message on. He's away right now."

Why the rush of disappointment? The man didn't live here, after all. "He's gone home?"

"Just had some business to attend to." Kit looked almost worried for a split second. "He'll be back."

When? None of her business! Time to get back to Sam. "Tell him I said 'hi' and give Dixie my thanks."

"I will. Be sure to come by the shop on Beggars' Night. Dixie's planning something special."

"We will." She stopped herself from asking if Justin would be back by then. It wasn't important and besides, Justin's business was not hers.

That didn't prevent her from wondering as she drove home, and telling herself she was *not* disappointed he wasn't there. The man had a life didn't he? About time she got one that didn't include fixating on sexy, smooth British accents and dark eyes warm enough to melt your bones.

"I'm glad you're back." Dixie gave Christopher a hug as he came in the door.

"Nice to be welcomed home. What do you have in mind? Hunting or . . . ?" He glanced up the steep stairs.

"Both! But first come talk to Justin. He won't tell me a thing."

Her partner grinned. "And I thought you were welcoming me for myself."

"I am. Every molecule of you, after you get Justin to tell what happened."

"He didn't say anything?"

"I asked him if things went well and if he'd worked things out and he replied, 'No and yes, or perhaps yes and no.' Didn't see much sense in persisting after that. I might not have any breath to waste, but I do have energy."

"Where is he?"

"Out in the backyard watching the moon. He's been out there a while."

"I'll wait for him to come in."

"Christopher!" Now she had a hard time staying patient. "Tell him you're here."

He shook his head. "I'm not disturbing him at prayer."

Dixie knew better than to be surprised. Praying to the moon? Why not? Artemis, Diana, or some Druid deity? "He might be out there all night." She needed to rest and wasn't sure she could wait another whole day before knowing what transpired between Justin and his old enemy. Especially if, as he and Christopher both intimated, the outcome directly affected their life here in Ohio.

"He won't. He knows I'm home." An insecure woman would be disturbed by the strong bond between these two men and Tom, the third of the group. Dixie found it irked her. She was part of the blood bond, but not as enmeshed as the three men and unsure she ever wanted to be. "Stella came by the shop this evening," Christopher added.

"Everything okay?"

He nodded. "Yes. She bought the story about an unclaimed order and the flaw in the cloth. Clever idea, that."

"Good. I'd like to see Sam in it. First time I've made a kid's costume."

"She promised to bring him round the shop on Halloween. It really is a big deal here, isn't it?"

"Yes." She still couldn't get used to the idea of British children not having exactly the same as she'd grown up with.

"You need to get Justin to talk about Samhain."

"I need to get Justin to talk about what went on between him and Dracula!"

"I said I would, Dixie, when Kit got back."

They both turned. Justin Corvus, one-time regimental

surgeon to the Ninth Legion Hispaña, filled the doorway, his face drawn and his skin gray. Did he need to feed? He'd looked worn coming off the plane. Now he was haggard. But he *had* just returned from negotiating with the vampire who'd stolen his soul mate, and come back, it seemed, with less than good news.

"Want to feed first?" Christopher asked. She hadn't been wrong.

Justin shook his head. "Soon. I need to. I refused our Central European acquaintance's offer of hospitality." He sounded as disgusted as she had in her mortal vegetarian days, when she'd once been offered grilled kidneys for breakfast. He did manage a semi-smile. "There's something you need to know."

Of course, neither he nor Christopher could talk standing in the kitchen like any normal friends sharing life-altering news. No, they settled in the living room—Christopher in his usual wing chair and Justin in the recliner, which he pointedly didn't recline. Since they wanted to get comfortable before possibly disrupting her life, Dixie took a little longer and turned on the gas fireplace. She hadn't yet acquired the others' skittishness towards fire. She still saw a fire as comforting, welcoming, and relaxing. But she hadn't survived the great fire of London; both Christopher and Justin had.

"Shoot," Christopher invited, when they all finally got settled.

"Want the good news first, or the bad?"

"Good news always comes first," Dixie said. Christopher didn't argue.

"Territory is not a problem." Justin explained the division of lands.

"Just like that?" Dixie asked. "We get use of six states. Don't the inhabitants and the U.S. government have something to say about it?"

"The government and the inhabitants don't believe we exist, Dixie," Julian said quietly. "Agreements among immortals don't involve them." He had a point, but the thought of a Transylvanian warlord and a Roman surgeon divvying up her country rather teed her off.

"We'll need space to roam, Dixie. We can't stay here more than ten, fifteen years—twenty tops," Christopher said.

That she wouldn't argue. Christopher had been doing this for four centuries, Justin much longer. "So that's the good news." Essentially it was. "What's the bad news?"

Justin paused. If he'd been mortal it would have been for a slow, deep breath. "Vlad Tepes is making ghouls."

Between Justin's tone and Christopher's shocked expression, she gathered this was *horrific*, not merely *bad*.

"By Abel!" Christopher said at last. "Are you sure?"

"I saw two."

Dixie resisted asking where the difficulty lay. It wasn't easy.

"Think Gwyltha knows about this?" Christopher asked.

Justin stared at him as if processing the question. "I doubt he'd tell her. She has rather strong feelings on the subject." He shrugged. "But if Vlad supports it . . . Hell, if I know."

"She wouldn't countenance the making of ghouls." Christopher spoke with certainty.

It was time to ask for explanations. "What's the taboo about ghouls?" Their existence she didn't question. Vampires and witches she'd learned about the hard way, ghouls she'd take on faith.

"Ghouls are mindless tools," Christopher said, "created by some vampires to use as menials, servants. It's abuse."

"Okay, help me out here." She paused as she thought a moment. "Ghouls are living dead . . . right?" Both men nodded. "We're dead . . . or would be if we weren't vampire . . . What's the big difference?"

Christopher looked less shocked the time she'd asked if

she couldn't just feed from him. One look at Justin suggested vampires sometimes needed CPR. "Dixie," Justin managed at last, "it's the difference between life and death!"

"I'm not sure I see it." She turned to Christopher. He'd always been willing to explain.

He didn't let her down this time. "You're right that we're both resurrected, so to speak, and yes, both vampires and ghouls are created by vampires. The differences are immense. We have reason, mental strength, physical power and endurance. When we're strong enough and old enough, we can transmogrify. We heal from hurt rapidly. Ghouls possess none of this. When they're made, or rather raised, those powers are withheld." He paused. "As Justin said, it makes for mindless, immortal creatures who can be used."

"They're chattel," Justin went on, "passed from one controller to another and used for whatever purpose the current owner chooses."

"Like slaves?" Dixie asked.

Justin shook his head. "Worse. Slaves, at least in my time, had rights and laws to protect them. Ghouls have nothing."

"Slaves didn't have much protection here," Dixie added, remembering back to South Carolina history in eighth grade. "But slavery was abolished a while back." Okay a century, and so a mere eye blink in time to these two. "So," she looked at both vampires, "Vlad's got these two ghouls, slaves if you like. What are we going to do about it?"

Chapter Four

They both stared at her as if she'd sprouted pumpkins from her ears. She recognized that look in Christopher's eyes. "We are going to do something, right?"

Justin spoke first. "There's nothing to be done." He paused. "Not now. Maybe later."

"Later?" Dixie waited for clarification. She managed, but only just, not to fold her arms and tap her foot. This was an elder vampire she was dealing with, not a recalcitrant third grader.

"Dixie, I know you're thinking!" Christopher said. Unfortunately, that was completely true. She veiled her thoughts. Fat lot of good it did now as he frowned at her. "We can't just barge in on his territory and offer them asylum. It doesn't work that way."

"Okay, how does it work?"

"Diplomatically." Dixie raised her eyebrows at Justin's reply. He went on. "Precipitous action, even if well-intentioned, would only backfire and result in the vampire equivalent of a territorial invasion. I just went to a lot of trouble to establish boundaries. They need to remain."

"And so those poor women remain too?"

He shook his head. "For now, yes." Okay, he'd pontificated before about time and immortality but even so. "It will be taken care of, Dixie. But not by us."

"Who?" She heard Kit gave a gasp of exasperation. Okay, maybe she was pushing it, but the thought of those two women in eternal bondage . . .

"Someone who has influence with Vlad." Justin paused. "Gwyltha." The leader of their colony. The woman who'd broken Justin's heart. "I'll talk to her when I get home. She has even stronger feelings than you in this matter, Dixie."

"She'll stop him?"

"If anyone can, she will," he replied.

Dixie nodded. "I know." Much as she hated to sit back and wait, she'd been vampire long enough to know Gwyltha's powers far exceeded her own.

"Let her handle it, Dixie. Don't go rushing off on a rescue mission."

Christopher's words irritated beyond measure. "I don't rush off on rescue missions. I plan them in advance!" She stomped out into the kitchen and stared at the never-used stove. She trusted Justin. If he said Gwyltha would handle it, she would. But something burned deep in Dixie's soul at the thought of those two ghouls . . . or were there perhaps more?

The whole thing seemed preposterous. Okay, Vlad and Justin barely tolerated each other, but the two times she'd met Vlad, he'd not struck her as evil. Not as books and movies implied. Powerful, intense and stubborn as any other male on the planet, yes. But if Justin said he'd seen ghouls, he had. He'd been willing to deal with Vlad to ensure she and Christopher had safe territory. The least she could do was follow his advice.

She'd let Gwyltha handle this. At least for now.

"Are you all right."

Dixie turned at Christopher's words. He stood in the

doorway, arms folded, eyes dark with worry. "I will be." She stepped closer and let him wrap her in his arms.

"Sure about that?"

She had to smile. He sounded so concerned. "Yes. I'm sure . . . Each time I discover the existence of another mythical creature, it gets easier to believe."

He stroked her head as he held her close. "Oh, Dixie, what did I drag you into?"

She looked up at him. "By my reckoning, there wasn't much dragging. I was the one chasing across England after you!"

"But you had no idea what you were chasing after."

"I knew what you were. I knew you were in danger and I loved you." She kissed him. "That was enough."

He kissed her back, his lips sure against hers as her mouth opened, his hands, in her hair and against her back, holding her flat against him. Her body responded as always, molding into his as if absorbing his old strength. "I'll never get enough of you," he said into her hair.

"Good." She grinned up at him. "I know Justin needs to feed, and hospitality and all that, but please don't stay out late."

He grinned back. "As if I could, with you waiting for me." His lips touched her forehead with a soft promise of later. "And Dixie . . ." He paused, smoothing her mussed hair. "Trust Justin in this."

She would, up to a point. "How different are ghouls from us? How can you tell one by sight?"

"I've no idea, Dixie. I've never encountered one."

Not in four hundred years! "But I thought . . ." What did she think? "I mean surely . . ."

"Dixie, when would I? Before I met you, I seldom strayed much beyond the colony, other than to make a presence wherever I lived. I never traveled except to change abode and the odd trip to see Tom, wherever he happened to be. We had reunions in Yorkshire every twenty-five years or so, or when a new vampire was created. But contact with other colonies—virtually never. We don't permit the making of ghouls, so I never saw one."

"But Justin knew. At least enough to recognize one, or rather two."

"He's been around longer than I have." Right! Well over a millennium more. "You're still worried about them." It wasn't a question. Christopher knew her too darn well.

"I can't *not* worry."

"Mom, please hurry up!"

"I'm hurrying," Stella replied. Heck, she'd already stabbed herself half-a-dozen times. She couldn't sew any faster.

"Everyone's going to be out ahead of me!" Sam hopped from one socked foot to the other. The combination of vampire cape, white face paint, navy tee-shirt and Rugrats underwear was novel to say the least—almost worth a picture, but she doubted he'd cooperate for that one.

"Give me fifteen minutes, Sam. Go set the timer on the microwave and I bet I'll beat the clock."

He scampered off, obviously delighted to be the one timing *her* for a change, and Stella took the chance to sew in peace. She'd shortened the cape last week, but forgotten all about the pants which looked as if they had about four years' growing room. Still, it was easy to pull in the elastic at the waist, and now she was tacking up the legs against the clock.

It wasn't the finest sewing job but Stella figured it would outlast the evening. "Come on, Sam," she called, "want to go out?"

He barreled into the living room, cape flying behind him, and had his pants pulled on in seconds flat. It took only a little longer to pull on his sneakers and snap the velcro tight. "All ready, Mom." He grabbed up his empty pillowcase. "Let's go!"

She crammed her disposable camera into her pocket, grabbed her keys and followed Sam out into the evening. She could almost taste the excitement in the air. Knots of children and parents wandered up and down the street, cautiously avoiding the end of the next block. No parent in their right mind took their kids up there. People were still talking about the trouble up there a few nights back. One of the older Day boys, in the middle of trouble as always, insisted a winged devil had attacked the lookouts. The entire neighborhood—including strict fundamentalist Mrs. Briggs—now held a passing admiration for winged devils.

Stella took Sam up both sides of the block and no farther; then she bundled him in the back of the car and insisted he wear his seat belt, as all good vampires did.

She parked in the Giant Eagle car park—they could hardly begrudge her the space given how much she spent on groceries—and she and Sam walked back and forth from Jaeger to Fifth, all the while making their way northward to the little shop on the corner of Jackson. By the time they were in sighting distance, Sam had a pillowcase of loot and Stella half-wondered if it was time to go home. No, she'd promised to stop by. It was just that . . .

She knew precisely what caused her to drag her feet. Justin! Not that it was his fault. It was all hers. A couple of nights back, Justin had starred in an incredibly vivid and downright erotic dream. She'd woken up panting and wet. Her wild imagination had rounded off the night with a most spectacular daydream, and now she was scared she'd blush when she met Justin face-to-face.

And so she should. The man had been a perfect gentleman and she'd turned him into a sex object! She'd just have to bite the bullet and get a hold of herself. She only hoped she could look him in the eye without imagining how his lips tasted, or how his cool fingertips felt on her . . .

"Come on, Mom!" Sam ran back to grab her hand. Stella pushed her inappropriate fantasies to the very basement of her mind and let Sam tug her the rest of the way.

Light spilled over the street from the open door. Kit sat by the steps, wearing knee boots and full-sleeved pirate shirt and looking as if his eye patch was part of the outfit. He dared passersby to come in—if they weren't scared of vampires.

"I'm not scared," Sam announced.

"Of course not," Kit agreed. "You're one yourself. Whoever heard of someone being scared of themselves?" Sam giggled. "On the other hand," Kit went on, "what if you scare away all our customers?"

Sam shook his head. "No one's scared of kids!"

Kit bent close. "Why don't you go in and find out?"

Sam needed no second invitation. He skipped up the steps into the packed shop. Given the size of the shop, ten was a crowd and Stella figured there were twice that many: kids with parents, a cluster of goth-clad twenty-somethings and a bunch of teenagers, a bit too old for trick-or-treating, but lapping up the atmosphere. And it was some atmosphere. A wispy cobweblike curtain cut off the back of the shop. One by one the teenagers took turns venturing beyond it while the others waited and listened to shrieks and yells. For the less brave, rows of bright, red apples hung from a ceiling beam. As Sam watched, mesmerized, a young woman tried to bite an apple as it swung and dangled just beyond reach.

"Thanks for coming."

Stella turned to Dixie who was wearing a grown-up version of Sam's cape. "Thanks for asking us and thanks a million for the costume. I still feel I owe you."

She shook her head. "Let Sam hang around a while and advertise for us and we're quits."

"I think my trouble will be getting him to leave." Sam was already edging his way over to the cobwebby curtain, scared but fascinated by the shrieks from behind.

Just then two wide-eyed teenage girls came out. "That's scary!" one of them said just as Justin appeared on their heels.

He, like Dixie, wore a long black cape. It accentuated his height and dark looks. He gazed around the shop, his eyes seeming to search her out of the crowd, and smiled. Stella smiled back. She hadn't meant to do so quite that eagerly, but the sight of him brought back her erotic dream and she half-suspected she was grinning.

"Anyone else dare to venture into the vampire's realm?" Justin asked. A couple of the boys nudged each other but no one volunteered.

"I do!" Sam piped up.

"You don't want to," one of the girls said. "It's too scary for a little kid like you."

Sam gave her a look that showed how he felt about being dubbed a little kid. "I'm not a little kid," he said. "I'm a vampire kid!"

Justin's mouth twitched. He gave Stella a fast glance that seemed to ask, "Okay with you?"

"Fine," she replied and realized he hadn't spoken but she'd understood.

Justin smiled down at Sam's upturned face and bright eyes. "Sure about this?"

Sam nodded. "Sure. Us vampires stick together."

Justin glanced across to where Stella stood beside Dixie. Any signal from her and he'd have refused, but he sensed her agreement. Now that was scary! "That's right. Vampires unite!"

Sam giggled and took Justin's offered hand. It was Sam's utter trust that humbled Justin. That and the swift young heartbeat that walked beside him as he parted the dark curtains and led Sam between the stacks of books and into the storeroom beyond. "Can you keep a secret?" he whispered as he opened the door.

"You bet!" Sam raised two fingers and drew them across his chest. "Cross my heart, hope to die."

How lightly the young speak of dying! Come to that, how lightly mortals speak of vampires. But Dixie had been right, vampires brought in the crowds. "Can we go?" Sam tugged at his hand.

Justin opened the door to the darkened room. Keeping hold of Sam's hand, he pulled the door closed and flicked on the light. Sam blinked in the sudden brightness. "Here's where I share my secrets," Justin said and took Sam over to the bowl of cooked spaghetti. "Monster guts." Sam ran his hands through them and poked the half grapefruit, or ogre's eye. Justin lifted him up to touch the strands of wet string that hung from in the doorway. "They hit people in the face," Justin explained, "and scare them." Sam had been short enough to walk under them.

Sam lapped it all up. Delighting in the frozen, water-filled, rubber glove hands of the corpse and the bowl of raw egg white dubbed "werewolf blood." "Want to try them with the lights out?" Justin asked. Sam did, keeping tight hold of Justin with his free hand.

"It's not scary when you know what it is," he confided.

"But remember, it's a secret."

Sam nodded. "That's right! Vampires unite!"

What had he started? Still, it was fun to see the amazement on the cocky teenagers' faces when Sam strolled out smiling.

"Hey! I bet he didn't go through the whole thing," one of the girls said.

"I did!" Sam wasn't letting that insinuation on his manhood pass. "I did it all: the ogre's eye, the monster's guts, the corpse. I wasn't scared."

Maybe not, but Stella looked worried. Justin needed to talk to her. Kit had come in while he'd shared trade secrets with Sam. "I'll take over a while," Kit said. Justin didn't wait for him to offer twice. He crossed to Stella, as Kit started his spiel. "Any of you lads got the courage of a nine-year-old?" It was an affront no one could ignore. Kit took the first two through the gap between the stacks. Good thing Sam had helped replace the thawing corpse hands with fresh ones.

"I brought him back safe and sound," Justin said, just in case Sam's grin and sparkling eyes weren't enough to reassure Stella.

"So I see." She gave Sam a hug and Justin found himself in the ludicrous position of stifling a stab of envy. Come off it. She was hugging her son! It was just . . . He knew exactly what it was. He'd been longing for her touch again since he'd climbed his way into her bedroom. The sound of her heartbeat had him longing for a taste of her sweet blood.

"Thanks."

She wouldn't be thanking him if she could read his thoughts. "Sam was my assistant."

Sam repeated the "vampires unite" line. "It was fun, Mom." His young eyes scanned the room. "Hey, can I bob for apples?"

Justin looked at Stella. "All right with you?"

"Can he reach them?" she asked. The teenagers were having a hard time getting to them.

"If I hold him."

She hesitated about two seconds. "Go for it, Sam!"

Stella smiled to herself as Justin swung Sam up on his

shoulders as easily as if he'd been a bag of cookies. Sam looked beyond cute, cape billowing behind him and Justin stood within easy reach of the apples. She just had to get a picture. Climbing onto a chair tucked in one corner, Stella angled herself just right and got a great snap between the crowd just as Sam grabbed a bright red apple in his teeth.

A couple of people turned at the flash but most eyes were fixed on Sam and Justin. As Justin set Sam on his feet, still with the apple between his teeth, a little girl dressed as Snow White came forward. For a while Justin did the honors of the apple grab, but he soon left it to Dixie to referee and made his way over to Stella.

"This is some evening," he said. "I'm glad you came and brought Sam."

"So am I," Stella replied.

"Me too," said Sam through a mouthful of apple. She suspected a couple of candy bars had sneaked out of his pillow-case into his mouth, if a chocolate smear on his lower lip was anything to go by.

"Chew first, before you talk, Sam."

He chewed fast. "This has been the best Beggars' Night ever," he announced once his mouth was empty, "and I have the best costume." He grinned up at Justin. "I wish I really were a vampire."

Stella just caught the questioning flicker in Justin's dark eyes. "What makes you say that, Sam?" he asked.

"I could wear a cape like this to school." He swirled it right and left as he spoke. In the crowded shop he missed the full effect. "Never mind," he went on with a shrug. "They are just make-believe anyway."

Justin's eyes wrinkled at the corners as he smiled. "Certain about that are you?"

"Oh, yes!" Sam nodded. "My mom told me."

Justin looked her square in the eyes. She sensed outright

interest and an odd emotion she couldn't quite place. "Don't believe in vampires? What's this?" He flapped a corner of his cape.

"Beggars' Night fun!" she replied. "And speaking of that . . . I think it's time the littlest vampire was going home."

Sam's pout suggested he disagreed.

"I agree," Justin replied. "Where's he going to sleep tonight?" He looked at Sam. "Are you one of those coffin-sleeping vampires?"

"No!" Sam shook his head. "I sleep in a bunk bed."

Justin smiled. Lord, that smile could melt chocolate. "Good idea. I always thought the coffin bit was odd. Has to be cramped. Tell me, are you flying or walking back?"

Sam giggled. "We came in the car. Mom parked in the Giant Eagle."

"May I walk with you back to the Giant Eagle?" Justin asked Stella. And waited.

She sensed he was asking for more than a few blocks' stroll down the narrow brick streets. "Fine," she replied and at once wondered why she hadn't refused. Because Sam was grinning like a drunken Dutchman at the prospect, that's why.

"Neato!" he said, jumping up with both fists clenched.

"That's what I thought," Justin replied. "This way your mother has two vampires to look after her. With all these goblins and I-don't-know-what about, you can't be too careful."

"Don't they need you to help here?" she asked. She didn't need anyone to look out for her. Never had and wasn't about to start now.

"The crowd's thinning," Justin said. "I believe Dixie and Kit, between them, can cope with anyone left here."

So she ended up walking down Fifth Street flanked by two vampires. And oddly, she did feel safe with Justin. Hadn't he taken care of the Day boys? Something about his presence convinced her he would keep her and Sam from harm. That was a dangerous thing to get used to. Sam had no such reservations. He had the costume of his dreams and a sack full of candy . . . At nine years old that was pretty close to heaven. They turned left on Lansing and walked side by side down the street towards the car park and her car.

"It looks weird," Sam said. Sam was right and Stella saw why. Three tires were flat and the car sagged backwards from the one good tire.

"What in heaven's name!" Justin muttered.

"Mischief night!" Stella groaned it. She was close to tears. Not this! There was no way she could afford a set of new tires.

"Mom, this wasn't an accident. I bet someone did this!" Sam sounded outraged. "How could they!"

"Never mind," Justin said. "Let's get you and Sam home so he can get to bed. Then Kit and I will take care of the car."

"It will need new tires." She could hear the panic in her voice.

"Stella," Justin rested his hand on her arm, "it's only a couple of tires."

He had to be rich to think of three brand new tires as "only"! "It's all I have to get to work!"

"It can be fixed. What matters most? Getting Sam home safely or standing here, fixating about three useless tires?" She couldn't deny he had a point. "I'm taking you home."

He did. In Kit and Dixie's Mercedes. Now Sam had yet another highlight to the evening. So, come to that, did she! It was nice to relax back on real leather and purr through the streets. Not that the surrounding luxury could ease her worry about getting her own car running again. Okay, Justin and Kit might get it fixed but she still had to scratch up the money to pay for it. As they turned onto her street, Sam discovered the automatic windows and was waving to everyone like an emperor in his carriage.

Justin eased into the curb. Stella pushed back the longing to ride longer in this cocoon of expensive engineering. Before she could hanker after it another minute, she opened her door and Sam's. Bad timing. As she closed Sam's door, Johnny Day and a couple of buddies sauntered up.

"Well, Stella, if that ain't a fucking pimpmobile you come home in! Got yourself a rich . . ."

The last word came out as a gurgle. Justin had him by the throat. Eyes bulging and feet dangling a few inches off the ground, Johnny Day, the scourge of the neighborhood was rendered speechless. "You do not speak to a lady that way. Do you understand me?" Something that could have been "yes, sir" burbled out from Johnny's mouth. Sam stepped closer to Stella and grabbed her hand. "I will not permit it! Don't ever forget!"

Johnny nodded as the sharp tang of urine filled the evening.

"He peed his pants!" Sam had meant to whisper it, Stella was certain, but the night air amplified his young voice.

"No shit!" said one of the others.

"You don't say that in front of a woman or a child!" Justin went on, still holding Johnny.

Then it hit Stella: Justin believed that! He lived in a world where gentlemen didn't swear in front of ladies. Were they light years apart!

He let Johnny down, not particularly gently, but he did allow him to land on his feet.

"God, man! You nearly strangled me!" The words came tight and muffled.

"Consider yourself fortunate I didn't," Justin replied. "Now scarper, the lot of you!"

Stella figured "scarper" meant disappear. Johnny Day

and his cohorts made the same assumption. Sam was grinning enough to split his face at the sight of the neighborhood tormentors running like spooked rabbits.

"You need a burglar alarm system with yobs like that about," Justin said as they stepped through the front door.

"I need a lot of things," she agreed, "but new tires will have to come first."

"Right." Justin paused just a second. "Give me your car keys and we'll take care of that. I doubt we can do it overnight. Let me take you to work tomorrow. With a bit of luck, we can have your car ready by the time you finish."

The thought of not having to cope with tire dealers, to say nothing of calling and waiting for the tow truck, seduced her. "I need to be there at nine."

"What about Sam getting to school?'

"He rides the bus."

"Yeah! And if I don't get to bed, I'll never get up in the morning!" They both turned at Sam's contribution to the conversation. "Mom, I'm going upstairs. Come give me a kiss when you're ready. 'Night, Dr. Corvus."

When would surprises cease? Stella stared as Sam went upstairs, toting his pillowcase behind him. "He never goes off to bed on his own like that."

"Maybe, he decided I needed you to myself."

Stella's throat went dry, as something stirred deep inside her. "Why would you need that?" Dumb, dumb question. She wasn't that far out of the loop!

He chuckled, deep, slow and sexy. If she'd had any smarts she'd have run a mile. Obviously, she had no smarts. She wanted to be kissed senseless by Justin Corvus, to be held by strong arms that could hold a child and terrorize a thug, to listen to his rich voice whisper in her ear. She didn't remember stepping into his embrace but could barely recollect her life before he pulled her close and locked his arms around her. She lifted her face to his, heart racing and lips parted in anticipation.

Anticipation was nothing! Her mind went off in a wild spiral of desire as his lips parted hers. She pressed herself against him, relishing the feel of a hard male body, the force of his chest against her breasts and the strength in his legs. His tongue found hers and she forgot all about his body, could only concentrate on his kiss.

Two could play that game! She matched him thrust for thrust and stroke for stroke. Meeting his desire with more. He was strength and comfort and need and want and he offered more than she'd ever dreamed. Or had she never had time to dream?

She didn't care, not with his hand on her breast. She gave her mind over to Justin and pleasure, angling her head back as he pressed a row of soft kisses down her neck. Her legs went soft with need and heat. Only his arms held her upright as he slowly licked the base of her neck. She clutched his sweater and gave a little moan as wild, sweet pleasure invaded her brain.

She could still stand. She'd half-expected to collapse in a boneless heap on the floor.

"I've got to leave, Stella," Justin said. "I'll wait outside while you lock up, and I'll be back to pick you up in the morning." She nodded. She wasn't too sure she could get her mind around words. "See you then."

"Wait!" She managed that much. Should she get adventurous and try a whole sentence? "Justin, thanks for bringing us home, and giving Sam such a great time and . . ." She paused, not sure if she wanted to say, "For kissing me witless!"

He seemed to understand. "The feeling's mutual. Don't worry about the car. Kit and Dixie have business contacts here. We'll find someone to give you a good deal."

The street was clear when he left. That was a relief! She'd half-expected Johnny Day to be messing up Justin's car, but they were nowhere in sight. Seemed a man ready to stand up to them was all it took to intimidate that bunch. She locked the door and went upstairs to tuck Sam in for the night.

He was half asleep. "Do you like Dr. Corvus, Mom?" he asked. What a question! And one she should have expected. "He's been a good friend."

"Wish he was a real vampire."

"They're only make-believe, you know that."

"I know." He opened both eyes and smiled. "But he looked like a real one when he grabbed Johnny Day like that. Lifted him off the ground!" She'd noticed. For a few seconds she'd been scared Justin would go too far, but she knew in her heart he never would. Even hurting a street punk was something Justin would never do without extreme provocation. "Can't wait to tell Tony, and everyone at school, how Johnny peed his pants on our sidewalk!"

She hoped there were no repercussions about that.

Stella fell into bed and all but collapsed into a deep sleep. If she'd overheard the conversation a few blocks away, she wouldn't have slept so easily.

"I'm going to get her . . . and him," Johnny Day hissed.

"Yeah?" Warty Watson, his right-hand man and part-time sycophant, muttered. He had a sore jaw from the punch he'd gotten earlier for laughing at Johnny's stained pants.

"I'm gonna see to the bitch," Johnny said. "She'll get what's coming to her."

"And him," Warty added. "You owe him too. What you gonna do?"

Johnny thought a minute. Thinking wasn't his strongest point. "Plug her with lead!" he announced. "Shoot her dead.

And him. Thinks he's so great with that big car and that stuck-up voice." He paused to smile. "Let's see how he sounds as he gets bullet after bullet in his chest."

"Maybe we should get them separate," Warty suggested. "One at a time like."

Johnny thumped him between the shoulder blades. "Maybe we just will. Of course, we could get the kid first."

Warty shook his head. Even he had his limits. "No, leave the kid. He's harmless."

Chapter Five

"You don't want much, do you?" Dixie raised her eyebrows at Justin. "Just a twenty-four hour tire store." She folded the cobweb curtain and packed it into a box. "I don't believe such a thing exists."

"You have all-night grocery stores and all-night discount stores," Kit pointed out as he removed the remaining apples from the beam.

While Justin took Stella and Sam home, the party had wound down and now Kit and Dixie almost had the shop back to normal. If a vampire emporium could ever count as normal in a mortal world.

"Yes," Dixie agreed, "but all-night tire merchants? I think not. Check the yellow pages if you don't believe me."

Justin believed her. He just wanted to get Stella's car running before morning.

"What do you think happened?" Kit asked.

"Random, senseless vandalism," Justin replied. "Nothing new in that!" He'd seen plenty over the centuries. "Damn it, though! She needs that car. She can't afford a set of new tires and I know she'll cut up rough if I try to pay for them."

Kit nodded. "Yeah, I can see that. We can't exactly claim Dixie just happened to have a spare set of tires, the exact size, that she never plans to use."

"Get the car fixed first thing in the morning and then worry about your fiction," Dixie advised. She looked right at him, her green eyes sharp as daylight. "You're not stringing her along, are you?"

Good question! He'd had liaisons over the centuries. Once, just after Gwyltha's defection to Vlad, he'd even left the colony to dwell with a mortal, until Charlotte had died of pneumonia. Much as the thought of courting Stella appealed, Justin knew he couldn't leave the colony, not when Kit and Dixie depended on him. Dixie was so new to their life and much as Kit loved her, she was only the second vampire he'd created. No, they needed the support of an elder vampire more than he needed to succumb to wild desires. Doing the right thing didn't get any easier with time.

"Well, are you?" Dixie persisted sounding every bit like the librarian she'd been as a mortal.

"Dixie . . ." Kit began.

"Never mind." Justin shook his head at Kit. "It's a fair enough question." He looked at Dixie. "I'm not stringing her along, at least I hope not. She's mortal. I'm here for a short while. If things were otherwise, who knows. But . . ." He shrugged, "As it is, I plan to do what I can. What I'd really like is to get her and Sam out of that hellish neighborhood, find her a decent house, and set her up for life." He grinned at Dixie. "And while I'm at it, burn that crack house to the ground. To think of that god-forsaken construction just yards from where Stella lives . . ."

Dixie nodded. "Can't say I'd argue with any of that, but you'd better start with a set of tires. The rest might be a bit harder." She didn't add "even for a vampire," but her eyes said it. Then, to his utter surprise, she stepped around the box she was packing and kissed him. "You're a good guy,

Justin," she said and turned back to gather up a row of furry black spiders decorating the cash register.

Not sure what to make of that kiss, Justin turned to Kit. He was grinning like a painted clown at Twelfth Night revels. "What's so amusing?" Justin asked and knew he didn't want to hear the answer.

"Nothing much." Kit Marlowe was a lousy liar but Justin was obliged to him for the effort. "Want to go hunting after we finish clearing up here?"

Justin shook his head. "Don't need to."

That got their attention! Dixie froze mid-stride, a life-size plastic skeleton draped over one arm.

Kit gave an annoyingly, knowing smirk. "Want to run off a bit of surplus energy?"

Talk about an offer he couldn't refuse! Decorations stripped down and boxed, they locked up the shop and walked Dixie back to their house on City Park Avenue.

"Want to run with us?" Kit asked as he unlocked the front door.

She shook her head. "Another time. I'm not in the mood for testosterone talk." She kissed Kit. "Take care, and while you're gone, I'll check the yellow pages and figure out the nearest tire place."

"You've got a damn good woman there," Justin said as the wrought iron gate clanged behind them.

"I know."

"Think she'd baby-sit Sam if I convinced Stella to come out with me?"

"You'd better ask her when we get back." He grinned. "Race you downtown!"

Kit started down Sycamore. Justin caught up with him seconds later as he turned on High, and they raced neck and neck towards downtown. A party of revelers outside Hosters noticed a sudden breeze, and a pair of cops parked in front of the courthouse looked up as a thud echoed on the roof of their car but no one else noticed the passing of a pair of vampires.

"Did you have to smack that police car as we went by?" Justin asked as they stopped on the grass in front of the capitol. "Not exactly discreet, was it?"

"No," Kit agreed, "but I thought lecturing me about appropriate and discreet behavior might get your mind off woman troubles."

"If you think it's that easy . . ." Justin muttered. Hell, he knew Kit didn't. He looked around. Behind them rose the marble steps to the capitol building and to their right a monument with a cluster of statues. "They don't have to worry about living around mortals, do they?"

"They don't have much fun either."

Justin wasn't sure what he was going through constituted "fun." "Who are they?" He took a couple of strides closer, Kit on his heels.

"Ohio's noble sons." Kit gave a little chuckle. "Dixie almost threw a wobbly when she saw this. Seems three of the noble sons are regarded as something less than heroic where she comes from."

"Right." Justin looked up at the dark shapes. "That war of theirs. She still hasn't adjusted her sights to immortality, then."

"I think she has her own slant on immortality." Kit elbowed him. "Come on, then. Want to climb the dome or the Huntington Tower?"

"Let's go for the taller one."

They jumped the street and climbed side by side. The capitol would have been easier—stone gave better anchorage than glass—but concentrating on handholds kept Justin's mind off his other quandary. At the top of the building, they found a perch overlooking the river. The water gleamed black far beneath their feet, the lights of the city spread away in all directions like a million glowing hopes.

They sat in silence for several minutes. An airplane crossed overhead, lights blinking, but few sounds drifted this high.

"Are you sure you know what you're doing?" Kit asked after a while. "With Stella, I mean."

"Hell, if I know," Justin muttered. "I know what I want to do, and what's best for her and Sam, and I can do it, but will she let me?"

"Most likely not."

"Thanks for the encouragement!"

Justin sensed Kit's smile. "Sorry, I thought you wanted the truth."

He'd ignore that. "Hell, the minute I mentioned getting tires, I could sense her adding up the cost and working out how the hell she'd pay for them." He paused. "Why can't she see common sense?"

"She does. She just sees a different common sense from yours."

"Full of clever answers tonight, aren't you?" That was unfair. "Kit, what the hell am I going to do?"

"About the tire problem or the more general question of you getting hooked up with a mortal?"

Justin growled, "Going to lecture me on ethics and morality?"

"No!" Kit shook his head. "You don't need my help for that. Shall we address the more immediate issue of a set of new tires?"

"Yes." What was he to do? Just get the tries, park the car in front of her house and disappear, make her accept them?

"Not necessary," Kit said. "And by the way, better practice veiling your mind, don't want Dixie peeking into your lascivious thoughts."

"All right, know-it-all, what do I do, then?"

Kit pondered a few minutes. "How about telling her the truth?"

Justin grabbed the side of the building to keep himself from tumbling off in shock. Kit's brains had to be turning to cream cheese away from his native soil. "Stella, excuse me, I'm a vampire and I'd like you for dinner tonight." He gave a dry laugh. "That will go a long way to reassure her!"

"For crying out loud Justin! I said tell her the truth, not reveal your nature." Kit ran a hand through his hair. "How about this: tell her you really fancy her. Maybe that's a bit much. How about you admire her and you wanted to give her a gift to remember you by. You thought about jewelry or flowers but thought she'd have more use for a set of tires."

"At least she won't think I'm trying to seduce her. No one ever offered tires as a courting present."

Kit chuckled and punched him on the arm. "With that outlook, you'll bowl her over."

"Wouldn't do me much good if I could. Hell . . . it's so much easier when they're just a source of nourishment. You make them feel marvelous, take what you need, and leave them with lovely memories."

"And then you meet one you can't dismiss that easily."

Justin stared up at the dark sky overhead. "I keep thinking how things worked out for you and Dixie, and then it hits me what that would mean for Stella!"

"It worked out for us because Dixie didn't consider her-self bound by our code. If I remember rightly, she rode roughshod over your plan to keep her safe."

"She always accepted your nature, didn't she?"

"After reality hit her in the face!"

"But she accepted you as you are."

"Yes." Kit went silent, his mind veiled completely, but Justin knew he was thinking back to the days he'd lived in fear that Dixie would reject immortality . . . and him.

"Right." The silence stretched out. Maybe "right" had been the wrong word.

"Dixie will baby-sit Sam. I'm certain. But what are you going to do? You can hardly take her out to dinner."

"I'll come up with something. Heck, you've got theaters and cinemas, haven't you? Art galleries and so forth." He suspected finding the perfect place would be the easy bit. Convincing Stella might well take all his vampire powers.

"Dr. Corvus is here, Mom!" Sam called from upstairs. "Can I let him in?" His footsteps scampered down the uncarpeted stairs.

Justin? She'd had no idea who'd be ringing her doorbell this early, half-expecting it to be one of the Day boys playing pranks. "I'll get it, Sam!" Stella met him at the bottom of the stairs. Sam was dressed except for his shoes. "You go start your breakfast. Your juice and cereal are on the table."

He went back towards the kitchen without argument. Was Justin right? Was Sam giving the time alone? That didn't mean she had to use it did she? No nine-year-old, not even her son, was picking her man for her! And in any case, she didn't want to get tangled with any man. The doorbell sounded again.

"Hi," she said, pausing to catch her breath. Justin was even better-looking—if possible—in the light of morning than costumed as a creature of the night.

"Am I too early?"

She wasn't sure she'd ever be ready for him. "I just wasn't expecting you." That sounded rude. "Come on in, please."

He wiped his shoes on the mat before stepping over the threshold. "Sorry if I'm messing up your morning."

He messed up her dreams, why not breakfast? No, that wasn't fair, the man had come to help get her car running. "I'm getting Sam ready for school. Want a cup of coffee or toast or something?"

"Thanks, but no thank you. I ate earlier."

"Hello!" Sam looked up from his cereal. "You're not wearing your vampire things."

"Neither are you," Justin replied.

"I've got to go to school."

"And I've got to take your mother to pick up her car. Didn't want to scare the mechanics."

Sam laughed. "You'd only scare the bad guys, like Johnny Day!"

Stella still worried that would come back to haunt them. "Sam, eat up and get your book bag ready."

Sam swallowed the last few mouthfuls of cereal and disposed of a slice of toast in a few bites. "Be ready in a minute, Mom," and he was gone.

Now she was alone with Justin. It wasn't smart to like it so much. "Sure you won't have a cup of coffee?"

Justin shook his head. Seemed coffee had no place in his morning plans. Made her wonder what did.

"Where does Sam get the bus?" he asked.

That wasn't what she'd expected. "Just on the corner of the block."

"How about I take him down there? That will give you a chance to get things together. They promised the car would be ready by 8:30."

This was too much to process before caffeine. Could she trust Sam to him? Why not? Why? And what did he mean about the car? "It's fixed already?" The man had to be able to work magic.

"I'm trusting so. I called one of those all-night breakdown places. They towed it away to a tire merchant. When I called them they promised they'd see to it first thing."

And now she had to pay for it. Well, she had her emergency plastic. She hated using it but she had no choice. "I'm not used to things happening this easily."

"Then I'm glad I was here to help."

It was a habit she could easily fall into and one she'd better steer clear of. "Thanks." It sounded woefully inadequate but what else was there to say that wouldn't dig her in deep?

"Think Sam will mind if I take him to the bus?"

Sam was overjoyed. He all but skipped down the porch steps, his little hand firmly locked in Justin's strong one. It would be so easy to rely on this man. And then have to do without when he went home. Not again! Stella closed the front door.

Justin looked down at the small hand clasping his. Mortals were so fragile, and a mortal child even more so. Not that Sam saw himself as fragile; he would no doubt be insulted at the suggestion.

"I want you to meet all my friends," Sam said as they approached the corner where a knot of children waited in the cold. Seeing them close-up was a shock. Two had no winter coats, and another looked half-starved.

"This is my buddy, Dr. Corvus," Sam announced to the group. "We were vampires together last night."

"You a real doctor?" a solid-looking girl asked.

"Yes, a real doctor," Justin admitted, omitting to mention he had been since long before Europeans set foot in the New World.

"You talk weird!" a little boy said and got shushed by a taller girl who looked like his sister.

Sam jumped right in to take up his case. "He talks that way 'cause he's British! He's here on vacation and he scared Johnny Day so much he peed his pants!"

That got attention! The whole group went speechless as young eyes widened with awe.

"I wish I were a grown-up," one little boy said on the tail of a long sigh.

"If you were grown up, Johnny Day would be too!" the stocky little girl pointed out.

"Yeah! But I could move away and wouldn't have to live next door to him."

"Tell you one thing," the half-starved little boy said, "you'd better watch your back. I bet Johnny Day and his lot are out to get you!"

"He ain't scared of Johnny Day!" Sam said, obviously feeling Justin's reputation needed a little bolstering.

True enough, Justin mused as the big, yellow bus pulled up and the cluster of children clambered aboard. Johnny Day couldn't do him much harm. But as he walked the few meters back to Stella's, he wondered if he didn't need to visit Johnny Day and his brothers one dark night and scare them better.

"Here we are." Justin pulled into the car park. "I'll wait a jiffy, just to make sure it is ready. I'd hate to leave you stranded."

"Thanks." What a lame, inadequate thing to say. Trouble was, her brain was occupied with worrying whether she had enough left on her card to charge a set of brand new tires. It was nice enough of Justin—heck, it was wonderful of him—to fix things up, but if it had been left to her she'd have bought retreads.

"Yeah, right. Schwartz you said?" the clerk at the desk asked. "Stella Schwartz. The '91 Mazda?"

Stella nodded. "Is it ready?"

"Yes, we did it first thing. Urgent, wasn't it?"

Now all she had to do was mortgage Christmas to pay for it. "Here's my card." She prayed it wasn't declined.

It was, but not by the bank. "It's all take care of." The clerk pushed her keys and their key ring across the counter to her. "All you need to do is drive it home."

He'd made a big mistake. "Are you sure?"

"Yeah. It was taken care of when it was left here. The wrecker left the American Express number."

Maybe, but it wasn't hers. She never even got junk mail from American Express but she could make a good guess who carried one—and probably a platinum one at that. "Thanks." She took the keys, found her car, complete with the best-looking set of tires it had worn since the day it left the showroom, and marched across to Justin, and the card he never left home without.

"Everything all right?" he asked, sliding his window down as she approached.

"The car's fixed," she replied, striving for clarity and calm.

"Good, they promised it would be."

"You paid for it!" It came out like an accusation. Darn! Now she was being rude.

Justin nodded. "I arranged it through the breakdown people. By paying in advance I made sure it was done right away. I knew you needed the car."

That she couldn't deny. "What do I owe you?"

He paused before offering a hesitant smile. "Not a thing."

"I can't accept . . ."

"Listen," he said, and then opened the door and stood beside her. "Stella. Would you please take them, as a present from me?"

No man ever gave something this expensive without wanting payment back. "No."

Hurt flicked behind his eyes. "Please."

This was worse than refusing Sam when he begged. "Justin, you must understand . . ."

"I understand you're reluctant to accept them because you fear I have an ulterior motive."

Right the first time! But how could she agree and not sound ugly? "You've been a great friend, Justin." Hell! Men hated that line when they were after more.

"Just give me two minutes, Stella, to explain." Justin paused, waiting for her nod to go on.

"Okay."

His whole face relaxed at her response. "Look," he began, "I'm sure you've picked up clues that I'm . . . attracted to you."

Her heart sank. Here it comes.

"I'm here on holiday, will be leaving in a fortnight. We've no future together, and our lives are worlds apart. I can't offer you anything . . . permanent."

At least he was up-front about it.

"But, if you'd be willing, could we be friends? Just while I'm here? Maybe go out a couple of times to the theater or the cinema. Perhaps take Sam with us to the zoo?" He paused. "Can we? No strings. No promises implied or understood. Just pleasant company and a friendly parting."

He went silent, waiting for her reply. He was scared she'd refuse.

She sensed that, and his sadness when he'd said he could offer her nothing. "I'd like to spend time with you," she said. His face, his whole body relaxed. She'd never realize how tense he'd been, waiting for her reply. "But that doesn't solve the question of paying for my tires."

"Of course it does!"

His old confidence was back in full flood. Give a man one "yes" and he assumed them all. "I don't quite see it!"

"Why not? If we're friends, I'd give you a present when I leave. The way I see it, you need a set of tires more than flowers or boxes of chocolates or little pieces of jewelry."

She wouldn't argue that but even so . . .

"You need them, Stella, and you'll be late for work if you stand here arguing much longer. Come out with me Friday night and we can debate it all evening."

"I can't leave Sam."

"Dixie will baby-sit."

"Planned it out in advance, did you?"

"Yes."

Drat him! Smug wasn't the word.

"You'll come?"

"Where?" She was only delaying, that she recognized. Why was it so hard to tell him yes?

"You pick. There's a middle-aged singer from the seventies at the Southern. A musical at the Ohio. Nothing at the Palace and a ballet at the Riffe." He'd obviously studied the paper.

"I haven't been to the ballet since I was a kid."

"The ballet it is then. I'll pick you up at seven."

She was halfway to work and stopping to drop off her roll of film with the Halloween pictures before she realized she'd never actually said yes. Didn't seem to matter to him one way or the other. Serve him darn well right if she took Sam shopping on Friday night and they were both out when he came around.

Not that there was any chance of that. Not once she mentioned to Sam that Dixie would baby-sit. "Can I go to the shop with her?" he'd asked, as if he only half-believed it was even possible.

Seemed that was the plan, they'd drop Sam at the Emporium. "If it's okay with you?" Dixie said when Stella dropped by the shop to make sure Dixie really had offered. Stella wouldn't put it past Justin to draft Dixie without her knowledge, but Dixie seemed perfectly happy with the arrangement. "Just pack Sam a toothbrush so he can stay overnight. Then you and Justin can stay out as late as you want and you won't have to worry about waking him."

"Are you trying to push us together?" Stella asked.

Dixie laughed. "Serve Justin right if I was!" she said. "Stella, he's a good guy. I've known him almost as long as I've known Christopher. He does have a tendency to think his wishes and the laws of the universe are one and the same"—

Stella wouldn't argue with that—"but he's good friend. He can be the same to you."

"But he's only here on vacation."

"Right, that's why I said be friends." Dixie paused as if deciding whether or not to go on. "He had his heart broken . . . a while back. I think just meeting you has helped him get over it."

Great! She was supposed to glue his heart back together so he could fall in love with someone else. The prospect didn't appeal.

Dixie seemed to sense her mood. "I said he was a good guy and I meant it. He won't expect more than you want to give. I promise that. He's what my Gran used to call a gentleman."

Stella had pretty much figured that out for herself, but she still appreciated Dixie's bluntness. "Thanks. To be honest, it will be wonderful to go out with someone who won't want chicken nuggets or hamburgers."

"I can guarantee Justin won't eat either!"

Thank the Lord for that! "You're right, he is a good guy." Much as she'd balked at his paying for the tires, his generosity had taken a load off her mind. She'd have to find some way to repay him. Bake cookies perhaps. Or have him over for dinner. Sam would like that. "He does tend to get overbearing at times."

Dixie agreed, "Yes, he can. So can Christopher, given half a chance. They're all like that." Stella assumed Dixie meant Englishmen.

Dixie shook her head as she watched Stella leave the shop. This was going to be interesting, if nothing else. At least Stella was tough and sensible and focused. She might care for Justin more than she admitted, but she wasn't about to lose her heart. Dixie did hope it all worked out well. Justin needed a little diversion. Stella needed a little coddling. A couple of weeks of both could hardly hurt either of them.

* * *

"Hey, Mom, can I look at them?" Sam reached for the envelope of photos she'd picked up on her way home from work.

"Sure." She'd dropped them on the table and forgotten about them. Her mind had been a bit overloaded with thoughts of Justin, new tires, Justin, fixing dinner for Sam, Justin, what exactly she'd let herself in for in agreeing to a date, and Justin. A couple of Halloween pictures on the roll of film that went back to summer had slipped her mind.

Stella put the chicken and a couple of potatoes in to bake, shook half a bag of carrots into a pot and set it on the back of the stove to cook later, washed her hands and walked over to the table to share the photos with Sam.

He had them spread on the table: three or four from the day they'd spent at Wyandotte Lake last summer, some even dating back to the Fourth of July picnic at church, his back-to-school picture all dressed up in his new clothes, and Beggars' Night.

"That's weird," he said, holding up one of the Halloween pictures. It was the photo she'd taken in the Vampire Emporium. She'd wondered at the time if the lighting was too dark. That hadn't been a problem. Sam showed up clear as can be, reaching out for an apple, a big smile across his face. But Justin, who she distinctly remembered was holding Sam, appeared a strange blur. "I wonder what happened, Mom."

Darned if she knew. "Maybe he moved at the wrong time, Sam. Perhaps his costume messed up the flash." She had no idea. Photography was a mystery to her and she didn't have time to worry about it now. "How about you get out your homework and we start on it while dinner's cooking?"

Sam slid the photos back into the pouch and dug his math sheet out of his book bag.

* * *

Justin Corvus, one-time surgeon to the Ninth Roman Legion Hispaña, wished by Abel and all his offspring that just this once he could see his own reflection. What if his tie was crooked? Or the darn cowlick he'd had as a child, a millennium and a half ago, decided to reappear? For all he knew he'd left blood on his teeth after his feeding last night. That thought had him grabbing the mouthwash for the third time.

"Justin, you look great." Dixie said as she gave his shoulders a quick brush. "If I weren't taken, I'd be competing for you myself."

"You think this shirt is the right color? Perhaps I should wear the linen one."

"Justin, they're both black."

Much as he was fond of Dixie, females didn't understand these things. "What think you, Kit? Is silk too much?"

Kit shook his head. "Not for the ballet."

That was another bone he had to pick with Dixie. "You might have warned me it was Dracula!"

"Stella wanted the ballet," Dixie said. "It was the only one, unless you wanted to drive to Cleveland."

Maybe he was getting a bit testy but . . . "It's such a cliché."

"Since Stella doesn't believe in vampires, it's hardly a problem," she pointed out.

"It's had good reviews," Kit added.

Justin didn't put too much stock in mortal reviewers. "What if I'm watching them feed on stage and my fangs descend? I don't want to horrify Stella."

"Justin." Dixie stepped close and to his amazement, hugged him. "They won't. You know you can control them. Heck, even I can do that much now."

She was right. He was dredging up needless anxieties. "It's just . . ."

"You'll be fine, pal." Kit thumped him between the shoulder blades and rested his other hand on Dixie's shoulder, to demonstrate his ownership.

Dixie ignored the gesture. She repeated the hug. "Get a move on," she said, giving Justin a light kiss on his cheek. "You won't impress her by keeping her waiting. You've got to drop Sam off and get there before the curtain goes up." She stepped back and gave a gentle shove. "Get going."

He got going.

This was ridiculous! He'd been less nervous as a child facing the wrath of his dictatorial grandfather. Abel, help him! Facing death in the shape of a black-tipped Brigante arrow had been easier than this. All he had to do was walk up the cracked concrete path and ring the doorbell, but despite all Dixie's assurances, Justin was next to convinced that a silk shirt was over the top and he had blood dripping down his chin from his last feeding. He felt so darn . . . mortal!

Sam pulled the door open. "Hello! Come in, come in, come in!" he said, dancing from foot to foot as his velvet cape billowed behind him. "Mom's nearly ready and she looks like a princess."

"Justin?" Stella called from upstairs. "Won't be long."

"Never mind, I'll just chat with this vampire here."

Sam grinned. "Mom looks lovely." Justin had no trouble believing that. "I wish she dressed up like this every day."

"Bet that would surprise her boss."

"Yes, but he's . . . Hey, Mom!" Sam had been right. Stella descended the worn carpeting in a swirl of royal blue. The full skirt of her dress caressed her thighs and brushed her calves as the bodice outlined her full breasts. "Doesn't she look like a princess?"

"Like an empress."

She wasn't used to compliments. "Give me a break, you two!"

"Where does your mom keep her coat?" Justin whispered to Sam.

"In the closet."

"Right." Before she had a chance to object, Justin had the door open. There was only one long, adult coat. "The navy one?"

"I'll get it."

Not while he was here, she wouldn't. "I have it." Justin reached for the coat. The fabric was rough cheap wool. If he had his way, she'd be wearing cashmere or the finest alpaca. He stepped close and held it for her. Short of snatching it from him, she had no choice but to let him put it on her. "All set?"

Sam watched openmouthed. "Do grown-ups get help getting on their coats?"

"When they look like empresses and princesses."

Stella fastened her buttons. "You really want to wear that cape?" she asked Sam.

"Sure! I want Dixie to see how great it is, and I want to be a vampire again!"

"Now, Sam . . ."

Sam gave a sigh. "I know, Mom, vampires are just make-believe, but can't I just make-believe for one evening?" Justin admired the way Sam put such a desperate plea in his voice and a glimmering entreaty in his eye. Could Stella resist it?

No. She gave Sam a quick hug. "Okay. But you promise to be really good?"

"Of course, Mom." He slid out of her embrace.

Justin indulged in a brief fantasy of taking Sam's place in Stella's arms. Later . . . "Let's get this show in the road. Got your portmanteau?" he said to Sam and then turned to Stella. "All set?"

For one brief moment he feared she'd back out on him, but she smiled. "Yes."

It was all he needed. They dropped Sam with little ado and barely a backward glance.

"I hope he's okay," Stella said as they drove the half-mile or so to downtown.

"Would you have left him if you didn't trust Dixie and Kit to take care of him?"

Stella gave a half-chuckle, half-sigh. "You're right." She paused. "Tell me one thing. You call him Kit, Dixie calls him Christopher. What is his real name?"

"Both. One's his given name, the other a nickname. When I first knew him, the crowd he was in called him Kit. Dixie has always called him Christopher. He answers to both."

"You've know him longer than her, then?"

"Years longer." No point in telling her it was centuries. "I just met Dixie a little over a year ago."

Justin parked in the same multistory car park he'd flown over a couple of nights back, and managed to foil Stella's efforts to open her own car door by zipping around the car at immortal speed. He had to stop indulging in these theatrics but this once was worth it for the look on her face. Was she so unused to anyone taking care of her? Of course. It was going to be different as long as he was around.

Once in the small theater, they settled in their seats in the stalls—only they didn't call it "the stalls" here, and they didn't charge for programs either.

"I seem haunted by vampires," Stella said.

"Sam makes a pretty good one."

"Yes, but I'm afraid he half-believes in them."

"Children need fantasy. After all, for the next couple of hours we're both going to be caught up in one."

"Good point."

Abel, help him! She wouldn't smile like that if she knew she was sitting right next to a creature she didn't believe in.

Justin spent the evening watching the sheer joy on Stella's

face and the ballet. He missed a lot of the ballet. It was good,
darn good in fact, and he almost forgave them for axing out
Quincy, one of his favorite characters. Quincy had a style
about him that boring Jonathan and the prune-faced Honorable
Arthur sadly lacked. Must be something about Americans!
Stella certainly had a style of her own. There wasn't a single
woman among the expensively dressed, immaculately coifed
crowd who could hold a candle to her.

It was going to be darn hard to leave her.

But he didn't have to . . . yet. He'd use what time they
had.

"That was fantastic." She'd said as they drove home.
She'd said the same words at least a half-dozen times since
the interval. "I can't tell you how much I enjoyed that."

"You have already, Stella." If he weren't driving, he'd
grab her in his arms and kiss her silly. Her sheer joy at the
ballet had hit him like the first taste of warm blood after a
long starvation. That he could so easily give her such pleasure with a couple of theater tickets . . . If she would only let
him show her what rapture really was. But now . . . He
reached over and opened the glove compartment. "Why
don't you grab the mobile and call Dixie? Make sure Sam's
settled. I'd like to take you out for supper."

Stella cast him a surprised glance. "Oh, the cell phone.
Thanks." She reached in and minutes later put it away, satisfied Sam was sleeping the sleep of a tired-out child. "I can't
get over Dixie, keeping Sam like this. Did you twist her arm
or something?"

"Just a smidgen. It wasn't an imposition, if that's your
worry. She knew I wanted an evening with you."

"She's a nice person."

Incredible might be a better word, but . . . "Yes, she is."

Justin took Stella to Barcelona. She accepted his "severe
food allergies" line. She refused supper but accepted a glass
of dessert wine and a rich, chocolate dessert.

She ate with such obvious relish, licking the chocolate off the spoon and closing her eyes to savor the full taste of the rich filling. A passionate woman. The woman he wanted.

"Look, this may be out of place, in which case, just tell me to button up, but would you tell me about Sam's father?"

She stared and swallowed quickly. "You want to know about Tarsim?"

The blighter had a name. Good. If he ever met him he'd scare the balls off him. What sort of specimen of humanity walked out on a son? "Yes, if it's not intruding."

She shook her head. "Not really. He was a grad student at OSU. An engineer. Good-looking, a bit older than me. His family, back in Turkey, had money. I'll be honest, he had me mesmerized. My mother thought he was after me to marry for a green card. She was wrong. He already had a wife."

"He knows about Sam?"

"I didn't realize I was pregnant until after he went home. I wrote to the address he left me, but he never replied." She shrugged. "His loss."

Her casual, brave words veiled heartbreak. Who would not ache at abandonment? "He sounds a foolish, stupid mortal."

"You could say the same about me."

"No way in heaven! You stand by your child and have a son to be proud of."

"You're right there." She moved her spoon through her dessert. "He's the love of my life."

Her loneliness snagged a trail across Justin's mind. She was beautiful, courageous and so alone. He wanted to protect her and keep her safe from worry and harm. If only he could stay near her . . . Impossible! They had no future and he had responsibilities an ocean away. But for now . . . "Stella, I won't make promises I can't keep, but can we be friends? Good friends?"

She was silent a few moments, as if weighing the odds and the risks. "I'd like that, Justin."

He felt like crying his delight to the heavens, but settled for a walk in Schiller Park in the moonlight.

As they stepped out into the street, Justin half-noticed a pair of teenagers loitering on the opposite corner and never gave them a moment's thought. Why would he when he was alone with Stella in the moonlight? The night was mild for November. Mild enough she had no need for gloves, and slid her bare hand into his. Their fingers meshed and as her wrist brushed his, the human warmth of her called to him through every pore in his body. He needed this mortal woman. Not just for the lifeblood coursing through her veins but for the life of her . . . the soul that made her Stella. He wanted to gather her in his arms and race at vampire speed to her bed. Unfortunately, that would no doubt ensure he'd never get past the front door.

He would have to seduce slowly, with tenderness. Give more than he took and offer more than her dreams ever had. He was vampire. He could do it.

As they strolled towards the *Umbrella Girl* statue, Stella stepped closer. Out of desire, the security a male body offered to a lone woman, or both—or something more? Justin measured his pace to match her steps. She seemed disinclined to speak. He was more than content to savor the rhythm of her heartbeat and the pulse of blood in her living body and plan the pleasure he'd give her . . . again and again.

It was then he heard the two heartbeats behind them.

He turned and faced two teenagers. For a second he relaxed, but then sensed the venom emanating from them. Muggers!

"Johnny Day?"

Stella barely had his name out before Justin recognized him and the lout replied, "Yeah, bitch! You and you's fancy man's gettin' it good." He reached inside his jacket.

"My God!" Justin felt Stella's fear as she clutched his arm.

"Pray, bitch!" Moonlight glinted on the barrel of a handgun.

Justin wasn't faster than a speeding bullet but he was faster than a hooligan. He stepped in front of Stella, as a loud retort broke the night. He felt the slam as the bullet passed through him, heard Stella's scream and the other lout's laugh in the same second, and turned to see her fall and sensed the life leave her as she lay, half on the grass and half on the hard, gray path.

The two hoodlums were very much alive. Another bullet hit Justin in the back, passing through him and into the tree behind him. He turned with grim determination as a third bullet ripped through his side and out his ribs. Pain clarified the mind wonderfully. He sensed a change in the two thugs. Astonishment perhaps that their bullets didn't work anymore? Justin deliberately showed his fangs and watched the assassin pale with disbelief. Justin didn't give him time to think, just leaped the few yards to grab him by the jacket and toss him into the air. His scream died in a crash of broken glass and the wail of a burglar alarm.

Justin turned as the other teen fled. Two strides and Justin had him by the arm and the boy was sailing in the other direction, bouncing off the tennis court fence.

It was then Justin realized he'd indulged in petty revenge while Stella lay dead. He raced back and gathered her lifeless body in his arms. She was still warm but her sweet blood no longer pumped in her generous heart. A wet patch on her coat marked where one spent bullet had slain her.

Justin looked up at the heavens, let out a wail that echoed off the houses around the park, and clutching Stella's body in his arms called his despair to Kit and Dixie as he ran towards their house on City Park Avenue, the only haven he knew in this murderous world.

Chapter Six

Justin leapt the iron railings and raced towards the open front door. He barely heard Kit ask, "What happened?" and didn't waste effort replying.

Dixie understood in seconds. "Take her up to our room. No, wait!" She stepped in front of him. "What if Sam wakes up?"

"He won't!" Kit shot up the stairs, Justin right on his heels.

Stella looked so utterly mortal lying motionless on the pale green spread. Justin wanted to howl his frustration at the futility of human life. Why here? Why now? Why had he taken her into the park? She was as lifeless as the bed she lay on, and it was all his fault.

The mattress gave a little as Dixie sat beside him. "I think you'd better change." She put his spare slacks and a shirt on the bedspread.

"Not now, woman!" Stella was dead and Dixie worried about bleeding on her bedspread!

"You've got blood all over you. I think we'd better burn those clothes. Just in case." He glanced at his chest. By Abel,

Dixie was right! Hell! He stripped and reached for the clean clothes and looked down at his already healing chest. "Is it all your blood?" she asked.

"Some is Stella's." A great shudder tore though his mind and heart. "I tried to protect her but the bullet cut right though me. What sort of guns do they have here?"

Dixie treated that as a rhetorical question. "Need a towel or a washcloth before you put on clean clothes?"

"Later!" Years, centuries later—after he got over losing Stella!

"Sam's out for hours." Kit had returned silently. "We've plenty of time."

"For what? To think about a mortal life gone?" All right for him to talk. He has his eternal love.

Dixie wrapped her arm around his shoulders. "For you to transform her, Justin."

The woman was mad! "Transform her! She doesn't believe in us! She thinks we're cartoon creatures to amuse children." If he'd only had more time . . .

"So what? Stella believing or not doesn't change our existence. And she'll believe right enough afterwards."

"How can I?"

"How can you not?" Kit asked.

"Justin, you have to." Dixie patted his shoulder. "She's all Sam has. She might refuse our life, but you need to give her that option."

He looked up at Kit, who nodded in agreement. "She's right."

So be it.

With Dixie's help, he pulled off Stella's bloodstained clothing. "You need to wash her off or something?" Dixie asked.

He shook his head. "Later. Before I do anything, I need to get rid of that bullet. It's still in her. There's no exit wound." The entry wound was bad enough. Mortals injured so easily.

His four bullet wounds were almost closed, but Stella's single one gaped like a red maw under her left breast. He'd seen a multitude of injuries and wounds in his long life, but never one that ripped his heart and mind as this one. He'd have wept long and hard if his body still made tears.

He had no time for human sorrow.

He had to focus his energies and his mind.

Resting his fingers on her still-warm breast, he focused on the inch or so of metal lodged inside. It took almost all his will, but with infinite slowness the metal eased through her flesh. When the flat end reached the surface, he pulled until the bullet rested in the palm of his hand.

It was so small to be so lethal. "Dixie." He handed her the bullet. "Get rid of this. Bury it. Deep. Right away."

"Okay." She took it with a grimace. "I'll take care of it."

"Trying to spare my woman's sensibilities?" Kit asked as her footsteps faded down the stairs.

"She doesn't need to see this," Justin growled in reply.

Kit's eyebrows rose. "Better get a move on, then. She can dig at vampire speed."

Right. "Go keep her company."

Kit shook his head. "Get on with it. Dither much longer and Stella will go cold."

He had to act now, and risk Stella's horror at what he'd done, or never hear her speak again. Justin eased his arm under her shoulders and raised her until her head dropped back, exposing her fragile neck. He leaned close and bit.

Her blood was rich and sweet, and from tonight he'd never taste it again. No matter. She'd be his. Of his blood. One with him. He savored the richness of her, tasted her spirit and lamented the life now gone. He drank. Deep. His body swelled with her lifeblood and still he sucked. He had to all but drain her. His feet and legs swelled first, bloating until his shoes pained him and his ankles were thick and heavy. Then his body engorged and his hands swelled so he had to concentrate to retain his hold on Stella's lightening body.

Not much longer.

With a concerted effort, he sucked, using all the force he possessed, until she was lightweight in his arms. He could barely move as Kit came forward, took Stella's drained body and laid her on the bed.

Damn good thing Kit had stayed. Without him, he'd have been stuck. His skin felt ready to burst, his lips were so swollen they wouldn't close, and his eyes felt ready to pop.

"I'll prop her up with pillows," Kit said, matching actions to his words. "It'll make it easier on both of you."

"I'll help," Dixie added. She was back.

Stella looked as pale as the pillows behind her and felt as cold as lost hopes. He had to bring her over to their life. "I need a knife or a blade."

"Here." Dixie handed him the scalpel from his bag.

"Thank you." His swollen fingers had difficulty grasping it but he'd manage. He owed this to Stella.

"You'll need this." Dixie spread a towel on his lap. "Just in case."

She was right. He was so full he'd no doubt spurt. There was also the problem of Stella's injured heart. Would it have strength to pump? It would heal, once she had blood, but what if she bled before her transformation was complete? What if he'd failed her after all?

He wasn't going to! "Kit, I need your help. You too, Dixie." She shouldn't be here. But she was, and he needed all the power he could summon. Right now, he'd ask Vlad for help if he were close!

"Yes?" Dixie was at his elbow. Kit beside her.

"I'm afraid her heart will lose blood as soon as it starts pumping. That damn wound gapes so. Kit, I want you to hold it closed, block it with your hand to stop any bleeding, and Dixie . . ." He paused, torn between knowing she shouldn't be here, the certainty she'd refuse to leave, and the conviction he needed more strength than he and Kit alone possessed. "I want you to concentrate on keeping her heart steady."

"How?" She sounded scared. He shouldn't be asking this of her.

"I understand what he wants, Dixie," Kit said. "It's not so hard, just tricky. Takes concentration more than strength. The second her heart beats, focus on the rhythm and keep it going. Think of it as CPR by mind power."

Kit had always had a way with words, but right now, words were nowhere near sufficient. Hanging the towel over his arm, Justin leaned close to Stella. Kit sealed her wound with his hands as Dixie watched. Their three minds touched briefly, an unspoken encouragement, a vote of trust. Justin took the scalpel in his free hand and slashed his wrist.

Their mingled blood gushed on the towel and splashed on the sheets. Justin had his wrist on Stella's mouth willing her to suck.

She didn't move. She lay like the leeched corpse she was. "Stella!" His mind screamed. He felt Kit flinch and Dixie shudder but neither faltered.

Three vampires waited helpless as the cut in Justin's arm slowly closed. "She won't take it!" He never spoke but the panic soared in his mind.

"Hold on!" Kit said. "Give it another try."

"It won't work! She won't suck!"

"She will!" Dixie spoke. Her words harsh in the silent room. "She will, Justin." Her voice was gentler now, but still lacked the slightest trace of doubt. "We just have to help her."

"Dixie . . ." Kit began, "sometimes it's difficult." Doubt etched in words, echoing Justin's despair.

"Sometimes, yes. But not this time. If I can will her heart to beat, why can't we will her to suck?"

Justin didn't waste thought or time answering. "Let's try! Kit, you still need to seal her wound. Dixie, you keep focused for her heartbeat the second it starts. Kit and I can will her to drink."

He had to reopen his arm. Not that it mattered, he'd slash his throat if it would help. Bending close to Stella, Justin took up the scalpel and cut. Blood welled up as once again and he pressed his arm to her lips. Nothing. She lay inert. Then Kit's mind linked with his. Two elder vampires focused their wills until Justin felt a soft flutter against his skin. Their united power bombarded her muscles and nerves. Forcing her lips and tongue to suck. Weak as a dying baby at first, her strength increased until she tentatively swallowed the first mouthful and the muscles in her slender throat undulated. A second later, she took over, her mouth clamping like a limpet as she sucked with all her might.

Kit's mind slipped the connection, leaving Justin alone with Stella and his desperate hopes.

Stella strengthened with each swallow. The blood flowed out of him. Now, if it would only stay in her. A little blood seeped though Kit's fingers. But barely a trace. He had the wound sealed. "Any heartbeat?" Justin asked him, not wanting to distract Dixie. She was far too inexperienced to do what he'd just asked.

"There will be," Dixie replied.

By Abel! If only she could be right. There had to be, and soon, given Stella's frenzied sucking.

"She'd not bleeding any to speak of," Kit told him.

It only half-reassured. If she wasn't bleeding, why in the name of sanity, didn't her heart beat? She had plenty of blood. His hands and feet were almost back to normal.

"Got one!" Dixie's jubilation echoed in his mind.

"Can you keep it up?"

"Of course! No . . ." His mind near to screamed. "No need to. It's pumping on its own."

"She's right," Kit added.

The world was right!

Tension Justin never imagined a vampire body could hold eased out with the last of his surplus blood. Color had returned to Stella's face, a pulse beat at the base of her neck. Her heart pumped, not too strongly as yet, but once the bullet wound healed in a few hours, she'd be fine. Her heart would keep going the few days necessary to complete the transformation.

But he still had work to do before he could face Stella and admit what he'd just done to her. Before she had a chance to wake, he cast a deep glamour on her. It was harder now that she was vampire. Her mind resisted his, but he was far more powerful.

His entire body slumped. He hadn't felt this worn since he was a mortal. Kit sat beside him, an exhausted gray tinge to his face, and Dixie flopped on the floor, leaning against the wall. She looked as if she'd fainted. Transforming Stella had spent all three of them.

"She's okay?" Dixie asked, lifting her head to give him a weak smile.

"She's fine, but I'm not quite finished. I need to clean her up. Don't want her waking up covered with blood."

"Good point." Dixie pulled herself upright. "I'll go run you a bath." She looked at Kit. "Sure Sam's out for the count?"

Kit nodded. "He won't wake until I tell him to, any more than Stella will until Justin's ready for her."

"Wish I could do that."

Justin smiled at her. "I think you can, Dixie. When this is all over, remind Kit to show you how."

She gave a chuckle as she walked out. Kit followed.

Tactful of them. He had darn good friends.

And a brand new fledgling to take care of. He had to prepare Stella to accept a vampire existence, and the less shocking he could make it, the better. Waking up and finding herself covered with blood came under "shocking."

He gathered her sleeping body in his arms and carried her down to the bathroom. Dixie had the bath filled with warm water and lavender oil. A stack of folded towels and a freshly laundered nightgown sat ready on a chair by the bath.

Justin lowered Stella into the scented water, bathing her with a soft sponge, smoothing it over her breasts, carefully washing the edges of her already-healing wound. Yes, Stella was fledgling all right, and it was his task to teach her the ways of the colony. But what a fledgling! Her breasts were full and firm, her body smooth with faint stretch marks from her pregnancy. She'd bear forever a scar from the bullet wound, but that would be all marring her skin. He shampooed her, twice, luxuriating in the feel of her short hair between his fingers. Taking a flannel, or as Dixie insisted on calling it, a washcloth, he wiped the last traces of sweat and blood and pain off Stella's beautiful face and dropped a kiss on her forehead.

He wanted to take her mouth with his, to possess it, but stopped. He wouldn't take his pleasure while she was under a glamour. She would know who and what he was, and what she meant to him.

Everything.

He dried her off with soft towels and placed a pad of gauze over her wound. She'd only need it a few hours, but if she remembered anything from the attack in the park, and instinct told him she'd remember every little thing, she'd expect to be injured. Might as well let one detail meet her expectations. Not much else would for quite some time.

"Can you maintain the glamour while you rest?" Dixie asked from the doorway. "Is it possible?"

"Why?"

"Because you need to rest. Kit is about to keel over and you look even worse."

"Where is he?"

"Downstairs, burning Stella's and your clothes. We're assuming there's other blood on them."

"I don't think so, but it's possible."

"It's all taken care of and the sheets are in the wash. I didn't want Sam coming across heaps of bloodstained laundry. So, can you sleep and keep a glamour?"

"Maybe, in close proximity."

"That's what Kit said. He's going to rest in the spare room with Sam. You'd better put Stella in your room." Dixie smiled as she turned to go. "Oh and by the way, there's an emergency supply of blood bags in the fridge in the basement. I put them down there so Sam wouldn't find them while looking for a snack."

By Abel, yes. How were they going to cope with Sam?

"You'll manage," Dixie replied. "Stella will figure it out. She's a mother."

Dixie left before he quite realized she'd answered his thoughts. She was beginning to link minds with him. Not that he had time to ponder that change. He tucked Stella into his bed and went down to the basement.

"Here." Kit lifted his head out of the refrigerator and tossed him a blood bag.

"Thanks." Justin bit the corner and drained it.

"Want another?" Kit asked, leaning on the open door.

Justin shook his head. "I need rest more than sustenance. Can't believe the effort it took. Thanks, Kit, I'd never have succeeded without you and Dixie."

Kit grinned. "That's what friends are for. You've got yourself a good woman there."

"Yes. I know. She's had it hard, bringing up a child on her own. She's not going to have to worry anymore. From now on things will be very different."

Full of plans for Stella and Sam, Justin went back upstairs. For a brief moment, he considered sleeping on the floor and letting Stella have the bed. No. He wanted to feel her soft body in his arms. He'd just be sure to wake before she did. No reason to give her a shock.

He wished he'd left her naked, so he could lie skin to skin with her. Later. For now he'd content himself with lying alongside Stella spoon fashion and letting the sweet scent of her body lull him to sleep.

It had to be the wine last night that made her head ache so. That and the late night. She wasn't used to such high-flying living. Stella burrowed her head under the pillow. She'd have to get up soon. Sam would be waking. No, Sam must have crawled in bed with her. Strange, he hadn't done that for months. She rolled over and opened her eyes. Something was wrong. The ceiling wasn't cracked. Not only was it not cracked, it had been wallpapered overnight.

Where was she? Stella sat up and almost yelped. No wonder the ceiling looked different! It wasn't her room. It wasn't her house. And it wasn't Sam snuggled beside her. It was Justin. Nude. With a raging erection.

Saints preserve her! What had she done? Gone to bed with him in a borrowed nightgown. She had to have been blotto last night. She had this vague memory of Johnny Day with a gun. Nightmares from too much alcohol, no doubt. She wasn't blotto now. She was getting dressed and taking Sam home and she'd start by finding her clothes.

She stepped out of bed feeling a bit wobbly, and looked around the unfamiliar room. No sign of her things. They couldn't be that far. As she walked towards the closet, her knees almost buckled under her. Weird sort of hangover. She took another couple of steps and keeled over, crashing onto the floor.

"Stella!" Seemed Justin had jumped over the bed. He was mere inches away and bending over her. "Are you all right?"

"No. You're naked."

Didn't seem to bother him. He bent over, his far too obvious erection bumping her hip, and scooped her off the floor. "What are you trying to do?"

"Get myself dressed—something that wouldn't hurt you!"

"You don't need to be walking around yet." He sat her down on the bed.

"Why not?"

He sat down beside her. "Stella, something happened last night. I'll try to explain."

She gave his naked torso the strongest glare she knew how and made a point of frowning at his erection and then met his eyes. "It's obvious what happened last night!"

Pure shock flashed across his face. "Stella, it wasn't what you think."

"Yeah, right! That's a real original line. Never been used by man or beast."

His mouth set hard and his forehead creased between his eyes. "Will you just listen, Stella?"

She stood up. Now she had the advantage of height and clothing—not that nudity hurt him one bit. "I don't think so." What was wrong? Standing upright was a challenge. "You did a great snow job on me. I thought you were a decent, up-front man, who wanted to be friends. Seems we have different ideas about what good friends means."

"For crying out loud, Stella!"

Getting irritated, was he? They had that much in common. And only that. What a shame . . . But she wasn't sitting here lamenting because he hadn't turned out to be Prince Charming.

She took a very wobbly step forward.

"Mom?"

Sam! Dear heaven, what now? "Get dressed!" she snapped at Justin, and ran to the door to head Sam off.

She had to cling to the doorframe to stay upright. What the hell was wrong with her? This was no ordinary hangover.

The sight of Sam in his footed pajamas was the only normal thing in sight. "Mom, you okay?" Sam asked.

"She's feeling a bit woozy," Justin said behind her. "She needs to rest up. How about I get your breakfast and we let her lie in this morning?"

Before she had time to refuse or protest, he had her in his arms again. He was dressed. Impossible! Unless she was hallucinating earlier. The way she felt that was more than likely.

"Is Mom sick?"

She pulled herself out of the fog long enough to reassure Sam. "I'm okay, hon. Just a bit sleepy."

"She'll be fine in a little while," Justin added. "Your mother works hard and we were out late last night." She was now back on the bed, Sam looking at her with worried eyes. "Hop in and give her a cuddle. I'll go down and see what Dixie has for breakfast."

Stella sagged back on the pillow and pulled Sam close. It wasn't just her legs, her head throbbed, her eyes ached, and she felt like crud. She had to be coming down with the flu. Her eyes closed as lassitude swamped her. She couldn't get the flu. She didn't have time to be sick.

Justin walked into the kitchen. "Something's gone wrong." Saying it aloud only underscored his dread.

Dixie shook her head. "You worry too much, Justin. I slept solid for three days after Christopher transformed me. Remember? Come sunset Stella will be perky as a puppy." She gave him a reassuring hug. It didn't work too well.

"Seems to me," Kit said, frowning as if sorting out his thoughts, "we need some sort of plan to handle things with Little Jack Horner in there." He angled his head towards the parlor where Sam watched TV and munched on toast. "How long can those cartoons last?"

"Twenty-four hours a day, if we pick the right channels," Dixie replied. "But I'll take him with me when I go to the shop. He can help price things, and when he gets tired of that, he can read. He'll be happy and too busy to worry. You need to concoct a story explaining why Stella's going to sleep through the next few days."

"A nasty bug going around?" Kit suggested. "The particularly nasty flu the papers are predicting for this winter."

"Why isn't she going to the doctor, then?" Dixie asked.

"Because you have one in the house," Justin said. "It would work." Assuming Dixie's optimism was correct and all Stella needed was a few days' rest.

"Okay, while I keep Sam occupied, you'd better go to her house, Justin, and pick up some spare clothes for her and Sam. I'd do it but I've never been inside, and I'm not sure Sam's invitation would work. I'd hate to get stuck on the porch unable to penetrate the barrier."

Dixie was right. He hated the thought of leaving Stella but she was in deep rest, and he could trust Kit to watch her. He nodded. "Good idea."

"There's still this evening to worry about," Kit said. "How about I pick up Sam from the shop and take him to the cinema. There has to be something on he'd like. If I time it to leave just before dusk and you shut up the shop early, then you and Justin can be here when she wakes."

"That would work." Dixie gave a little smile. "This is getting complicated."

"And so far we've only covered one day," Kit said.

"Once Stella wakes and feels fine, it will get easier. Although"—Dixie frowned—"I don't know how she's going to cope with her job."

Stella wouldn't have to cope with her job, not anymore. He'd take care of all she and Sam needed.

* * *

It had been the hardest day of his long life, tortured by the memories of her anger and fear, and his own worries about her well-being. He'd swung by her house to fill a suitcase with spare clothes and now he waited for Stella to wake, tearing his soul with the hope she'd look at him with something more than fury.

She must have had a shock, waking in a strange bed and finding him in his skin. He should have been prepared but he'd never imagined she'd wake before him. It didn't make sense. He was the one resting on alien soil. He shook his head. Just one more thing about Stella to utterly confuse him.

"It's almost dusk." Dixie came in quietly. "Want me to stay or go?"

"Stay." Dixie's presence might help allay Stella's fears.

Dixie nodded and pulled up a chair. "I almost had a brain spasm when I woke up vampire, and I knew what you and Kit were. She's in for the ultimate culture shock."

"I'm afraid she'll hate me for it."

Dixie shook her head. "I don't think she's the hating sort. More like punch you in the gut and then get over it, but she may well be utterly confused and worried. Be sure to tell her right off that Sam is safe and well."

"Right." Dixie was on most things self-willed, stubborn and opinionated, but also loyal and courageous. Kit considered her the best thing to happen to him in four hundred years.

"She'll be fine, Justin." Dixie squeezed his hand. "Just you wait and see."

Yes she would . . . If he hadn't taken too much blood—or too little. If his own metabolism had mingled it properly. If he'd given it back fast enough. If her injured heart had repaired itself. By Abel, was that why she'd been unable to walk? Was her heart unable to heal? He was a physician, an elder vampire. He should be able to take care of everything.

"Sam?" Stella's eyes were wide with worry as she sat upright.

"He's okay," Dixie said. "He's been really good all day. Christopher's taking him to the movies as a reward."

Dixie was right. The tension leeched out of Stella's face at her reassurance. "Stella . . ." Justin began.

She looked. It was the only word for it. "So, you're dressed this time around. Good."

"Look, I'm sorry about that. It must have been a bit of a shock." And she was in for a far worse one.

"A bit of a shock!" Her mouth dropped open. "I all but peed on myself. Do you make a habit of climbing nude into other people's beds?"

"Actually, it's my bed." That was the wrong thing to say.

"Well, excuse me. I'll let you have it back right now." As she spoke, she tossed off the covers, stood up and marched toward the door. She almost got there before her legs quivered under her and she stumbled.

He grabbed her. What was wrong? "Stella?"

"Put me down."

"If I do, you'll fall again." Rest had not helped one iota.

"If you don't, we've got a problem. I've got to go to the bathroom."

Of course, her body would still function for another day or so. "Don't worry." Before she had a chance to object, he was down the hallway and sitting her on the loo. She wasn't too happy about making the trip in his arms, but he wasn't letting her fall again. "I'll carry you back when you're finished."

"You might give her a moment of solitude," Dixie said.

He'd forgotten about women and their need for privacy. "Call me when you're ready," he said and exited, dragged by Dixie.

Chapter Seven

Embarrassment and anger took second place to sheer relief. Much as she still smarted at the indignity of Justin carrying her here and sitting her on the toilet, Stella had to admit that, without his assistance, she'd have had an embarrassing accident.

What was wrong with her? Flu? Some awful virus going around? Outside was early evening. Did that mean she'd slept away an entire day? She half-remembered collapsing on the floor earlier, but maybe that was part of the nightmare about Johnny Day. Without a doubt, she was sick. Her head ached, her muscles were sore and she dreaded trying to walk again but whatever he might say, she was not calling Justin to pick her up off the toilet.

There wasn't a mirror in the bathroom. Odd really. Maybe just as well, she probably looked like death warmed over. She tentatively checked out her body. No bruises. No cuts. Still had all her limbs. And was wearing an unfamiliar nightshirt. She hoped it was Dixie's not Justin's. If she could get a feeble laugh out of it, she wasn't dying. Not yet at least. She felt a soft pad just under her left breast. Had she hurt herself falling earlier? She eased off the thick gauze, half-scared of what she'd find. A fading bruise and an odd round of puckered flesh where she'd never in her life had a scar. What had happened last night?

Good question.

She'd like some answers. Stella stood up and made for the door. She'd just managed to half-open the door when she fell over again. Justin was in like a shot and grabbed her as she fell.

"Didn't I tell you to call me when you were ready?"

"Maybe I wasn't ready!"

"If you think I'm going to stand here and watch you kiss the carpet, you'd better think again." He strode down the hallway, sat her back on the edge of the bed and turned to Dixie, who was a couple of paces behind. "Something's wrong."

"What's wrong, is I've got some sort of bug."

Justin seemed not to even hear her. "We've got to work out what happened."

"Yes? Hello there!" Stella felt like screaming but with this awful headache it hurt too much.

"Justin." Dixie stepped forward and sat on the bed beside her. "Let Stella get dressed. No one feels their best wearing borrowed nightwear."

He looked—no, scowled—at Dixie, but nodded and brought a large suitcase from across the room, and set it on the bed. "Okay. But I need to work out what's going on."

She wouldn't argue with that. With Justin gone, Stella frowned at Dixie unsnapping the locks on the suitcase. "How did you get my things?"

"Justin and Sam used the keys in your pocketbook. Sam needed fresh clothes and I told Justin to pick up some odds and ends for you."

"I hate to sound ugly but I'd rather be sick in my own bed."

"Don't blame you. But Sam couldn't be left on his own and I don't think he'd feel happy parted from you."

Good point.

"Here you are. You'll feel better in your own clothes." Dixie opened the suitcase and stared.

Stella leaned forward, looked, rummaged through the contents, met Dixie's eyes and they both burst out laughing. "I don't believe it!" Stella got out between cackles.

"I should have gone myself," Dixie said. "I'm sorry, I just wasn't sure about getting in your house and . . ." She shook her head. "Justin must have . . ."

"Had a wild rummage through my underwear drawer. I swear every pair of panties I own is here." And a bunch of worn out stuff she should have tossed out months ago. Maybe the man intended to keep her in bra and panties. He was going to be disappointed. "Aren't there any clothes?"

There were: a pair of slacks she'd been keeping in case she lost twenty pounds, a couple of sweaters, a pair of high heels she'd last worn to a friend's wedding, a spaghetti-strap sun dress with a miniskirt, a seventy-five percent off sale purchase that she'd never had the guts to wear.

Dixie let out another whoop of laughter at that. "I'm sorry," she said. "I would have picked out clothes you could wear." She shook her head at the daring dress. "You'll freeze in that. Mind you, you could wear it with the navy sweater. Would certainly be a new look!"

"But only if I added the shoes and"—she reached into the case—"wool socks." It felt great to laugh. For a few wild seconds her worries evaporated. Even her head hurt less. She felt well enough to get up, but what to wear?

"I've got a pair of sweatpants you can borrow." Dixie offered. "You're taller than I am so they'll hang at half-mast, but at least you'll be covered. Now shoes . . . well"—she giggled again—"I'll find flip-flops or something."

Standing still made her dizzy, so she dressed sitting on

the bed. Dixie's loaned sweatpants were too short but they met around the waist, which was more than her pair would, and covered more than the minidress. She felt halfway human, at least until she stood up to put on the flip-flops and had to grab the bed for support. "What is wrong with me?" She was panicking, she knew, but . . . Dixie caught her. Her arms were almost a strong as Justin's. "My feet don't work on the floor!"

Dixie sat her back on the bed. "I think I can guess. Where were you born, Stella?"

"What?" Here she was, falling all over the place and Dixie wanted her life history.

"Bear with me, Stella. It's very important. Where were you born?"

Since Dixie insisted and was grabbing Stella's arms so hard she couldn't move, Stella told her. "On Mildenhall Air Base, in Britain. My father was in the Forces."

"I just knew it!" She released her pincer grip on Stella's arms and hugged her. "Thank heaven it wasn't Germany or Outer Mongolia. England we can take care of it. No problemo." She turned her head. "Justin, bring Christopher's slippers? Stella needs them."

"Got them," Justin called through the door seconds later. "Are you going to let me in?" He sounded as if he'd beat the door down if they refused.

"I'm decent," Stella called. Not that that seemed to bother him either way.

He strode in and handed Dixie a pair of soft, leather slippers. "What's going on?"

"Stella was born in England."

For the first time since she'd met him, the man was lost for words. "By Abel!" he muttered a moment later.

"Here." Dixie handed them to her. "Try them."

Might as well humor her. What difference would a pair of slippers make? All the difference in the world. She could stand, even take steps and . . . "This is crazy! Why a pair of shoes?" Double crazy, her aches had disappeared and her head was perfectly clear. She walked back and forth across the room. She was fine. The slippers were far too big and had soles as heavy as sneakers but . . . "What's in them?"

"Kit's native earth," Justin replied.

"What? Oh yeah, right! You're vampires. Ha! Okay, what is it really?"

"Why don't you see if you can walk downstairs?" Dixie suggested. "We've at least got chairs for everyone there."

Walking downstairs was a breeze. Whatever had been wrong with her earlier was cured now. When Sam got back, she could take him home. She liked Dixie but she wasn't parking herself and Sam on her for the weekend.

Dixie pulled the blinds in the parlor that overlooked the street and switched on the gas logs. Stella had half-expected Dixie to offer her coffee or pop but she wasn't the least bit thirsty. Weird.

"Stella?" Justin asked from the other end of the sofa. "What do you remember about last night?"

Oh dear, she never had thanked him for the evening. "I had an incredible time. Haven't been to the ballet since I was a kid. Thanks so much."

"I enjoyed it too, and the company." He gave one of his sexy smiles. "What do you remember about afterwards?"

Odd question, but heck, she'd humor him. "We had dessert at Barcelona. Or rather I did. You watched me gorge myself on that incredible choclate concotion. And then we went walking in Schiller Park." That was where it got confusing. "Did I pass out or something? All I can remember is what must have been a nightmare. Maybe a fever dream."

"What did you dream?"

"Crazy dream. Johnny Day was in it and his friend Warty Watson. I remember them clearly. It so vivid. Johnny had a gun and shot at us. You did the gentlemanly thing and stepped in front of me, I felt as if I'd been slammed in the ribs ... and then I woke up in bed here." She gave a sigh, or tried to, it just didn't come. "See what I mean about wild dreams? I must have passed out or something."

"Stella." Justin reached over and took her hand. "There's no easy way to say this and I'm not quite sure which end to start from. But it wasn't a dream."

She stared at him for a full minute. "You're nuts! If he shot me, I'd be in the hospital. Injured." Dear Lord, the bruise and scar by her breast. "Have I been in a coma for weeks and healed?" How long had she been out of things? Dear heaven! "What happened to Sam?"

"He's all right, Stella, honestly he is. He's at the cinema with Kit. I promise you, on my word of honor, he's well. And no, you have not been in a coma. This is Saturday evening. We went out last night, but you did sleep most of the day away."

She believed him. Not sure why, after his other preposterous words, but she did. "Okay. Make sense for me please. Johnny Day did not shoot me. I'm here. Alive. The same as I was yesterday."

"Stella, what I'm about to say is incredible and unbelievable but every word is true. Please listen. Johnny Day did shoot you. And me. I got four bullets. One passed through me and killed you."

"Then why am I sitting here thinking you're crazy?"

"Because that's only part of what happened."

"I got up and made a miraculous recovery, I suppose."

"Not quite." He hesitated. "Remember your comment upstairs about vampires?"

"Yeah. You made a crack about these slippers having Kit's native earth in them." And that didn't make sense either; why could she walk wearing them but knocked the dust out of the carpet when she didn't?

"I wasn't joking, Stella. They do contain Kit's native

earth, and yours as it turns out. You were both born in England. He has his shoes lined with it because he's . . . a vampire."

She laughed. "Be serious, Justin! Halloween is over."

"I am being serious. Halloween is costumes and capes and plastic fangs. This is reality."

"Vampires don't exist!" Why didn't Dixie say something? She knew Justin was talking nonsense.

"We do."

"What do you mean, '*we* do'?"

"Kit, myself, Dixie, and others. Why do you think Dixie opened a Vampire Emporium? It was her idea of a joke on mortals. Have you noticed there are no mirrors in this house? We avoid them. We don't appear on photographic film either."

A horrid possibility hit her. The blurry figure of Justin in the photo she'd taken at Halloween—she'd thought it was ruined by bad light.

"You're all three vampires?" He nodded. "My child is out, alone, with a vampire at night!" She leaped up, grabbing Justin by the upper arms. "Where is he? Where did he take Sam?" She was shrieking but didn't give a damn. If one of them dared touch Sam . . .

"He's safe, Stella. Didn't I tell you that?"

"Yes, on your word of honor as a vampire!"

"Sam is perfectly safe, Stella," Dixie said. "Christopher would no more harm Sam than you would."

"I'm supposed to believe that?"

"Yes."

Stella looked from her to Justin. What chance did she have against two of them? "I don't care who or what you are. If anything happens to Sam . . ."

"Stella," Justin said, "Sam is safe. Kit can protect him far better than any mortal could." He eased his arms out of her grasp and held her hands. "Kit will never harm him. This is reality, not Hollywood or a television special. We do not harm or kill. It's against our ethics."

"Right, I supposed you don't drink blood either."

"We do. But we don't kill for it. We take small quantities from mortals or animals, and occasionally use blood bags."

Stella turned to Dixie hoping she'd deny all this. "Got a fridge full of blood bags in the kitchen then?"

"I moved them all to the basement. Didn't want Sam finding them if he was looking for a snack."

It was true! Impossibly and hideously true.

"We keep to ourselves," Justin went on, "look after each other and try to stay uninvolved in the lives of mortals. Over the centuries we've had more to fear from breathers than they ever have from us."

"Then why, exactly are you sharing all this with me?"

"Because, as I told you, Johnny Day shot and killed you last night."

She plonked right down on the sofa, her mind not quite in sync with her body. Dixie sat beside her and held her close. "Justin, you have the finesse of a clodhopper!"

"I did my best!"

"Back up a bit here." Stella had to get this last bit straight before she went crazy. "You're telling me, you two and Kit are vampires and that I died last night. Now I'm sitting here talking to you. If I'm not dreaming or hallucinating . . . what does that mean about me?"

"You've already worked that out, haven't you?" Justin said quietly.

Stella looked from him to Dixie, searching their eyes for a lie, their faces for a trace of amusement to betray this as a twisted joke. She saw nothing but truth and concern. Her mind turned flips as it grasped the incredible. "I'm a vampire." She felt time had stopped while she accepted the shock and neither of them denied it. "What happened?"

"You were shot and killed. I transformed you. Your weakness was because I mistakenly thought you were on your native soil. We have a network to take care of things like that."

"Vampire's Aid?" she asked.

"We all need it from time to time. It's like . . ."

The front door opened. "Mom!" Sam called.

From learning she was a vampire to getting Sam ready for bed was too big a leap. How was she going to—

"Be a mother now, Sam needs you," Justin said. "You've a long time to learn the rest of it." She'd heard every word and Justin hadn't spoken. "He needs you. He's been worried."

"Sam!" Stella hugged him tight. He was warm and living, his face cold from the outside. His soft hair brushed her cheeks. She heard his heart pump, felt the thrum in his veins and the rhythm of his life. She could smell his blood, rich and warm and . . . She stopped right there. She was not thinking this way about Sam. Ever! "Did you have a great time?" she asked him, smoothing back his ruffled hair.

"We had pizza for dinner. Kit doesn't like pizza so I ate all of it . . . and Mom, he said I could call him Kit, really. And I've got a new book. Will you read it to me? Please! I'm so glad you're okay. I was scared you were sick."

"I'm okay, honey." She gave him another hug, to atone for lying. "Now gather up your things and say 'thank you' to Kit and Dixie, we need to get home."

His face fell as if she'd said there'd be no Christmas. "Mom! Kit said we'd be sleeping over."

He had, had he? She paused just long enough to glare at him. Not content with changing her into one of them, now they were managing her life for her. Or rather the life she had, after dying. Which meant . . . what? She shook her head trying to clear her confusion and make some sense of the chaos that passed for her present life—or death.

"How about it?" Dixie asked. She'd stepped across the room and stood beside Stella. "Once Sam's tucked in and asleep, we can talk."

Once Sam was tucked in and asleep, she'd more likely scream.

"Scream if you want. Take a couple of slugs at me, but give me time to explain. You can't survive if you don't know how to." Justin spoke but he didn't. She heard him but he hadn't said a word. Was she hearing voices? Stella scowled in his direction. They were rearranging her life, her death, and now getting into her mind.

Dixie put a hand on her arm. She didn't say a word, just rolled her eyes in Justin's direction. "Don't let anyone bull-doze you," she said. "But you're more than welcome. You feel fine now, but if you wake up feeling lousy, one of us can help out with Sam while you rest."

"Okay, but just tonight. We have to be home tomorrow, as Sam's got school on Monday."

They spent the evening playing War and Go Fish. Bloodsucking vampires and kid's card games struck Stella as an unlikely combination. But now she was one of the bloodsucking vampires—something she had to get her mind around. If she didn't go utterly crazy first. Not that that was an option right now. She had to go see Mom next Saturday and how in heaven's name . . . ? She'd worry about that when the weekend came. She had more than enough on her mind now.

It was an incredibly long evening, but in some ways it was no time at all before she had Sam bathed and tucked in bed in Dixie and Kit's back bedroom. Sam nestled close, warm from his bath and smelling of soap and clean boy, as Stella began to read. She read three chapters, partly to compensate for not spending the day with him, and partly because of anxiety about what waited after she tucked Sam up for the night. She had questions, she wanted answers, but she knew in her gut she wouldn't like what she heard.

"Mom," Sam said at last through a yawn. "I think I need to go to sleep."

Wasn't often that happened. Wasn't often she had three vampires waiting for her either. "Good night, honey," Stella said hugging Sam and giving him a last kiss. "Sleep well."

"I will, Mom." Sam smiled and kissed her back. He snuggled under the down comforter. "I like this house, Mom. Thanks for letting me stay another night."

She would not let that hurt. But it did. Not that she blamed him. Even a nine-year-old could see the difference between faded hooked rugs on floorboards and wall-to-wall carpeting. He'd have to be blind not to notice that the freshly plastered ceiling didn't have a single crack, and she didn't want to dwell on how warm it was in a bathroom where the windows fit perfectly.

That was the way it was. No point in hankering after what she'd never be able to afford. Kit and Dixie were rich. She worked in a dry cleaner's. Big difference. "It's a nice house, Sam, but won't it be nice to be back home tomorrow?"

He wrapped his arms around her neck. "I love you, Mom." He gave her a last kiss, completely avoiding her question. After all, she'd brought him up not to tell lies.

Tomorrow night they darn well would be home. Tonight she'd find out from Justin whatever it was she needed to know to live as a vampire and she'd work out how to do it. Even if she had to live in Kit's borrowed slippers until her promised shoes arrived. She shuddered to think how much they'd cost.

No point in standing up here worrying. Might as well go downstairs and find out. "'Night, Sam," Stella said and opened the door.

Justin was waiting, sitting on the floor at the top of the stairs and effectively blocking her way downstairs. He smiled.

"Hi," Stella said. Though she'd rather have said, "Get the hell out of my way," it seemed rude.

"Hi." It sounded different with his accent. "Want to wait a little while until Sam's asleep?"

"And then what?"

"I thought we could sit on the roof and talk. That way, you can hear Sam if he wakes up." He sounded so cool and casual but she couldn't miss the hesitation in his voice.

"That's the first time anyone's made that offer."

"Interested?"

"I do have some questions." Some? She was getting to talk like him. She had hundreds!

"Thought you might." He held out his hand. "Come and sit next to me. I won't bite, I promise."

She couldn't help smiling as she sat down. "Is that a vampire joke?"

"A bad one."

She had a dozen smart replies on the tip of her tongue but none seemed worth the effort. "I'm terrified."

"I know." As he spoke, he pulled her close and wrapped his arms around her, "you wouldn't be human if you weren't."

"Am I human?"

"Of course you are. You don't stop being human."

She looked up at him. "But I'm a vampire." Each time she said the word, it became easier.

"I took your blood, not your humanity."

She thought on that a moment. A long, sweet moment with his arms around her and her body aligned with his. A fierce longing for more fought with her determination to keep this casual . . . but it would never be casual again. "I have your blood?"

"Our blood is mingled. That's how I transformed you," he paused. "We have a bond between us, Stella."

That was one of the zillion things that worried her. But . . . "Sam's asleep."

"How do you know?"

"I heard his breathing change."

"Through a closed door?" His look was almost a challenge.

"Yes, through a closed door." The thought chilled her. "Is that part of it all?"

He nodded. "Yes. Want to climb on the roof?"

"In borrowed slippers, three sizes too big?" She already knew what happened without them.

"We can improvise." He reached into his pants pocket and pulled out a roll of duct tape. "I'll tape them on. You don't want to lose one halfway up."

Stella sat on the stairs as Justin knelt at her feet, taping the slippers on snugly. When he finished, she stood and tried walking. It was awkward but at least they didn't slip. "You really think I can climb in these?" Or in anything else for that matter.

"Yes. We're just going up the side of the house. We'll let the Capitol and the Leveque Tower wait until you have shoes that fit properly."

He spoke as if climbing a tall building was as easy as a stroll in the park. Yeah right, look what the last stroll in the park got her! One good thing, she had no fear of falling to her death. But . . . "What if someone sees us?"

"We'll climb up the back." He took her hand and led her out of the house. "Don't worry about being seen. Few mortals ever look above eye level."

They were in Kit's backyard. Stella wore borrowed sweatpants and a tee-shirt. It was nearly nine o'clock on a November evening, and she didn't feel cold. "Why aren't I freezing?" she asked but guessed the answer before he replied. "It's part of it, isn't it?"

"Yes." He paused. "And so is this. Watch what I do. Lean into the wall and use any handhold you find. Your fingers are stronger than your arms and legs used to be."

He wasn't kidding! The moment she reached for the first windowsill and levered herself up she almost fell in shock. Instead, she sort of hopped on the sill and spread her fingers wide on the bricks for support. She felt every little ridge and hollow. A hand on the top of the window frame, a foot braced on the brick and she was climbing as easily as walking. The wide box gutter delayed her briefly, but following Justin's suggestion to curl her fingers and reach over it, she was up onto the roof. Seconds later she was perched astride the ridge of the hip roof, her back against the chimney with Justin facing her, his foot resting on a vent cover.

"Comfy?" he asked.

It wasn't the word she'd have chosen but . . . "Yes, I thought it could be scary, but it isn't."

"Stella," he replied, "there aren't many things that will ever scare you physically again. You're faster and stronger than any mortal."

Sobering thought, that. What was she going to do? She looked out over the rooftops and across to the trees that marked the park. The park where she'd died last night. She ran her hands though her hair. Why not? She'd be having bad hair days the rest of her unlife, but since she couldn't look in a mirror . . . or could she? But there wasn't one in the bathroom. This was too much, but she had to find a way to cope. She had Sam to take care of.

Justin watched the emotions crossing her face. Now was not the time to tell her he could read her thoughts. She was scared, but not of heights, of facing her new life. "So, the thought of being a vampire gives you the heebie-jeebies."

"If it were just the thought, I could handle it. It's the reality that has my brain spinning."

"You're not alone. We don't make fledglings and leave them to survive or extinguish on their own."

"Who's 'we'? You mean there are more vampires?"

"Many more, and I prefer the term revenant. 'Vampire' has been sensationalized by Hollywood."

She paused, thinking that one over, and he knew her reply before she spoke. "I'll stick with what I know. I'm a vampire." She went silent and he saw the shock rippling though her mind at what she'd just said.

"It has some advantages over mere mortal existence. I brought you up here to show you one. When you have your shoes tomorrow, we'll go down to the river and jump over it. We can climb any building downtown. Run faster than any car or train. I'll show you how. You're my fledgling. I'll take care of you."

Wrong words. Her mind snapped at that. Irritation sparked like power arcs. "When I have those shoes tomorrow, I'll go home. Sam has school to get ready for and I've got work on Monday." She stood up and stared at him as the shock coursed through her. "How can I go to work if I sleep all day?"

"You can't. You don't need to."

"Like hell I don't! I need my job. How else can I live?" She was close to shaking with worry.

"Stella, I'll take care of you."

"Like you have already, I suppose!" She moved. Too fast. Unused to her speed she lost her balance and fell.

Justin leapt after her, caught her halfway down and landed on his feet, his arms tight around her as her soft breasts pressed into his chest. By the time they landed he had a hard-on and she was doing her best to clobber him.

He let her go.

She stood and glared.

She was torn between her anger at his offer to look after her, and her innate politeness that demanded she thank him for catching her. She didn't realize she could have landed on her own.

Innate politeness won. "Thanks. Next time I get mad at you I'll make sure I'm standing on the ground."

"Learn to jump down from the roof. It's not that hard." She was counting . . . looked like to a hundred. He'd handled this all wrong. "Stella," he said as she got to seventy-eight. "I didn't bring you out here to get you angry. I wanted to show you what you can do."

She stopped counting and listened. That was progress. Or was it? Panic flared through her mind. "Seems the things I can do and the things I need to do are at odds. I can leap tall buildings but I can't get up in the morning to fix Sam's breakfast. I can move faster than a speeding bullet, even stop one if I need to but I can't get up and go to work, and even if I could, I can't see to put on my lipstick."

"Mirrors are a bit of a problem. It's something about the silver in them, we don't reflect, and if we look straight at them, we see our lives reflected back at us. So we avoid them. Talk to Dixie about doing your hair and all that, she came up with using dark, polished Plexiglas."

"Okay, so I can brush my hair, but . . . how about getting up in the morning and going to work?"

"You'll be able to, in time."

She clutched that thought like a lifeline. "How much time?"

He hesitated, remembering Kit's telling of Dixie's shock at the reality of feeding. "That depends."

"On what?"

He was going to have to tell her. And soon. He wasn't ready and he suspected she wasn't either, but . . . "Let's have a seat." He nodded towards a teak bench under a half-bare tree.

She considered refusing—he read that much—but she nodded. "Okay."

As he sat beside her, she looked right at him. He read her hesitation and worry but brushing it aside, she asked, "What does it depend on?"

"How soon you feed." Direct yes, but she was in no mood for delay.

"You mean drink blood?" Her mind recoiled at the thought, but she wouldn't back away.

Her courage gave him pause. "Yes. Right now you're what we call a fledgling, a young, newly transformed revenant. You're relatively weak. Blood sustains us. Enables us to walk in day. Gives us strength to transmogrify . . . change into animals if need be. Lets us fly. Helps us heal from injury."

"And you use blood bags, right?"

"From time to time, but fresh blood is more sustaining, and you, as a fledgling, need fresh blood."

She never paused. "Seems I'd better go find some." And she had no idea where to start.

"It can wait."

"Not if I'm going to work Monday morning, it can't."

"There's no need for you to go to work Monday morning. Didn't I tell you I'd take care of all that?"

Wrong again. She glared at him. "Get this straight, Justin. I need my job. I'll have to live once you go back to England."

"When I go, you and Sam will come with me."

"What? You have some nerve! I'm not going anywhere with you. In fact if only I hadn't gone on the damn date last night, my life would be fine!" She marched back into the house and left him sitting in the moonlight. He looked up at the sky and called on the gods to help him straighten this out.

Chapter Eight

"Stella, are you aware? Can you understand me?" It was Dixie. That much Stella realized but her eyes prickled with fatigue and her limbs felt heavy and it was still daylight.

"What's wrong?" Stella asked, her voice sounding groggy and halfway to incoherent.

"Nothing's wrong. Nothing at all, I promise. Sam's okay."

Stella trusted Dixie not to lie. "I've got something for you. The shoes Justin ordered arrived an hour or so ago. I'm going to put them on you. It's going to make a big difference."

Dixie wasn't kidding. Just sitting up in bed, her head cleared and every ache disappeared and when she stood up, she could walk. Stella took two turns around the room before she came right back and hugged Dixie. "I'll never thank you enough. It's like magic." She bounced on the carpet, feeling the spring in her feet. "I feel I could fly."

Dixie smiled. "One of these days. That takes time. I've only just started being able to do that alone."

Stella stared. "I hadn't meant that literally. You're telling me I'll be able to fly?"

"Yup. Justin and Christopher can just about anytime. Usually they transmogrify into bird or bat form to conserve strength, but they can do it in human shape too. I've just started learning. It takes time to acquire the power and strength, and you have to feed both before and afterwards. It drains energy."

"Flying or changing into animals?"

"Both."

Stella sat down on the edge of the bed. "I only half-believe I'm having this conversation, and . . . Where's Sam?"

"Taking Christopher and Justin round Cosi, the new science museum." She sat down beside Stella. "I suggested they scoot off while you get used to your new shoes. You've got several pairs." She had four. Another pair of black leather sneakers like the ones she was wearing, a very nice pair of Sunday shoes which Stella doubted she'd have much use for and a pair of rubber thongs. "You'll need those for showering," Dixie said. "They'll save you from clinging to the granny bars for dear life."

Stella hefted her new shoes. They were heavier than they looked. That must be the earth in them. The soles were a good half, three-quarter inch thick. "They don't feel heavy when I walk."

"They won't. You're vampire. Not many things will feel heavy anymore."

"You mean I can move out the refrigerator to clean behind it?"

"With one hand."

That took thinking about.

"I went with Justin and fetched you some usable clothes," Dixie said at last. "I figured you'd feel better wearing your own things. Holler if you need me."

Dixie was darn well right. After pulling on her own blue jeans and sweatshirt, Stella did feel more normal. Or as normal as she was likely to, being a vampire. She allowed herself a little chuckle. She had no idea how she was going to cope, with life, with Sam, but most of all, with Justin, but she sensed a major ally in Dixie and right now she needed a friend.

"How about some retail therapy?" Dixie asked as Stella came downstairs. "I think a trip to City Center might be what you need."

Bless her! The mall might be Dixie's answer to melancholy, but a shopping spree was the last thing Stella could afford. "I'm not that big on shopping."

"What I had in mind wasn't plastic money madness," Dixie went on, "but a nice stroll. It's cloudy out. You can get into the car with no problem. We'll park underground and be indoors in the mall. You won't have to worry about the sun." Dixie paused. "It might help get you used to being around mortals en masse."

They spent hours in City Center, walking back and forth, and up and down the escalators, and pausing in one of the coffee shops to watch the mortals stroll past. Dixie bought them both cups of coffee. "Don't take more than a couple of sips," she warned. "In time you'll be able to drink cups of it. It doesn't have any effect, any more than alcohol does, but it helps us pass as mortals."

Stella remembered the cup of coffee Justin drank in her kitchen that day he'd confronted the Day boys the first time. She picked up the white coffee mug with both hands and sipped. Twice. Either this was the blandest coffee in the world or . . .

"Doesn't taste the way it used to, does it?"

"It tastes of nothing."

Dixie nodded. "I know. I miss chocolate truffles and some mornings I hanker for a nice, sausage biscuit."

"So nothing tastes anymore?" Well, duh! Of course not. She'd never eat again.

"When we feed," Dixie paused, "it tastes."

"Yes. Justin mentioned feeding, a little while before I marched off in a huff. I never got any details."

Dixie paused, taking a small sip of her coffee. "Yes, he was a bit bent out of shape over that."

She bet he was. But mind you, he had respected the closed door. Taking refuge in Sam's bed had been a bit cowardly. "It was too much! He just announced I would have to quit my job, and then up my life and toddle off to Britain in his wake. I left there when I was three years old! It's not my home and I'm not hauling Sam over there."

"Look, I'm on your side," Dixie said, reaching across the table to squeeze Stella's hand. "Honest, I am."

"He's so damn . . . dictatorial!"

Dixie nodded. "They tend to be like that." She took another sip of coffee. "I frequently have to remind Christopher we're not in the sixteenth century anymore."

Stella blinked as she got her mind around that fact. "When was he born?"

"Fifteen sixty-four. Walter Raleigh was one of his friends. Hard to imagine, isn't it." Dixie smiled. "He's that Christopher Marlowe."

Stella knew she must look blank and confused. "Who was he?"

Dixie gave Stella's hand another squeeze. "Sorry, I'm speaking like the old librarian here. He was a playwright and a poet. I still have a hard time completely accepting that the dead, white, Elizabethan playwright I used to read in college is the man I love."

"You love Kit though. I don't love Justin."

"He loves you."

"Oh, come on!"

"I'm not kidding. He was smitten from the first time he met you in the shop. If you'd seen his face Friday night when he carried you through the front door, you'd never doubt it. He was utterly distraught."

"He has a funny way of showing he loves me. He could try asking instead of telling."

"He could, and he will. If you give him the chance. Remember what I said about attitudes set in the past."

"Is Justin as old as Kit?" It was Dixie's turn to stare. "He hasn't told you?" Stella shook her head. "You two need to have a good, long talk. Let's say Justin is a lot older."

Stella wasn't sure she wanted to comprehend that. "How much older?"

"You've got yourself a much older man, but you do have the edge on him in mortal years." She wasn't sure it was a big advantage. This did need thinking about. "You really need to talk to Justin, you know."

Stella took another sip of tasteless coffee. It didn't help. As she set her cup down she looked at Dixie. "Okay, I'll ask him. Sometime. Meanwhile, I have to feed before going to work tomorrow. Will you show me how?"

"Justin transformed you. It's for him to initiate you."

"You make it sound like some sort of fraternity or sorority."

Dixie shrugged. "I suppose, in a way, it is. Just our select group and the rest of humanity."

Stella went silent. Watching the passersby, she became aware of the heartbeats of the couple at the next table. Above the buzz of humanity, she sensed a hundred pulses thrumming with life. A life she'd had cut short by a vengeful delinquent. And now . . . she leaned back, looking out over the vastness of the mall. She'd taken her anxiety and uncertainty out on Justin. Hardly fair . . . but . . . did he love her? Could she love him? And was there any point anyway? She could not hotfoot it off to Britain, even if she wanted to. There was Mom . . .

Through the sounds of mortal heartbeats, Stella caught a faint aroma of . . . "Can you smell something?" she asked

Dixie. "It's not unpleasant. It's rather nice but it seems to get stronger as we sit here."

"It's human blood," Dixie replied. "You notice it in crowds, or closed-in spaces." And she thought it smelled good!

"Maybe we should get back, and you get a bunch of questions ready for Justin."

Made sense. Perhaps. "Will I be a vampire forever? Or can't you tell me that? Are there magic herbs like in books that will turn me back?"

"No magic herbs that I know of. Maybe I shouldn't tell you this but heck, you might as well know. The transformation isn't permanent . . . yet." Dixie had her complete attention. "If you don't feed, you won't remain a vampire."

So, she wasn't stuck like this. There was a chance of normal life again. "So I just don't feed." Suited her, the idea wasn't exactly appetizing. "That's easy. Why didn't Justin tell me this?"

"You didn't give him much of a chance to."

Okay, she hadn't but . . . "So I just don't feed and then I . . ."

"Revert to the way you were before Justin transformed you."

When she was shot! "I'll be dead!"

Dixie nodded. "Right. Not much of an option is it?"

It wasn't any sort of option. She was not going to choose death. "I'd better just get used to feeding. What's it like, the first time?"

"Go with Justin, let him teach you. You don't want to do what I did. I lost my temper and lost control. That is not recommended. Do no harm to mortals and all that." She paused. "The colony has some strict rules and that's one of them."

"What's the colony?"

"It's our immediate group, adopted family you might say. Vampires who are linked by blood. Justin made Christopher. Christopher made his friend Tom and me. Justin made you.

There are several others. Gwyltha, the vampire who made Justin, is the leader. Most are in the UK. But at least one, Toby, is an American too. They have a network set up. That's how Justin got your shoes made and flown over. Sometimes they work with other colonies, but mostly we keep to ourselves. Our colony is pretty small and . . ."

Dixie paused and looked up. Stella followed her gaze. A man stood a small distance away. He smiled and inclined his head. In a flash, Stella realized he wasn't a mortal. He was a vampire. Was Columbus full of them and she'd been too wrapped up in herself to notice?

"Vlad," Dixie said. She sounded wary, almost worried.

"Forgive my intrusion." He gave a little bow. "I have a message from Gwyltha. I had planned on calling on you but on seeing you here . . ." He paused. And looked right at Stella.

She looked right back. He wasn't as tall as Justin but very thick set. You could imagine him hefting tree trunks or wielding a battle-axe without much effort.

"Oh," Dixie hesitated a few seconds but then went on. "Stella, this is a close friend of Gwyltha, Vlad Tepes. Vlad, this is Stella Schwartz."

He took Stella's hand and bowed. It was like a scene from an old movie. "A pleasure to meet you. Give Doctor Corvus my felicitations." While Stella wondered what exactly that meant, he turned to Dixie. "Please tell him Gwyltha will be here next weekend, if all goes to plan."

"I'll be sure to." Dixie paused as if wanting to ask something, but went on. "I don't think you were expected."

"I was not, but presumed on the same courtesy of passage I gave Corvus. I will be here until I leave with Gwyltha . . . unless anyone objects." He gave them each an abrupt nod and a surprising smile. "My best wishes," he said and turned and walked away in the crowd.

"Who was that vampire?" Stella asked as Dixie drove out of the parking lot and up the ramp to the fading afternoon.

"Someone Christopher and Justin mistrust and who's always treated me with his odd, old-fashioned courtesy," Dixie replied. "He's . . . well his full name is Vladr Tepes, Prince of Wallachia, otherwise known as Count . . ."

"Dracula!" Stella almost gasped it.

Dixie nodded as she eased into a gap in the traffic on Third. "Yup, Dracula. Gave me a bit of a turn when I first met him."

"This is going to take getting used to." Wrong! She was never going to get used to a character from a movie appearing in real life. "I thought Dracula was fiction."

Dixie chuckled. "A couple of days ago, you thought vampires were."

"I couple of days ago, I had a nice life!"

Dixie took a hand off the steering wheel and squeezed Stella's hand. "You still have. It's just on its ears right now. When you think about it, the advantages outweigh the snags. You'll never grow old. Won't get sick. Never run out of energy, and your strength will increase with time, not diminish. No more having to shell out for haircuts, and you won't ever have to worry about getting fat."

Put that way . . . "You mean my body will stay just like this forever?"

"Yes."

"Makes me wish I'd lost that ten pounds I'd been meaning to."

Dixie chuckled and gave Stella's hand another squeeze. "You'll make it, Stella."

"Maybe . . . but what about Sam?" He was the heart of all her worries.

"You're not alone, Stella," Dixie said as she turned off Third towards City Park. "The colony is with you. I'm here.

Christopher is, and Justin will do just about anything for you and Sam. You know that, don't you?"

Stella nodded as Dixie slowed the car and then backed into a space a couple of houses down from hers. "Maybe that's what irks. He wants to do and manage far too much."

"We're back where we started, aren't we?" Dixie turned off the ignition. "It's up to you sometimes to look him in the face and say, 'No.' Okay, they have time-honored rules, most of which make sense, but once in a while . . ." She grinned. "Let your gut instincts prevail. I have and always intend to."

Stella tried to keep that in mind an hour or so later.

"If you insist on going back to your house, I'm coming with you," Justin said.

"You are not!" She was whispering, hissing almost, so as not to be overheard by Sam, happily coloring in a book about space exploration.

"You cannot manage on your own."

"I can if I feed."

"You don't know what you're talking about."

Stella folded her arms under her breasts. "And you do?"

"I know about survival for our kind."

"And I know I have Sam to think of."

"Of course you do it's just . . ."

"You're not moving in."

"Hi, you two." Dixie walked over to them. "Perhaps I can help?"

Justin frowned at her. "I'm trying to get Stella to see reason." Reason! Stella almost spluttered. "She can't possibly go off on her own so soon."

Dixie nodded. "You're right." Stella clenched her fists. And she'd thought Dixie was on her side! "I'll stay with her and Sam. That way someone's with her."

Stella gave Dixie a hug that would have broken a mortal's ribs. "Thank you." But through her relief, she sensed Justin's hurt. "I just need to get settled, don't you understand?" she asked him.

"Frankly, Stella, no."

His barely disguised annoyance set her temper off. "I'm sorry about that." She stepped back. "I need to get packed." She walked through the living room. "Finish that picture, Sam, we have to leave in a little while," she said and walked on up the stairs.

Justin looked ready to explode. He grabbed Dixie's arms and pulled her into the kitchen where they would be out of Sam's earshot. She didn't resist. "Dixie." His voice was clipped and tight. "At the risk of insulting a hostess, you have no business intruding between us. You women!"

"What's wrong?" Christopher appeared in the doorway.

Justin snarled. "Dixie is interfering with Stella and me. Seems, Kit, you can't control your woman!"

Kit's mouth twitched at one corner. "Sorry about that. Got any pointers for me? Any tips?"

Dixie could feel the testosterone sparking. Another minute and they'd be at blows. "Hush, the pair of you! Sam's got darn good ears for a mortal!"

They followed her lead, exchanging thoughts instead of speech.

"What's going on, Dixie?" Christopher asked.

"I've helped resolve a problem."

"Resolve!" Justin's response all but vibrated her skull.

"Yes, resolve. Think a minute. Stella, not unreasonably, doesn't want the neighbors to think you've moved in." She sensed Justin's hesitation at that. He hadn't seen it from Stella's point of view. "We all know she can't be alone. So, I'll be there."

"Don't I get a say in this?" Christopher asked.

"Yes, dear," Dixie replied. "It won't be for long, and it will help out Justin."

Christopher's eyes met hers. His mouth twitched again. "I see." She knew darn well he didn't.

"Would you care to explain how this will help me?" Justin asked.

"Of course. You won't have to tear your mind out worrying how Stella is doing on her own. Plus, I'll be in the house to watch Sam whenever you and Stella want to go out." He only looked half-convinced. "Have you thought how much privacy you'll have in a house with a nine-year-old?" He obviously hadn't.

"Dixie," Justin began, "I see your point." He offered his hand. "I apologize."

She took his hand, and smiled. "No problem, but I think you have a few fences to mend with Stella."

He ran his free hand though his hair. "I seem to have a knack for angering her."

Dixie couldn't help it. She gave Justin a bear hug. "It will work out. Trust me. You've got a week to sort things out between you."

"I've got as long as it takes. You think I'm leaving here without her?"

"I wasn't talking about leaving. I'm talking about . . . I forgot to tell you both Gwyltha will be here next weekend."

"Did she call," Christopher asked, "while we were out?"

Dixie shook her head. "Stella and I ran into Vlad in City Center. He gave us the message."

Christopher looked ready to erupt this time. "You just 'ran into' Vlad Tepes?"

She'd had it up to everywhere with this male stuff. "We didn't exactly run into him. Stella and I were sitting having a cup of coffee, I was showing her one easy way to pass as mortal, when he came up and spoke to us. I introduced Stella." Justin would surely hyperventilate if his lungs still functioned. "And Vlad delivered the message. Said he was assuming the courtesy of passage he afforded you, Justin, and he'd see us with Gwyltha at the weekend. He didn't say how many others were coming." There had been a couple of dozen at her introduction to the colony but that was in Yorkshire. Besides, numbers didn't matter. Vampires were easy guests. No cooking needed.

"That man is everywhere," Justin muttered then turned suddenly. Stella was coming down the stairs, bag in hand. She looked at him with such longing. "I'll give you a lift home," Justin said.

"Thanks. Pack up your things, Sam, it's time to go."

Now it was Justin's turn to gaze bereft. Dixie shook her head. They had better sort things out or they'd both end up miserable. "I'll go grab a few things. Shan't be long." She made her escape before Christopher could stop her. She'd miss him, yes, but getting Stella and Justin together was a darn good cause.

"Did you get them all set?" Kit asked as Justin walked back into the house.

"I left Stella and Dixie gabbing over hairstyles and how to apply mascara without a mirror!" He flung himself into an easy chair. "I'm not sure how good an idea this was. Yes, Dixie will be there to baby-sit, and it's darn nice of her to step in, but I need to be the one with Stella. Showing her what to do, teaching her."

"You can't really show her how to put on mascara."

"There are more important things needed for survival."

"And you'll get to them." Kit smiled. "Dixie's been through this herself. She can help Stella."

"So the hell can I!"

"Yup, but you seem to have a gift for rubbing her the wrong way."

That was the trouble. "She won't listen."

"She's listening, alright. She's just not doing exactly what you expect."

You could say that again! "I'm scared I'll lose her, Kit."

Kit shook his head. "Don't be. She's got it as bad as you have. Just go easy on the instruction and try courting her instead."

"I'm worried about her."

"Of course you are. I worry about Dixie but in reality they can both cope with just about anything that comes up."

"Maybe that's what's wrong."

"Hell, Justin, you can't have it both ways. You've got yourself a vampire woman there, and a modern one at that. You're going to have to adapt."

"There are so many things . . ."

"Yup, and talking about things, I'm half-expecting a visit from our Transylvanian acquaintance, sooner or later. I'm rather glad Dixie is out of the house for the next day or two."

Justin would second that with regards to Stella. "What does he want? Dixie might believe he came just to deliver Gwyltha's message. I don't."

"Neither do I. He wants something."

"Justin's coming over tonight, right?" Stella asked as she came down from putting Sam to bed.

Dixie nodded. "That's the general idea. You've been saying you want to feed. He's going to show you how."

Stella sat down. "Somehow I don't feel the least hungry."

"Blood hunger isn't like human hunger for food, it's more like a physical longing. I didn't feel it at all until after I fed the first time."

"What did happen your first time?"

"I lost control and halfway killed someone." Stella's eyes widened with horror. "Don't worry, you won't do that. Not with Justin to guide you. The colony has strict rules about not harming humans. Revenge or meting out arbitrary justice are definite no-nos."

Stella appeared to think on that one. "So I can't go around scaring the boys who used to tease me in junior high."

"Afraid not. But you can be the youngest looking at the twenty-year reunion."

Stella grinned. "That's a thought." The smile faded. Fast. "I don't know how I'm going to cope. Sam's going to notice if I don't eat."

"Tell him you're on a diet. That will last for a while. After then, I don't know but between us we'll come up with something. We can talk to Gwyltha when she's here. I bet you're not the first vampire to have a child."

"You know of another one?"

"No, but if any of the others had had kids, they'd be long dead by now." That didn't seem to reassure in the least. "Take it one day, one week at a time." She paused. "At the risk of making you mad, Justin's right about your job. You can't work all day in daylight. I can't even and I'm on my native soil. You'll have the most strength at night. You can go out once in a while, like we did this afternoon, but you were tired weren't you? And now it's evening, your energy is coming back."

Dixie was right, since sunset her energy had returned. "I was thinking of getting a night cashier job at the Giant Eagle."

"And leave Sam every night?"

Could she? "I have to have money."

"You could help out in the store. I might not be able to pay what you get now, but you could save on baby-sitting by bringing Sam along. I can't offer you any benefits, but you won't have an old age to provide for and you certainly don't need medical insurance, but Sam will."

Sobering thoughts indeed. "I don't have insurance with my current job. Sam gets his through the state program."

"That's it then. You work for me. You'll still have a job that will keep Sam in hot dogs. Justin will be happy and I've got another pair of hands."

It seemed too perfect to work, but it would—Stella hoped. She had one quandary solved, only a couple of thousand still to go, like spending an evening with Justin, feeding, satisfying what Dixie said was akin to physical longing and no doubt setting off other physical needs.

Justin was coming! She sensed him! Stella crossed the room and opened the front door. He paused on the steps. As handsome as sin in the porch light. He would be so easy to love. His face lit up as he watched her.

"Stella," he said, holding out his hand. "Is Sam asleep? Can you come out?"

This was it. Saying "yes" meant she'd accepted what he'd turned her into.

He looked worried. "Should I come back later?"

"No." She reached out for his hand and he stepped into the house.

"Here. For you." From behind his back, he produced a bunch of pink rosebuds. Stella stared, first at the flowers and then at Justin. His mouth curled up at the corners. "Do you like them?"

She got her senses back enough to take them from him. "Thank you. I'll put them in water."

He followed her back to the kitchen as she searched the cabinets for something to hold them, settling finally on a jug she used to mix lemonade in the summer. "They're beautiful," she said as she arranged the long stems. "Thank you."

"My pleasure," Justin replied.

"I love roses, one of the best parts of summer."

"My grandmother used to grow roses," Justin said. "She would have one of the house slaves gather the petals to strew on the table at dinner. My mother died young so I lived with my grandparents when I was a boy."

"When were you a boy, Justin?"

"I was born in AD 110, the son of a Roman centurion posted to Britain and daughter of a British merchant. My mother died when I was born. My father did the honorable thing, acknowledged me and sent me to be raised by his parents. By an odd twist of fate, I was posted back to Britain and died there."

When Dixie said much older, she hadn't been joking. "You're nearly two thousand years old."

He nodded. "Yes, but I'll never be more than twenty-five."

His hair was a young man's. Not the slightest trace of graying. His olive skin still smooth but his dark eyes had creases in the corners and slight furrows marked his forehead. "You look older than twenty-five."

"They were harder days. Men were old at forty—if they lived that long."

"There are days I feel old at thirty-two."

"Not anymore, you won't."

Now that was a sobering thought. "I'm still trying to get used to that idea."

Slowly his mouth turned up at the corners. "So am I."

"It doesn't get any easier?"

He shook his head. " 'Fraid not, but having friends helps."

And Justin would make it a whole lot easier. Could she let him? He'd be gone soon. She had to learn to cope with this on her own. Others had survived for hundreds of years, why shouldn't she?

She placed the roses in the center of the kitchen table. "Shouldn't we be going out?" She might as well get this over with.

He insisted on fetching her coat from the hall closet and holding it for her. "Do I need it? I'm not cold."

"Of course you're not, but going out in November without a coat is liable to attract notice. Always blend in with the breathers."

As if he blended in! Still, he had a point. She buttoned up her coat and, after a final look in on a sleeping Sam, stepped out into the night with Justin Corvus, one-time regimental surgeon to the Ninth Hispañia.

He took her to Cup o' Joe and they settled in a sofa by the window overlooking Third Street.

"What's this? A let's-get-to-know-each-other date?" Stella asked, as he took her coat and laid it over a spare chair.

"More of quick chat before dinner."

She couldn't help smiling. "Yeah, right!"

"And we'll talk over coffee and pass as mere mortals."

Anything that delayed the moment when she had to bite someone's neck was fine with her. She had to do this. She had no choice, but no one ever said she had to like it. It would be like eating meatloaf at school. It tasted bad, it made her want to barf but it wouldn't kill her. The utter reverse in fact.

Justin stepped from the counter, a large white mug in each hand. He cast a smile in her direction and then started back to the table.

Stella watched his shoulders as he moved toward her. Nice shoulders. Nice body come to that. That she knew already; she'd seen all of it. She wasn't the only woman watching him. The skinny rich-looking girl in the armchair couldn't keep her eyes off Justin. She might think he was eye candy, Stella knew so much more. Looks were just the beginning. He was great with kids, sexy as all out, and he was coming back to her. Let the mortal drool.

Justin gave Stella a guarded look as he set down the mug. "Remember, just a sip at a time."

She picked the mug up in both hands and sipped. "So, what do I need to know, Justin?" He looked even more uncomfortable. Instructing beginners on the intricacies of blood sucking was no doubt grunt work for master vampires.

"Look, there's something you have to know before we go any further."

"What?"

"I can read your thoughts." After Justin wiped up her spluttered coffee, he apologized. "By Abel, I'm sorry. I didn't mean to do that to you."

"I didn't mean to either." She bet the sweet rich thing in the corner didn't spurt coffee out her nose. "It just . . ." Incredible! She'd soaked her shirt with near-boiling coffee, and after the first burn, she didn't feel a thing. She should be half-scalded. She clutched at her still-damp clothes. "Justin . . . ?"

"You're recovering already. What was a severe scald is healing." He smiled. "You will from now on. Cuts, broken bones, bullet wounds. "

Yes. She knew that, it just hadn't completely registered and this was getting her distracted. "I know. Now about reading my mind? Please stop doing it."

"It's up to you to veil your mind. I'll show you how." He paused. "I agree, she's far too skinny. Not my sort at all."

"If you're trying to wind me up, you're succeeding!"

"I'm not. I'm just agreeing with you. Mortals that skinny tend to have bland blood. Nothing wrong with slim but avoid the anorexic sort."

She'd make a point of it. "Any other helpful advice?"

He pulled a pack of cards from his pocket. "First, you need to learn how to do this. Kit used cards to teach Dixie, so let's see how it goes. Take a card." She cut the deck and took the top card and turned it over. "Five of hearts." She almost dropped it. "Try another." He saw the ten of spades and the queen of diamonds as clearly as she did.

"Remind me never to play poker with a vampire."

"Why not? You'll be on equal footing."

She kept forgetting that. "Not completely, right? I'm still a fledgling."

He shuffled the cards. "Yes, but this is very elementary stuff. You'll pick up the rest over the next couple of hundred years or so." He cut the deck and took a card. "What do I have?"

"How am I supposed to know?"

"Focus and concentrate. Our minds are linked because of the blood bond. I'm going to open mine completely. Think with me."

Easy to say. But she did sense his thoughts as if feeling her way through a fog. "Three of clubs!" She all but shouted it. She'd known. Not seen it but sensed what he held.

"Good." He reached for another card. "Again."

She was halfway to having a headache before he let her rest. "See what I mean about simple?"

"More like incredible! So, I can see into your mind. Fair enough, now what about teaching me how to close off mine?"

"That's a little trickier." She bet it was! He grinned. "I said tricky, not difficult—but it takes practice. You just shut it off so I can't link with you."

Easier said than done, but she managed after ten minutes or so. She pretended her mind had a heavy oak door, like the one to the church, and just locked it shut. It worked! She was holding the ten of hearts and Justin said, "I can't see it. You've done it." At last. "Now, five more cards, and keep your mind closed."

Now that she knew how, it was easy. "Thanks for showing me that."

"It comes in handy. As you get stronger, you'll catch more and more from the mortal minds around. It gets over-powering at times."

"You mean I can read other people's minds, not just yours?"

He chuckled. "Yes. You can control them to a degree. You'll need to, to feed. Total strangers don't hold still while you bite."

She bet they didn't.

Justin stood up and help out his hand. "Let's go have dinner."

Chapter Nine

Justin took her beyond German Village to a rundown neighborhood on the east side. Perched on the roof of a boarded-up house, they looked down on a razed lot. Two dark shapes sat huddled under a shack of scrap wood and old cartons.

"Let them get settled," Justin said, "then we'll jump down at the far corner. I'll soothe them both. You open your mind to me and you'll sense how I do it." Stella nodded, still uncomfortable with the idea of Justin in her thoughts. "Keep your mind open. When I tell you to stop feeding, stop. I don't want your introduction to the colony to be a discipline for killing a mortal."

"Is it that easy to kill?" Her mind and stomach roiled at the thought.

"Not when you know what you're doing."

And she didn't—yet. "When will I know what I'm doing?"

He looked out into the night and at the human shapes below. "In about five or ten minutes. One important thing: after feeding, you must remove all trace of memory of it from the mortal's mind. That's how we remain undetected."

"How do I do that?"

"Keep your mind open to mine. You'll know."

After the last couple of days, she didn't doubt him one little bit.

They waited, side by side, perched on the sagging roof as the two vagrants below huddled under newspapers against the November wind. Justin squeezed her hand. "Open your mind," he said. "Good. Not long now. Follow my signals."

The last sentence wasn't spoken. He'd been in her mind before, but this time she opened to him utterly, like a surrender. That thought scared and aroused her, until he soothed her fears. She was alert and ready for his signal.

They climbed down the far corner of the house; Stella waited in the shadows for Justin's signal and then followed. He crouched beside one sleeping form; she took the other. Justin had been so right. His knowledge flowed through her mind. She knew how to cast a glamour so her target sank into deep sleep. She knew just where to bite, brushing long hair aside to bare the skin, and following Justin's lead, she slid an arm under the man's shoulders to let his head drop back and expose his neck to her itching teeth.

She bit, confidently, surely, as if she'd nipped necks all her life. She sucked slowly at first, the blood warm and strange to her tongue, until the sweet taste of human life-blood hit her like wine on an empty stomach. She drank deep. This was a feast for gods, a banquet for immortals, sustenance and reason and she had to stop before she took too much. Reluctantly, she moved away and, at Justin's cue, lapped the skin with her tongue to seal the wound.

Removing the memory was the work of seconds before she covered the sleeping man back up with his newspapers and tattered quilt. Justin handed her a bundle of bills to tuck in the man's pocket.

That was all there was to it? Justin and Dixie had been right. It was easy! Neither of them had mentioned the wild and heady buzz that roared through her senses. Stella leapt rather than stood and turned to Justin. His lips were stained red and a wild light burned in his dark eyes.

He handed her a folded linen handkerchief. "Always wipe your mouth after feeding."

As she handed it back, their hands touched and he didn't let go. His fingers closed over hers, grasping the crumpled linen. "Shouldn't you wipe your mouth, too?" It sounded like reminding Sam to clean up after eating spaghetti, not standing in the night after feeding with a master vampire. A master vampire who was as aroused as she. She knew that, as surely as she knew her name and the taste of mortal blood.

Justin's grip loosened. Stella eased her hand from under his fingers and stepped closer. Reaching up, she wiped Justin's lips clean. A thrill rose from her chest to tighten her throat as she watched his mouth curl up at the corners and his lips part just enough to glimpse his fangs before they disappeared. She ran her tongue over her own descended canines and felt them retract. There was no going back now. She'd crossed the line between mortal and vampire. She was truly a creature of the night hunt. The realization set a wild surge through her. She would no longer feel cold or weariness. Never fall sick or die. She'd heal from any wound or hurt. She was vampire. Revenant. Immortal.

The wild power of the ancients flowed through her veins. A fierce desire shook every cell of her body as her mind melded with Justin's. He knew her desires. His yearnings became hers. Her wants were his needs. His eyes gleamed with the hunger that echoed in her soul.

His mouth came down as his arms closed around her. Just a brush of his lips and her mouth opened for his kiss. His first kiss was gentle, almost hesitant, as if still unsure of her needs. His second was a furnace blast. She literally left the ground, caught in his embrace as she curved her neck under his kiss and her tongue met his. Fire and need and longing rose in her like a wild conflagration. Her idle imaginings were nothing. Her mortal fantasies, shadows of the sensations that poured though her. Now she clung to him, needing him and everything he had to offer. Eternity was too short to love Justin. To feel his hair between her fingers and his tongue dancing with hers. She pressed herself against him, wanting her breasts flattened against his chest, needing his erection against her belly.

With no need to pause for air, their kiss drove on with a heat and passion that fired her body with crazed yearnings. She needed him deep inside her. Longed for his skin on hers and his hands branding her with his touch.

"Not here." He was in her mind and she rejoiced. There would be no misunderstanding ever between them. They shared thoughts and needs and hungers.

She complained as he broke off the kiss, but not for long. "Come," he said aloud taking her hand. "It's time you tested your speed. Let's run."

Hand in hand they raced, past sleeping houses, boarded up buildings and near-empty streets. Through downtown, leaping over parked cars, jumping up to touch the underside of a railway bridge, until finally they left the streets behind and were in open country. Above them, the sky rose like a great star-sprinkled canopy and beside her stood the man who would make her wildest dreams come true.

"See the copse at the end of the next field?" She did—if he meant the clump of trees, perched like a bunch of dark skeletons. "Just beyond them is a small incline; I'll race you there."

He took off and she was close on his heels. At one point, she grabbed his coat and it came off in her hands. He laughed and pulled her coat off, tossing it in the air as he grabbed his coat back and raced on. As she caught up with him, he was waiting, arms open and pulled her close.

"You're mine. You know that, don't you?" Stella nodded, his words driving her desire to fever pitch. "I made you vampire, Stella, and now I'll make you mine forever."

She wanted, no, needed to belong to him. She was his. She was him. His desire raced through her veins and her needs were as clear as the night sky overhead. She rested her hand on the hard wall of his chest. In a wild frenzy of need, she pulled his shirt open and pressed her face against the skin beneath. The soft hair caressed her cheek as she rubbed her face across his chest, relishing the touch of his skin and his male scent. She let out a little growl and raised her head to meet his eyes.

"Stella." He drew her name out like a slow sigh.

Knowing with all her soul his needs and hers, Stella pulled off his shirt and tugged at his leather belt. They moved fast as the wild night creatures they were, stripping each other. Her clothes fell to the ground. He stepped out of his pants and kicked off his shoes. In moments, they were naked and Justin had their coats spread on the ground.

He was magnificent in the moonlight. His erection pointing at her as the center of his desire. A slow ache within her yearned to be possessed by Justin Corvus, vampire. The heat in his eyes sent her crazy with need.

He gave her another mind-stopping kiss and then stepped back, looking at her as if he'd never seen a naked woman before. He rested both hands on her head, stroking her hair. Slowly trailing his fingers down her head to her neck, he skimmed over her shoulders and cupped her breasts in his hands.

His touch lit a blaze in her. Her mind was on fire with desire and her body hurt with wanting. "Justin!" she groaned.

He smiled up at her as he trailed his hands over her belly, and lower. But she was beyond caresses and foreplay, nothing but animal loving would quench her needs.

"I know," he said. "Soon."

"Now!" She all but screamed it.

He grinned and lifted her up, spreading her on her back on their coats. He stood over her like an ancient god, tall and potent. Then he was on her, covering her with his length, touching her until her skin seemed to burn. Kissing her until her earlier needs were nothing compared to the ache and yearning that seized every fiber of her consciousness. Her hips rocked and jerked of their own volition. A stream ran between her legs until she smelled her own arousal. If he didn't come into her soon, she would yell her frustration.

He shifted. Moving swiftly he parted her legs and she raised her hips to meet him as he settled between her thighs.

"Justin!"

"Stella!"

It was all the affirmation either of them needed.

He came into her, hard and deep and she burned with the need that fueled his desire.

Stella shifted, angling her hips to meet his thrusts, opening her eyes to the great arc of the night sky and the beauty of the vampire atop her. Justin moved inside her in a steady, sure rhythm. Each thrust took her higher and faster in her own desire. Each lunge brought them closer together in mind and need. She was moaning, tossing her head from side to side in the effort to keep her body one with his. She rocked as he drove into her, and clung to him. She wanted him embedded in her forever. He was taking her like the wild creature of the night they both were and she gloried in their shared heat and passion.

He was as tireless and insatiable as she. He rolled on his back, taking her with him so she sat astride him moving with the same frenetic pace, driving her hunger higher and wilder. The night air on her breasts only served to fuel her desire, stirring her mind to greater needs. She looked at the man beneath her. Justin. The man who'd given her the gift of immortality and was now taking her to the pinnacle of human pleasure.

He opened his eyes. She read his need.

He rolled her over on her back and, levering himself up on his arms, came into her. His eyes blazed with a wild and savage light as she felt herself drawn into his mind and his heat. She was climbing as if pulled by a wild force, closer and closer to the edge. With a feral scream she climaxed just as Justin thrust harder and deeper than ever before and his heat and passion filled her.

After a while he rolled off, brushed the hair from her face, and grinned. "Satisfied?"

Satisfied? Way beyond her wildest fantasies! Her body still throbbed with wild waves of pleasure and for the rest of her life she'd feel him stretching and filling her. No one had ever come close.

"I should damn well hope so!" He growled it at her. There was no other word for the irritation in his voice. She'd been too sated with exhilaration to think of veiling her thoughts. "Forget breathers. You're vampire now. Mine."

His last word set off a frisson of joy and anticipation. She reached out and hugged him tight, closing her eyes to better inhale the perfume of satisfied male. She was naked, in the middle of a field, miles from home, and she'd never in her life felt this protected or secure.

"I want you again so much it aches," he said, "but we have to go back. Since you insist on going to work to give notice in the morning, you need to rest."

"I don't feel the least bit tired." The reverse in fact.

"Of course not. You've drawn strength from feeding and sex energizes, but daylight saps strength fast and you'll need all you can conserve."

She didn't imagine she'd ever feel tired again. Justin stood, looking like a primitive god in the moonlight. And he was hers. She indulged in a moment of sheer gloating. Never in her wildest teenage dreams had she imagined a Justin Corvus. She leaned up on one elbow and let herself leer at his strong legs and firm butt as he turned to pick up their scattered clothes. "Justin!" She was on her feet in a second. His back was a mass of bleeding scratches.

"What?"

She rested her hand on the largest gash. "Did I . . . ?" Surely not? She'd grabbed him tightly, yes, but . . .

He turned and dropped a kiss on her forehead. "Yes, you did, my love. We vampires get a trifle rough at times. You'll soon learn your own strength."

"Justin, I never meant . . ."

His chuckle rang through the clear winter night. "No matter, they're already healing."

She walked behind him, still only half-convinced. As she watched, the scratches closed and healed—of course, if his body could heal from multiple bullet wounds, scratches from her fingernails were nothing.

"Does that set your mind at rest?" He grabbed her hand. "A few scratches are a small price to pay for the ecstasy you gave me."

"You might say it was mutual."

He broke into a grin. "By Abel! I hope so! I need you, Stella, and I hope to heaven you will always need me." He pulled her close. She was female enough to relish a strong man like Justin needing her. She refused to consider the implications of her needing him. This night was magic, whatever the morning might bring, and right now, she refused to consider how long his "always" might be.

She dressed quickly, her hands and arms moving faster than she'd ever imagined possible, but he was ready before her. "We'll go back at a steady pace," he said. "No need to run like demented revenants."

"We were a little demented, weren't we? I've never felt so driven."

"I'll get you demented again soon," he promised as he helped her coat back on. He held out his hand. "Come on, we've a fair way to go back."

"Where exactly are we?"

"About ten miles north of Jeffersonville."

"You know where we are?"

"Of course. I wouldn't run like that without knowing exactly where I was going." He shrugged. "Besides, I wanted the right spot for our first time."

And he'd picked it with the night quiet around and the moon and stars overhead. "Did you lay on the weather too?"

He shook his head. "Sorry, can't do anything about the weather. If I could, I'd put in perpetual cloud cover for you." He held out his hand. "Let's go."

They ran steadily, across country at first, hand in hand zigzagging across the fallow fields, then following the Interstate, racing the trucks and winning until Justin insisted they slow as they reached the outskirts of Columbus. They crossed High Street into German Village, and as they skirted Schiller Park, Stella glimpsed yellow police ribbon but they were past in a flash, and in minutes they stood at her front gate, ready to part like a teenage courting couple.

"I'll be back over at first dusk," Justin said and kissed her. "Go in."

She wanted to. She needed to check on Sam. Heaven alone knew what time it was. Justin stood on the path until she closed the door. Stella waited in the hall and listened as his footsteps faded down the sidewalk.

Justin wanted to whoop, shout, and dance on the rooftops but settled for a high speed run. No point in wasting energy when he had a willing Stella to pleasure tomorrow evening . . . or rather later today. He felt as wild and lightheaded as a lad downing his first wine, as reckless as he had after his first battle and more contented than ever in his long life. Not only had Stella filled his heart and mind with joy, she'd erased the void and hurt left by Gwyltha's defection. In his joy, he wished Gwyltha and Vlad well. He had Stella. What more could man or vampire need?

Justin vaulted the iron railings in Kit's front garden and took the front path in two strides.

"You look more than a trifle pleased with yourself," Kit said as Justin closed the door. "I assume felicitations are in order."

"Very much." Justin sank into the wing chair opposite Kit.

Kit nodded. "At the risk of destroying the moment with mundane affairs . . ." he began.

"What mundane affairs?"

"Vlad called while you were out." Justin nodded and waited for Kit to go on. "Bearing a message from Gwyltha."

"Who's coming?" Not as many as if they were home, granted. But she'd bring someone with her besides Vlad, who wasn't a true member of the colony.

"Toby and some of the others, but I don't think that was why he came."

Kit's hesitation and his fully veiled mind alerted Justin. "Why then?"

"He wouldn't say. Just said he'd come back at a time convenient to you. A matter of business, apparently."

"What sort of business would I want to do with Vlad Tepes?"

"Maybe you impressed him with your negotiating skills."

Justin snorted. "I'll negotiate him!" But the old antipathy was hard to rouse. He was too full of joy and new pleasure to feel true rancor over their past. If Gwyltha and Vlad found half the joy he shared with Stella, they were welcome to it. Once, he'd loved Gwyltha with all his being and the hurt at her loss had rankled for decades. But tough Stella with her bright eyes had laid to rest the ghosts of his lost and long ago love. Justin gave a sigh. "I suppose we'll find out what he wants sooner or later."

Monday mornings were not any easier as a vampire. Sam couldn't find his book bag, and when it finally turned up among his things brought back from Dixie's, he remembered he needed two empty yogurt cups for science. Stella had one but it was full of yogurt which Sam didn't want for breakfast. She dumped the yogurt into an empty canning jar while Dixie fished the empty can from Sam's supper last night out of the trash. Stella washed and dried them as Sam gathered his things together. They made it on time to the bus stop and once Sam was safely on the bus, Stella set off to give notice at the Village Laundry.

Justin had been right, working in daylight would be impossible. As it was, she already felt weak in the morning sunshine. Trouble was, Stella knew her leaving would cause problems both for her coworkers and the owners who'd bent over backwards giving her hours when Sam was in school and never complaining when she needed time off if he was sick. She was going to be leaving them in the lurch and she hated that. But . . .

It had to be done. She opened the door, nodded to Annie, the other clerk, and walked back to the office.

"Giving notice?" Old Mr. Lynch looked ready to have a heart attack.

Stella fought with her guilt. "I'm sorry, something came up."

"That all you can tell us?"

"It's a bit difficult. It's been great working here and you've been so good about Sam and everything, but I have to leave."

"We'll match any offer you have."

Now she felt even worse. "It's not the money. I've found a job that will work better for Sam and me. I've already accepted it."

She half-expected him to ask where it was but he just shrugged. "You'll work out your week's notice, won't you? Give us time to find someone else?"

She couldn't refuse and now that she was indoors, she felt fine. She could manage a week. She'd worked here five years, she owed them that much. She left her coat in the office, went up to the counter, took in the first load of shirts and then helped Annie get the first batch of laundry ready to go.

"That was something else over the weekend, wasn't it?" Annie said as she pushed a wheeled basket in from out back.

"What happened?"

"You didn't see it on the news? It was all over the papers, too. They still have part of the park taped off."

"I was sick. Never turned on the TV."

"Jim was called out Friday night and didn't get back until after breakfast. It was weird, if you ask me." Annie shook her head as she stuffed shirts into another linen bag. "Police think it was some gang fight or other. But there were odd things. One kid was found near the road, the other over by the tennis courts. One or other of them threw a gun through a window of a house on Reinhart. That was what brought the police in. The alarm went off. A couple of uniformed cops went to investigate and found the whole mess."

"They were killed?"

"Nah! Beat up and taken to hospital. One of them was raving about the devil attacking them. They figured he had to be on something." She tossed the full bag into the basket. "Can you get the rest of them? I need to make some phone calls."

Stella bundled the rest up while her mind did cartwheels. This had to be Johnny Day and Warty. What had Justin said about harming mortals? Stella didn't feel too much sympathy for Warty or Johnny. They'd killed her and tried to kill Justin. Her head began to ache. She'd try to get hold of an old paper and talk to Justin later. Meanwhile, with the shirts bundled up, she had the dry cleaning orders to get ready.

A couple of hours later, her head throbbed and her joints ached and she longed to find a dark corner and curl up and sleep.

Dixie and Justin hadn't lied. She didn't have the strength to work in daytime and she'd committed to a whole week. Maybe she should go back and tell Mr. Lynch she was sorry but she just couldn't and . . .

"Hello."

She had a customer. Better pay attention. She wrote up the slip, but had to ask him twice to spell his name. She wouldn't feel so bad but she darn well knew how to write Brown. He gave her a very funny look when she told him they'd be ready tomorrow, Thursday, and just about gaped when she asked him if he wanted his shirts washed as well as starched.

She wouldn't have been surprised if he'd cut and run, but he stayed just long enough to hand her a couple of coupons and made her repeat that they would be in tomorrow, Tuesday. He gave her a wary look as he left.

Stella bundled up the shirts and she saw the customer's wallet sitting on the counter. Without thinking she grabbed it up. She was weak and wobbly as she stepped out the door into the sunshine but the man was just unlocking his car. "You forgot your wallet," she called, taking a couple of steps towards him, and then the world around seem to shatter and she felt herself dropping.

"Justin, help me!" was her last thought before everything went cold and black.

* * *

"Stella!" Justin leapt to his feet. He called to Kit. "She's in trouble."

"Where?"

Justin made his senses focus. "Somewhere just beyond the park."

"Must be the laundry where she works," Dixie said, "down on Thurman."

Justin tried to enter Stella's mind. He couldn't. "I'm going to her. Bring the car after me."

Before Kit replied, Justin was out the door and running at vampire speed. If anyone saw him pass, he'd be a blur. Discretion be damned! Stella was in trouble. He slowed to a fast mortal speed as he passed the park and ran the rest of the way. He knew the shop the minute he turned the corner. A crowd of people gathered on the pavement around a prostrate Stella. Oblivious to caution and discretion, he had moved them aside with his mind.

A woman was leaning over her, calling her name and a gray-haired man was standing by saying, "If she'd only said she was feeling bad."

Justin brushed past the kind-looking woman, scooped Stella up in his arms and carried her into the shop and out of the sun.

"Who are you?" the man asked, running alongside.

"A friend of Stella's and I'm a doctor." That last word opened doors. It didn't fail now. "The name's Corvus. Justin Corvus," he added as he sat Stella in a chair and forced her blank mind to open to his.

"Justin?" She smiled at him. "I knew you'd come."

He felt his heart tighten at her words. Impossible. But it had. Stella faded back into unconsciousness but he willed her back awake. The last thing he or she needed was a concerned mortal feeling for her pulse. He turned to the kind-faced woman at his elbow. "Could you get her some water, please?"

"Of course." She scooted off and now all Justin had to deal with was the elderly man.

"Seems she just ran out to give a customer his wallet and fainted."

Ran out in the sun as if she were mortal or a master! He'd make darn sure it was weeks before she went out in daylight again. "She's been feeling poorly all weekend, some sort of flu," Justin lied. Well, the first part wasn't exactly untrue. "She shouldn't have come into work this morning." He'd say that twice. "She needs to be home in bed."

The man looked genuinely concerned. At that moment, the woman returned with a glass of water. "Do you think she's well enough to drive?" he asked.

Not until sunset. "I'll take her home. I'm a friend," he added as the man looked even more anxious.

"I think perhaps . . ." Gray hair began.

Justin gave up any attempt at pretending normalcy. He cast a glamour on the pair of them, imprinted in their mind the idea that Stella had gone home ill and would not be returning anytime soon and gathered her up in his arms just as Kit pulled up outside. He came in with a blanket over his arm. They wrapped it around Stella and Justin handed her to Kit. As Kit settled her on the backseat, Justin removed the glamour, wished the two mortals "good day" and walked out the door.

Stella started recovering before they'd gone a hundred yards. She pushed off the blankets and frowned around her. "What happened?"

"You didn't do what you were told to." Justin was too far gone with worry and the rush of relief to catch the flash in her eyes. "I told you to stay home and not go to work. For Abel's sake!"

The relief and pleasure at seeing him that he'd glimpsed minutes earlier were nowhere to be seen. She scowled at him. "I'm listening now. It's hard not to when you're yelling."

Was he yelling? Probably. "Stella, you can't go out in sun. We've all told you that. Why didn't you listen?"

Her lips parted as if to answer him but her jaw tightened. "Why don't you stop trying to run my life? You made your point about sun. Trust me, I won't forget that in a hurry." She turned to look out of the window. "Kit, where are we going?"

"I'm taking you to our house."

"No!" she almost snapped it. "Please," she calmed with obvious effort. "Take me home."

"By all means." He slowed and made to turn right at the next corner.

"Take us to yours, Kit!" Justin snapped. "I'm going to make darn sure she stays indoors . . . for a week!"

"I can do that without your help!" She leaned forward. "Home, please, Kit," and gave Justin the full benefit of her frown. "I'm going home. If I need to be indoors, I need to be where Sam is."

Kit turned the car. Justin said nothing. The way Stella was acting, she'd most likely try walking home if he insisted. He'd just go in with her and lock her up if he had to.

"Like hell, you will!" Stella said. In his anxiety, he'd forgotten to veil his mind.

She had no intention of veiling her feelings. They were wide open. "When Kit gets me home, I'm going in and resting. Alone. So when Sam gets home I'll be waiting for him. Just as always." She couldn't have made it clearer if she'd written it in the sky.

The sun was still shining as Kit pulled up at her gate. "I'll wrap you back up and carry you in," Justin told her.

She looked ready to argue but her recent memories were too clear. She let him cover her and carry her up the path. "Thanks," she said as he pushed open her front door and stood her on her feet. She smiled. "I really mean it."

He just had to spoil the moment by pushing too hard. "I'm staying to make sure you rest."

"No, you're not! I can get myself into bed and trust me, I'm not going back out in the sun anytime soon!"

"You're going to need to feed to replace your lost strength."

"Then ask Dixie to bring me a blood bag. Goodbye!"

He left before she summoned her last strength and tossed him out on his ear. He couldn't believe it! He stood on her porch staring at the locked door. He was a master vampire, damn it and he'd just been thrown out by a fledgling. Ask Dixie to bring a blood bag indeed! Stella was coming feeding tonight whether she felt like it or not.

"You handled that one wrong, pal," Kit said as he drove away, Justin muttering in the passenger seat. "Really got her in a mood, you did."

"Thanks for the advice! If I want any more I'll ask!"

"Nice woman, Stella, got guts, like Dixie," Kit went on, totally ignoring Justin. "You need to be careful what you say to them though, a 'please' or 'would you' works a lot better than laying down dictums." He seemed not to notice Justin's snort. "Dixie's got an old Southern saying, 'You can catch more flies with honey than with vinegar.' Sort of applies to women, too."

Justin fumed for a few seconds. The fact Kit was right didn't help his state of mind one iota. "She had me terrified, dammit! I thought for one hideous second she'd expired."

"Must have terrified her, too. Last night she ran halfway to Cincinnati and back, stopping off on the way for a bit of fun, and today she can't take three steps along the street. Bit of a shock for her, I'd say."

"You think I acted like an ass?"

"I'd most likely have done the same but I do suggest you gift wrap the blood bag and send it with flowers."

He'd buy up the florist shop if it would help. "Why did I get so angry at her?" he asked, more to himself than Kit.

Didn't stop Kit. "Because you were scared blind. You

need Stella, Justin, the way I need Dixie." He gave a soft chuckle. "Better get used to the feeling."

He would, if Stella ever let him within touching distance again. He'd thrown orders and demands at her as if she'd been a surgeon's assistant in his distant army days. Honey instead of vinegar. Good thought! Pity Stella no longer ate sweetmeats, or the chocolate Dixie still murmured wistfully about.

"What the hell is he doing here?" Kit's exasperated question drew a stronger response from Justin. Vlad Tepes waiting nonchalantly at Kit's front gate was the last creature in creation Justin fancied seeing right now. "Better find out," Kit said as he turned off the ignition and opened the door. "Something about Stella's welcome, no doubt."

Or a vulture come for the kill. Vlad had appeared in London the first time right after Justin and Gwyltha had a wild disagreement. If Vlad thought he was getting anywhere near Stella, he could go right back to Transylvania and not bother to stop to feed on the way.

Chapter Ten

Stella wanted to spit. Screaming and stamping feet might help but she no longer had saliva, and standing upright took all her strength. Justin had rescued her, come when she needed him desperately and she'd acted like a horse's patootie.

She walked into the kitchen and picked up the phone to call him and apologize but her mind was too fogged and confused to remember the number and the thought of lifting and opening the phone book made her shoulders ache more than they did already. Justin was right, she had to rest, but she also needed some answers. Summoning her last dregs of brain energy, she scribbled a note to Dixie to please wake her before picking Sam up from the sitter. They had to talk.

Finding a magnet to stick the note to the fridge took more energy than Stella imagined possible. She made in upstairs and into her room on all fours, and with her last vestiges of strength, dragged herself onto her bed. Sleep came as swiftly as a slammed door.

* * *

"Good morning, Vlad. To what do I owe this pleasure?" How could Kit be so cordial? Vlad Tepes was just about the last person, living or undead, that Justin felt like seeing right now, but the man stood by Kit's gate, obviously waiting for them.

"Marlowe, Corvus." Vlad smiled and inclined his head.

Justin offered a curt nod. "Vlad." Whether he thought of Gwyltha or the two ghouls, this creature was a world menace.

"Dixie gave me your message," Kit said. "We'll expect Gwyltha on Saturday."

Vlad gave another nod of acknowledgement. "I felt certain she would but, as I said the other evening, I come on another matter. I wonder if I might presume to ask a considerable favor of you and your mate."

"I question what I can do for you, Vlad," Kit said with just a suspicion of sarcasm.

Vlad chose not to rise to that. "I can explain here if you wish."

Justin was hoping Kit would take him up on the offer to spill his demands right here on the brick pavement, and then get lost. Before Kit could reply, Dixie opened the front door and called, "Are y'all going to debate out there on the sidewalk or come inside?"

Vlad actually had the grace to hesitate, his eyes on Kit, waiting for him to ask him in. Or maybe he was reluctant to take on the two of them despite Dixie's invitation.

Kit shrugged. "If we need to talk, let's go inside. No point in standing out here all morning."

Was it only morning? It seemed at least a decade since Justin received Stella's desperate summons. He was not disposed to cope with Vlad's impositions, if there was a way to gracefully back out. He couldn't. Minutes later they were all seated in the front parlor. Vlad, Justin noticed with a wry smile, avoiding the gas logs as much as he did himself, their caution landing them side by side on the sofa.

"I will not intrude long," Vlad said, the necessary niceties over. "I imagine Dr. Corvus told you after his visit to Chicago that I have recently acquired a pair of dependents."

"A pair of ghouls, you mean," Kit replied.

Vlad nodded, obviously choosing to ignore the implied criticism. "Two ghouls. Young women. I am reluctant to take them to Britain with me." The man was impossible! To callously discuss this in front of Dixie! Did he really think by leaving his two creations behind him, he'd square things with Gwyltha? "But I will not see them abandoned and rootless."

"Why did you create them then?" Good for Kit to ask.

Vlad's face was a study in astonishment. Hit where it hurt. Good. "I did not create them!" He sounded more shocked than offended. "Marlowe, we may not be friends but would you think that of me?" He turned to Justin. "You too, Corvus?"

"Given the evidence of my own eyes, what else was I to assume?"

Vlad looked ready to burst. Whether from outrage or guilt was a matter of debate.

"Vlad," Dixie said, speaking for the first time, although she'd obviously been following every word. "Why not tell us how you acquired them?"

"Yes." Justin wanted to hear this one.

Dixie looked right at Vlad. She never could quite see what Kit and Justin disliked about him so. Okay, Justin and he had fought over Gwyltha, but heck, did he still carry a torch for her? He had Stella now. He'd better wise up. "Tell us then, Vlad," she repeated.

"By all means, lady." He gave her one for his courtly bows and then looked at Christopher as if waiting for his go ahead. That irked, couldn't he answer her question without applying to Christopher first?

Christopher nodded. "Should be interesting."

"More disturbing than interesting," Vlad replied more sharply than Dixie could ever remember him speaking. "I found them, abandoned. Or to be precise, they found me a month or so back, wandering in a park in Chicago. Seems their creator either discarded them or, by some untimely turn of fate was extinguished. They were rootless, lost, and confused and latched onto me as their only hope of existence. Despite your low opinion of me," he cast a sideways look at Justin, "I could not see my way to relinquishing them to whatever fate might lurk. They were once intelligent young women by all appearances, and possess some, admittedly insubstantial, memories of their life before.

"Since I took responsibility for them, they've been working for one of my creations. In a Goth bar, as Dr. Corvus will no doubt attest. It was neither elegant nor delightful but they were safe. Unfortunately my brethren no more possess the resources to support them than they would human servants or maids. Plus, they are young women who, I suspect, would welcome female companionship." Vlad paused. "I know you are establishing yourself here as entrepreneurs and I wondered if you could employ them in some capacity?"

"Despite the colony's policy of never taking dependents?" Kit asked.

"You prefer the alternative of leaving them as waiting prey for the first pimp or pusher who comes along? That I will not countenance! They're not mindless automans but living, feeling humans in need of protection." His eyes flashed as he spoke, giving Dixie a glimpse of his wrath when roused.

"If we were to agree, how would that stand with Gwyltha?" she asked. "If the colony's laws forbid taking ghouls." Privately Gwyltha could go sing if she objected but Dixie knew the deference the others paid her and tact never hurt.

"As I understand it, your colony forbids the making of ghouls, not the protection of abandoned ones." The "your colony" was inescapable. Dixie tended to forget that Vlad governed himself and his vampires by a different set of ethics.

"Isn't that rather splitting hairs?" Christopher asked.

Dixie wanted to kick him.

"No," Justin said before Dixie could reply. Was he saying "no" to Kit or Vlad? "We've had no hand in their making and in this Vlad is right. Alone they will either perish or become victims. You've never encountered a ghoul, Kit, and I've only met one other besides these two. They need protection."

Vlad looked ready to lose his lower jaw. "I thank you for your support, Corvus."

Justin gave a curt nod. "Our differences are one thing. What's right is another." He looked in Dixie's direction. "Can you find them employment?"

"Yes."

Her reply was half-muffled by Kit's, "Of course." She wanted to hug him for his support. "Where do you think we can use them?" he asked.

Good question. "Not too sure. If it were last week, I'd still be needing help in the shop but that's taken care of. But . . ." She paused and looked at Vlad, "I don't know the first thing about ghouls, other than what Justin would call 'Hollywood sensationalism.' Can they go out in sunlight? Move around as mortals? Do they eat?"

"Light does not harm them. They possess our immortality but not our strength or powers. They do not feed as we do. They eat as mortals but prefer their meat raw. They possess more than mortal endurance but are incapable of much independent thought and will follow any direction from a stronger mind. Hence their vulnerability to abuse."

"Hummm." Dixie mused on this a second or two. "I wonder if one could take Stella's old job? She was worried about leaving them in the lurch. If she could say she had a friend who wanted the job, I bet she'll feel better about it." She looked back at Vlad. "They were working in a bar, right? Well, there are scads of restaurants around here. We'll find something."

Vlad bestowed on her a smile that would most likely raise Christopher's hackles. No wonder he'd gained such a reputation as a seducer. "I will be forever in your debt, lady. And now, if you will forgive me, I will leave you." At the door he hesitated. "Perhaps in a day or two I can contact you again and make our final arrangements?"

"I'll call you, Vlad," Christopher said. "You're staying at Southern Hotel, right?"

A flash of surprise crossed Vlad Tepes's dark eyes. "That is so. I will await your call."

"How the hell did you know where he was staying?" Justin asked after the door closed.

"Wasn't hard. Just took a few phone calls. After Dixie said she met him yesterday, I thought it made sense to know where he lurked. I'd dearly like to know what he's up to." He shook his head. "Beats me what he thinks he'll learn."

"Wait a minute." Dixie had to get this sorted out. "You think these ghouls are spies? Then why accept them?"

"Might as well know who to watch," Christopher replied. "This way we know who he's planted."

"Could it just be what he said, that he doesn't want them left helpless and unprotected?"

They both looked at her as if she were weak-skulled.

Dixie left early, under pretext of paperwork to do before opening the shop and having to go by Giant Eagle to get something for Sam's supper. In truth, it was to get out of the house before screeching at the pair of them. They were so darn convinced that Vlad was up to no good. She could understand Justin's caution. He'd lost a companion he loved to

Vlad but that was a hundred years or so in the past. Besides, Justin had Stella now. Christopher's antagonism she put down to good old male solidarity. Or were they right? Had Vlad seduced her with his legendary charm? She laughed. Pretty bland seduction if he had! Christopher beat him hands down any day or night of the week.

She'd cleared off her small desk and unpacked two new orders of books, when Justin opened the door.

"Mind if we change our arrangement?"

"Is Stella okay?"

"Yes. I just went by her house. She's deep asleep and likely to stay that way for hours. She's taken no lasting harm. But I want to be there when she wakes and . . ." He paused as if uncertain what to say next. "She has to learn to trust me, Dixie. How else can we live together?" He shook his head. "I couldn't have made it clearer that she was not to go out in daylight, she ignored me, and look what happened. I tell you . . ." He gritted his teeth. "She will drive me to perdition and back!"

By the look in his face, he was halfway there. "Justin, a couple of words to the wise: try asking nicely instead of telling. Works wonders."

He stared at her. "Kit said much the same thing!"

God bless him! "Two of us can't be wrong. And Justin, before you go off all barrels blazing about this morning, talk to her and find out what happened."

"What happened was she ignored my directions!"

This was one of those times Dixie missed not being able to take a nice, slow, deep breath. "Justin, talk to her first. The one thing Stella isn't, is stupid."

He nodded. "Fair enough. Will you come over later, after you close up, and watch Sam? Stella will have to feed again tonight."

Dixie gave him a hug. "Of course. Oh, and one thing. I

promised Stella I'd run by the Giant Eagle and pick up something for Sam's dinner and breakfast the next couple of days and they're out of milk. Want me to get it for you?"

Justin shook his head. "I'll get it on my way. Stella and I parted a bit stiffly. Might help soften things if I come bearing gifts."

It was only after Justin left that Dixie stopped to wonder just how many hundreds of years it had been since Justin had entered a grocery store.

Talk about humbled. Justin walked from the Giant Eagle to Kit's borrowed car, his hands full of plastic sacks of food and a bunch of pale pink roses in one hand. The Giant Eagle didn't stock olive branches but they had just about anything else a mortal might need at short notice. The sheer volume and variety had stunned him as he maneuvered his way through the passages stocked high with consumables, cleaning chemicals and everything from kitchenware to pencils. He'd no doubt still be there, wandering between the rolls of toilet paper and the toothpaste, pushing that benighted metal barrow with the rattling wheels, if he hadn't importuned help from a unsuspecting young housewife who accepted his story of buying for a nephew. She'd been bemused but helpful and now he had hot dogs, pizza and hamburgers, which apparently small children lived on here. Plus a box of what passed as cereal and a few additions he'd recognized as treats from his boyhood. How anyone with mere mortal strength endured grocery shopping on a weekly or daily basis astonished Justin.

He drove past the Barcelona on the corner. Had it only been three days since they'd walked there hand in hand and Stella had met her fate? Praise the gods he'd been there to transform her but if he hadn't taken her there for dessert that night . . .

No point in thinking along that vein. He'd better preserve his energies for peace-making.

He drove down Jaeger and past the park. Loops of yellow tape still hung in limp festoons from tree to tree to metal post. What had happened to those two thugs? He hadn't read a paper since Friday. Life had been too full. Between worries about Stella and Sam, and now the added crimp of Vlad and the two ghouls, who had time to read a newspaper or watch the news? Still, he'd better find out what had happened. His memories were unclear of anything but purple rage.

He made a point of driving past the crack house. That was something he intended to take care of. Soon. The house looked as deserted as it had that first morning, but in a few hours things would be different. He'd bring Kit back here, then between them they'd jam a wedge in the wheels. No point in mentioning it to Stella or Dixie, they'd want to join in too, knowing them, and it was far too dangerous.

As Justin parked and walked up to Stella's gate, arms full of paper bags and roses, the old woman from next door was waiting on her porch. "How's Stella? Heard she was taken ill at work. Did go over this afternoon to see if there was anything I could do. I expect she was sleeping."

Sleeping more deeply than this good woman would ever believe. "She had a touch of flu over the weekend and went back to work too soon."

"That's just like Stella. She does too much." She nodded at the bags in Justin's arms. "See you brought her some groceries. Nice of you. You make sure she rests up." She paused a minute to wrap her coat around her chest. "If I can help with keeping young Sam, you just let me know. He's a joy to have around. And you tell Stella I'll be counting on keeping him Saturday, if she's well enough to go see her mom as usual."

"Indeed, I will," Justin replied. "Stella is fortunate to have you as a neighbor."

The woman shook her head. "She's a good neighbor, too.

I tell you, with the trouble around here, we need to stick together. That house down there . . ." She jerked her head
down the street. ". . . and now police in and out of the Day
house all weekend."

Day! The name of the boy who'd shot Stella. "What happened?"

Mrs. Zeibel shook her graying head. "Lord alone knows!
Those boys are trouble through and through. Just like their
father, come to that. Seems Johnny and some other boy got
into more than they could handle. Both ended up in the hospital. Found someone meaner than they are." She gave a
harsh laugh. "Don't wish harm to anyone, but those boys . . ."
She clucked her tongue against the roof of her mouth. "You
know them. You had a run in with Johnny on Beggars' Night,
and earlier with the younger ones over smashing bottles on
Stella's garage. She told me about that." She smiled and
stepped back out of the wind. "You tell Stella to take care
and I'll bring a casserole over for you tomorrow."

Why a casserole? From what he'd seen, Stella had plenty of
cooking pots. "You're very kind, and if you'll excuse me . . ."

"Lord, yes! Here I am gabbing and you're laden with groceries." She turned back to her front door. "See you."

Justin balanced the bags on the porch railing while he
fished out the key. He had to find out what lasting harm he'd
done those boys. How could he have so lost control? Why
had Stella never mentioned her mother before? Presumably
she lived within driving distance. Justin fit the key in the
lock. In truth he knew so little about Stella. But one thing he
was sure of—he needed her.

Stella knew the minute Justin opened the front door.
She'd been hung in a strange twilight between sleep and
wakefulness for the last hour or so, her mind half-alert for

Dixie and it was Justin. Her every sense was attuned to his progress in and out of the kitchen and up the stairs. She was sitting up, feet on the floor and ready to stand when he burst through the door, a bunch of roses in one hand and her note to Dixie in the other.

"Justin!" She was torn between delight at seeing him and irritation he'd read her note. Not that he could have missed it, but it was clearly not addressed to him.

"Stella!" The smile stayed but his eyebrows quirked up. "Oblige me and stay in bed."

"Really?" They should sit down and talk, but after last night she wouldn't object to sharing a bed with Justin. This was terrible. Hormones had invaded her brain. She grinned. "Got any plans?"

"Yes. To tie you to it if you won't listen to sense."

"Yeah, right!"

"As an alternative to seeing you in a crumpled heap and wondering if you've extinguished, I'll chain you down and lock the door." He sat down beside her. "I never want to go through that again. I'm not sure I can. Have you any idea what I went through?"

She was beginning to understand. "Believe me, I didn't plan it that way."

He seemed ready to respond but looked as if he was biting back his words. "What happened?"

"I ran out after a customer who'd forgotten his wallet. I never even thought about the sunlight. It had been overcast and cloudy earlier. I went about three paces and it was as if I hit a black wall. I half-remember crashing into the sidewalk. I couldn't move and I hurt all over but I could hear everything that was said. I knew the minute you came. I hurt less."

Justin put his arm round her. "I opened my mind to yours. Just as you opened yours when you called out to me as you fell."

She remembered her panicked need for him. "I don't think I've ever been so scared or hurt so much. It was worse than the bullet."

He kissed her. "Now will you believe me about staying out of the sunshine? We're potentially immortal but not indestructible. You were scared. What do you think I felt? For a few hideous minutes I thought you'd expired." His dark eyes glinted with remembered panic, but then he smiled as he rested a hand on her leg. "I waited centuries to find you Stella. I intend to keep you. Eternity isn't long enough to spend with you."

She couldn't help but grin. "You vampires don't have any trouble with commitment, do you?"

"Not when we find the right soul mate." His hand eased up her leg to her waist, and then up to cup her breast, bringing back a wild rush of sensual memories.

"Justin . . ." she began but his mouth blocked out her words and every trace of conscious thought.

His mouth opened her lips followed by the soft, certain warmth of his tongue. She felt his fingers skimming her breasts until she moaned, the sound lost between their lips, swallowed in the vast need that burst deep within her and threatened to drown her in want.

Her hips rocked against his leg. She arched her back to fill more of his hand with her breast. Great waves of desire flooded her and she knew a touch and a kiss would never be enough. Ever. "Justin . . ." she began but as she spoke, he raised her sweatshirt and unhooked her bra and she had trouble thinking straight. When his lips found her breast she gave up trying to think and lost herself in sensation. He suckled her breast, each lave of his tongue and every press of his lips setting off wild waves of pleasure.

He switched back and forth, his fingers playing her as his lips crossed from one breast to the other. "You're the most

beautiful creature on Earth," Justin said as he paused between nipples.

As Stella looked into his dark eyes, she believed him utterly. "You're pretty incredible yourself, you know," she
replied, pulling his head back to her breast. He was. Heck,
incredible wasn't enough to describe how she felt as his lips
worked her nipple and his hand eased down her jeans. She
barely remembered him touching the snap and zipper but
they were open and his hand was flat on her belly and moving south. She rocked her hips to move his fingers closer to
where she needed them. He responded, tangling his fingers
through her curls and gently easing a finger between her folds.
His skin felt cold against her heat and the contrast wrung a
moan from her lips. "I want you inside me," she muttered,
her voice sounding desperate and hoarse.

"All in good time," Justin replied and stifled her objec-
tions with a kiss. "Why rush a good thing? I want to see you
naked first before I take you."

"You saw me naked last night!"

"Yes!" The man had her shirt and bra off in less time than
it took to grin. As he bent to kiss her belly, he tilted her hips
up with both hands and eased down her blue jeans and
panties. He hadn't been kidding about getting her naked!

She meant to protest that he was still clothed and things
were far from even, but as she started to complain he put his
mouth between her legs.

She was lost in a fierce spasm of exquisite pleasure that
waxed and magnified with each lap of his tongue and every
brush of his lips. Never in her life! Not even in her randiest
dreams had she imagined anything like this. She gave up trying
to speak. Even thinking was impossible as her mind and body
became a total pleasure zone, the instrument of their loving.

As if that wasn't enough, his hands smoothed across her
belly to find her breasts again. Her nipples were hard and

sensitive and his touch was almost more than she could stand, but she never wanted him to stop. He knew exactly what she needed, a soft feathery touch on her nipples, gentle pressure on her nub, and a light scratch of his fingernails across her belly. He never slowed or tired as she moaned and sighed under him, but took her deeper and deeper into her own passion and faster and higher to a pinnacle of sensation until she came with a great surge of joy and a cry that echoed off the ceiling.

He gathered her into his arms as the shudders of her climax gradually eased. She fancied she could speak if she tried, but to lie close to Justin, inhaling the scent of his vampire body, and rubbing her face against his broad chest, was quite enough effort for now.

"Did that please you, my love?" Justin said after a while.

She couldn't help the little giggle. As if he could have any doubt! Aftershocks still rippled inside her.

"Well?" he asked.

Stella leaned up on one elbow and looked down at him. One look at the smug smile on his handsome face and she darn well knew he needed no reassurance. "Pretty much," she said.

"Pretty much!" His eyebrows shot up. "What does that mean?"

"It means," Stella said, getting up on her knees, "that things aren't even between us. I'm naked and you're still dressed." She straddled him.

He looked up at her and raised one eyebrow, his mouth twisted in a wry smile. "What of it?"

"So, I'm fixing that." She took hold of his shirt front. "I'm stripping you as naked as I am, Justin Corvus."

"You are, are you?" he replied. "Let's see you do it!"

He might put a note of defiance in his voice but the erection rubbing against her bottom showed exactly how he felt. "You bet!" His shirt was gone in seconds. His beautiful naked chest was hers. She ran her hands over it, brushing her fingers through the pelt of dark hair. He was approaching two millennia in age and he would always have the body of a hard-muscled twenty-five-year-old. She bent to flutter her tongue over his nipple and grinned as it hardened at her touch. She turned her attention to the other one. Might as well play fair—sort of.

"Enjoying yourself?" Justin asked, his voice a little rough.

"Yes," she replied, her mouth full of nipple. Lifting her head, she grinned at him as she sat back. "Every bit as much as you are." She rubbed herself over his erection. "Mmm, seems your clothes are getting tight. Better fix that. She planted a kiss right dead on his navel and then, because she just didn't feel like stopping herself, she blew on his belly. Interesting, grown vampires reacted just like babies. She tried to hide her smile.

"Find that funny, do you?" he growled.

"Just a little detour on the way." To prove her point, his pants and underwear, socks and shoes all hit the floor, and Stella squatted back on her heels to get full advantage of the view. What had been impressive by moonlight was downright breathtaking in the confines of her bed. As she watched, Justin slowly waved his erection at her and her body clenched in response.

She settled between his spread legs. She was no doubt grinning like a fool and her eyes popping like a Pekinese's, but who cared? The man she loved was naked in her bed and he was all hers.

"Stella," he said, tension and need lacing his voice as she kissed the inside of his right knee. He let out a little moan and she ran a line of soft kisses up his thigh.

She paused as she kissed the warm skin beside his testicles before kissing down his other thigh. She fluttered kisses up and down his legs until he began to mutter with frustration. She looked up at his poker-stiff erection and promised herself it wouldn't be long. She trailed fingers up his leg and gently cupped his balls in her hand and kissed them. His sigh became a slow drawn-out groan and before he quieted, she raised her head a little and lowered her mouth over his erection, taking him in up to the hilt.

Justin let out a long moan of satisfaction.

"Good?" Stella asked, her voice muffled by his erection.

His hands tunneled in her hair as his hips rocked. She eased her mouth up a little, circling him with her lips as she moved her head up and down, running her tongue over his flesh, savoring the smooth roundness of the tip of his penis and the ridges that circled it. She lapped and kissed along the underside and then came back to the smooth and heated head. Her tongue flicked over him, feeling every detail before taking him in deep again. Her mind all but flipped. Here she was Stella Schwartz, laundry clerk, holding in her mouth the manhood of a master vampire. She was almost dizzy with power.

Slowly she lifted her head, met his dark gleaming eyes and smiled.

She shifted, poised over him, her feet flat on the mattress, and lowered herself on his magnificent erection.

His entire body shuddered with anticipation. His eyes shone with a dark light and a slow groan of utter pleasure came from deep in his belly. His strong hands rested on her waist. "Stella," he said.

She might be on top, but there was no mistaking who led. He moved under and inside her, as he lifted and lowered her. She was his woman and she wanted nothing more than to pleasure her vampire lover.

He worked her up and down, coming deeper each time until all she knew was the touch of his hands on her skin and the power of his flesh seated deep in her. She was woman and he was man and they'd been created to come together this afternoon and forever. Across time and ocean, he'd found her and she never wanted to part. He made her woman and she gloried in her power.

It was at that moment, she opened her mind to his. She felt his pleasure. She was at once, vessel and contents, fire and flame. His approaching climax became her own building orgasm. Together they came, screaming in unison. Her body ignited with need and want, power and satiation in the same split second and then she knew, she could never, ever, part from him.

They lay together, spent from their mutual passion. Somehow they'd slipped under the sheets, maybe she even dozed, her mind too full of joy to think much beyond the power of his body and her own needs. She was hungry for more sex and needed blood. The two thoughts shocked her. She truly was changed beyond all recognition.

She must have slept. The next thing she knew was Justin kissing her. "I'll be back soon," he said. "I have to pick up Sam from the sitter. Want to explore the shopping I brought and see if it will do?"

Stella sat up in shock. She'd been so lost in lust, she'd all but forgotten she had a child to take care of. Justin was dressed in seconds and she didn't take much longer. She kissed him goodbye in the hall. Parting seemed so hard but he'd be back in minutes . . . with Sam.

Time to behave like a mother again.

Chapter Eleven

"You can't be serious, Toby!" Kit looked across at the dark-skinned vampire who'd knocked on his front door twenty minutes earlier.

Toby gave a little smile. "Sorry, Kit. I was just sent to gather facts. It would have been a lot simpler if one of the three of you had told Gwyltha what happened right from the start."

"To be honest, Toby, if we'd stopped to think, and knew about it, we would have."

"How could you miss it? Justin had to know what he'd done. It was in the paper."

Kit shook his head. "Honestly, Toby, since Friday night, we've had to cope with a dead mortal, transforming said mortal to our life—the latter being somewhat complicated because Stella didn't believe we existed. Among the three of us we had a fair bit of public relations work on our hands. And, I'll add as an aside, Stella is not the sort to just take anyone's word for anything. On top of that, it transpired she wasn't on her native soil, as we'd supposed, so I had to email to John to overnight us shoes. We did all this while taking care of a nine-year-old boy and making darn sure he never got an inkling of what was happening under the same roof. And let me tell you, after an afternoon with Sam, beats me how any mortal keeps up with a child.

"Just when things seemed to be settling down, the fledging forgets her limitations and goes running out on the first sunny morning in three weeks. Justin and I got to her in minutes, but we had a few bad moments. He's with her now, as it happens. Oh, and if that excitement wasn't enough for one day, Vlad himself comes visiting this afternoon, begging a favor. So between one thing and another we're a bit behind on the local newspapers and somehow never managed to turn on the TV."

Toby raised a slim-fingered hand. "All right, Kit. You made your point, but the fact remains two mortals were injured, one seriously, by all accounts." He looked at Kit and gave a shrug. "I'm not here on a witch hunt. I'm to collect facts and present them to Gwyltha when she arrives."

"When is she arriving?"

"Late Friday. I'm to give her a report when she arrives. She plans on holding the inquiry Saturday afternoon and attending Stella's welcome in the evening."

Kit gave a wry smile. "Between you and me, Toby. If Justin ends up expelled from the colony, there won't be much point bothering with a welcome for Stella." That he was sure of. He'd seen more than enough to convince him that whatever misgivings Stella might have, she'd darn well stand by Justin.

"Like that, is it?"

Kit nodded.

Both vampires sat in silence for several minutes. Kit wondering if he could send a mind warning to Justin without Toby noticing. If he could, what earthly good would it do?

Better use his energy digging out old newspapers and finding out what happened. "By the way," Toby looked up as Kit spoke, "mind if I ask what or who alerted Gwyltha to the injuries?"

Toby shrugged. "Vlad."

Damn him! "And he had the gall to come here asking favors!" Toby looked more than interested. Why not satisfy the curiosity in his eyes? "Seems he has two ghouls." Kit ignored Toby's look of shock. "Found them, to use his own words, 'rootless and abandoned.' He wants us to undertake their protection."

"You agreed?"

Kit coughed. "Yes. Mostly on the grounds that the colony only forbids the making of ghouls. Plus, Dixie sees herself as their champion."

"I hope she has a champion."

"She has me."

Toby stood up and walked over to the window. "This gets trickier at every turn." He turned back to face Kit. "Look, I'm here to collect facts about the injuries to those two mortals. That's all. If we get Justin through this, then we worry about ghouls."

"What are his odds?" If they knew this, they could perhaps make plans.

"That depends on the prognosis for those two mortals."

Kit swore. Just when Justin had found happiness, everything was about to blow up in his face. Not if Kit Marlowe could do anything about it.

"Look here, Kit," Toby went on, "no one holds Justin higher in esteem than I do. I've come to ascertain the truth, that's all. I hope . . ."

"No more than I do." Kit interrupted. He shouldn't have. Toby was an honorable man. It was just that the truth could damn Justin. Still . . . "Thank you for coming, Toby. And for warning me." No matter how he felt, he owed Toby hospitality. "Do you need to feed? We have blood bags, hidden in the basement away from the inquisitive eyes of a nine-year-old, or if you prefer, we can go out tonight."

"Tonight . . ." Toby paused. "Is there any chance I might meet this new fledging?"

"That would be for Justin to decide, but I'll pass on your request."

Toby smiled. "Protective is he? Understandable. I'll be off then. See you tonight."

He was gone with a wave and his own distinctive smile. Kit gave him ten minutes to be out of sight and then set off for the shop. He needed to chew this over with Dixie, and then they'd both better warn Justin. Would life ever get uncomplicated? So far in four centuries, it hadn't.

Interesting wasn't the word! Stella stared as she unpacked the groceries. Justin hadn't quite hit it on everything, but considering he hadn't eaten for well over a millennium, he hadn't done too badly. He'd bought six different pizzas—thank heaven she had plenty of freezer space—hot dogs and a family size pack of frozen hamburgers—enough to see Sam well into the New Year, but no buns. There was bread, but it was raisin cinnamon. He had cheese and eggs, good, but the only cereal was oatmeal, and the old-fashioned sort at that. She'd better read up the directions on the box to figure out how to make it. He hadn't bought any milk. It was all relatively healthy stuff, no chips or cookies. That would disappoint Sam. She dug into the second bag for fruit: oranges, grapes and pomegranates! She doubted Sam had ever tasted one. She hadn't and never would.

She sat down with a slump as that thought hit her. Never again to taste a fresh-baked cookie, sausage gravy and biscuits for breakfast, or sour cream on a baked potato! But she was alive—in a manner of speaking. If it hadn't been for Justin, she'd now be in a casket. Seemed a bit silly to mourn sausage gravy and pomegranates . . . but she did need milk before the morning.

She gave Dixie a quick call at the Emporium, asking her to please grab a gallon of two percent on her way over. "Anything else Justin forgot? I don't think grocery shopping is his usual thing."

As she was telling Dixie she'd manage, Sam came bursting through the front door. "Mom, have you heard?"

She told Dixie a quick goodbye and gave Sam her attention. "What, honey?"

"About Johnny Day. He broke both arms and his leg and his mom has to help him pee like a baby!" He dropped his book bag on the floor. "What's for a snack?"

"Raisin toast and fruit." She popped a slice in the toaster and, just because she had four of them, cut a pomegranate into quarters.

"What's that?" Sam asked.

"A pomegranate," Justin replied. "I loved them when I was a boy."

Maybe that underscored all their differences. He'd been a child who ate pomegranates and she was raised on canned fruit cocktail.

"Never had one, Sam?" Justin asked.

Sam shook his head and eyed it suspiciously. "Uh-uh."

"Feeling adventurous?"

Sam didn't look too convinced but gamely took a bite, his young face scrunched up with concentration. "It's good," he said, "but do you spit out the seeds?"

Justin shook his head. "Only barbarians do that. Chew them up."

"What's a barbarian?" Sam asked through a mouthful of pomegranate and a dribble of pink juice down his chin.

"Someone who destroys what other people build, can't read and doesn't want to learn, and doesn't try to understand new things."

Not a bad attempt. Stella was darn glad she hadn't been asked that one. "And someone who doesn't wipe their chin when they dribble," she added, handing Sam a paper towel.

"Aw, Mom," Sam said as he rubbed juice all over his chin. "Are Johnny Day and his gang barbarians?"

"Perhaps," Justin replied. He looked at Stella. "Wasn't that the name of the lad who . . ." Stella nodded. The toast popped up and she started buttering it.

"Pete Day got arrested for stealing from the school!" Sam was in full force. "And Johnny got smashed up last Friday."

Justin seemed to freeze for a minute. A cold knot of worry twisted Stella's stomach. Last Friday! "What happened?"

She'd just handed Sam his toast. Bad move. She had to wait endless seconds while Sam chewed and swallowed. "Everyone's talking about it at school. Carrie Day told us on the bus. She's okay. It's not her fault she has mean brothers." Sam paused to take another bite.

"Got knocked about badly, did they?" Justin asked. "Broken bones?"

Sam nodded. "I told you! Johnny Day has three casts and his mom has to dress him and take care of him like a baby. Carrie said so. She says he's meaner than a snake now and her mom said she wished they'd kept Johnny in the hospital." Sam paused to chew again. "Warty Watson is still in the hospital. He's hurt real bad."

"This happened Friday?" Justin had a knack of asking just enough to get Sam going again.

"They're saying they got attacked by a monster." Sam rolled his eyes. "In the park. Even kindergartners know there's no such thing! Matt said he bet they'd been eating pills but Carrie says no, Johnny swears it was a monster." Sam took another bite of toast. "I think Matt's right."

Maybe Johnny and Warty had been on mind-altering chemicals but this went along with what Annie had told her earlier. Stella looked at Justin. Shocked was not the word for the look in his eyes. "What happened to the other boy?" he asked.

Sam shrugged, obviously getting bored with the subject. "He's still in the hospital, coming out on Wednesday. But guess what?" Sam paused for effect. "Sally Watson told Carrie that Warty says he saw the devil and he's been asking to see a minister, 'cause he's afraid he's going to hell." Sam took a long drink of juice and smiled up at Stella from under an orange moustache.

"Some weekend," Stella said. Heck, she had to say something. Justin nodded. His mind was obviously running on the same lines. She reached across the table and put her hand over Justin's. He grabbed it as if it were a lifeline. Would he feel worse or better when she passed on the talk at the laundry this morning? Her fingers meshed with Justin's.

"Oh!" Sam caught the movement and his eyes almost popped. "May I leave the table? I've got lots of homework."

"Need any help with it?" she asked.

He stared at their linked hands. "Maybe."

Stella eased her fingers from Justin's. "If you do, just ask. Dixie's coming over later, remember? If you get your homework done before she gets here, you can watch a video or play a game together before going to bed."

"Will she fix dinner, or will you?"

"That depends. You've had a good snack so I don't expect you'll be hungry for awhile. I've got you pizza when you're hungry . . . and your homework's done."

Sam was silent a moment or two as he looked from Stella to Justin and back. "Are you two dating?"

She should have expected this. Were they dating? Did being transformed into a vampire and having incredible sex count as dating? Friday night started as a date but since then . . .

While Stella still struggled for an accurate answer to

Sam's question, Justin asked, "Would it matter to you if we were?"

Sam chewed his cheek over that one. "No," he replied at last, "that would be cool." He slipped out of his seat, placed his glass and plate in the sink and then spread his homework on the kitchen table.

He seemed set for a while, so Stella took the chance for a quick shower. Her body smelled of sex and Justin. She could still sense his skin against hers and his erection deep inside. She was definitely not the woman who'd walked out on Friday evening. But what now? Her new job might well work out fine, once she figured out the baby-sitting side, but how much longer could she get away with telling Sam she was on a diet?

She turned on the shower, taking care not to look in the mirror and stepped under the warm spray. Soaping her breasts, she wondered more about Justin's offer. Should she go to England with him? Sam could go to school as easily there as he could here, and she bet Justin didn't live in a neighborhood with a crack house down the street and a family like the Days as neighbors. He was a doctor. Doctors were rich. He most likely lived in a mansion.

Why even think about it? She couldn't leave Mom—and she'd promised to take care of the house until Mom got out, and that was another nineteen years! Why had she ever made that promise?

Stella lathered up a washcloth and scrubbed the rest of her body. The house aside, if she wasn't here to visit Mom, no one would. Stella shampooed her hair, letting the water run down her body, taking away the scent of Justin and their wild afternoon. She'd talk to Mom when she visited this weekend. Maybe she could find someone to rent the house . . .

Stella turned off the shower and reached for a towel. Here was yet another problem: how would she get to Marysville if the sun was shining?

She wouldn't solve that one standing dripping on the bathmat.

Justin knew he had to be grinning like an adolescent fool. Even in blue jeans and a sweater he knew for certain wasn't cashmere, Stella carried herself with dignity. The dignity of a beautiful, confident woman. His woman. His vampire.

"Have fun!" Dixie said with a grin.

"Yeah, Mom!" Sam gave Stella a goodbye hug. He stepped back, a worried expression on his face as he looked Justin square in the eyes. "You're not trying to get lucky with my mom, are you?"

"Sam!" Stella all but gasped, and Dixie made a noise that might have been a cough, but by her eyes was a strangled laugh.

Sam just looked at him—man to man—demanding an answer.

"Sam, let's have a quick word." He offered his hand. Sam took it but didn't grasp it. He was still the anxious male defending the honor of his family. "Tell me first," Justin asked as they stepped into the living room leaving Stella and Dixie standing in the hall, "what you meant by 'get lucky.'"

Sam chewed his cheek. "It means . . ." He frowned. "That, well . . . you know . . . when men and women . . . get lovey with each other. Mom says when people love each other they take care of each other and make 'em feel good. But when the kids at school talk about it . . . it sounds gross." He gave Justin another stern frown. "You're not going to try it with Mom tonight, are you?"

He couldn't lie to this child but neither could he admit to getting singularly lucky this afternoon. Justin scrunched down so they were eye to eye. "Sam, your mother's right about people looking after those they love. She looks after you, doesn't she?" Sam nodded. "I want to look after your mother and you."

"You love her?"

"Yes, I do."

That earned him another cautious scrutiny. "You gonna move in with us?"

"Not right now. I'll come and visit your mother and we'll go out together. Maybe sometimes we'll go out with you, too. Does that sound all right to you?"

Sam nodded. "Guess so." His voice didn't sound so sure. "You gonna get her pregnant and then go away like my dad did?"

The hurt and skepticism in the young voice shocked Justin. "Sam. I'll never get your mother pregnant and leave her." No chance of that, but Sam needed more reassurance. "I swear it. Understand?" Sam nodded, his eyes still uncertain. "Something else the matter?"

"It's just . . . well . . . Friday night she looked so pretty when she went out with you and then she was sick on Saturday and all weekend and . . ." His earnest dark gray eyes demanded an answer just as his anxieties needed soothing.

"Your mother had something like flu." Stretching the truth, yes, but Sam needed to know his mother was not sick. "It meant she had to sleep to get well. She'll still get drowsy at times and need to rest a good bit. Do you understand?"

Sam nodded. "She's not going to die, is she?" he blurted out after a longish silence.

That Justin could answer with certainty. "Your mother is not going to die. She'll be here for as long as you need her." And at some point would have some very tricky explaining to do. Surely someone in the colony had come against this problem. Anyway, it could wait a few years. "I'm going to take good care of her."

Sam smiled. "Okay."

"All right with you if I take her out now?"

"Sure." As Justin stood up, Sam gave him a quick hug. The feel of the slim, young body touched something deep in Justin. Memories of his own boyhood and his long-dead half-brother, stirred deep in the mists of his long memory. He gathered up Sam in his arms and returned the hug.

"It's okay with me if you want to kiss her," Sam whispered, his mortal breath warm against Justin's ear.

Justin held Sam even closer, so he wouldn't see his grin. It was good to have the man-of-the-house's blessing! He stepped into the hall. "Here," he said to Dixie, and handed Sam over. "Better take good care of him. We'll be back in a little while."

Dixie caught Sam and hugged him close. "Sure will."

"Hey, you're strong!" Sam said looking at Dixie with admiration. "Mom can't pick me up anymore. She says I'm too heavy." Not any longer she wouldn't, but Sam had better not realize that any time soon.

Dixie caught Justin's eyes and put Sam down. "I think your mom's right," she said. "You weigh a ton!" Good move. No point in letting him suspect exactly how strong they all were.

The sky was clear. A cold night for mortals. Colder still for injured mortals lying in plaster casts in hospital beds. Justin couldn't get that out of his mind. Just when his life seemed perfect, the gods chose to teach him humility. He hadn't needed a slave in the chariot reminding him. A child had told him he'd transgressed vampire law. And now . . .

"Something the matter?" Stella asked.

"Just thinking over what Sam said about those two boys." By tacit agreement, they avoided Schiller Park, walking along Thurman and then turning up Pearl, heading for the Cup o' Joe on Third.

"Annie, who works in the office at the laundry, is married

to a policeman and she said much the same. So it's most likely true."

"What?"

"That Johnny Day and Warty Watson were found injured in the park some distance from each other. The police are a bit mystified how they got hurt but think it must have been some sort of gang retaliation. Both of them were known to be mixed up with drugs." She paused. "Someone, no one knows who, threw a gun through the window of a house on Reinhart. It set the burglar alarm off, the police were alerted to answer the alarm and that's when they found Johnny and Warty. Also, and I suspect Annie shouldn't be passing this around, but seems the gun was covered with fingerprints, mostly Johnny's and almost all the bullets had been fired."

That didn't leave much room for conjecture. "Stella, let's skip the coffee shop tonight and go somewhere we can really talk." Kit was manning the Emporium; Dixie was busy making Sam's supper. They'd have the house to themselves. They turned left on Columbus and turned up City Park.

"You need to feed, to replace the strength you lost this morning," Justin said as he closed the front door behind him. "I had planned to take you to the zoo, but Dixie won't grudge you some of her supply. Want to feed first or talk?"

"Why were we going to the zoo? To see the sights?" She looked at him and her face changed as she understood. "To feed?"

He nodded. "It's an alternative. Kit much prefers it to human feeding. As a fledgling, you really need the extra sustenance of human blood, but any animal will do at a pinch. Dixie, now, has a few issues with this, she was a life-long vegetarian before her transformation. She prefers blood bags when she can get them. She has a stash in the fridge. So, want to eat first?"

Stella shook her head. "Later. I'd like to figure out what really happened Friday."

"That's clear enough. That hobbledehoy shot you. I lost control and injured the pair of them and somehow the gun ended up breaking a window. Come to think of it, I remember hearing the alarm go off as I carried you here."

"And they are now rambling about monsters and the devil. I think I do need to feed after all." As she hefted the chilled bag in her hands, watching with strange fascination as the dark liquid slurped within the thick plastic. "Where do I start? It's not exactly like unwrapping a candy bar."

"Watch me." He took another bag, tilting it over his head, he bit off one corner and sucked. Stella did pretty well for a first time. She drained the bag quickly and only dribbled a little down her chin. "Here." He handed her a paper towel.

"What do I do with the empty?" Stella asked as she crumpled up the used paper towel. "They can hardly go in the trash."

"Dixie collects them up and every so often, on a dark night, takes a trip to the landfill."

"You think of everything."

"That's how we survive the centuries."

"Yeah, I've been thinking about that a lot and just how long I can convince Sam I'm on a diet." She gave a wry smile. "It's not going to be easy."

"We'll help you." And if he wasn't around, Kit and Dixie wouldn't let her down . . . but he'd not worry Stella with that —yet. "Let's have a seat. There's some things you need to know." Not about ghouls, or the problems he faced over those two youths, but Stella needed to be prepared for Gwyltha. They sat side by side on the sofa. Stella's head on his shoulder. He shut his eyes a second, to block out everything but the scent of Stella. To find her like this, the woman he loved and to face possible exile. What the hell could he do? Pray to the gods both boys recovered? Even so, he'd harmed them. No getting away from it.

"You're very quiet," Stella said. "Thought you wanted to talk."

"I think I'll kiss you first. I have Sam's permission."

"You what!" Her laugh was deep and earthy and sexy.

"When we had our man to man talk, he said it was okay for me to kiss you."

"He did, did he? Do you think it's okay with me to kiss me?"

He didn't bother to answer that. He just tilted her head back and took her mouth. He tasted the last traces of fresh blood on her lips and his body went into overdrive. He kissed with his mouth, his mind and his soul and she responded with the same wild passion she'd given earlier. By Abel and all the gods! To find this woman across the centuries and to be so near to losing her again . . . that, he refused to think about tonight.

"You look very pleased with yourself," she said when he finally broke off the kiss.

He loved how her gray eyes gleamed. "You don't look exactly disappointed yourself."

She let out another lovely, earthy chuckle. "I thought we came here to talk."

They had. And after he took her home, he'd have to do some thinking. "It's like this. You understand about our vampire colony. Kit, Dixie, myself, now you and several others. We're all joined by blood and by custom. We support each other for our mutual survival. When I realized you'd need shoes with your earth in them, I contacted someone in the colony who makes them. He did an overnight special order and flew them over here. Things like that. Part of it is welcoming new fledglings. Our leader, Gwyltha," amazing how he could now think of her without hurt, "will be coming with several others to meet you."

"Coming from where? When?"

"Mostly from England. They'll arrive in a day or so."

"They're coming all this way just to meet me!"

"Not just to meet you, to welcome you as a new member of the colony." The colony that might well expel him.

"The thought of a vampire reception will take some getting used to."

He squeezed her hand. "At least you believe in us now."

"Oh yes, Justin Corvus, I believe in you." If only her faith could carry them through. They sat in silence a few minutes, her head on his shoulder. "When's this big reception, then?"

"Saturday."

Stella broke from the circle of his arm and turned to him in shock. "It can't be. I can't be there on Saturday."

"What's happening Saturday? Something with Sam?"

It would be so easy to lie but she couldn't. Not to Justin. "No, not Sam." She stood up and walked over to the window.

"What is it, Stella?"

Up and down the street porchlights cast bright pools of light on trim yards and swept sidewalks. The iron fence around Dixie's front yard was newly painted and the path wasn't missing stray bricks. Stella shook her head. What was she doing in this world of clean streets and neat lives? Enjoying it! Wanting it for Sam! But people who lived here didn't visit incarcerated relatives on alternate Saturdays.

She'd hoped never to have to tell Justin, but what the heck. Stella turned to face him. "Every other Saturday I go to see my mother. I can't miss it. I'm the only visitor she ever gets."

His dark eyes clouded as he digested her words. "Is she sick? In hospital?"

"She's in the Women's Correctional Facility at Marysville." Might as well tell it like it is.

His eyebrows rose, just a tad. "In prison?"

She nodded. "I don't suppose your friends get arrested or imprisoned, do they?" It was unfair and too sharp, but . . .

"Not recently." He wasn't kidding. His voice and face were utterly serious.

"When?"

"Kit was arrested, not long before he died. He wasn't detained long though, but his friend Tom, whom you'll meet on Saturday, was arrested and tortured."

"Tortured? What for?"

"He was accused of blasphemy. They racked him to get information to incriminate Kit. That's what killed him. That and the weeks in Bridewell afterwards."

"For blasphemy? This was in England?" And he'd expected her to move there with him!

"Blasphemy was a serious crime back then."

"When?"

His mouth twitched a little at one corner. "In 1593."

She stared while her brain got around that fact. Would she ever get used to this?

While she stood and gaped, Justin stepped closer. "Tell me about your mother."

"Mom is what they call an habitual criminal. Has been since she was in her teens. Shoplifting, stealing from employers, using other people's credit card numbers. She's been in and out of jail ever since I can remember. Six years ago, she got herself involved with a really bad lot and took part in a bank robbery. She got twenty-five years."

"So now you go to see her every fortnight?" Stella nodded. "How are you going to get there? You can't drive in daylight." Dear heaven! She'd forgotten about that!

"Dixie can drive. You can lie on the backseat and cover yourself with a blanket if the light bothers you."

"I can't ask her. She's done so much already. Can't you drive me, if I can't do it myself?" Justin's support would make the day so much easier.

He shook his head. "I may not be free that afternoon. I'll ask Dixie. She'll get you there and back safely."

Stella gave a slow sigh. She should be relieved. This way she'd get there without passing out at the wheel or anything terrible like that, but Justin's refusal stung. It shouldn't. He didn't owe her. He'd done more than enough already and maybe she was being a nuisance. Passing out at work and needing his help. She ran her hand through her hair. "I hate to bother her."

He dropped a kiss on her forehead. "Remember what I said about helping other members out? This is one of those times. One day you'll be the elder vampire aiding a fledging."

"And what will you be? A senior citizen vampire?"

"I'll be the one who loves you. Never forget that, Stella. Whatever might happen, I love you." His words warmed the cockles of her heart; she believed him utterly. How could she not with his arms around her?

"I'm in trouble and I'm afraid it may rebound on you and Dixie by association," Justin said when Kit came in from hunting.

Kit frowned. "Could you be more specific?"

"Those boys who shot Dixie. Seems I went berserk and injured them both. One has broken limbs, the other I'm not sure of the details."

"A broken neck, leg, pelvis and arm, and internal injuries."

Justin rounded on Kit. "You knew and you never told me!"

"I did not know until this afternoon. I planned on telling you this evening when you came back. Did you read the papers?"

"No. I got part of it from Sam—apparently school buses here are hotbeds of gossip and conjecture—and Stella told me the rest. One of her former coworkers is married to a policeman." Saying it aloud to another vampire who understood the gravity of this made the whole thing seem even worse. "I don't remember much, just a blur of fury before carrying Stella here. Seems I paused long enough to attack and maim two mortals." He let out a long mutter of exasperation and worry. "I'll have to inform Gwyltha . . . and soon."

"You don't need to bother."

"What?" Something cold seemed to settle permanently in Justin's heart. "How? Is she here now?"

"Not yet . . . but Toby is. He came to 'gather the facts,' as he calls it. Seems Vlad just happened to mention it to Gwyltha."

"Damn him to perdition and back! I bet he'll dance jigs when I'm exiled."

"You're not exiled yet." Kit walked over and clapped him on the shoulder. "You didn't intend harm, that's got to count for something."

"If I'd only had a chance to tell her first, admit my culpability and ask for clemency, for Stella's sake if not mine. But now . . . She'll be asking why you and Dixie didn't report it." Damn the man!

"Toby seemed to accept our ignorance. I did my best to persuade him of yours."

"That makes it worse. I'm going around attacking mortals and forgetting about it. A vampire with memory problems!" He laughed and heard the near-hysteria in his voice.

Kit shook him. "Justin, you can't give up. There has to be a way to fight this."

Justin shook his head. "How, Kit? I was one who helped frame those laws."

"There's a fair bit of uninhabited country in our territory . . . plenty of wildlife."

Did Kit know what he was suggesting? Yes, and would take friendship that far. "Kit, I can't ask that of you. You'd risk exile yourself. Dixie would never survive in the wild this young. And what about Stella? I need you two here to keep her safe and arrange for her to go to England, to Tom. He'll keep her safe. If she refuses to go, keep her here but give her all the protection you can. Will you promise me?"

"You don't need to ask, Justin, that's a given. But I refuse to give up hope like this."

"Better not dispute it. I have no defense and this way there will be no repercussions on you two or Stella." Justin slumped into a chair and closed his eyes. Somewhere he had to find the strength to do what he had to do: face his culpability and keep all taint of suspicion from Stella.

Chapter Twelve

Dixie looked the dark-skinned vampire in the eye and dared him to prevaricate. "Okay, Toby, are you going to tell me what's going on?"

He gave Dixie a cautious smile. "Why should something be going on?"

"Give me a break! You're staying here virtually incognito . . . in the same hotel as Vlad, as it happens." She had to get that in, wondering if it was all part of it. By the flash of surprise in his eyes, he hadn't known. Interesting. "I know darn well you seldom ever come over to this side of the Atlantic, but you just so happen to be in the same city as Christopher and I. And you try to tell me it's all just a coincidence?"

She had him! She just knew it by the shock on his face. Now to press home with a nice bit of guilt. It had always worked in her librarian days. "Toby, we've just got settled. Kit likes it here and I was so worried he wouldn't. Things are good. I can't bear the thought of you coming over and disturbing things . . ." She almost embarrassed herself with the whine that broke off the last sentence. Talk about shades of Scarlett O'Hara! It was a very long shot, but . . .

"For heaven's sake, Dixie! It's not you or Kit I'm investigating. It was never suggested either of you were involved."

Involved in what? Vlad's ghouls? They hadn't done anything yet. To buy herself a little thinking time, she stood up and walked over to the window. The City Center parking lot wasn't exactly an enthralling view. "Toby, do you promise me that?" What had just happened that the colony would involve itself? Stella's transformation? Why would Toby be investigating—to use his own term? "Toby, please . . ." she began but decided not to push it too much. A whining Southern Belle wasn't likely to cut much cake—reminding Toby of his days as a slave wouldn't help her cause.

"Dixie." He'd crossed the room to her but stood a few feet away. "You have my word. The investigation does not involve you two other than sources of information, and as I learned from Kit, you knew nothing about it. Justin alone bears responsibility."

For what? Transforming Stella? That didn't make sense. "Is it really that big a deal?"

If vamps spluttered that would have been a splutter. "For heaven's sake! Haven't you learned anything about our ethics?" Quite a bit, as it happened but . . . "Justin attacked two mortals. Maimed them." The thugs who'd shot him and Stella. "There's no denying it. He admits it."

She knew almost everything now. Except . . . "So when are you holding the inquisition?"

"The inquiry." He sounded almost miffed at her choice of words. "On Saturday afternoon. Gwyltha wants to get it out of the way before Stella's welcome."

"I bet she does!" She might find it wasn't that easy.

"Dixie, don't take this on as a crusade. You can't thwart the law. It's unfortunate, but . . ."

"Unfortunate!" Dixie all but lost it. "One of the most decent, honorable men I've ever met is about to get thrown out of the colony because he was defending the woman he loved!"

"Heaven help me!" Toby made no effort to hide his exasperation, but in his cultured Oxbridge accent it really did sound like an appeal to Providence. "Look here, Dixie. You think I'm enjoying this? Justin's my friend, dammit!" Toby let out a sigh as he shook his head. "We have no choice. If we relax the rules, what next? We permit feeding to the point of leaving a dying corpse? We kill like the vampires in horror novels? We can't permit that to happen. Gwyltha is right on this."

And Gwyltha had no more need for her discarded lover! No, that was unfair. Gwyltha had never shown rancor or spite of any sort. "Toby, it just seems so unfair!"

"Girl," he put his hand on her shoulder, "you're right there."

The colloquial address was so unlike him, she turned. His eyes were misting and a wry smile twisted his wide mouth. Toby no more wanted this than she did. "And it's doubly unfair you got stuck doing this!"

He shrugged. "I won't argue with you. I didn't volunteer. I was conscripted but at least I'm on his side, not pulling the other way."

She hugged him. Tight. He returned the hug and patted her shoulder. It was all-out unfair. "Toby," she said, for once not too sure what to say next. Try to get him on her side? Launch a counter inquiry? Plead extenuating circumstances?

"I know, girl. Some things we can't do much about." Maybe he couldn't, but she had other ideas. "Look," he gave her another quick hug, "promise me you won't start some counterattack of your own, mount a defense or something like that. Promise." She pulled back from his hug and gave him her best outraged look. By the angle of his eyebrows, she hadn't lost the knack. "You can't change vampire law single-handed."

"Maybe two of us can?"

"Dixie, Justin was one of the group who laid down those laws. He won't thank you for defying them." She'd defied Justin before and got away with it. "Promise me, Dixie."

She weighed her options. Fast. Toby was between her and the door, he still had the longshoreman's physique from the years he'd worked on the Liverpool Docks and he was older than her by almost a hundred and fifty years. She couldn't beat him by speed or power. "Okay, Toby . . . on one condition." He let out what sounded like a growl. She decided to ignore his vampire posturing. "One condition. That's all. I promise not to interfere during the inquiry and to be a good little fledgling. Fair enough?"

"Depends on the condition."

"I just want to know who told Gwyltha."

He shrugged. "That's no secret. Our Romanian acquaintance."

Vlad! Dixie was ready to spit nails but instead she gave Toby a last hug. "Thanks for telling. Now I must be off."

"Goodbye, Dixie."

Toby saw her to the lift—he'd never get into the habit of calling it an elevator—and went back to his suite. He'd planted the seed. He hoped something would come of it. What could Dixie do? Maybe nothing, but she'd rattled the colony and the establishment before and Toby darn well hoped she'd find a loophole for Justin. She'd only promised not to interfere during the inquiry. That gave her two good days. He doubted Dixie would let the moss gather on her native earth.

* * *

Dixie longed for the effects of a nice stiff gin and tonic. She toyed with ordering one just for the aroma and old times' sakes but decided, no. She had too damn much else to do to and she might as well start with Vlad Tepes. She was close to seething as she strode from the elevator to the house phones. The man had the nerve to ask favors at the same time as he was deep-sixing Justin and his chance of happiness! "Mr. Roman's room, please," Dixie said, using Vlad's traveling name. As it was ringing on the other end, she realized she had no idea what she was going to say. She'd come up with something after she got invited into his room.

"Hello?" The voice was sweet, hesitant, and female. The wrong room perhaps?

"Is Mr. Roman there?"

"Not right now."

Right room, but the man she wanted was . . . Wait a minute. This had to be . . . "I'm sorry, I don't know your name but I think you must be one of the two women Mr. Roman, Vlad, asked us to help."

"Oh, yes!" She could hear the relief over the phone. "I'm Angela and Jane's here, too. We've been wondering what's going to happen."

"I'm Dixie LePage. Mind if I come up?" It was pushing her luck a bit but heck . . .

"Please do!" It wasn't exactly begging but was the next best thing. "We've been wondering what's happening."

They weren't the only ones. "I'll be right up."

As the elevator made the short journey to the third floor, Dixie decided it was a good thing Vlad wasn't there. She'd be tempted to clout him one and that would be a bad move and now she had the chance to see what all this ghoulishness, if that was the right word, was all about. Then she'd go home and talk to Stella. Between them they had to be able to do something. Dixie had a pretty strong suspicion her role might be restraining Stella. But heck . . .

"Dixie? It is you, isn't it?" They were both waiting by the elevator, and greeted her as if she were the answer to their prayers . . . assuming ghouls prayed . . .

"Yeah, it's me. I'm Dixie LePage."

They introduced themselves as Angela Ryan and Jane Johnson.

"Let's go talk," Angela said leading the way down the hallway.

"Perhaps we'd better find somewhere we won't be disturbed," Dixie said. Heck, Vlad might be back any minute.

They both gave her an odd look.

"We'll just shut our door," Jane said. "Vlad would never intrude without knocking."

"We've been after him since we got here to let us know what's going to happen. He'll be glad to know you're here."

Dixie wasn't sure she shared Jane's conviction but Vlad had asked for her help. Well, okay, Christopher's, and so far neither sounded like the mindless slaves of Justin's description.

Dixie scrutinized them as they got settled. They insisted she have one of the two very comfortable chairs. Jane took the other and Angela stretched out on the bed. If Dixie had legs like hers, she'd want to show them off at every opportunity too. The woman look like a model: tall with legs that went up to her armpits and honey-colored hair pinned up in a French pleat. Ghouls must not have to cope with the same mirror inconvenience vampires did.

"Well," Angela said with a smile. "No point in beating around the bush. What's your offer?" Mindless slaves! Dixie couldn't help smiling. Justin definitely had it wrong. But Justin was her reason for being here and if she could help out with these two women, Vlad would darn well owe her.

"You're not exactly subtle, Angie," Jane said. "How about, 'Would you like a drink?' before you attack?"

Angela, stiffened her shoulders and raised her eyebrows.

They were light brown, like her lashes and framed her blue eyes. "I'm not attacking. I'd just like to know what Dixie has in mind."

"To be honest, I don't have anything specific in mind." Might as well say it like it is. "I know you need jobs and somewhere to live but . . ." she paused, "since you're the first ghouls I've ever met, I've no idea what your skills are or what sort of jobs you want. How about you give me a quick Ghoul 101?"

"It's not easy . . ." Angela began only to be interrupted by Jane's, "I'm not sure where to start . . ." They both paused, looked at each other and then at Dixie and waited. Maybe not mindless but indecisive and confused seemed to fit.

"Okay," Dixie said, "how about you tell me what jobs you are trained for."

"We don't know," Angela said. "That's what's driving us both crazy. It's a black void."

Jane nodded agreement. "We can't remember a single thing before meeting Vlad. Not where we came from, what we did. Even our names."

"How did you know your names then?"

"We didn't," Jane replied. "We picked them out of a telephone book."

"Whoa! Back up a minute. You're losing me here." She half-expected to hear *Twilight Zone* music. "Let's forget job skills a minute. You two remember nothing until meeting Vlad." They both nodded. "Start there, when did you meet him and where and what happened?"

"It was just over a month ago," Angela began, speaking for both of them. "He found us on a park bench. We still can't remember how we got there but we both agree we'd been there days." She looked at Jane who nodded agreement. "Several days. We hid in the bushes at night because of the street people."

Angela went on. "Then one afternoon, Vlad appeared. He

walked by a couple of times. Didn't look our way but we sensed he was watching us."

"We could feel his power," Jane said, "Like an aura. He seemed so safe after the streets. He walked over to us and asked where our controller was and what his business was in Chicago." Vlad protecting his territory? "We told him we'd no idea where we came from. That seemed to surprise him. He told us to be patient, he'd return for us."

"We thought he was nuts at first," Angela interrupted, "and wondered if we should make ourselves scarce, but we couldn't. He'd told us to wait."

"That sounds so wimpy," Jane said, "but I can't explain it, he emanated security, so we were waiting like good little ghouls when he returned and didn't hesitate when he told us to come with him."

Angela nodded. "He took us in a taxi to his hotel. To this day I'll never understand how he got us through the lobby without being stopped. We must have looked like scarecrows and it was one of those marble floors, oriental rugs sort of places." Dixie knew exactly how. Not hard for a vamp of Vlad's powers, but seemed these two didn't know any more about vamps than she did of ghouls.

"He took us up to his suite and he told us to take a shower and wash our hair. We did half wonder if we'd let ourselves in for some sort of pervert," Jane said. "But he told us not to worry, that he was leaving us alone. We were quite safe and he was going out to find us nourishment. Then he left and we went hog wild with soap and hot water." She grinned. "Have you ever felt so dirty you felt you needed sandpaper to get clean?"

Dixie nodded. She had. "I know what you mean."

"We almost fought over the shower," Angela went on, "until we realized there were two, one in the parlor. I stood under the water for ages, until I started feeling weak. I couldn't stand putting back on my filthy clothes so I grabbed one of the lovely thick toweling robes the hotel provided and found out later Jane did the same."

"It was weird," Jane said. "We both stood there staring at the coffeemaker trying to remember what it was. Took the two of us about fifteen minutes to work out what to do with it. It was like fumbling through thick gel and finally grasping hold of the right idea. We eventually figured out how to make a cup of coffee and were sitting drinking it, remembering the taste, and trying to remember what the TV was for, when Vlad reappeared."

Angela took up the story, "I could smell the meat almost before he opened the door to the suite. He had six chickens in a grocery sack, and we all but tore them out of his hands. I devoured one, tearing at it with my teeth, pulling the bones apart with my fingers. I sensed Jane doing the same but was too hungry to care. We were like ravening beasts."

"Hardly surprising, we were ravenous. Lord alone knows how long it was since we'd eaten," Jane said. "I ate the other chickens a little more graciously but I was still starving. After that, Vlad gathered up the few bones we hadn't chewed up, gave us milk to drink and told us to rest. We slept over twenty-four hours and woke like new women."

"Refreshed and rested, full of energy, and able to think— but with all our memories gone. That was when Vlad suggested we pick names, so we took a pin to the phone book." Angela smiled. "I first hit Wayne J. Leatherbarrow so I tried again. I'm glad I didn't hit Doris or Elvira someone-or-other."

"Okay, feeding gave you back strength and energy . . ." Made sense, she'd weaken without feeding, so did mortals come to that. "But your memories?"

Jane shrugged. "Gone. Whoever abandoned us took our memories with them. You see why we're in a hole?"

"But Vlad found you a job," Dixie said, remembering what Justin said about the vamp bar.

They both rolled their eyes.

"It was so tacky!" Jane said with a shudder. "I hate to sound snobby, but honestly all these mortals pretending to be vampires and all thinking they were the answer to any woman's prayer. I finally learned to spill drinks on the most persistent but . . ."

"It wasn't just the mortals, the vampire who ran the place had creeping hands," Angela grimaced, "and they knew darn well we couldn't file for sexual harassment . . ." She broke off, eyes wide. "Good heavens! I've just remembered about sexual harassment." She walked over to the bed and took Jane's hands. "Do you remember? It's when you sue someone for making unwanted advances at work." Jane frowned. "What's suing?"

Angela shrugged. "Beats me. It's what you do over sexual harassment." She paused, eyes scrunched up with thought. "I wonder if I ever sued for sexual harassment . . ." She looked at Dixie. "This is how it is: odd things come back and sometimes I understand them and other times I don't."

It was a marvel they hadn't both flipped. "Suing is taking someone to court, if you win, you get restitution, usually in money. Angela's right about suing for sexual harassment, but I don't know how you'd go about it if you don't even know your own names."

"That's the trouble all around," Jane said. "That sleaze had us over a barrel. We don't exist. He got out of paying our Social Security too, because we don't have numbers. That's why we jumped at Vlad's offer to come with him here."

"Finding jobs shouldn't be hard, if you're not too picky. Columbus has a shortage of potential employees. Until you remember what your skills are and what you can do, we'll find you something, but not having Social Security numbers is a problem." Dixie sighed. How were they going to get over that one?

"Vlad said there was a member of your colony who could take care of that," Angela said.

Dixie wondered what Tom would think of that! Brother, would Vlad owe for the rest of his life! Which suited her fine right now . . . She smiled. "I can't speak for anyone else, but I'm willing to do what I can about a job. Either of you fancy clerking at a laundry?"

"Beats getting your bra strap twanged by drunks," Jane said.

Dixie wouldn't disagree there. That bar sounded a whole lot worse than Justin painted. "I can't promise anything, but a friend of mine had to quit her job recently and they need someone to replace her." And thinking of Stella, "Angela, how would you feel about baby-sitting?"

"You really think some mother would trust her baby to a ghoul?"

"I can ask. Since the baby is school age and the mother is a vampire, she might agree." And it would make things easier all around having another pair of hands. How Stella would pay, they'd work out. She'd been paying a sitter before.

"Seems too good to be true," Jane said.

"It isn't carved in concrete but I'll do what I can. No promises. If these don't work out, we'll find something else." She'd never been hugged by ghouls before. Another first . . . "I'll call you back as soon as I know something."

They insisted on walking her to the elevator, heaping thanks on her all the way down the hall. "Don't start counting paychecks already," Dixie cautioned. "I can't write any guarantees, only that I'll do the best I can."

"Vlad said you would," Angela said.

He had, had he? "I don't answer to Vlad, or Mr. Roman, as he calls himself here . . . and I had hoped to see him."

"He's coming," Jane said.

Moments later, the elevator doors opened and Vlad Tepes, the one-time Prince of Wallachia stepped out.

He greeted Jane and Angela with an interesting mixture of affection and concern. Dixie got an amused smiled and a curious glint in his brown eyes. "Ms. LePage." He inclined his head. "An honor."

"Hi, Vlad. I dropped by hoping to have a word with you, and I met Jane and Angela." No point in snapping his head off. She wanted to negotiate after all.

"I'm glad you made their acquaintance. I gather you're here at Corvus and Marlowe's instigation?"

Not exactly, but he needn't know that. "I came to talk to you on a different matter entirely, as it happens."

That piqued his interest. His wide eyebrows rose slowly. "Indeed?"

"Yes. How about you buy me a drink and we can discuss things?" No way was she negotiating with him in that suite where the other two might overhear. In a public place, she'd be safe—most likely.

Vlad nodded. "By all means." He turned to Jane and Angela. "Wait in the suite. I won't be much longer."

They nodded, hugged Dixie a last time and walked back down the hallway. Vlad watched them, the way a parent might watch a child crossing the road. When the suite door shut behind them, and only then, he pressed the elevator button. "Are you beginning to understand their predicament?" he asked. "Two attractive, intelligent, young women, with the survival skills of three-year-olds."

The elevator arrived, he stood back to let Dixie enter. They were alone. "What do you think happened?" she asked.

He raised both hands palms up. "My conjecture is some vampire made them and then, for whatever reason, wiped out their memories. It's not hard to do."

No, she'd done the same but . . . "To take the entire memory isn't like taking a few fragments."

"But done the same way. It just takes longer and requires a considerable expense of power. Way beyond a fledgling."

That irked. "But not beyond a master vampire, like yourself."

He looked surprised. Heck, he looked outraged, but before he could respond, the elevator stopped and a couple got in. He fell silent. Fair enough. This was not a conversation for mortal ears. Vlad remained silent as they crossed the lobby and found a secluded table in the bar. They pretty much had it to themselves at this point in the afternoon. After a lengthy discussion with the bartender, Vlad got a bottle of vintage port and two glasses. Dismissing the server, Vlad slowly poured a glass and held it up, eying the ruby liquid against the light. He took a brief sip before pouring a second glass, which he handed her with a short bow. He raised his glass and hesitated.

She read it as a challenge. Was she really going to drink with him? "To Jane and Angela, and a resolution to their predicament." Predicament! Heck, she was hanging around Brits too much. She sipped. Vlad didn't drink cheap stuff. The liquid flowed over her tongue like velvet, warming her mouth before it eased down her throat.

"So. You think I stole their minds and memories?"

At least he had the decency to wait until she'd swallowed. Or had she just been lucky? "You said that. I didn't!"

He raise a very dark eyebrow. "No?"

"I asked if a master vampire could wipe their minds clean . . . that's all." Bristling might be a good word to describe his body language. Heck, she might as well go for broke. "Did you?"

"No." He almost whispered, but the insistence in the one syllable sent shivers down her spine. She'd pissed off Vlad the Impaler. He didn't need a stake with eyes like his. "Thank your gods you are a woman, Miss LePage. There was a time when I killed men for lesser insults."

What now? He was waiting for her to reply. Now was not the time to point out his comments were sexist, but she wasn't apologizing. He might be a fifteenth century despot but she wasn't one of his serfs. "Who did then?"

"If I knew that . . . they would be suffering as we speak."

She halfway agreed with him. She took another sip of port, letting the rich liquid slide down her throat. "Have you tried to find out?"

"Of course. He's either left Chicago or gone to ground." He sipped again and set his glass down silently. "I'll find him. One of these centuries. Meanwhile we have two ghouls to protect. That's partly why I brought them here. They will not fall into this monster's clutches again."

"I'm with you there, but is Ohio far enough away?"

"For now. Will you help them?"

"Of course. I think Jane could do Stella's old job and Angela seems willing to start with baby-sitting until we find something else. I don't know where they'll live but we'll work that out." She paused. "The biggest obstacle is their identities. They're nonpersons, they need birth certificates, Social Security numbers, high school diplomas . . ."

"That's where I'd hoped Kyd might help. He took care of Marlowe's green card, after all."

Okay, Tom's computer skills were incredible—felonious even—but if Vlad thought . . . Dixie smiled. "He might, but he's hardly likely to want to do favors for anyone who fingers his best friend." Vlad stared. "You did tell Gwyltha about the fiasco last Friday, didn't you?"

"You think I did that out of malice?"

"Let's say the suspicion crossed my mind." She took another drink, a long one, as she watched him over the rim of the glass.

He leaned back in his chair and gave her a look of extreme exasperation. "You are so easily convinced I'd do that?"

"Unconvince me."

He looked close to stalking out, but he stayed. Sure proof he needed her help. Fine. Let him earn it. "I came here to Columbus the day after Corvus left Chicago, bringing Angela and Jane with me. I intended to scout out the city and if it seemed suitable for them, approach you and Marlowe. After the generous apportion you received, I hoped you'd feel obligated."

"And if we didn't?"

A shadow of a smile flickerèd across his mouth. "I felt certain you would not refuse them."

He thought she was a soft touch, did he? "And?"

"I called Gwyltha daily, about Jane and Angela. Gwyltha had considerable misgivings about adopting these two but agreed that the alternative would mean their demise or victimization. When I read about the attack on those two thugs, I suspected immediately it might be a vampire attack. A conversation over beer with one of the reporters convinced me. I suspected it was my ghouls' creator stalking them and playing with a few mortals for sport, and mentioned as much to Gwyltha.

"She sent Toby out to investigate, fearing a psychotic vampire might pose a threat to your safety. He found there was no other vampire, only you and Marlowe and Corvus and his new fledgling. The truth unfortunately surfaced almost immediately."

It could be, but Vlad could just as easily be lying through his fangs. "I see."

"You doubt my word!"

"Not at all." She paused to drain her glass. As she set it back on the table, she looked him in the eye and smiled. "The deal is simple: I'll do everything I can for Jane and Angela, you find a way to get Justin off this hook."

"And if I can't?"

She stood up. "You can."

He rose as she did. "If I fail?"

"I can't imagine Vlad Tepes failing. You do have Gwyltha's ear." And a whole lot more of her, if gossip was true.

Vlad nodded. "I will do what I can."

Dixie held out her hand. "I'm counting on it, Vlad."

"As Jane and Angela are counting on you."

Damn the man! He was right! No way could she walk away from Jane and Angela. "See you, Vlad." She turned and strode out, wishing she had Stella's height to really walk out with dignity.

She'd just about had it up to her fangs with macho male vamps but she now knew a whole lot more than either Christopher or Justin had cared to share. Drat them! They knew all this and hadn't told her—or Stella, she'd be bound. A good, long talk with Stella was the next thing on her agenda and then . . .

"Dixie!" Christopher stepped in front of her as she marched across the lobby. "What the hell's going on?"

"I could ask you the same!"

"I'm not cozying up with Vlad Tepes and I've not been drinking his wine."

"For crying out loud!" Christopher had her by the arm. Dixie banked on him not wanting to make a scene in the lobby of the hotel. She yanked her arm away and marched on.

He waited until she'd gone a couple of blocks and stopped her again. With both hands this time. "You were drinking with him, Dixie. Why?" His eyes blazed fury. "You said you had errands downtown and you went to meet him!"

"And you followed me to check up! Or you just happened to be lollygagging around the lobby."

"I was not following you. I had business here and walked out of the elevator to see you tête-à-tête with Vlad and hanging on his words."

"Business with Toby?"

That stopped him a second or two. "What do you mean?"

"I've been employed on the same 'business.' I talked with Toby before Vlad, and a couple of ghouls in between." It wasn't often she rendered Christopher speechless. She wished she had time to enjoy it fully. "I wanted to know what the hell was going on, and since you and Justin were, shall we say . . . reluctant to share information, I went to the primary sources."

He looked relieved and exasperated all at once. "I didn't want you to worry."

She almost laughed but felt more like slugging him. "You failed miserably there. Because I was worried I had to track down Toby and Vlad."

"That was it." It wasn't a question. He believed her.

"Yeah! That was it. Old Vlad wasn't romancing me." She couldn't help the chuckle. "The man is pompous and patronizing."

"Hell, Dixie, when I saw you two together . . ."

She couldn't help it. She kissed him, right there in the middle of Front Street. "Let's worry about the real stuff. Justin is in deep doo-doo, and if he's in trouble so is Stella. You really think I'm going to sit by and let that happen?"

Christopher sighed. "The fact is, dear, he broke our laws. He has no defense."

"We'll find one. We need to talk."

He gave her the grin she loved. "Want to talk at the top of the Leveque Tower?"

"There's too many people around."

He shook his head. "They're all going home, it's getting dark and no one will see. We'll go through the car park, like respectable mortals, and get across from there. I guarantee you, no one will even look up."

He was right, as he always was on these things. A quick hop from the edge of the third level to the walkway and then hand over hand up the side, past the marble carvings and the towers to the top. It was dark by the time they got there, and a million lights lit up the panorama in all directions.

Christopher put his arm around her shoulders and pulled her close. "Not exactly the view from St. Paul's, but not bad at all."

It was beautiful, red taillights from thousands of cars, meandering along the interstates, house lights of countless homes and the reflection of streetlights that bordered the river. But she hadn't come to admire the view. "Christopher, please listen."

Bless him, he did. Barely saying a world, apart from the odd "damn" or "hell" until she got to the end.

"You believe Vlad?" he asked when she finally finished.

"You mean about Justin?" He nodded. "Not altogether, but it could be true. After all, he's the one who took Gwyltha from Justin. He shouldn't be the one bent out of shape and besides, if Justin's now in love with Stella, it leaves the field clear for Vlad. He should be glad to help out."

"Not entirely . . . When we established the last set of laws, Justin proposed we not be allowed to mate with vampires from other colonies. He didn't get it through. Didn't expect to. He only did it to rile the pair of them, and Vlad isn't likely to have forgotten."

Christopher was right there. "Yes, but he wants our help with the ghouls."

"Wants to dump two liabilities in our laps. You're a bit of a soft touch, my love."

"These are two intelligent women, Christopher. I met them, without Vlad. It's as if they have amnesia. They remember snatches and odd bits. Maybe one day they'll get their memories back."

"They might not."

"True. But either way they need help. Can you really refuse?"

"Hell, you know the answer to that."

She hugged him. "I knew you wouldn't let me down."

"It's Gwyltha you need to think about. I'm none too certain she'll accept the subtle differences between making and keeping ghouls."

"Maybe we can persuade her they're not as mindless as she thinks. But first we have to settle things for Justin."

"Love, he doesn't have a leg to stand on."

"He has two, plus Stella's—that's four. We'll find a way."

"Don't drag her into this, Dixie. Promise me."

"Christopher, she has a right to know. She loves him. His problems are hers."

"Then in that case, it's for him to share them with her. Not you." He held her face in his hands. "Promise me you'll wait for him to tell her."

"Okay, but I'm telling her about the ghouls. Heck, I have to if Angela is going to baby-sit. And between us, we're going to help them. They don't deserve to get shunted off just because of colony policies!"

She expected him to argue. He didn't. Just kissed her and said, "Don't defy Gwyltha too much, will you, love? I don't want to have to defend you in front of the council."

"But you would, wouldn't you?"

"For eternity, Dixie, with the last words in my heart."

She was darn well certain Stella felt the same way about Justin.

Chapter Thirteen

Her new job at the Vampire Emporium was working out better than Stella have ever imagined. Okay, this was just her first week, so perhaps she shouldn't hold her breath. She chuckled. That would never be a problem again. This job was a whole lot more interesting than tagging shirts for starch or no starch. She was saving baby-sitting money while Sam did his homework in the back room and Dixie seemed more than willing to shuffle working hours as needed, even in the spring when Sam played soccer. It was turning out to be a dream job and to top it off, seemed Dixie and Kit knew someone moving into town who was interested in the old job. That eased her guilt over not giving notice.

Stella reached for a carton to pack three books for shipping. Wrapped in bubble wrap, the books fit snugly. She'd just finished taping the box when the door opened.

"Justin!" It had only been two days, but it felt like weeks since she last saw him. "I've missed you."

In seconds he was behind the counter. "Stella!" he said as his arms locked around her. She lost herself in his kiss. He was strong and loving and as she pressed her body against his hard frame, she shut her eyes to lose herself in his male presence. His tongue caressed hers and his lips pressed hard. She wanted to engulf him and be engulfed. In her mind they were once again running at vampire speed across open fields, or looking down at the sleeping city from their perch on the rooftops.

Slowly he drew his mouth off hers. "We'd better watch out. I'd hate to shock the populace."

"Sam's in the office doing homework."

"Better not shock him either." Justin smiled. His mouth looked so luscious she wanted to kiss him back, long and hard, but he was right. "How's the new job?"

"Marvelous. I was afraid it wouldn't work with Sam coming in after school, but so far it has."

"Why shouldn't it? He's a good lad." She wouldn't argue with that. "Think he'll mind if I sweep you away tomorrow night? You need to feed again and . . ." He paused. "I need you."

Something caught deep inside her as his last words echoed in her mind and she looked up and into his dark eyes. "I love you, Justin." She couldn't quite believe she said it, but no words she'd ever spoken had felt so right.

He stared down at her, as if in shock or hurting. "What's wrong?" Was it her words? But he'd said he loved her days ago.

"Just someone walking over my grave." He grinned, squeezing her as he said, "Vampire humor, Stella." She wanted to believe him but . . .

"Hi, Dr. Corvus." They both turned. Sam stood in the doorway to the back room. "Think it's okay if I use the electric pencil sharpener, Mom?" He held up a pencil with a broken point.

Stella instinctively took a step away from Justin. A bit late, but . . . "I'm sure it's fine, honey, but you were right to ask."

"Okay." Sam smiled and looked from her to Justin.

"Hello, Sam, how's the homework?" Justin asked.

Sam shrugged. "Fine. I'm almost through." He paused. "You gonna kiss Mom again?"

"Sam . . . !"

"Would you mind if I did?" Justin asked.

Sam tilted his head to one side and considered the question. "Fine with me if you want to," he said. "I think she likes it a lot."

While Stella gasped and Justin stood openmouthed, Sam gave them both an encouraging smile and strolled back into the office, throwing a grin at them over his shoulder as he closed the door.

"Dear heaven, Justin! He must have been watching us!"

He brushed the hair back from her face. "He didn't seem scandalized."

Maybe not, but she was. Or was she? What could Sam have seen? His mother kissing the man she loved. "I just think . . ."

He stopped her with a finger to her lips. "Maybe we're both thinking too much." He dropped a soft kiss on her forehead. "Until tomorrow. We'll go somewhere Sam isn't because what I plan is not for his eyes."

Getting back to taping cartons seemed a major anticlimax after a promise like that but she got all six boxes packed and ready to ship and was straightening out the bookshelves when Dixie came in.

"Everything okay?"

Other than getting caught in passionate embrace by Sam . . . "Fine. I got the boxes ready to mail and the new tee-shirts came."

"I don't know how I did this before you, Stella. Honest, I don't. Thanks a bunch." She put an armful of envelopes on the counter. "Just been by the post office to pick up another shipment of junk. That'll keep me busy for a while."

"Want some help?"

Dixie shook her head. "No, I'm late arriving as it is. You get Sam home." She hesitated and then went on. "Seeing Justin tonight?"

Stella shook her head. "Tomorrow. He came by a little while ago." She probably had a silly grin on her face, but she didn't much care. "Just dropped by."

Now Dixie had the grin. "Just dropped by? You mean he didn't take off his coat and stay awhile?"

"He stayed long enough for Sam to tell him it was okay for him to kiss me again!"

Dixie roared with laughter. "Caught in flagrante delicto by Sam and then he gives his blessing! Oh Stella, he's wonderful!"

"Yes, but . . . Well, it's a bit awkward."

"Life's awkward, come to that." She wasn't about to argue with that. "Look, if you're out with Justin tomorrow, okay with you if I don't come over this evening until later?"

"Of course. I hadn't thought! All the time you spend with me . . . you're not with Kit."

Dixie shrugged. "Hasn't hurt. He's missed me." She gave a wicked grin. "I thought tonight I'd remind him exactly what he's been missing."

"Shouldn't you move back with him?"

Dixie shook her head. "Not yet." She paused. "We'll work it out. Right now you need to get Sam home."

After they left, Dixie leaned her elbows on the counter, rested her chin in her cupped hand and frowned at the jet jewelry under the glass counter. Stella was utterly oblivious to the impending disaster. Both she and Sam would be devastated, there were no two ways about it. Dixie's gut reaction was to tell Stella what hung over Justin—and all of them. She'd argued this point with Christopher all the way back from downtown and long after they got home.

Christopher insisted it was Justin's dilemma and he was

the one to tell Stella. Maybe he planned to, tomorrow night. Poor Stella! She was expecting a nice romantic evening. Dixie swore quietly. They had to find a way around this. Vampire ethics were well and good, but not when they confounded common sense.

Stella wasn't sure how she'd handle it when Sam got too old for stories and bedtime snuggles.

"I'm ready," Sam said, opening the book and balancing it on his knees. "Last night you stopped right here." He pointed to the top of the page. To the exact paragraph she'd stopped on because he'd been so tired he could barely keep his eyes open.

"Right, let's finish the chapter, shall we?"

It was only three pages and Stella expected negotiations to start, or even finish, another, but Sam seemed content for her to stop, and they went through their rituals of prayers and night lights. As Stella snuggled him close, he wriggled under the blankets and then went very still. "Mom," he said, "will you marry Dr. Corvus?"

What next? Would she? Did vampires even marry? She was pretty sure Kit and Dixie weren't and heaven help her, Sam was watching her, waiting for an answer. "What made you ask that?"

He shrugged. "Just wondered. He's around a lot and you seem to really like him."

"Yes, I do really like him, Sam."

"Will you marry him then?"

"Sam, he hasn't asked me to marry him."

"But if he did, would you?"

Was there no putting him off. "I might, Sam."

He reached up and put his hands round her neck and pulled her close. "I'm glad. He's a cool guy." He kissed her.

"He's okay. He promised he wouldn't go away and leave you pregnant."

Stella's heart would have stopped, if it had still been beating. "When exactly did he say this?"

"When we were talking. I told him I wasn't having him messing around and making you sad and he said he was going to look after us." That seemed to settle it for Sam.

It didn't for her. Justin was right. Sam was matchmaking. And as for asking Justin about her getting pregnant . . . What if he did? She needed to ask a few questions. She kissed Sam as he snuggled under the covers. Outside the night called, but she wouldn't budge until Sam slept. It didn't take long. Stella stayed by his bed and watched his soft breath brush the covers as his heart pumped his young blood though his body and made a list of questions to ask Dixie.

"I've got to talk to you or I'll burst," Dixie said as she walked in the front door.

"Maybe, but I have to ask something or I'll burst."

"Make it quick," Dixie said. "I don't think I can hold this in much longer."

"Okay, can I get pregnant?"

That surprised her. "Didn't Justin tell you that?"

"We never got round to talking about it. Can I?"

"Not now. Not ever again come to that. Were you getting worried he hadn't taken precautions?"

"It wasn't that. Sam brought it up; apparently he's been telling Justin not to play fast and loose with me and then I got to wondering . . ."

"Sam was asking him if his intentions were honorable, like a Victorian father?" Dixie couldn't hold back the grin.

"More like a getting above himself!"

"I think it's cute. You've got a great kid there."

She wouldn't argue with that and Dixie had answered her question. "What was your news?"

"It's not news exactly. More like . . . Oh hell! Christopher has already had his say and I can guess what Justin will add. I want you to listen while I spout off."

Stella listened while Dixie told about her afternoon's investigation. "What exactly are ghouls?"

"I'm none too certain. Seems they died as we did and are now immortal. Christopher said something about dying violently at a vampire's hand but since he also insisted, like Justin, they were mindless machines, I've beginning to think our men don't know as much as they think they do." She smiled. "Those two women were neither automatons or sycophants!"

"But they're in a mess."

"Yes, but nothing that isn't fixable. Think your old employer would take one on? They don't have our inconveniences with sunlight."

"I bet they would. Especially if I call and give them her name."

"That's what I hoped, and I thought Angela could solve our baby-sitting crunch. If you could pay her what you used to pay the sitter who kept Sam after school, she could fill in when we both need to be in the shop. With the holidays coming, we should get busier."

"They've got to live somewhere, too. I've got one spare room but it's not much . . . but if cold and heat don't bother them, we could fix up the attic."

"You sure?"

Stella shrugged. "Heck, why not? Christopher's going to want you back home soon. I'd sort of enjoy the company. As long as it doesn't end up too disruptive for Sam." She shook her head. "This is going to be some weekend, getting to know ghouls and going to a vampire reception."

"Trust me, the vampires you can handle. I was nervous as a newborn virgin when I heard we were being invaded by a bunch of vampires, but it was no big deal. Most of them are really nice. They just dropped in, literally, hung around an hour or so and then flew off. We were staying in a cottage in the middle of the North Yorkshire Moors. I doubt they will drop in, in quite the same way in the middle of a city. They're big on not being too conspicuous. They'll most likely come by cab."

"I still can't get over them all flying over here to meet me."

Dixie hesitated a second or two. "The colony is pretty close-knit. Support and that sort of thing."

"I'm used to Justin and Kit, but the thought of a room full of educated Brits is intimidating—to put it mildly."

"Don't be. Anyway, they're not all Brits. One of them is from South Carolina." She paused. "Long before my time, though. He was a slave and stowed away on a blockade runner and worked his passage to England."

"I should be used to it by now, but I haven't readjusted my sense of time. I used to think ten years was a long time, now I'm learning a hundred years is nothing."

"Sobering isn't it?"

Stella nodded. .

Kit kept the shop open another hour after Dixie left. He wasn't sure why, just that he wanted to linger a little longer in the surroundings that were so . . . her. What had he ever done before he met her? Better not go into that. He loved her, plain and simple. Loved her energy, her strength, and her . . . loveliness. And, he had to admit, her knack of ignoring the rules if they clashed with her idea of common sense.

Kit thought about her, and Justin, as he strode along Jackson towards City Park Avenue and home. Her suggestion that they all join Justin in exile perhaps wasn't as loony at it seemed at first. He bet Tom would join them. They did have the territory Justin negotiated. Dixie was on her native land. But Stella . . . Yes, there was a problem. She needed

her native land to reach full strength but was steadfastly refusing to uproot Sam. Even Justin had ceded defeat on that
point—at least for now. What would they do about Sam?
Caring for him was not a problem but it wouldn't take long
for an intelligent child to notice the rest of them had hair that
never grew, that they never ate, healed miraculously and
went out at odd hours of the night.

And how could they take care of him, if Gwyltha got
stroppy and claimed the territory for the colony? It was
enough to give even a vampire gray hairs. Maybe Justin did
have the right of it, to accept his exile, and leave Stella in
their care, but Kit had a sneaking suspicion Dixie was right.
She'd insisted in no uncertain terms that Stella would never
accept Justin's banishment as a fait accompli and just go on
with her life. Kit wasn't sure what Stella could do about it,
but he didn't doubt Dixie was spot on. That was why he'd all
but coerced her promise not to tell Stella what loomed. It
was Justin's place to handle that and he didn't envy the poor
bastard. If he lived another five hundred years, Kit would
never quite obliterate his pain at parting from Dixie. He'd
done it, yes, because he feared for her safety, given certain
lethal individuals, but it had all but ripped out his heart. He
knew what misery Justin was going through.

"Good evening!" Justin was lounging at the front door,
his foot propped on the curve of the limestone steps. "I
thought you'd never get here."

"The responsibilities of an entrepreneur . . ."

A loud snort of a laugh greeted that. "Pull the other leg,
it's got bells on! More likely been dawdling along, trying to
find a solution to old Justin's predicament."

"I'd be a lousy friend if I wasn't."

Justin stood up. "Did you find a solution?"

Kit shook his head. "Not yet."

Justin slapped him on the shoulder. "There isn't one,
mate," he said, in a fair imitation of the Air Raid Warden per-

sona he'd adopted during the Second World War. "Let's just
have a bit of fun while we're still standing."

"Got anything special in mind?"

"Let's start at the zoo. I'm taking Stella there tomorrow. I
want her to learn about feeding from animals."

They ran there, following the riverbank and intruding on
more than one expensively maintained garden before turning right and crossing the dam. It was pure exhibitionism on
Justin's part to leap the dam, but maybe he was practicing to
impress Stella. The poor chap didn't have much else left to
enjoy.

Kit wasn't quite sure why Justin fed as deeply as he did.
If he was feeding again tomorrow . . . why?

"I've got a bit of fun planned for after," he said as he patted an antelope on the haunch as it lay still half asleep.
"Better drink up yourself, I'm counting on your assistance."

"What exactly do you have in mind?" Kit asked as they
ran back, with the wind this time.

"Tell you later," Justin replied, and put on a spurt so Kit
had to push to keep up. Justin didn't let up until they reached
Berliner Park and then he agreed to stroll up towards
German Village. They ambled along Thurman, past the café
emptying of its late night patrons. Justin turned right and a
little while later, Justin said, "I'm doing something for Stella
and Sam."

"What?"

"Closing down that crack house."

Definitely a move to raise house prices. "Exactly how do
you plan to do that?"

Justin paused mid-stride and quirked an eyebrow.
"Scared I'm going berserk and deciding I might as well get
exiled for a massacre while I'm at it?"

No, he hadn't been. He knew Justin better than that. "Just
wondered how you plan to encourage them to shut up shop."

"Simple . . . it's winter. Mortals need heat and light; I intend to disrupt both of those. I won't hurt a soul but the house won't be much use by the time I finish with it." He paused. "You with me?"

Kit gave a short bow. "I'm honored to be invited."

That got him another slap on the back and an unexpected hug. Abel help him, how he'd miss Justin! "Let's start with a little bit of teasing and filch a few guns."

At a slow dog trot, Kit followed Justin through a maze of narrow streets until he paused in an alley, vaulted a fence, leapt up to the porch roof and climbed hand over hand to perch against a chimney. They had a grandstand view.

"You take these two lookouts," Justin said, "and I'll take care of the others. Just grab guns and run."

"What do we do with them? Run them down to the river?"

"Let's leave them right near the house. Toss a couple through windows, drop one on the lawn. If I'm right, we'll attract the law and it might be helpful if they found something interesting. We shouldn't destroy evidence, after all." As they watched, a car drove up and parked. "We need to do something to discourage that, too."

"One of us could always jump on it. That would get it moving."

"Be my guest."

Kit leaped down from the roof, jumped the fence and landed square on the car. The roof buckled, yells from inside got plenty of attention but Kit was off and racing for lookouts. With an armful of weapons and leaving one lookout flat on his face, Kit raced towards the house. Justin had been a bit slower, he'd paused long enough to let them get a glimpse of lips drawn over fangs before racing behind the house.

Shouts and yells echoed from the road. "Three, perhaps four minutes, that's all," Justin said. "Let's take care of the meters first, then dispose of the arsenal."

By marvelous convenience both meters were side by side.

It took both of them to destroy the gas meter. "Hell, this wasn't intended to budge!" Kit muttered as they tugged side by side.

Justin snickered. "All the more likely to get attention then. Here, I think it's giving. Pull on three. One . . . two . . ."

It gave on three, bending forward until pipes were twisted and severed and the sick, sweet smell of gas poured into the night.

"Think that's dangerous?" Kit asked.

"Bound to be, but it is out in the air, not in a house, and help will be here soon. If it isn't, I'll borrow your mobile and call."

"And get it traced to me? Not likely! Find a ruddy phone box."

"Stop belly-aching and let me get the other one."

Electric meters were less well attached, but ripping out wires was rather sparkly. Tossing the detached meter up in the air so it hit the transformer on the pole in the alley behind was more spectacular than expected. Every light in the street went out.

"Damn," Justin muttered, "didn't think that would happen."

As he spoke, another transformer down the alley blew with a rain of white sparks that lit up like a rocket. "Hell! Let's get rid of these damn guns." Easy enough. The noise of breaking glass barely got noticed among the shouts and the excitement of a third transformer popping.

That seemed to be it, at least as far as electrical sights and sounds went. "Think we'd better be on our way?" Kit asked as the sound of a distant siren heralded the approach of the law. "No point in hanging around."

"Right," Justin agreed. "Looks as if half the neighborhood is dark and—" He broke off. "Stella!" he yelled, just as Kit shouted, "Dixie!"

Together they ran down the alley, across the street and behind Stella's house. They leapt the fence together and raced through the dark garden. "Let's go round the front, don't want to scare them," Kit said.

"He's still fast asleep," Stella said as she came downstairs from checking on Sam, "missing all the excitement. Thank heaven! Is it out all over the street?"

"Looks like it," replied Dixie from the front porch, "and I . . ." The wail of one siren and another interrupted her. "Seems as though it's more than a power outage."

"Another advantage of being vampire, but Sam isn't. Let's keep what little heat we have."

"Fair enough." Dixie stepped back but then froze. "Christopher?" she said as he and Justin appeared around the corner of the house. Stella wanted to rush up and hug Justin but Dixie blocked the doorway. Hands on hips. "You did this, didn't you?"

Kit ignored her irate librarian voice. "You bet!" he said, grabbing her and kissing. "Justin wanted to do something for Stella."

"You disrupted power to the whole street for me?" Stella asked, torn between amazement and irritation.

"The wholesale power outage was an unplanned extra," Justin replied. "Mind if we come in?"

"Beats standing on the porch and letting out what heat we do have. Did you really do this?" Stella asked as she shut the door behind him.

His smile could melt polar ice caps. It had much the same effect on her. "Yes. I wanted to put that crack house out of business."

"And you did it by taking out the power?"

"And the gas supply. Didn't mean to disrupt the whole street."

"The whole street!" Stella let out a roar of laughter. "You

took out the neighborhood. I looked out when I was upstairs. There isn't a streetlight in sight." She looked up at Justin. "I wish you'd let me join in."

"It was too risky for a woman."

"It what?" She launched herself at him.

He caught her, grinning as he wrapped his arms around her. "You are so easy to get a rise out of."

"Who are you to talk about getting a rise!" She rubbed against him, lust taking over from anxiety. Sam was asleep and unafraid. Justin and Kit were safe. The blot on their neighborhood was out of action and . . . Justin lowered his mouth.

His lips tasted of man and power and the sharp touch of risk. She opened her mouth to take it all in, his power and his presence. His lips and tongue matched hers, touch for touch and stroke for stroke. His hand rested on her hip. She pressed herself against him as his hand closed on her breast.

She was wobbly and wet between the legs when he finally broke the kiss—but not his hold on her. "The others . . ." she began. "Kit and Dixie."

"Have gone home," Justin said. "I'm staying. Can't leave you here alone."

"No," Stella agreed. "You can't."

Chapter Fourteen

The house was pitch dark but that didn't make an iota of difference. Justin smiled, his mind wide open, not even trying to hide his desire. He needed her. Wanted her. Longed for her. Lusted for her. "So," she said, "you're staying?"

"Yes." He brushed his lips over her mouth as she opened to him with a sigh. His arms lifted her to him as the power of his kiss seeped through her body. She pressed against him, closing her eyes to better sense the hard muscle of his chest, the strength in his arms and the power of his erection pressing into her belly. He kissed slowly, as if sipping the desire from her lips.

He wrapped his arms around her and deepened their kiss. She tasted his need as he caressed her mouth with his tongue. He held her face in his hands and rained kisses over her cheeks and eyes. "You need me," he whispered, "I can smell it."

"And you don't need me?" she replied, rocking her hips into his erection. "You seem very glad to see me."

"That line's been used before!" he growled. She giggled as his hand slid under her sweatshirt and the tips of his fingers teased her breasts and unsnapped her bra. "That's better. Why you modern women wear such things, I'll never know. They only get in the way."

"Didn't stop you for long!"

"Nothing will stop me when I want you." Nothing stopped her sweatshirt and bra from hitting the floor either.

"What about when I want you?" Her hands slid up his chest and pulled open the buttons of his shirt. He eased his hold on her just enough to let her spread her hands over his chest.

"You want me?" he asked.

"Yes!"

"Good." Justin scooped her up in his arms. Ignoring her gasp, he took the stairs at a run. Held tight against his chest, she rubbed her face against the soft hair and inhaled his scent. Justin pushed open her bedroom door and all but tossed her on the bed. She was still bouncing when he plastered his body on hers and anchored her to the mattress. She was flat on her back as he showered her face and throat with kisses, his hands tugging at her jeans.

"Trying to get me naked?"

For reply, he fastened his mouth on hers. She all but saw comets as his lips heated hers and sent pleasure rippling down between her legs, right where he rocked his erection against her wet heat. When she moaned, he broke off the kiss and looked down at her with dark and steamy eyes. "You're too damn impatient. This is going to take all night."

The next kiss was slow and teasing and left her shaking. If she had breath to catch, she'd be gasping for air. He eased off her to kneel up and straddle her waist and look down as if he'd been starved for her all his life.

"Like what you see?"

" 'Like' doesn't begin to describe it." His fingers teased a line up her chest. She expected him to cup her breasts but instead he brushed his fingers over the tips of her nipples. She hadn't thought they'd harden more. She was wrong. She now had two aching points of flesh that needed more than a fingertip.

"Kiss them . . . please." She was begging as she arched her back, begging and ready to grovel, until he bent down and licked, first one nipple then the other. Pure pleasure rippled through her and then came in a wild rush as his mouth closed on her breast.

She heard a long, slow moan as if from a distance, and knew the woman she heard was herself. "Justin!"

"I'm not going anywhere." Maybe not, but his hands were everywhere. They stroked and teased and caressed, taking her deep into a wild mist of pleasure as her shoes hit the floor and her socks and jeans ended up gone. All she had on were her high-cut, cotton briefs. She half wished she wore a black lace thong, something seductive but . . . so what! It wouldn't have lasted any longer.

She was naked, her mind floating on desire and her body humming with need. "How come you're still dressed and I'm naked?"

"Good question. Could be because I like you naked."

"I like you naked, too." And she'd do something about it if he didn't still have her as good as pinned to the bed. She did reach out for his shirt, but he caught her hands in one of his. She could have broken his grasp but she waited, wondering about his next move.

He kissed her fingertips.

"Wait here, just like this, and I'll get naked for you."

"Just like this?" she asked as he shifted off the bed.

He looked her up and down from her face to her toes. He definitely liked what he saw. "Almost," he replied, moving her ankles so her legs were spread and placing her other foot flat on the bed so her leg was bent and her body open to his gaze. "That's better!" His hand cupped her raised knee. "Yes, I like that. Stay still and watch me."

Instead of the vampire speed he went for vampire tease. With exasperating slowness, Justin took off his shirt and hung it over the back of a chair. He sat on the same chair to untie his shoes and carefully placed them side by side before rolling up his socks and tucking them inside and never once taking his eyes off her.

Stella lay back and watched as he stepped out of his pants and folded them to keep the meticulous crease. He was down to underwear now. The minute he was out of them she moved, leaping towards him, but he'd anticipated her move and was faster. They met in mid-leap and his force and weight propelled her back to the mattress in a rattle of bed-springs.

"Trying to get a move on me?"

"I stayed still while you undressed. Now, I want to touch you."

"Soon," he promised. "I guarantee you won't mind the wait. Let me make love to you."

How could she refuse? His mouth skimmed her skin with light butterfly kisses that sensitized every inch. He took her hands in his and kissed and sucked each fingertip. He licked and tasted her nipples until she rocked with need, and then he rained kisses on her belly as his fingers brushed the curls between her legs. She was sighing and moaning, caught in a maelstrom of sensation, wishing time would stop still so that forever she'd feel his tongue teasing her skin and his fingers stroking the inside of her thighs.

The mattress shifted as he moved between her legs. She arched her hips, aching for his slow penetration, and felt his fingers opening her. She was wet and ready and needed him filling her, but instead he bent his head between her thighs and lapped. Every nerve ending responded to his soft caress. Her head sagged back. She knew nothing but the joy build-ing between her legs. Justin paused, then touched her nub with the tip of his tongue. He brushed her again and again, a little faster and harder, and her hips jerked as she climaxed in a wild rush of heat and satisfaction.

She was still shaking as he wrapped his arms around her. Wild ripples of pleasure still possessed her body and as for her mind . . . She wasn't sure it still worked, or if she'd ever need it again. She sagged into his arms, lost in his strength and maleness.

"Worth a little bit of patience, wasn't it?" Justin asked as he kissed her.

She tasted herself on his lips and smelled her arousal on his face. The raw sensuality of it pitched her desire higher. "Yes," she replied, "and now I'm repaying in kind." As she spoke, she moved fast and pinned him on his back.

He grinned up at her in the dark. "Full of yourself, eh, fledgling?"

"Soon I'll be full of you! But first I think you need to wait a bit."

If he minded her dominating him, he sure didn't show it. His nipples hardened as she kissed them and he gave a slow groan as she licked a slow line from his shoulder to his ear. She smiled as he shivered under her tongue . . . and this was just the beginning.

She settled back on her heels, perched astride him, his erection brushing her bottom. She slowly licked round his nipples as her fingers stroked up and down his arms, and across the muscle of his chest. She gave him a long, drawn-out kiss on his lips, opening his mouth with hers. When he started moaning, she broke off the kiss and sat back, looking down at him. She ran her hands over his chest and reached behind her to feel his hard-muscled thighs.

If all Roman soldiers had bodies like this, no wonder they'd conquered all the known world. But now it was her turn to conquer. She moved down the bed. She was flat on her stomach between his spread legs, admiring his impressive erection. She smiled and looked up to meet Justin's eyes. He was propped up, his elbows and forearms resting on the bed, and his eyes blazing with a wild need. Keeping eye contact, she licked her lips. Slowly.

"Stella!" It came out like a groan. "Have pity on a desperate man!" He moved his erection back and forth as if in salute.

"Soon." She slithered down the bed and kissed the inside of his ankle. Out of the corner of her eye, she saw his penis twitch and kissed the other ankle, just to see if it would happen again. It did.

Heady with the power to so arouse him, Stella kissed a slow trail up the inside of each leg up to his knees. He spread his legs wider. In anticipation? Hope? She wouldn't let him be disappointed, but she wasn't anywhere near ready yet. She licked a rather wobbly line from the side of his knee up the inside of his thigh, stopping just short of his balls and skipping over to send a matching trail down his other thigh.

"Playing games are you?"

"Yes," she replied, as her fingertips tunneled through the dark hair between his legs. "Ball games are a great American tradition." As she spoke she reached for his testicles. They were as soft as his penis was hard and filled her cupped hand. Awed by their fragility and vulnerability, she bent and kissed each one.

Justin let out a great groan.

His whole body tensed and before he had time to relax, Stella opened her lips and circled the hard, smooth head of his penis.

He let out a long, sweet moan of yearning.

Stella ran her tongue over the taut skin and gently caressed his rim with her lips. Heady with power, she slowly took him into her mouth. Her lips brushed the tight curls in his groin and his hard flesh filled her. She moved her mouth up and down, caressing him with her lips and tongue as his hands cupped the back of her head.

She closed her eyes. Nothing else in the world existed but her mouth, his penis, and their two bodies joined. She lost track of time. The world seemed to slow as she slowly moved her head up and down with the gentle rhythm of his fingers in her hair. She tasted his flesh, his power, and his manhood, and knew he was hers. Forever. That thought thrilled her to the core and drove her own need higher.

She eased her mouth away and smiled up at him from between his legs. Suddenly remembering she was no longer mortal but possessed vampire power, Stella moved at vampire speed and straddled him, before lowering herself on his penis.

Her eyes closed again as she let out a slow sigh of joy. She was filled, possessed and possessing, owning and owned. She opened her eyes. His were dark with desire and heated her body as he stared. His hands settled on the curve of her hips, and then he took over. She was on him, but he was in her and he lifted her and lowered her at his pace. His hips rocked in cadence. Each thrust took her a little higher. Each rock of his hips increased her sensations. Each touch of his hands sent her nerve endings singing. She was climbing the peak with him, racing towards pleasure, joined in their mutual lust and passion.

She sensed his coming climax. Knew his desires. Felt the same rush of need. Then she was him! His mind locked with hers. She tasted his longing, felt his passion. With a wild cry of joy, they came. Together they rushed and soared above the world of mortal pleasure, and together they found peace and delight as they drifted to sleep content in each other's arms.

Stella woke as Justin disentangled his legs from hers and prepared to get up. "You're leaving?" Her heart snagged at the thought.

"It's after seven," he said. "One of us had better get up and get breakfast for Sam."

"I will. I . . ."

He kissed her. "I'm going to shower first. When I finish, you get up and wake Sam. I think I can manage cereal. It seems easy enough on the TV."

Heaven help her! This was a man who'd never tasted cereal! Never had pizza, and had no idea what a corn dog was. That last wasn't a great loss, but . . .

"You look worried. What's the matter?"

She shook her head. "Nothing. Go shower and be quick. I want to be dressed before Sam wakes." Now she faced a whole new set of problems: How would Sam react to Justin at the breakfast table?

Pretty well it seemed. The novelty of eating breakfast by candlelight and wearing his coat at the same time probably had something to do with it.

"You been here all night?" Sam asked halfway through his cereal.

"Yes, I have," Justin replied. "The lights were out so I decided to stay with your mother."

Sam took another spoonful of Cheerios. "You think maybe school is out?"

"Good try," Stella said, "but it's open. I called to be sure. The power is on over there. It will be a whole lot more comfortable than here."

"Yeah, I suppose so." He didn't sound too convinced. "What are you going to do? It's freezing in here."

As if the cold would ever bother her—but she couldn't tell him that. "I expect it'll be on in a couple of hours and if it isn't, I'll go into the shop early."

That seemed to satisfy Sam. He finished his cereal and slowly chewed on his bread and jelly. "You going to be here tonight? Or Dixie?"

"I'll be here a while and then I'm going out."

"With Just . . . I mean Dr. Corvus?"

"Yes."

Sam chewed slowly, his eyes going from Stella to Justin and back. "You two got a thing going?"

Where did he pick up these things? And what to say? "No" was a lie but she just couldn't say "yes."

"Do you mind the time I spend with your mother?" Justin asked.

Sam thought a minute. "Nah! It's okay with me. She smiles a lot now you're around. Just don't keep her out too late." He chewed the last mouthful of bread and carried his plates to the sink.

"Go fetch your book bag," Stella told him, "and we'll check you have all your homework and go over your spelling words."

He came back minutes later, his bookbag in one hand, and her bra in the other. "Mom," he said, holding her bra at arm's length, "I found this by my book bag."

Dear Lord in heaven! She was sure she had to be purple. She grabbed the bra and stuffed it in her jeans pocket. "I must have dropped it in the dark. Now let's have a last look at those words."

Having a child in the house changed all the rules. Justin watched Stella help Sam practice his spelling. Hell! He should have checked the hall, not left evidence all over the place. Next time—there wouldn't be a next time. Tonight he'd have to tell Stella he was leaving. Forever. Saturday his life in the colony would be over. Just when he'd found his lifemate.

"You look mad," Sam broke off in the middle of spelling "pilgrim." "What's wrong?"

"Just thinking about something that made me sad."

"Don't worry, it may never happen. That's what my mom always says." If only he could share Stella's optimism.

"Come on, Sam. Last two." Stella got Sam's attention back on his words. "Now pack up and I'll take you to the bus."

"How about let Dr. Corvus?" Sam asked.

"I'd be delighted. Is that all right with you?" Justin asked Stella.

"Fine with me."

"There is something going on, isn't there?" Sam asked before they were halfway to the front gate. "With you and my mom." He gave Justin a stern look. "You took her bra off in the front hall. You had to have. She never drops clothes on the floor. She doesn't let me!"

He had twenty meters to come up with an honest, plausible answer. He wouldn't lie, but he sure as hell couldn't tell him the truth. Or could he? "Sam," he began, "I stayed with your mother last night because she was worried about the power outage." As if even a child would believe that!

His skepticism was well-founded. "Yeah, right! My mom's never been afraid of the dark!"

"There were things happening in the neighborhood." Things he and Kit had instigated. "Lots of police and trouble at that house down the street."

"Oh, there!" Sam nodded. "Sorta makes sense now. There's mean people there." The child stopped and looked at Justin. "You are going to do right by my mom, aren't you?"

"Yes, Sam. I promise I will always do the best I can for her . . . and you."

"Good. I like you. I don't want you to be the sort of loser who walks out on their friends."

Sam's words slashed into Justin's already shredded conscience. He couldn't promise not to leave them. He couldn't promise not to hurt Stella. And he darn well couldn't explain to a nine-year-old boy, the intricacies of the vampire code. "You are very fine son," Justin told Sam. "Your mother must be so proud of you."

"Yeah, she is," Sam agreed, pausing as they approached the corner and the knot of children waiting for the bus.

"Goodbye, Sam." Justin couldn't believe the rush of emotion clogging his throat. After tonight, he'd never see this child again. After tonight he'd be the sort of loser who walked out on his friends.

As if catching something in Justin's voice, Sam stopped and turned. "I do like you," he said and gave Justin a bear hug.

Justin hugged him back, feeling the small fragile body in his arms. "Take care of yourself, Sam . . . and your mother," he said as his heart twisted with emotion.

Sam gave him a wave and skipped off to join his pals.

Justin waved back and dragged his feet along the road towards the house.

It was even worse when Stella greeted him like a conquering hero. "You're something wonderful," she said as he walked in the door. She gave him a wicked grin. "I'm going to feel great all day. I should be worn out, but I feel the reverse."

He should tell her sex energized a vampire, but he wouldn't. He was selfish enough to hope she never found another man, mortal or immortal, to share what they shared. "I'll see you tonight."

"You bet!" She wrapped her arms around his neck and kissed him. Hell, no! She kissed him and took his mind and body into overload. He was ready to take her then and there on the hall floor. Maybe they'd make it to the sofa. He eased off her lips.

"I have to go." If he didn't leave, he'd blurt out the whole truth. "Tonight, Stella." He dropped a soft kiss on her hair. "Tonight."

"I'll be ready." Not for what he had to tell her.

He almost ran down the street, uncaring who might notice the wind or the rush of air, but he didn't. He had one more thing to check before totally indulging in self-pity.

Halfway down the street, a pair of workmen were aloft in a cherry-picker, working on a burnt-out transformer. Two more crews were busy around the now-deserted house.

"So that was the problem last night," Justin said to the closest workman. "I wondered what all the to-do was about."

The man shrugged. "Some crazy on drugs ripped the meters out. We'll get the power back to the street in an hour or so but . . ." He shook his head. "I've never seen such a mess. Looks like the Incredible Hulk was here. They had to be on some new-type of speed or something."

A lone police car parked on the corner seemed to be doing nothing more than keeping an eye on the proceedings—or watching out for someone returning to the scene of the crime. Either way, the last thing they were alert for was a couple vampires. That thought cheered Justin up for a good ten seconds.

His feet got him to the park. He had to be a masochist to want to walk these paths, but walk them he did. In front of the school, a row of yellow buses disgorged chatting and smiling children. How he'd miss Sam. It had been centuries since he'd really known a child; his mind drifted back to his younger half-brother. He couldn't even recall Lucius's face. Would he one day forget Sam's earnest eyes and tilted chin when he'd demanded to know if there was "something going on"?

The yellow police tape had finally gone from the area near the *Umbrella Girl*. Only tire tracks showed where last week—was it only a week? How could life move so fast? From a quiet dessert, to a hopeful stroll, and gunshots that changed everything. If only he'd just grabbed her and run, leaving those two hobbledehoys stunned and starting . . . but no, he'd let the purple rage possess him.

Strange, but the thought of transforming Stella never entered his grief-stricken mind, until Kit insisted. How right he'd been. Stella would make a fine addition to the colony but he'd not be there to see it. Justin walked across the grass, kicking stray piles of dead leaves and wishing he could just turn back the clock, relive last Friday. He let out a harsh laugh. As if he hadn't learned by now, that was one thing even a vampire couldn't do.

Pain burned in his chest at the prospect of leaving Stella. How blithely he'd counseled Kit about parting from Dixie. Now he was paying the price for his own trite advice! But what earthly choice did he have? He'd attacked and injured two mortals in blatant contravention of the laws he'd helped promulgate. He had no defense and no recourse, but exile from the colony was bearable compared to the loss of Stella.

And before he left her, he'd hurt her. He didn't delude himself that a few harsh words would make her stop loving him. She was too constant, too loyal for that. He'd hurt her and she'd soldier on, for Sam. At least she had one man who'd stay with her. He didn't dare tell Stella the truth. He'd have to tell her goodbye and walk, dragging his heart and soul with him. He'd learned enough about these women from Dixie to know what stand Stella would take if she knew the truth. She'd insist on staying right beside him and following him into exile and she'd never survive. It was going to be hard enough for him without the support of the colony but for a fledgling like Stella, it was impossible.

No, he had to leave Stella behind. Kit and Dixie would stand by her, teach her what he'd not had time to. Tonight, he'd take her out to the zoo and explain how to feed from animals. He'd give her a taste of flying and then tell her goodbye. Abel give him strength!

Tomorrow she'd be gone all day visiting her mother, and by the time she and Dixie returned, he'd be history.

* * *

The moment the door closed behind Justin, Stella punched Dixie's number in the phone. She had intended to do the laundry this morning but that was now impossible so they might as well put their afternoon plans into operation early.

"Hi, power still out?" Dixie said.

"Yeah, and all over the street. I was going to do wash this morning but since I can't, I thought either I'd go into the shop early or perhaps we could go meet those two . . . ghouls." She had to work hard to get the word out, and she was considering having one baby-sit Sam!

"Sure . . . Give me an hour or so and I'll pick you up."

Christopher reached out as Dixie swung her legs off the side of the bed. "What are you two concocting?"

"Stella wants to meet Angela and see if she'll make a suitable baby-sitter. She needs to meet Jane, too, if they're going to stay in her house."

He sat up and looked at his lifemate. "Are you certain this is a good idea?"

"Getting up or taking Stella to meet the ghouls?"

"I can think of something better than getting out of bed for a couple of ghouls . . ." She turned back to him and kissed him. He longed to pull her back and bury himself in her warm woman's scent, but he knew Dixie when she was on a mission.

"I'm tempted, Christopher, but we do need to sort this out."

"This early?" It hadn't been light more than an hour or so. "They'll still be gnawing on pigs' thigh bones . . . or whatever it is they eat for breakfast."

"Stella's stuck in a house without light or heat, because of your and Justin's little prank last night. So we might as well get going."

He reached for her hand. "We could!" He watched the turmoil in her eyes: the tug between her own physical need of him and her sense of justice—for two ghouls! "How about later?"

"I promised Stella I'd baby-sit tonight."

"I thought she was hiring a ghoul."

"She is, but she may not be ready to leave Sam with one yet."

"I'm not sure I'd ever leave a defenseless child in the care of a ghoul."

"Not much difference between a ghoul or a vampire, in most people's minds."

Would he ever get it through to her? Dixie was so darn stubborn. All right, her stubbornness had saved him from expiration but this was different. "We are sentient."

"They're not exactly brainless, you know. They're more like amnesiacs. Their minds are wiped clean but not obliterated."

"We have ethics."

Bad choice. She snorted with disgust. "Right, and look where your precious ethics got Justin. He's about to be pilloried by your vampire ethics."

Reminding her they were her ethics, too, wouldn't be a good move. "Dixie, if there was anything I could do, I would. He helped frame those laws. They're what we've lived and survived by all these centuries."

"Maybe that's the problem. It's time to modernize a bit. This is the twenty-first century, not the sixteenth."

"They were old when I was transformed. We can't permit killing and maiming. We'd end up as travesties: Hollywood-type vampires, characters in cheap horror stories."

For once she didn't argue. "Is there nothing anyone can do?"

He was tempted to say "no" outright, but he couldn't lie to her. "Tom and I, and even Toby, have discussed the possibility of standing with him." Her eyebrows creased as they always did when she was confused. "We'd take his part and in doing so, accept the same sentence."

That, she understood, and it pleased her! "You mean we'd stick together with him. That's marvelous!"

It hurt to have to burst her bubble. "We could." He emphasized the "we." "Maybe." She looked set to argue her way to reason and back. "We're old enough we might manage to survive. You wouldn't be able to and Stella wouldn't have any earthly idea."

She straightened her shoulders and glared. "I don't need the colony to run my store!"

"True . . . but what happens in twenty years when people start noticing you still look thirty? We need the network to reestablish ourselves. What happens when Stella needs more native earth and we don't have access to John's supply channels? I could manage without but I'd be weakened. She'd perish. How about if another nasty group sets up shop near us?" That wasn't fair, she went pale at the memory, but he had to make his point. "And where could we live? This is colony territory."

"That Justin negotiated."

"And who would back that claim? With Gwyltha's recognition gone, we'd be vulnerable to every rogue vampire on the continent." He paused. "The sort of vampire that made and abandoned those ghouls." Her face showed he'd shot home.

"So there's nothing we can do?"

"Not right away. I've promised Justin I'll take care of Stella. Being fledgling alone is hard enough, but with a child as well . . . I'm counting on you to help."

"You know I will."

"You won't help if you go off on a wild crusade to rewrite our code."

She was silent a good minute. He was tempted to read her thoughts, but if she were scheming, she'd block him anyway. "Okay, I won't go on a crusade to save Justin. I'll settle for a crusade to take care of Stella."

"That's what Justin wants. He's hoping the whole tribunal will be over and done before you get back from Marysville."

"He'll be gone?"

"He won't have much choice. This way Stella can be welcomed into the colony without prejudice."

Her brow creased again. "I see." He doubted she did. "He is planning on sharing this with Stella, I hope."

"Of course he'll explain things."

She frowned deeper. "Mmmm."

"Now, don't you go telling her. I know what you women do when you get together. Let Justin do this his own way."

He'd shoved his elbow in the inkpot there. Dixie got right out of bed and turned to him, arms folded over her rather luscious breasts. "Let me tell you one thing, Christopher Marlowe, you have no idea what we women do when we get together." She gave a most unladylike, thoroughly Dixie snort, and marched out of the room. The sight of her firm, round bottom and smooth thighs striding down the landing almost had him running after her but he knew when Dixie needed time to stew.

Chapter Fifteen

"I'm dropping you right at the door, Stella. Wait in the lobby. I'll be back as soon as I've parked."

"Okay." She was not wimping out. It was cloudy and overcast, a typical Columbus day. No sun to worry about, but still she did. She hadn't been out on the street in daylight since Monday and was still nervous about hitting the sidewalk again.

Dixie pulled up right opposite the doors. This was going to be easy. Except Stella was sure blue jeans were nowhere near smart enough for a hotel like this. Too bad and too late. She opened the car door, stepped out, and didn't kiss the sidewalk. The doorman held open the door and in seconds Stella was standing in the marble-floored lobby, staring around and trying to remember not to gape. Other people came to places like this, but she was here to meet two ghouls and find a baby-sitter. The clerk at the desk was looking her way, so she straightened her shoulders. She was vampire, let mortals stare. Including the old man looking her way and who was now standing and coming towards her.

"If I may presume, it is Ms. Schwartz, is it not?" Stella

agreed it was. "Forgive me. I should re-introduce myself. I use the traveling name of Roman, but you may have heard of me by another name. I am Vlad Tepes." He was, was he? He held out a manicured hand. "Otherwise known as Dracula."

Stella knew she had to be showing him her naked tonsils. She did manage to shake hands, but other than a strangled "Hi," her voice had quit on her. Dracula! Shaking hands in the lobby of the Southern Hotel.

"Oh, Vlad, hi!" Dixie said as she swept in through the door. "Didn't expect to see you here."

"Good morning, dear lady," he said with a slight bow. "How could I not be here? You have the future of my protégés in your hands." He gave Stella a brief smile. "Are you ready to meet them?"

"That's why we came downtown." It was good to get her voice back. On the other hand, getting into an elevator with Dracula—if only she could tell Sam.

"We're not making any promises, you know," Dixie said. "There's all the problem of Social Security numbers and so forth."

"I still hope to intrude on Tom Kyd's goodwill for that. He said . . ."

"You spoke to him?" Dixie asked.

Vlad shook his head. "We emailed. He'll be here for to-morrow."

He must mean the vampire party. Stella had another set of misgivings about that. Tomorrow was going to be one busy day. Visiting Mom always left her drained, and now she'd have to come back and smile at a bunch of vamps.

"How did you get them on the airplane without IDs?" Dixie asked.

Vlad gave a shrug as he raised his palms. "I didn't even try. I hired a car and drove. And Dixie, forgive any implied criticism of your native land, but the countryside is hardly picturesque."

Dixie chuckled. "You've seen the wrong part, Vlad. Next time you come, try the South."

"Alas, it is some other colony's territory, but the Northwest is beautiful and for what you are doing, you and yours will always be welcome there."

"We haven't done anything yet, Vlad," Dixie pointed out.

"You've given them hope," he replied. "When was that ever nothing?"

Stella had to hold back a snort. Talk about master of the guilt trip! So, if they didn't help they were destroying hope. "We can help find them jobs, only they can keep them."

Vlad nodded in acknowledgement of her point. "They will not disappoint you."

He hadn't lied.

Stella sat in a hotel suite like ones she'd seen on TV and looked across at Jane and Angela. "I don't get it," she said. "You're college educated. Anyone could see that. Why do you want jobs as store clerks and baby-sitters?"

Angela gave a twisted smile. "Until we remember what we know, how can we do much else? What can we put on resumés? 'Job skills: Temporarily forgotten. Previous experience: Can't remember. Edu . . .'" She broke off, mouth open. "I remember about resumés!" She took a breath and shook her head as if to clear it. "This keeps happening."

"To me too," Jane added. "Maybe one of these days I'll remember who I am."

"Yeah, in about a hundred years," Angela said.

The sadness behind her words, cut through Stella. "Not that long. The more you see, the more you both seem to remember."

"You really want someone who doesn't know their own name to keep your kid?" Angela asked.

Good question. Did she? "I think we need to see how you do and see if we all feel comfortable about it. Tell you what. Why don't you come over this afternoon when Sam's home from school. Meet him and see how you get on together. Then tomorrow, Dixie and I are going out of town for the day. My next-door neighbor is keeping Sam; I'll talk to her about you spending a couple of hours with her and Sam. It might be easier for you if another adult is there." And Mrs. Zeibel could be counted on to tell anything that wasn't up to her exacting standards.

"Not sure what we can do about you, Jane, without ID of some sort. That may take a little while." Dixie stretched her legs in front of her and frowned at her feet as if thinking. "But you could surely go and talk to them the first of next week, couldn't she?" Dixie looked at Stella.

"Why not? Offer to bring your ID in later. Tell them it's packed and hope this friend of Dixie's can fix you up."

Jane gave them both a wide smile. "It seems too good to be true. We're out of that bar and have a chance of a job, but I'm scared I'll mess up because I can't remember something all the world knows."

"Don't borrow trouble," Stella said. "If this doesn't work out, we'll find another. There's no shortage of jobs here."

"You make it sound so easy," Jane said.

"I don't see why it should be hard. You're smart. All you have to do is fill out a tag, mark for starch or no starch on the shirts and put a sticker on the stains for the dry cleaning. It's not exactly brain surgery." More likely she'd die of boredom—if she wasn't immortal. Immortal boredom sounded even worse.

"Okay, we've got you jobs. We hope. We'll have to talk to Tom about ID. For the time being, we can put you up either in my house or Stella's. I've got a small apartment over my garage. Stella has a spare room. We can work out the logistics later." Dixie paused. "Vlad's going to be here through the weekend, right?"

Angela nodded. "Yes, and he said we could stay on here as long as needed." Stella almost choked. She couldn't imagine even sleeping in a place like this, much less be able to just stay on as long as she needed.

"We'll sort it out later," Dixie said. "What else do you need?"

"We need clothes," Jane said. "This is all we have. We have to sit around in the hotel bathrobes when we send them out to be washed."

"Ah!" Vlad spoke for the first time since they'd sat down, "Ms. LePage and Ms. Schwartz, could I presume on your goodwill further to ask you to outfit my two protégés?"

"I guess so," Dixie said. "They'll need stuff but . . ." She gave him a very hard look.

What was that about? "I would be indebted," Vlad said carefully.

"I was thinking the same thing," Dixie replied. "Okay, Vlad. We'll take them shopping but you'd better bankroll the trip."

"Of course." He handed a credit card to Dixie. "Get them whatever they need."

Jane stepped forward, staring at the plastic rectangle. "Let me see." She frowned at it, turning it over and biting her lip as she scrutinized. "I had one of these." She looked at Vlad and Dixie. "I was worried about it, as I'd charged it up to the max . . ." She turned to Stella. "Whatever that means."

"It means you had a job and credit and owed money," Dixie replied. "It's a start."

"You can figure out who I am from that?"

"Not by that alone. There must be millions of women with cards charged up to the max but if you keep remembering we'll piece it together."

"Like a patchwork quilt," Jane added and grinned. "Another thing I remember—patchwork!"

"It gets better every day," Dixie said. "Let's see if you remember how to shop."

They left by the side entrance and crossed to City Center,

Stella praying the sun wouldn't come out halfway across the road. It didn't. Once inside, Jane and Angela remembered how to shop. Stella had to squelch more than one flash of jealousy as they went from store to store, going through racks of clothes, trying on, and buying everything from lacy bras and thongs to new coats. Stella lost count of the dresses, sweaters and slacks they bought. She knew they had nothing but the things they stood up in, but to buy whole wardrobes on someone else's credit! Perhaps it was a loan and they were paying it back. Hah! At seven dollars an hour it would take them years—but of course, they had eternity.

"Why don't you get something, Stella?" Jane asked.

"Maybe later. I didn't come out to shop." And she had to pay her own bills.

"You know, there are some good buys on the sale rack," Dixie said. "A new outfit for tonight wouldn't hurt."

It would at the end of the month and with Christmas coming . . . But the markdowns were great and Stella finally let herself be persuaded to buy a pair of black pants and a matching top in a wonderfully soft knit.

They were making their way back through the mall when a wheelchair came towards them. Stella glanced at the occupant and had to use all her self-control not to stare. It was Warty Watson, still recognizable under the bandages and casts. He was doing more than staring, his eyes looked ready to pop out of the sockets and his mouth gaped as he let out a strangled, "Ms. Schwartz!"

The others had wandered into the Gap. She was alone and face-to-face with the boy who'd seen her die. "Why, hello, Walter," Stella responded, remembering just in time not to use the time-honored nickname the kids used.

"You're dead! You're dead! I saw you die!" It came out like a scared mewl as Warty shook his head and tears gathered in his eyes.

"Hush! Walt!" his mother said patting his shoulder. "You

can see she isn't dead. Look at her. Now would she be standing here if Johnny really shot her?"

She would and she was, but that was more than Warty and
his family needed to know. A bit of damage control was
needed here. Stella smiled at Warty, squatting down so they
were eye to eye. "Look at me, Walter. Do I look dead?"

He shook his head. "But I saw! Johnny shot you. In the
park! By that fountain thing."

"Walter, I'm here and I'm talking to you. You had a really
nasty accident and got confused."

"That's what I've been telling him," Walter's mother said,
patting his shoulder again. "Am I glad we ran into you. He's
been on and on about you getting killed. Wouldn't believe us
when we said you weren't. Even when the police said there
was no one dead, he still insisted."

"I thought . . ." Walter began and seemed to give up on
thinking, his eyes still glued on Stella.

"Don't worry about me anymore, I'm fine."

"Your hands are cold."

Heck, she'd forgotten that. Stella pulled her hands from
Warty's and tucked them in her pockets. "They get cold in
the wintertime. I am glad to see you're out and about."

"He came home yesterday. He wasn't as badly hurt as
they feared at first."

"That's good news."

"I ain't gonna believe another thing Johnny tells me!"
Warty announced to the world in general.

"About time, too!" his mother replied with a grim smile.
"He's nothing but trouble and you know it!"

"But I swear I saw the devil. All red eyes and fangs."

"Maybe it was the Lord giving you warning. Just like the
minister said."

Warty nodded. "Yeah." Silent for a minute, then looked
up at Stella. "Ms. Schwartz, I sure am sorry about throwing
things at your garage."

"No problem, Warty—sorry, Walter."

And it wasn't a problem . . . Not now.

Stella dropped her clothes on the floor, slipped her feet into her earth-lined rubber scuffs, and stepped into the shower. They had power back on and with it, hot water. Sam was busy with homework and at last she had a minute to herself. Some afternoon! Some day, come to that! She might as well say some life! She had to get back into routine soon. If Angela worked out as a baby-sitter, and this afternoon she and Sam had hit it off, then working regular hours for Dixie shouldn't be any problem. She needed a settled life, not one that resembled the *Twilight Zone*! But how settled could life be for a vampire who hired a ghoul as a baby-sitter?

Stella gave up, turned on the warm water full blast and reached for the soap. She lathered up her breasts, her nerve endings still sensitized from last night's lovemaking and the anticipation of more. She'd once been so leery of Justin, mistrusting him and his intentions and now, at long last, she'd found a fine, honorable man, and a lover with skills way beyond her wildest fantasies. A good man, who was fifteen hundred years old! Experience helped.

Stella reached for her razor from habit before she remembered there was no need. Her legs were as smooth as days earlier when she'd last shaved, vampire life developed new benefits by the day. She rinsed off and slathered her body with the flower-scented lotion that had been another indulgence this morning. After all, she'd be saving a small fortune in trips to the beauty parlor. She half-wished she'd indulged in some of the lacy underwear Angela and Jane had bought by the handful, but she settled for her practical white cotton and pulled on her new pants and sweater. The soft knit caressed her skin as she rubbed her hands down her arms and legs, wishing she could see herself in the mirror. Once was enough. She'd made that mistake earlier in the week when cleaning her teeth. She'd all but choked on mint-flavored gel at seeing her life's mistakes reflected back at her. She'd have yanked out every mirror in the house, but Sam would notice and ask. The full-length one on the door, she'd covered with a towel and the one over the sink, she avoided.

"Hey, Mom, that's beautiful!" Sam looked up from his paper and crayons.

She didn't need a mirror when she had Sam. "You like it?"

"Yeah!" He gave her a sideways look. "You're going out on a lot of dates these days."

No pointing denying it. "Yes. You're okay staying with Dixie, aren't you?"

"Yup." He gave Dixie, sitting at the opposite end of the table, a big smile. "We do fine." And bent back to his coloring. "Is Dr. Corvus staying over tonight?"

"That's something he and I will decide." But, please, she hoped so.

Sam carefully selected a green crayon. "I hope he does. You look pretty in the morning when he's here."

Stella all but choked. She didn't dare look Dixie's way or she'd lose it. Judging by the strangled cough from the end of the table, Dixie was having the same problem.

By God's good grace, the door rang at that instant, and Stella made a fast exit.

Walking in the night with Justin was an incredible pleasure. It wasn't just his company and the touch of his hand in hers and the promise of later. The night itself was different. Or was her awareness heightened?

They'd parked in a dark corner of the zoo parking lot, in less than three minutes they were over a high cyclone fence and slipping through the shadow towards the animal enclosures. In the dark of night with the wind rustling the half-bare trees, Stella became aware of the life around her: the heartbeats of a hundred different animals, the call of a night owl in the trees and the distant hum of a car engine. Justin squeezed her hand and led her through the ankle-deep grass. He showed her how to soothe a wild animal so it lay still as she fed. Having a lion lie docile under her hand gave her the same thrill of power and strength she'd felt climbing on rooftops and racing across country. What else could she do? What other wonders and powers would Justin share with her?

Having both fed, they lingered under the trees. Justin talked about his clinic in Yorkshire and the beauty of the countryside around. She felt the pull of what was, after all, her native soil. Should she go with Justin? Surely for a few years Sam would be fine in England. Kids went to school there too, didn't they? Perhaps in a few months, after school was out, they could go visit and if Sam seemed happy . . . She had no doubt she would be. A life with Justin was all or more than she could ever want.

She'd made a promise to Mom, yes, but surely if she found a tenant for the house . . . Perhaps let Angela and Jane stay and look after it. Maybe she'd been too hasty refusing to go with Justin. Tomorrow she'd sort it out with Mom.

"You're very quiet."

Stella smiled at Justin, her eyes feasting on the sight of his dark hair, the eyes that glinted in the night and his mouth curved in the beginning of a smile. If ever there was a mouth made for kissing . . .

She stepped close to him and put her arms round his neck. He looked down, a surprised look in his eyes, but he didn't object in the least. She chuckled as her lips came up and his came down. They met in a sweet, hard kiss that sent Stella's mind off in a wild spiral of lust, and to judge by the body pressed into hers, did the same of him. She heard a little sigh, as if from a long way away, her mouth opened to his, their tongues met and she left the ground. She was airborne, with the wind rushing through her short hair, but no breeze in creation could cool the heat that flared between them.

They soared several yards higher and then descended with a rush, Justin landing first and absorbing the jolt before he set her feet back on the ground.

"That was flying!" They couldn't have, it was impossible, but they had flown as sure as blood was sweet.

"Yes, it was," he agreed.

"Can I do that?"

"Not on your own, not yet. Give yourself ten years or so. Feed well and regularly, build up your powers and . . ."

"Will you know when I'm ready to fly?"

He stilled for several seconds, looking down at her as if imprinting her face in his mind. "Oh, I'll know, my love. You're my blood, my creation. By Abel, I'll always know."

"Why do you and Kit always say 'By Abel'?"

"By our tradition, Abel was the first human to defy death and return to life."

"Vampires, revenants have been around that long?"

"We're as old as the hills, Stella."

This time he took her aloft before he kissed her. His hands were tight around her waist and his lips sweet and forceful against her ready, open mouth. This was more than she'd ever dreamed, ever imagined, ever . . . She gave up on thinking and lost herself in his lips and the soft passionate caress of his tongue.

Then they came down to Earth.

"I need to take you home," Justin said.

She wouldn't argue. Home and bed. Especially bed . . . She smiled up at him. "Sounds good to me."

Justin barely said a word on the drive back. Not that it bothered Stella. She too busy thinking about the night ahead and thanking Providence and the line workers that power had come back on in enough time to wash her sheets. She hadn't rested much during the day but between an abundant feeding, the exhilaration of Justin's kisses and flying in his arms—literally, she felt as able to do without sleep as she now lived without mortal food.

Even when he pulled the car up in front of her gate, she never suspected a thing. He pulled her in his arms and kissed her tenderly and deeply. "I love you," he said as he lifted his lips from hers. "If ever there was a time to be thankful Gwyltha transformed me after that arrow hit my throat, it was when I met you." He brushed back her hair and kissed her forehead.

He looked more like a man condemned than a lover, as he reached into the glove compartment and handed her a black leather box. She snapped open the lid and stared into the velvet lining. She'd seen jewelry like this in shops in the mall, but to hold it in her hands . . .

"For you." Justin said. It was a locket—a polished back heart on a silver chain, the stone cool to her touch, it was a deep black, like the oval stone Dixie wore—the same stone Justin wore on his little finger—and a pin, with a larger stone, set in a silver star. "Whitby jet," he said. "It's mined in Yorkshire, near where I have my clinic." Where she would one day live with him. "We wear it to help anchor ourselves to the earth. The locket is for every day. The brooch is for you, for being Stella, my star."

Her chest tightened. Her mind seemed to lighten in a rush of happiness. It was beautiful beyond measure: a silver star set with pearls and rows of rubies. No, they had to be garnets. In the center was a large, polished round of jet that felt smooth and warm under her fingertip. "It's beautiful, Justin."

"Like you," his voice came harsh and tight in the quiet. "A star. I want you to have them, to remember me by."

Something in his tone, his words, snagged at her heart. "To remember you by?"

"Yes, I'm leaving tomorrow. When you get back from visiting your mother, I'll be gone."

His words felt like cold acid in her eyes, burning her brain, etching scars into her soul. Only half-comprehending, she stared at him. His impassive face and stone-hard eyes hurt as much as his words. "I see." It was an outright lie. She didn't, but looking at the pearl-edged star against the dark velvet, she understood. She'd once read a story where a rich man paid off discarded lovers with a diamond bracelet. She'd thought it incredible and ridiculous and now it was happening to her.

If only she'd never let herself get caught up with Justin Corvus! But she had. It was done. Nothing she could do about that. But from now on . . . !

She snapped the jeweler's box shut and tossed it into the glove compartment.

"Stella!" Justin said as she unbuckled her seat belt and opened the car door. "It's yours! I want you to have that."

"I don't want it!"

He beat her to the gate. He'd even stopped to grab the leather box. "Please, Stella. I want you to have something to remember me by. To remember us. Please take it."

She almost laughed in his face. Boy, was he good! If she hadn't known better she'd think he was the one hurting! "Forgetting you is what I'd rather do!" He took a step towards her but she side-stepped. "Get the hell out of my way!"

"Stella!"

"No! I've a better idea! Go to hell and don't come back!" With a leap, she was over the fence and halfway up the path. If anyone saw . . . too damn bad! She half-expected him to follow, so she could find out if a knee to the groin hurt a vampire, but he just stood on the sidewalk, staring. She caught a glimpse of his shock-struck face as she slammed the door behind her.

Dixie got up from her seat by the TV as the front door

slammed. Even before Stella rounded the corner, Dixie felt her fury. "What happened?"

"I can't believe I fell for it! That I was so stupid! Such a fool!" She paced on the worn, living room carpet. "I'm thirty years old. I've heard enough men spin lies to recognize one a mile off!" She stopped pacing, clenched her fists and bent her neck back as if in agony.

"Justin, huh?" What had the idiot done and said?

Stella frowned until her brows all but met. "Who's Justin?"

"The bozo who just acted like a horse's rear end."

It didn't get a smile, at least not one that counted, but it eased Stella's clenched jaw, just a tad. "I'm trying to tell myself it's a bad dream! That it didn't happen! That he really didn't!"

Dixie put her arm around Stella. "How about we have a seat, and you tell me what happened?"

Seemed Stella's whole body sagged as she sat down, confusion and bewilderment replacing her earlier fury. "Dixie . . ." she began, a dry sob cutting off her words.

Dixie moved closer, wrapping her arms around her. At her touch, Stella's sobs resumed. She didn't cry, that relief was gone with her mortality, but her shoulders heaved with grief and Stella muttered angry phrases until her misery eased and she just sat limp beside Dixie.

"Now that you've got that over with," Dixie said, hugging her, "and we agree men have the sensitivity and intelligence of slugs, tell me what the hell he said and did."

Calmer now, Stella told her.

Tom Kyd frowned up at Justin. "You're not paying attention."

"I'm trying to." He forced his attention back to the laptop

and the changing screens as Tom's twisted fingers skimmed over the keyboard.

"This web site I set up for you has all the information I could get together at short notice. I'll update as needed. In case you can't get web access, most of the info is on these CDs." He indicated a stack by the computer. "The hard drive also has a list of URLs and emails. See this file?" He clicked on an icon to open it. "You need to memorize the top few. That way you can still access them from a cyber-café or another computer."

Justin stared at the laptop in his friend's hands. Tom must have spent hours loading up details of all Justin's widespread personal finances, records of the clinic, and two alternate identities. "How did you do this?"

Tom shrugged and gave the same grin Justin remembered in a tavern in Southwark four hundred years earlier. "Just brilliant."

"Wouldn't argue with that. I planned on going back to Havering. The clinic is mine, not the colony's, and it will give me ten, fifteen years more before I need to assume a new identity. But now I have this . . ." He could go anywhere. Lose himself.

"I'd still say go to Havering," Kit said. "You've got your life there. Take a few years and plan your next move. Besides, if something comes up, we'll know where to find you."

"Nothing's going to come up." He'd given up believing in miracles more than a millennium ago. "The sooner this is over, the better. Less fuss for everyone and less upheaval in the colony."

"You still could fight it, you know?"

Justin was tempted not to dignify that with an answer but . . . "No. I'll not put myself above our laws. Just give me your word you'll protect Stella."

"You need to ask twice?" Tom asked.

Justin gave him a twisted smile. "No, my friend, but her safety and that of Sam are my main concerns."

"She understands what's going on?" Kit asked.

Justin's chest cramped at the memory of their parting. "I told her I would be leaving tomorrow."

They both stared in silence.

"That's it?" Kit asked, sounding shocked to the core. "You didn't tell her why?"

"A bit abrupt, wasn't it?" Tom added. "I mean to say, a bit off. Didn't it upset her?"

It cut her to the quick and he still hurt from the pain in her eyes. "It was the only way."

"You could have told her the reason why."

And they claimed they were here to help! "How the hell could I?" He all but snarled at them, and they darn well deserved it.

"Well," Tom began, "you could have started with: 'Stella, there's a bit of a problem.' Explain things to her, like."

Justin's harsh laugh slashed into Tom's words. "Explain it all to her, you say! Ah, yes. I tell her the whole involved mess, and she'll just nod docilely and say, 'I see, Justin, goodbye. I'll miss you,' and then go on with the washing-up! Tom Kyd, you need to get out and about more! Remember what Dixie did when I explained the need to leave the country for her own safety?" Tom's shocked face showed Justin had made his point. "Beginning to understand are you? Good! Stella is cut from the same mold. If possible, she is even more bull-headed. If I'd told her the full story, I'd wager anything you care to name she'd be, right this minute, banging on Gwyltha's suite demanding she refashion the tenets of our colony, and when that failed, she'd be off canvassing every revenant she could find to take my part. We'd end up with a civil war!" Justin strode over to the window. He'd be weeping if his body could. Just saying Stella's name cut to his soul. He dreaded existence without her but what earthly choice did he have?

"He's right, Tom," Kit said. "Hell, I had to practically twist Dixie's neck to get her to promise not to tell Stella. I had visions of the pair of them joining forces and taking on the colony. Civil war isn't even it! We'd have World War Three. You just don't know what these women are like."

Under his words, Justin heard the pride and love. Kit knew what he had in Dixie. Just as Justin knew exactly what he'd lost in Stella. He turned away from the window to look at the comfortable parlor with its wide sofa and twin wing chairs by the fireplace and his two oldest friends. He'd lost Stella and tomorrow would part from them. All he had left was the few hours remaining tonight. "Tom, Kit, let's not waste the night arguing might-have-beens and what-ifs. Let's . . ."

"Have a glass of fine port?" Tom suggested. "It's what we've always done together."

It was like old times—Old times they'd never share again. Justin refused to dwell on that. What mortal friendships lasted as theirs had? He raise his glass and sipped. Not exactly Tom's famed aged port but rich enough. In fact, pretty darn good. He was tempted to swig the glass and half the bottle too, but why bother? Alcohol lost its effect on him back in the second century. There was nothing in creation to ease his pain.

"You will keep contact with me," Tom said. "Use the emails I've set up for you."

"And if word gets out?"

"How the hell could it? No one could crack my computer, trust me, and in the unlikely event anyone did by accident, heck it's just spam. Everyone gets it. If you don't sign it, who'll know where it comes from?"

He should refuse. Tom's suggestion approached anarchy

but the earnest look on his face and Kit's was more than he could deny. "I will, in emergencies, if you promise me news of Stella and Sam."

"It goes without saying," Kit said. "She will be safe, I swear it."

And safe was the best he could offer her.

The room was quiet, only the tick of the clock and their thoughts when a rap on the door brought them all to their feet.

"At this hour of the morning!" Tom went stock-still. They all knew he'd never forget the knock on his lodging door, the prelude to his arrest and torture.

"It's all right, Tom." Kit squeezed his shoulder. "Most likely some early tourist looking for Schmidt's."

Tom stared at Kit as if he had willow trees growing out of his ears. "It's a local joke, Tom," Justin said. Explaining it was beyond him right now. "Want me to get it, Kit?" If it was trouble, he could handle it. If it was a the tribunal convened ahead of time, he'd survive it. And if it was a lost tourist, he tell them, "Sorry, the sausage house doesn't open until lunch time."

It was Vlad Tepes.

Chapter Sixteen

"Pardon the intrusion," Vlad said, inclining his head. "Would you would permit me a few minutes of your time?"

He was going to hell in the proverbial handbasket, why not let his old nemesis join in the show? But looking at Vlad, Justin saw no rancor or even a trace of a gloat. That would no doubt come later, and at this point, he hardly cared.

But the others did.

"Vlad Tepes!" Kit jumped to his feet. "What does he want?"

"He wants to turn around and scarper before I see him," Tom said.

Justin waved them away with a flick of his wrist. "He says he only wants a few minutes. What more can he do anyway?" Justin looked at Kit, legs apart in a fighter's stance. "It's your house, Kit, can he come in?"

"Five minutes," Kit replied not shifting position one hairsbreadth.

Vlad took a couple of steps into the room. "Three will suffice." He nodded to acknowledge Kit and Tom and then turned to Justin. "Dr. Corvus, apologies at this point are trite and useless but even so, I proffer them. We have had our differences and rivalries, but at no time have I ever wished on you a disaster of this magnitude. That my actions caused it is to my shame. My ignorance of your colony's laws is my embarrassment and your tragedy. If I could undo it, I would, but seems your laws are as immutable as your leader is inflexible.

"Since it has been made clear the outcome is not in question, I have only one thing I can offer. It is a poor alternative and no replacement for your loss, but I offer you the shelter and services of my colony, wherever and whenever, for as long as you might wish to avail yourself of our support."

Whatever any of them had expected, it wasn't this! Justin sensed the others' utter astonishment. Why not? It matched his own.

Vlad offered a deeper bow this time. He glanced at Kit as he raised his head. "A little less than three minutes, I believe, and I will trespass on your goodwill no longer. The dawn comes soon. Goodbye."

"By Abel!" Justin said as Vlad turned towards the still ajar door. "Vlad!" As Vlad turned back, Justin held out his hand.

Now it was Vlad's turn to stare but he only hesitated a second before clasping Justin's hand. "I meant every word," he said.

Justin nodded. "I know."

Kit stepped past them to push the door shut. "Come on in, Vlad, I'll find another glass."

A century and more is a long time to bear a grudge. Justin and Kit and Tom raised their glasses with Vlad and toasted the future. Now he had a glimmer of a future, thanks to an old rival. He'd still be parted from Kit and Tom, but he'd no longer be a rootless wanderer without a home. He had somewhere to take Stella.

He couldn't wait to share the news with her.

*   *   *

When Dixie finished, Stella sagged back against the sofa pillows and stared at her. "It's medieval!"

"Much older. They drew up the code long before the Middle Ages."

"It's high time they modernized things a bit! Punishing Justin for defending me."

"As they see it, and Christopher pushed this point, you were already dead. Justin wasn't defending you, and therefore there's no defense for his attack."

Stella wanted to attack someone herself. "What was he supposed to do? Walk away?"

Dixie pushed her hair back. "In a nutshell, yes. They have this thing about no revenge or retaliation. You were dead, no question of it. So Justin's actions were retaliation. The fact is he put those two in the hospital. I'm not saying it's right or I agree but that's the way it's written."

Stella let out an exasperated hiss. "It's nonsense, do they expect Justin to be superhuman?"

"He is. So are we."

She wouldn't, couldn't deny that point. "We're human too!"

"We're human in our emotions and superhuman in our abilities; it's a potent mix and, from what Justin once told me, was at one time hideously abused. That's why they drew up the code and enforced it. There was a reason they called those days the Dark Ages."

They weren't over yet. She was sucked right into a twenty-first century dark age. "I can't let it happen. I've got to do something."

"I thought you'd see it that way."

"We'll leave early for Marysville. Arrive at the very start of visiting times, and then get back here in time to disrupt this farce of a trial!"

* * *

"By Abel, we're too late!" Justin had sensed it as he walked up the path but the empty house confirmed it. "Why didn't I come earlier?"

"This is early," Kit pointed out. "Most of these houses aren't even awake yet. Sure she's not resting?"

Justin shook his head. "I swear there's no one there. I'd hear Sam's heartbeat." Hell, I'd sense Stella's presence. Feel her being. She was gone. Where? Run away because he'd hurt her. Taken Sam with her and fled, and how in creation would she survive? Last night his heart ached to the roots, now it was ripped and shredded.

"I still think you should check the house," Kit said. He didn't add, "just in case . . ." but Justin could read it in his face. Hell, he was thinking it himself!

Justin got in via the same loose bathroom window he'd used—was it only three weeks ago? Three minutes confirmed the empty house, but did nothing to allay Justin's anxiety. Stella's bed hadn't been slept in. Sam's had, but the covers were pulled back and cold as if he'd left in the middle of the night. Open drawers and clothes scattered about both bedrooms suggested hasty packing before flight.

"I have to find her!" Justin said as he and Kit sat on the porch steps. "How far can she have gone?"

"Not far," Kit said, "Dixie is with her." Justin almost shook at his friend's words. He'd been so preoccupied with Stella, he'd clean forgotten Dixie. "She wouldn't go away without telling me."

Justin tried to relax. There had to be a reasonable explanation for this but he was darned if he could see what it was.

"Hello, looking for Stella?" They both as good as jumped at the old woman leaning over the porch next door. "You missed her."

Accurate but useless information, but Justin forced a courteous smile. She was old, and female and mortal, and . . . yes, he remembered her name. "Mrs. Zeibel, remember me? I was hoping to catch Stella."

"She left early, with that friend of hers."

"To see her mother?" That made some sense, but this early?

His question earned him a cautious nod and a wary look from beneath gray brows. "You're that young man of hers who took care of the Day boys and Warty, aren't you?" By Abel, how did she . . . "I'll never forget that. This street owes you one. Those boys did nothing but break fences and smash windows all up and down the alley. You did the whole street a good turn when you took care of them." She was talking about the afternoon when he'd caught them pitching beer bottles, not more recent events.

"I was glad to help. But I was hoping to catch Stella . . . ?"

"They left early. Called me before I was up and asked if she could bring Sam over early. Carried him over in his pajamas. He's still asleep on my sofa."

If Sam was there, Stella would return. "Can't be helped then—I'll see her when she gets back." Lightheaded with relief, he smiled at Mrs. Zeibel in her pink, quilted dressing gown. "Let me get your paper for you." He jumped over the fence between the two yards, grabbed the paper off the path and presented it to her with a flourish and a bow that would have done justice to Kit's old friend, Walter Raleigh.

She laughed aloud, showing she'd left her dentures in the house. "Young man, if you were closer my age, I'd give Stella some competition."

"I'm older than I look, Mrs. Zeibel."

That she treated as a huge joke. "You go behave yourself, young man. I'll tell Stella you came by."

He was about ready to vault over the fence again when Kit called from the gate. "I think we might as well walk back." Kit put a lot of emphasis on the walk, and Justin just realized what he'd done.

"Kit, I think I'm cracking up. I almost went berserk at the thought of Stella having run away. Then I was so relieved, I . . ." he shook his head. "My mind just caved in on me. That old woman . . ."

Kit chuckled. "Was amused and thrilled out of her curlers. You have quite a way with you. I stopped you before you went too far."

"I wasn't thinking."

"I'd go along with that assessment but since you're a bit, what they call nowadays 'stressed out,' it's understandable."

"Kit, stressed out is what I felt trying to track those Brigantes in the mist, or switching that pauper's body for yours. What I felt just then was cerebral meltdown."

"Just cerebral, not emotional?" Kit asked with a twist of a smile.

"Where do I keep emotions, if not in my brain? In my feet?" Justin said.

"I did wonder at one point last night!"

Kit didn't know how lucky he was they were in a public place.

Justin's relief lasted about two hundred meters. Passing the shell of the one-time crack house gave him a bit of a boost. The neighborhood had more to thank him for than stopping a bit of vandalism and graffiti, but some things only revenants knew. Just as well, too. Knowing Stella was safe was a relief. Hell, it was a sanity preserver. Imagining her gone, he'd have been a quivering wretch by the time he faced the tribunal. Now he could look them all in the eye, knowing he'd have to take the blame and the consequences, but secure knowing he had a place to take Stella. They had a future. All he had to do was learn to live with the shame of expulsion from his colony, assuming of course that Stella wanted to spend her life with an outcast.

By the time they turned up City Park, the black mood was on him again. He'd have Stella, perhaps, but how would they make their way in a strange and unfamiliar colony? How could he protect her and Sam when he didn't know the rules himself? Should he go off after all and leave her safe with Kit and Dixie? He could feel cerebral meltdown approaching once again.

"You're early."

"I know, Mom . . . but I need to get back to town."

"What's more important than visiting your mother?"

Stella prayed for patience. Incarceration would no doubt make a saint snippy. "Mom, it's because it's important to see you that I got up before it was light and came over. I didn't want to miss it."

"I should hope not! You know I count on your visits. No one else bothers."

Was there anyone else who cared? Most of Mom's friends were either in jail themselves or unlikely to visit voluntarily. "I always do, Mom."

"Yes." Her mother seemed to lose a little of her sharpness. "You're a good girl, Stella. You do come and you're looking after my house for me, aren't you?"

"I do the best I can, Mom."

"I want a home to go to when I come out. Don't want to end up in some homeless hostel somewhere. I plan on coming to my own place and my own things."

Stella did not want to dwell on the house, the leaky basement or the geriatric appliances. "I've got a new job, Mom."

"You have, now? You quit the cleaners?"

"This works better. It's in a new shop at the top of Fifth Street. Nice people to work for and hours are good. I can switch around if need be and I'm getting a new baby-sitter."

Mom was quiet a minute. "Sam doing okay?"

"Fine."

"Good . . . you're right not to bring him here." She glanced over where two toddlers played on their mother's lap. "This ain't no place for kids. I've been a bit harsh sometimes about him not coming, but you're right."

"I understand, Mom."

She listened as her mother talked on about gossip and happenings among the other inmates. Stella smiled at intervals, and agreed when it seemed appropriate, but all the time wondered how soon she could graciously leave without getting accused of not staying long enough. She was weary from missing rest and had a confrontation awaiting her back in Columbus.

". . . so Jimmy's brother may be dropping by."

"What, Mom? Joe?" Jimmy Holt's no good brother! Wasn't he in jail too? She should have been paying better attention. "Why is Joe Holt coming to see me?"

"He's going to need somewhere to stay a few days. You've got space."

Not for Mom's criminal pals, there wasn't. "Mom, he is not staying in my house. I don't care if the alternative is his sleeping in the streets."

"It's my house." Mom's eyes flashed.

"And my kid lives there. I won't have him coming home to Joey Holt entertaining him with tales of his stay at the big house! There's enough bad things out on the street." Although fewer now, thanks to Justin and Kit. "I sure as heck won't have one sleeping on my sofa!"

"Okay, okay." Mom waved a hand at Stella, as if she were the awkward one. "No need to get your panties in a tangle. I was just asking."

"I know, Mom, but it's impossible. No way!"

"Sometimes I wonder how I gave birth to you, Stella. You're such a goody-two-shoes. Keep the rules. Do what they tell you to do. Don't you ever hanker for a bit of fun and excitement?"

Stella laughed aloud at that. She'd had more excitement in the past week than Mom could ever imagine. She was half-tempted to look her mother in the eye and tell her that her only daughter had just become a vampire. Better not. "I do fine, Mom. I do fine." Or would once she took on the colony and got her man out of a pinch. "One thing I must tell you, Mom. I've met this man . . ."

"So that's what it is." Mom came back with a smug look. "Shoulda guessed. Thought there was a different look about your face. Getting it regular then, are you? You're on the pill, I hope."

"Mom!"

"Now don't you go all shocked on me. I know you. You never did handle men right. Look what happened with Sam's dad. Walked out on you. I can see it happening again, and you'll end up with two little Sammies to buy shoes for."

"Don't worry, Mom. I will not be getting pregnant."

"Got yourself fixed, did you? Makes it easier all round if you ask me." Stella didn't ask her, but . . . "Now I understand why you don't want Joe sleeping over. Men can get funny over little things like that."

"Went badly, huh?" Dixie asked after they'd driven a good twenty miles in silence.

"No more than usual. We never really have gotten along but she is my mother . . . and . . ." Stella gave up. How could she explain her mixed emotions about her mother when she didn't understand them herself.

"She's the reason you balked at going to England with Justin, isn't she?"

"Pretty much. I always leave there feeling shattered. She is my mother; she just happens to be a convicted felon—one of those details missing from most families."

"May be more common than you think. Some just don't get convicted."

Stella nodded. "I guess that's true. So, what's it like in England?" Surely not miles of cornfields and a distant flat horizon.

"Very green, and everyone talks funny but they think you have an accent." Dixie glanced from the road. "Seriously thinking about it, are you?"

"I've been thinking about it . . . and other things . . . Life seems to have gotten a bit full these days."

Dixie laughed. "A bit full! You've been hanging around Christopher and Justin too long. I'd say it was overwhelming!"

"That too! I'm beginning to feel if I get through today, I'll live forever."

"Living forever is a given, barring some awful mishap. Concentrate on this afternoon."

Good point! "You think Justin will be barred from the colony?"

"If they apply the letter of the law, yes. Unfair, unjust, but there you are."

"So he gets thrown out. Can't he just stay here?" Seemed simple enough.

"That's what I said. Christopher came out with a lot of rigmarole about needing to protect me and not exposing me to censure. I told him to stick his head in it . . . but . . . well, you can imagine the rest." Stella could. "Thing is," Dixie went on, "Justin, in a pinch, could survive most places; he's old, doesn't depend on his earth the way you and I do. But you need yours—that's why he's been on you so much about you moving to England with him."

"Fine, we'll move to England, someplace where Gwyltha and the colony aren't."

Dixie shook her head. "Stella, Gwyltha is Britain. There isn't anywhere."

"Then she'd better see sense about Justin."

"You go tell her, girl! There's no hope if you don't try. Justin is hell-bent on no defense and doing the gentlemanly thing and making a dignified exit. Someone has to get up and fight."

"Here I come." She was ready to take on the lot of them if need be.

They were both silent the rest of the drive. Stella got the feeling Dixie was praying. She darn well knew she was.

"I'm going to drop you by the alley," Dixie said. "I don't think they will be watching the front door but with this many vamps under one roof, I wouldn't be surprised."

"How many do you think will be there?" Stella tried to ignore the tightness in her throat. She was not going to chicken out on Justin.

"Maybe a dozen, fifteen. Perhaps nowhere near that many. Could be just a half-dozen."

Stella decided to fix on the half-dozen. She felt fine with Justin, Kit and Dixie, that was three. Six was just another three. She wouldn't dwell on the big difference. These were hostile vamps she was talking about, not friends. Hostile vamps who were out to get the man she loved. Not while she lived and breathed! She had to suppress a smile. Not breathing was part of the problem.

"I'll give you ten minutes, then I'll park in front and walk in as if I own the house."

"You're not coming in, too!"

"You bet I am!"

"No way, Dixie. If the shit hits the fan, I don't want you caught in the fallout."

Dixie grinned. "I'm caught in it already. I doubt you can fool anyone into believing it was chance that you climbed over the back fence, snuck into the house and just happened to stroll uninvited into a tribunal."

Good point. "I still . . ."

"Look, if this does get really nasty, I'm darn certain Christopher will come down on Justin's side. If he does, I do. So we're all in this up to our necks anyway." Dixie grinned as she slowed down and turned left off Third. She eased the car to a stop. "Hop out, I'll take a couple of turns around the block and then walk in the front door."

"How about you check on Sam for me?"

Dixie shook her head. "Sam is fine with Mrs. Zeibel. You've got five minutes."

Stella was over the fence in seconds. She dropped to the ground and looked around the immaculate yard, neat winter-bare flowerbeds, a smooth newly-laid brick path and a circular iron bend around a half-leafless tree. Right! She hadn't come here to look at dead flowers! She sprinted up the path to the back door, unlocked it with the key Dixie gave her and stepped inside.

She'd half-expected to have to brave a receiving line of vampires but the kitchen was empty. The house wasn't.

"Who just entered?" an unfamiliar voice asked.

"I did!" Stella replied, moving fast through the dining room towards the gathering of vampires in the parlor. Everyone except the two women stood up as Stella walked in.

"Stella!" Justin and Kit spoke at once.

"What are you doing here?" Justin asked.

"Where's Dixie?" Kit asked

"Parking the car," she replied, ignoring Justin's question.

There were seven, no, eight, vamps standing in a circle. Stella hardly had a chance to look at them.

"Is this the new fledgling?" someone asked. No one else spoke.

The speaker was short, tiny and dark-haired, and power rippled off her in waves. She was old, very old, Stella could sense it, and pretty pissed. Too damn bad. "I'm Stella Schwartz. You must be Gwyltha." Offering a hand might be pushing it. Stella settled for standing up straight and looking her in the eye.

A rush like water shot from a high-powered hose hit Stella square in the chest. She staggered but kept her balance. What in hell?

"Gwyltha, don't do that. There's no need. She will leave." Stella turned her gawk as Justin came towards her. What did he mean? What sort of powers did this woman have if she could attack with her mind.

"Justin," Stella said, the shock receding, "I . . ."

"Leave, Stella. This has nothing to do with you. Go."

She shook her head. "No way, José."

"You don't belong here. Leave us," Gwyltha said. Stella decided that didn't deserve any response.

Justin gave her an exasperated frown. "Stella, go! Get out! I don't want you here!"

"Tough cookies."

"Go, fledgling. This has nothing to do with you." Gwyltha spoke quietly but with an authority and certainty of obedience. Refusing her soft-spoken order wouldn't be smart.

"I'm not leaving. If it concerns Justin, it concerns me."

"It doesn't, Stella," Justin said. He was close enough to touch her but made no effort. "I don't want you here. I don't need you here. This has absolutely nothing to do with you."

Could he possibly mean that? That he didn't want her help or support. Tough shit! He was getting it. "That's not what I heard!"

"What did you hear, fledgling?" Gwyltha asked.

"It was Dixie, wasn't it?" Kit asked, not even trying to hide his exasperation. "She told you!"

"She didn't tell me! I wormed a few details out of her and figured out the rest for myself." No point in getting everyone mad at Dixie as well.

Gwyltha laughed. "Fledgling, I doubt any human, mortal or immortal, has wormed anything out of Dixie she didn't choose to share." Her voice changed back to the one woman judge and jury. "What did she tell you?"

Stella squared her shoulders to at least pretend courage. "I learned that Justin is being blamed for what happened last weekend. I was there; none of the rest of you were." She glanced round at the stony faces in the room. "I guess that makes me a material witness."

Gwyltha raised an eyebrow. "Does nothing intimidate you, fledgling?"

"Would you let yourself be intimidated if someone you loved was in danger?" As she spoke, Stella remembered what Dixie told her about Gwyltha and Justin's past. Maybe that wasn't the smartest thing.

"Justin is not in danger, fledgling," one of the other vamps said. "He's being called to account for his actions." The man was tall and broad and built like a linebacker.

"And I was in the middle of the action."

"You were dead at the time, I believe."

"Still am, for that matter, and so is everyone else in this room!"

"Stella," Justin all but growled. "For the last time, will you leave?"

"You really think I'll just walk away and let them hang you out to dry?"

"You really believe you can stop us, if we choose to?" That was linebacker again.

"Probably not, but I'm sure as hell not sitting by while you do." Swearing most likely wasn't a good idea.

"Let her stay. Why shouldn't Justin have her speak in his favor?" That was a shorter, thin man. He looked older than most of the others, his face drawn and lined.

"Tom . . ." Gwyltha began but as she spoke, the front door opened and Dixie walked in.

"Hello, everyone," she said, as easily as if she found a

gathering of vampires in her front parlor every day of the week.

Christopher gave her a lopsided smile and a raised eyebrow. "You're back early, dear."

Dixie crossed the room to kiss him. "Yes, Stella had something she needed to take care of."

"So I understand."

"Are we expecting any more interruptions?" Gwyltha asked.

Kit looked at Dixie. "Are we?"

"Not that I'm aware of." She turned to Gwyltha. "You're letting Stella stay?"

There was silence a few seconds as Gwyltha fixed a stare at Stella and then Dixie. "Can she add anything besides pleas for mercy?"

"Perhaps you should ask her?" Dixie replied.

"I will."

Stella took that as consent to remain.

"Let us proceed," Gwyltha went on. "We were all but finished when we were interrupted."

So they'd arrived just in time. Stella glanced at Dixie and got an encouraging smile and a surprising thumbs-up sign from Kit.

Everyone sat down, Justin offering Stella his chair with a look that dared her to refuse. He stood behind her, both hands grasping the smooth wood, and Stella sensed the tension strumming his body. She tried to meet his mind but it was slammed shut against her. That hurt, but she had no time to dwell on it.

"Go on from where you left off, John," Gwyltha said and linebacker stood up.

"The facts are clear and undisputed: Justin Corvus ignored our laws, and in a fit of rage, injured two mortal youths." He made Justin sound as if he'd been the attacker instead of the attacked! Was no one arguing this? Stella looked around the room. Kit shook his head as she caught his eye. Telling her to keep quiet? Or that there was no hope? Or . . .

"You have something to add, Stella?" Gwyltha asked from her seat in the high-backed wing chair.

"Yes, I do." She'd half-expected Justin to deny it, but his only reaction was to tighten his grip on the chair back.

"You are saying it didn't happen this way?" John asked.

Smart-ass. "No, I'm saying it's the truth but not the whole truth." No one tried to stop her, so she went on. "Johnny Day and Warty Watson are both bad news. Johnny in particular has been in trouble with the law since he was in kinder-garten."

Gwyltha looked right at Stella. "You're saying that justi-fies injuring them?"

"No, I'm not, but I'm saying they weren't innocent by-standers. Johnny had that gun for a reason—to shoot us. He had it in for Justin because he got him good for smashing my garage door and for dissing me on Halloween. Justin didn't hurt him either time." Better add that! "But he made him look small. Johnny doesn't like being bested and decided to get back at us and got himself that gun.

"I remember him yelling and calling me a bitch, and a noise, then a great thump in my chest. It hurt like hell and then everything went black, so I don't know what happened immediately afterwards, but I do know both boys were hurt and in the hospital. They're both out now. Johnny Day has a leg and both arms in casts and will be unable to cause any more trouble for a while, plus, his credibility with his gang is a bit low. He kept boasting how he'd shot me, but I turned up alive.

"And as for Warty Watson, who never was as mean as the Day boys, before he even left the hospital he asked to see a minister. Seems Warty believes he saw the devil. He con-fessed to the cops to killing me and then they told him I wasn't dead. I saw Warty yesterday." Lucky break that was. "He's not as injured as they feared at first but he's what you might call confused. However, he's sworn off a life of crime and wants to be saved. So, seems some good came of it."

"So," Gwyltha's dark eyes looked right at Stella, "one youth repenting a life of crime, and another incapacitated. Interesting . . . But the fact still remains that Justin attacked mortals."

"Mortals who'd just shot me dead!"

"We vampires do not indulge in revenge."

Dear heaven, give her strength! "It wasn't revenge. It was instinct. Justin loves me." Or so she hoped after this. "I'd do the same if someone hurt Sam."

"Who is Sam?" John asked.

"My son."

That raised Gwyltha's eyebrows. "You have a child?"

"Yes, he's nine years old." The look on Gwyltha's face suggested a possible vampire law against having children.

"Well, Justin, when you roil the waters, you don't do it by halves," Gwyltha said.

"Sam is part of the reason I transformed Stella. My despair at seeing the mortal I loved, struck dead, was part of it, I admit. It was certainly a great part of my fury, but also, I couldn't leave Sam without a protector. Sam needed her as much as I needed Stella."

Stella felt the world rise and float. She wanted to grab Justin, hug him and kiss him until she tasted all he was, but they were smack in the middle of a vampire court martial.

"Very touching," John said, "but as Justin is about to be exiled . . ."

"He's not exiled yet!" Stella jumped to her feet and looked around the room. "What's wrong with you people? How many good doctors do you have that you can calmly throw out Justin? And what would the rest of you have done? Asked Johnny Day to please hand over his nasty gun? You really think he would have? More like shot someone else:

the valet parking attendant in front of the Barcelona, other people leaving who'd perhaps wondered what was going on, the police. It could have been bloodshed and mayhem."

John seemed unconvinced. "Unlikely. Justin could have easily disarmed him."

"Maybe, but while he'd held them and waited for the police, he'd have had a lot of questions to answer as to how he managed to move faster than a speeding bullet and why his wounds self-healed. I'd have been dead and Sam headed for foster care. As it is, I'm here, Sam's safe, Warty has forsworn a life of crime, and who knows, maybe even Johnny Day will think twice before shooting the next person who pisses him off." Stella folded her arms and glared. They might be vampires and centuries old, but damn the lot of them!

"Sit down, my love. I think you're making some of them nervous." That last was ridiculous, but she was so relieved at the mind contact from Justin, she sat.

"I love you."

"I know."

His words rang so in the turmoil of the mind that it took a few moments to realize the total silence that greeted her outburst. She heard a car pass, traveling south on City Park and the tick of the carved clock on the mantelpiece, but no sound, nothing even as faint as a breath or a heartbeat from the crowd around her. Of course not! It was still as the tomb. She held back a smile. That might give a total wrong impression. Stella looked Gwyltha in the eyes. Willing her to find in Justin's favor.

"Are you finished?" Gwyltha asked.

"I think so." Maybe in more ways than one.

But the nod from Gwyltha was neutral rather than hostile. "Does anyone else wish to speak?"

"I do!" Everyone turned to look as the short, haggard-looking vamp stepped forward. It was then Stella noticed his deformed fingers. Another ancient injury like Kit's eye?

"Tom." Gwyltha turned to him. "Well?"

So, this was the Tom that Justin had mentioned.

"Gwyltha, other members of our colony." Tom nodded to Gwyltha and the rest of them. That must be the polite way to address vamps. Now she knew. "I will stand with Justin, whatever your findings. He helped transform me. I cannot remain in a colony that excludes my mentor."

The closest thing to a vampire gasp greeted this quiet announcement.

"You'd withdraw your skills from us?" a dark woman blurted out as if in shock. Then she looked at Gwyltha. "Apologies."

"I share your shock, Antonia," Gwyltha replied.

"I would not withdraw them!" Tom almost snapped. "When have I ever refused any vampire who needed my help? But I will stand with Justin. Make no mistake about it."

The silence hummed with tension. Stella felt it like a breeze over her skin and then realized that was Justin wrapping his thoughts around her. What was happening? "Be still and wait," his mind whispered to hers. "Let others speak." She felt so safe as his mind melded with hers, but were they?

"Indeed, Tom, you make yourself clear." Gwyltha frowned. "Are there others who wish to part from the colony and it's laws?"

"Gwyltha," Kit stepped forward. "None of us wish to part ways but I, too, cannot break the bond with the vampire who transformed me."

Dixie stepped beside Kit. "I'm with Kit in this."

"And I." That was a tall, black vampire who looked sort of familiar. Had she seen him around German Village?

In the shocked quiet, two other voices declared solidarity with Justin.

"No!" Justin's voice broke the tense silence. "Toby, Kit, Dixie, Simon and Rod, and most of all Stella." He squeezed her shoulder. "Your support overwhelms me but we cannot create schism in the colony. Division wouldn't work to any-one's advantage. If I need to leave, I leave alone."

"Like hell, you do!" She'd meant to think it to him, but it came out aloud. Too damn bad!

"Stella," he half-growled.

Gwyltha stood up and took a couple of steps towards Stella. She stopped. "So, you'd exile yourself from the colony before you even join it. Have you any idea of the dif-ficulties you'd face as a fledgling vampire alone with a child?"

Stella stood up to meet Gwyltha eye to eye. "I won't be alone. I'll have Sam and Justin, and okay, I'm darn sure there will be difficulties, but heck, being a single mortal with a job and a child wasn't exactly a piece of cake. I'll manage some-how."

"I don't doubt you would, if you had to." What did that mean? Would? If? Gwyltha looked at Justin. "Where did you find her, Justin?"

"She found me. I was minding the shop for Dixie and Stella walked into my life." His hands cupped her shoulders, holding her steady, anchoring her to him. What now?

Gwyltha scanned the room. "So, to include Stella in our numbers, we have to overlook Justin's transgression." She looked back at Stella and Justin, a smile curving her mouth. "A fair enough arrangement in my mind."

It took Stella a few seconds to realize exactly what she meant. Dixie's whoop of delight convinced her. Justin was safe! Moments later he swept her up in a hug tight enough to crack ribs on a mortal. She hugged back every bit as hard and kissed him. He pulled away and grinned.

"By Abel! You are wonderful! What did I do to deserve you?"

"You don't!" Gwyltha said as Justin set Stella's feet back on the floor.

Stella shrugged. "You're right there. But he is great with kids," she added and grinned.

After that, the tribunal degenerated into a gabfest. Stella was introduced to everyone, and promptly forgot at least half their names. An almost party-like atmosphere filled the little house. It didn't take much brain power to figure out Justin was well-liked and respected. Seemed vamps had a lot of sense as well as physical strength and liked to talk. They hung around the house in groups chattering at the tops of their voices and looking as if they were set for the night. Maybe they were.

The bell rang, and Kit opened the door to a vamp Stella did recognize. It was the one Dixie had called Vlad. "Do I intrude?" he asked.

"No, Vlad, your timing is impeccable." Kit stepped back and the group parted as Gwyltha came forward.

"Come in, Vlad." She held out her hand and Stella sensed the bond between them.

"Why has he come late?" Stella thought to Justin.

"He isn't part of the colony," he replied. "He's Gwyltha's lover."

Just then Vlad approached them. "Corvus, may I offer my good wishes on the favorable outcome of the tribunal and . . ." He smiled at Stella. "My felicitations?"

"My thanks, Vlad, for your good wishes." Justin held out his hand. The whole room seemed to wait as Vlad nodded and clasped hands with Justin.

"Have you any idea of what you've just done?" Stella turned as Tom spoke. She'd somehow been separated from Justin.

She smiled at Tom. So this was Kit's close friend. "What have I done?" she asked, looking at the intelligent eyes in the worn face.

"Only faced down our fearless leader, who incidentally,

has the power to blast you through even these thick walls if she chose. You may conclude she liked you. But most amazingly, you've turned Justin from a growling curmudgeon to a lover. I felicitate you."

"I'm not sure I had much to do with it."

He tossed back his head and roared with laughter. "Don't delude yourself, Stella. You had everything to do with it. Justin is one lucky vampire." He gave her a hug.

"Take your hands off my woman!"

Stella grinned up at Justin. "Who said I was your woman?"

"I do." He grabbed her hand. "Since no one seems to want to leave, I suggest we do." He nodded to Tom. "You're staying a few days?"

"Dixie asked me to, told me I could have your bed."

"Keep it, I don't need it anymore."

It took a matter of seconds to say goodbyes and they were running hand in hand down City Park. Justin had all but invited himself to move in, but she couldn't refuse. Not now. Heck, she didn't want to. She needed him tonight just as she needed his help to cope with the next few weeks and the move that she knew in her heart she had to make.

Chapter Seventeen

"Enjoying the honeymoon?" Gwyltha seated herself on the park bench beside Justin as he watched the leaves change color and fall to the ground.

Gwyltha had a near-twisted sense of humor. "Is that what it's called? Sharing a house with the woman I love, a nine-year-old boy and a couple of ghouls? And don't forget Mrs. Zeibel next door, who keeps coming around with cookies and pound cakes as an excuse to chat and try to work out what's going on. Damn good thing Sam and the ghouls eat or we'd be burying cookies in the back garden after dark."

"At least your problems have diminished in size, if not in number."

"You can say that again!" He turned to smile at his one-time love. "My big worry right now, and one I sought the solace of nature and the inspiration of Schiller to contemplate, is how much longer we can keep up the pretense to Sam that things are normal."

"Doesn't that depend on your definition of 'normal'?"

"Let's word it another way: how much longer can we maintain the fiction that life is as it used to be before his mother became a vampire and he acquired a ghoul for a nanny?"

Her laugh hadn't changed over the centuries. "Only, an arrogant, conquering Roman would even try!"

"What option do we have? Tell him the truth?" Her silence seemed to suggest she'd advise that course. "We can't, Gwyltha!"

The thought was preposterous. He shook his head and went on. "It's driving Stella nuts! In less than a week we've got Thanksgiving. Apparently everyone cooks for days before feasting like Lucellus. Stella's already invited Angela and Jane but how the heck are we going to put on a family feast when two of us won't eat a morsel?"

"Stella doesn't have a solution?"

"No, she was half-expecting me to come up with one, on the basis of my vast experience and knowledge of vampire life."

"Must gall not to be able to live up to her expectations."

"Gwyltha . . ."

She smiled. The beauty in her eyes was still there, but it no longer held the same appeal. "Don't fret over it. I'll wager Stella will find a way. A fledgling who can face down a room of masters can surely handle minor domestic details." He wished he shared Gwyltha's optimism, for Stella's and Sam's sakes. "She'll cope. Trust me. I'm almost disappointed I won't be here to see how."

"You're leaving?" Obviously. He was surprised she'd stayed this long. She hated being away from Yorkshire.

"This evening. My soil calls. Doesn't yours?"

"Yes, but it will wait for me."

"It's Stella's, too. She needs to come home."

"She's beginning to see how restricted she is and how much Dixie can move in daylight."

"Don't let her take too long."

If it were up to him they'd be long gone. "She needs to

make her own decision and Sam's a big part of it. I can't force her." No point in going into the promise to her mother.

"I'm glad you realize that, at last." Gwyltha stood up and gave a half-smile. "She's a wise, strong woman. You should have told her the full story of your troubles."

"I was afraid she . . ."

"Would take on the assembled colony on your behalf?"

He couldn't help smiling. With pride. "Something like that. I wanted to protect her from hurt. From censure."

"Far better to stand beside her. In a few years, you may have to run to keep up. You have a fine partner." She flashed a smile. "Not that I need to tell you that. A blind mortal could see you're besotted." Besotted? Yes! He couldn't deny it. Didn't want to. It was a wonderful sensation. Gwyltha stood up and smoothed her black cashmere coat against the breeze. "I hope to see you for Yule."

"We'll be there when Stella's ready."

There was a tinge of sadness in her eyes. "I know. I seem to be losing half the colony to the New World: Kit, Dixie, you, Tom . . ."

"Tom's staying?" News indeed.

"For a while at least. Seems he's not just taken on the task of providing working identities for those two ghouls you've adopted, but discovering their original identities."

"How?"

"I'm not about to ask. If he breaks mortal laws, that's their concern. Keeping up with this colony is quite enough." She held out her right hand and grasped his elbow in the Roman style. "*Vale, Justinius Corvus.*"

The Latin of his youth seemed out of place in this time of moonwalks and supersonic air travel, but he grasped her forearm as they had once on a misty hillside in Roman Britain. "*Vale, Gwyltha, Sacerdotissa Britannicorum.*"

Justin watched the one-time priestess walk away. Once he'd loved her with his heart and soul—or had he? Nothing he remembered matched his love for Stella. If Vlad felt this much for Gwyltha, he was a fortunate vampire, but in his heart Justin doubted that ever a man, mortal or immortal, had ever burned with the wild and tumultuous emotions that had restored the soul of Justin Corvus. An unexpected peace erased the long years of hurt and rancor. A blessing, yes, but he was no nearer to helping Stella solve the Thanksgiving dinner quandary.

"You want to see our old clothes?" Angela obviously thought his request more than a trifle peculiar.

Tom nodded and gave her his best smile. "Sounds a bit odd, I know, but I really think it might help."

"Sounds downright kinky, if you . . ." She broke off, deep blue eyes wide. "Heaven! I've remembered what kinky is!" She gave a little gasp. "I'm not crazy, honestly, but this keeps happening all the time." A beautiful rosy tinge flushed her pale skin. "I've also remembered kinkiness isn't something to talk about on the front doorstep with someone I barely know!"

"Ask me in and we can talk about clothes. Let's save the kinky stuff for when we know each other better." Now she did think he was one of the unhinged. "You have to actually invite me in."

"Oh!" Understanding flickered across her face. "Sorry." A glimmer of an awkward smile curved her wide mouth. "Come in, please."

He followed her nice rear into the living room and sat down on an easy chair just across from her rather spectacular legs. That was the easy bit. Now he had to convince her he wasn't loony. "Is Jane here?"

"No, she's at work. They grabbed her the first day. The tale about losing her social security card worked." She grinned. "And it seems the fake driver's license convinced him."

"I don't like the word fake. I prefer 'special creations.' "

She had a lovely laugh. "Doesn't sound quite so felonious either!"

"The prices are!"

Her eyebrows creased in a quick frown. "I hadn't thought about that. How are we going to pay?"

She didn't need to worry about that. "Vlad set aside a fund to cover your expenses."

She did worry. "Hardly seems right, he rescues us, takes us in, feeds us, brings us here, buys us clothes and now shells out more."

Vlad would hardly miss ten or twenty thousand dollars, heck he could hand over ten times that amount and not notice, but Tom understood her reluctance to be beholden to Dracula. "It's his responsibility. He undertook your protection and in doing so assumed the obligation of providing for you."

"Seems a bit unfair. He could just have easily walked by and saved a lot of money."

"But he didn't."

"No, thank God!" It came out with a long, slow sigh of relief. "That grungy park was not one of the better tourist attractions." She paused, a crease forming between her brows.

"Makes me wonder what Vlad was doing there."

"Scouting for supper, perhaps?"

The frown momentarily deepened before her eyes lit with understanding. "Good heavens! I bet you're right. That missed supper has cost him a bunch! I still think we should pay him back."

"No hurry. You've got plenty of time."

"Right. Eternity!" She stood up. "You wanted our old clothes? I'll go get them."

She was back with two carrier bags. "Here they are." She put the bags on the coffee table between them. "I sorted the things out. Mine are in the white bag, Jane's in the blue one. Not much to look at but all clean, I promise. We were going to donate them to the Kidney Foundation. You were only just in time."

"Is that everything?"

"You want our old coats, too?"

"Might as well."

She added two coats to the pile. "I wouldn't mind mine back when you've finished. It's actually quite a nice coat. Could use a good cleaning though." She sat back down opposite, crossing her ankles. "Will they help?"

"I hope so. In detective novels they always seem to be getting clues from clothing . . . and teeth, come to that."

"You want to look at my teeth?"

That wouldn't be so bad. "I'll start with the clothes. Maybe we can find out where you bought them or something."

"How would that help? They could have been bought by whoever changed us. We could be hundreds of years old like you and Kit and Justin."

"I don't think so."

"What makes you so sure?"

"I'm not. It's just a hunch." He wasn't about to commit himself until he was sure.

"What gave you the hunch?"

He didn't want to say. It seemed so tenuous, but the eagerness—no, hunger—in her face was more than he could refuse. "The other day, when we were at the computer, you knew what you were doing. You knew about the web, about Altavista and Google. You knew how to operate Unix. You wouldn't if you'd been made even ten years ago."

"Maybe I was made a century ago and just learned it."

She was playing devil's advocate. "I don't think so. It

came back to you, just like your other memories. I'll wager
you knew it not long before he wiped your memories."

"He?" Her dark eyebrow went up, just a little. "Couldn't
it as easily have been a she?"

"Yes," he conceded the point, "it could. But wiping your
minds seems a bit harsh for a woman."

"You think women are all sweetness and light and dainty
femininity?"

"I did once!" The last year or so had shifted some long-
held notions. "Look, thanks for these." He stood and gathered up the bags and coats. "I need to get going."

"Let me know what you discover." She preceded him to
the door and took the knob in her slender fingers. "If you
find any clues."

"I will," he promised.

He tossed the two bags onto the passenger seat and drove
away in his hired car. His mind, rounding on one big question: who was Angela Ryan? He wanted to know her past,
where she came from, who she really was, and most of all, if
she was single.

Angela closed the door. That was one fascinating man!
Not exactly handsome in the conventional sense; he looked
more as if he'd been through the mill at least twice. But talk
about a sexy mouth . . . and when he smiled . . . !

Yes, right! She'd better keep hold of what brain she did
have. He was one of the others, a vampire. Vampires had
given Jane and her identities, put a roof over their heads and
found them jobs. Was she being hideously critical and un-
grateful? Maybe, but vampires were the rulers. The con-
trollers. Tom and Kit and their partners were offering friendship
and support, but some deep instinct warned Angela to stay
distant, to protect herself from falling into another vampire's
thrall.

With that firmly in mind, she stood up, smoothed down her skirt and went into the kitchen. Time to get on with the oatmeal cookies she'd promised Sam. Busy shaping the dough into balls, Angela had both hands covered with cookie dough when the phone rang. She wiped her hands as fast as she could. Talk about impatient machines! "Hello," she said, grabbing it on the fourth or fifth ring.

"Took your time answering!" The voice was female, rough and brusque.

"Can I help you?"

"Stella?" It was hard to hear her reply above the background noise. Was the caller in an airport, or a busy shopping mall? "You there, Stella?"

"Stella's not here right now." Or rather she was, but in deep vampire rest. "Can I take a message?"

"Where is she?"

Time for a white lie. "She slipped out. Can I have her call you back?"

"No, she can't!" Snappy wasn't the word. "Who are you?"

"I'm the baby-sitter." There was a pause while the background noise rose. "I'll be glad to give her a message." Who was this odd woman? "Who shall I say called?"

"I'm her mother!"

Surprise. Stella had never mentioned her mother. Still if vampires had kids, presumably they had mothers. "Hello, Mrs. Schwartz. What message shall I give?"

"You tell her Joey Holt is coming around in the next week or so. She's to let him get what's his and not cause problems and if he needs to toss down on the sofa a couple of nights . . . she's to let him. Tell her that. I don't want her making any trouble. Y'hear?"

"Yes . . . Just a minute. Let me get a pencil and write this all down." Stella kept a pad in the drawer by the phone, but the pencil was broken. Just her luck! Angela grabbed one of Sam's magic markers. "Okay. I'm ready."

"Took your time! There's people waiting for this phone."

And she had cookies ready to get in the oven. "Just let me make sure I have the whole message." Angela scribbled as the old woman snipped down the phone.

"Got that?" she said.

"Yes, I think so . . . What is it he's picking up?"

"None of your damn business! Stella doesn't need to know either. Might be best if you just go away for a few hours and let him be. Safest all around."

"I'll tell her." What on earth was going on?

"And one last thing . . ." The voice softened a little. "You tell Stella to just make nice with him, okay? Joey can get mean. I don't want no trouble for her or the kid. Y'hear?"

She heard but she didn't understand. "I'll pass on the message, Mrs. Schwartz."

"You do that!"

What an odd woman. Angela stuck the note on the fridge with a Rugrats magnet and went back to the oatmeal cookies. Some afternoon! She'd been hit on by an attractive vampire on a mission to uncover her past, and had a weird conversation with a rude old woman—who claimed to be Stella's mother. Angela slid the first tray of cookies into the oven. Life as a ghoul certainly wasn't dull. Mind you it hadn't been dull as . . . She slammed the oven door closed. As what? She'd almost had it. The answer hovered somewhere on the edge of her memory, just out of reach. She knew who and what she'd been but the answer was just beyond her reach. She felt as if she were in a dark room and reaching out blindly, feeling nothing but cold air. It was hell!

No, it wasn't. Hell was being nameless and living on a bench in an unkempt park. Right now, she had a name, a roof over her head, friends and a job. It would be lovely to know who exactly she was, but she was immortal wasn't she? She had time.

*   *   *

"Good heavens! Is this what you get up to when I'm out of the house?"

"Hello, Dixie," Tom said.

Christopher blew her a kiss. Neither got up for her as they usually did. They were engrossed.

She set her bag and keys down and walked over to the dining room table. "Tell me, love, is this underwear fetish something new, or have you just not mentioned it before?"

Tom stared at her with shocked eyes. "Dixie! It's not that! We're . . ."

"Give us a break, love," Christopher said. "Can't you see we're busy?"

Busy wasn't the word, they were totally occupied. "Okay!" She pulled up a spare chair to the dining room table. "Nice stuff, some of that . . . Is it yours or Tom's?"

Christopher frowned in her direction. "It's Jane's and Angela's. Satisfied?"

Not really, but it obviously made sense to the two of them. Just another proof that men's minds were different. She watched as Tom unfolded a tee-shirt and spread it out on her polished mahogany tabletop, but when he got to the well-worn white lacy bra and set it on top of a pair of pink cotton briefs, she couldn't keep quiet. "Would one of you please explain what you're doing." She'd sensed Tom was attracted to Angela, but playing with her underwear . . .

"We're going though it," Christopher replied. "It must have looked a trifle odd when you came in."

"It looked downright perverted, but I'm sure you have a good reason. Do they know you have them?"

"Of course." Tom shot a frown in her direction. "Angela gave them to me!"

This was it! "Okay, humor me. Please stop for a second

and one of you tell me why you're decorating my dining room table with a heap of Victoria's Secrets?"

Christopher looked up and grinned. "We're trying to unravel Victoria's Secrets! Or rather Angela and Jane's secrets."

"You think their clothes might contain clues as to who they really are?"

Tom looked up as he unfolded a worn, red, quilted parka. "If it works in the detective novels, why shouldn't it for us?"

Why not indeed? "Want some help? You could take me on as consultant."

"Can you cut out the cheeky comments?" Christopher asked.

"For you, love, anything."

"When you two stop billing and cooing, can we get back to work? This stack is Angela's." He nodded to the pile at his right elbow. "The other lot is Jane's. Have a look through, Dixie, and tell us what you think."

She took her time going through both stacks. The men watched as if they expected her to do a Sherlock Holmes's style deduction from a random heap of clothes, except it wasn't random. These garments were what they were wearing when Vlad found them, and presumably when they were abandoned. "Did Jane and Angela give you any clues, hints? Anything they've remembered?"

"Nothing," Tom replied. "It was Angela I spoke to. She, in fact, wondered if they were their clothes, if they hadn't been given them, like Vlad bought their new clothes."

"No." Dixie paused as she looked at a Hard Rock Cafe sweatshirt. "I'm pretty sure they were their own."

"How?" Tom was looking at her as if she'd just calculated the square root of minus one.

Christopher gave him a smug smile. "I knew she'd help us."

"Hold on a minute. I didn't say I could divine their pasts. Just that I think they're most likely their own things."

"How do you know that?" Tom was staring at the jacket her hands.

"Educated guess. Think about it. If you looked through the clothes Angela and Jane have now, they'd all be very new, not even a week old. These are mixed, just like most people's wardrobes." She picked up Jane's cotton bra. "This is worn, the elastic has almost gone and the same with the briefs." Looking over them brought to mind her grandmother's warning about wearing nice underwear to get run over. Jane would most likely have a cow when she realized her ratty panties had been passed from hand to hand. "Look at her sweater, the hem is frayed but her slacks are new. See?" She turned a pocket inside out. "The pockets are still stiff and very clean. None of the fluff and lint you collect after wearing for months.

"Angela's things are a mix too. The bra and panties look like they've been washed a fair bit, but they're not limp like Jane's and the elastic is still good. Her blue jeans are old. See how washed-out they are and rubbed white at the seams and hems? Her tee-shirt is well washed but not old, and this . . ." Dixie picked up the Hard Rock Cafe sweatshirt, "is pretty new. Only washed a couple of times."

"And look!" Tom pointed to the city name under the logo. "Chicago. She must have bought it there."

"Maybe they live there," Christopher said. "That would narrow the hunt."

"I don't think so." She hated to smush his enthusiasm. "People go to a Hard Rock Cafe on holiday, when you're visiting places. I went to one in Atlanta. I'm not so sure you'd go to the one on your doorstep."

"You think they were visiting Chicago?" Tom asked.

He was hanging on her reply. "At a guess, yes." She looked from Christopher to Tom. "Doesn't it make sense?"

"Yeah." Christopher nodded. "So we've narrowed it down to all the young female visitors to Chicago in the past goodness how many months."

"It's not that long." They both looked at her. "These are winter clothes. They wouldn't have been walking around in the summer wearing sweatshirts and ski jackets."

"Hey, you're good at this!" Christopher said. "See anything else? In detective stories they're always on about laundry marks or tailor's labels."

Forget laundry marks—Dixie bet they both did their own wash—but labels might help. She rechecked every garment. Jane's underwear and tee-shirt were good brands sold in every department store in every mall in the country. Her pants were an upscale national name and her sneakers were available just about anywhere. Her sweater was handmade. That might be some sort of clue but Dixie wasn't sure how. Jane's quilted down jacket was another top quality brand, but again, nothing that couldn't be bought in any city in the country or by mail order, for that matter, as long you could afford it. Hadn't Jane said she remembered maxing her cards?

Jane was Ms. young-professional America charged to the limit. Angela was a conundrum. Her black leather sneakers were even more widely available than Jane's. Her familiar logo blue jeans could have been bought almost anywhere in the world, and they already knew where her sweatshirt came from. But her black leather jacket, that was a bonanza. Maybe. Dixie ran her hands over the glove soft leather. This was definitely not from some chain department store, not with heavy silk lining hand sewn to matching piping. She spread it open on the table and looked for a label. Bingo! There it was, hand sewn on the inside pocket. "Do either of you know a place called Totnes, Devon?"

They did.

"Totnes?" Tom asked.

That was what the embroidered label said. Dixie ran her

hands over the lapels. It was a beautiful coat. "I'll bet she bought this at a small, expensive, leather shop in Totnes. Looks like she's at least been in Britain."

"She bought her underwear in the UK, too." Tom turned back the elastic on the pink cotton panties to show the St. Michael label. "Same as the bra and shirt."

"There are Marks and Spencers in Canada," Dixie said, playing devil's advocate. "She could have gotten them there."

"But the jacket she didn't. Unless they sell by post or the Internet." Tom sounded certain. "Look at the blue jeans and the trainers. She could have gotten those in the UK too."

Christopher shook his head. "She doesn't speak like a Brit. More like a midwesterner. Certainly not like Dixie."

"Maybe that's how ghouls speak no matter where they're from," she suggested.

Tom thought about that a minute. "We don't change our speech. You still have your accent."

Now was not the point to argue who had the accent. "Yes, but we're vampire. They're ghoul. What do we know about ghouls?"

"Diddly squat!"

Christopher was right there. "Can't we find out? There has to be someone who knows. Isn't there ghoul lore like vampire lore?" By his face, Christopher seemed to have the same thought.

Tom was only a skip behind. "There might be something in the library." Maybe in one of the books Dixie had sold Christopher when she first met him in Bringham.

"Where are they all now?" she asked.

"I have most of Kit's for safekeeping. Justin has some." Tom smiled. "Seems I need to do a bit of ghoulish research." A wide smile creased the corners of his eyes. "I'll tell Angela what you've discovered." He stood up. "Thanks, Dixie. You're a peach! Bye, Kit!"

He was gone. Dixie couldn't resist a smile. "He's got it bad!"

Christopher's brows creased. "What do you mean?"'

"He's in love."

"Come now, Dixie! You imagine everyone is in love." He grinned. "I agree it's very pleasant and all that." He ducked from her mock feint to throw one of Jane's shoes. "But not everyone you know is going to succumb. You claimed Justin was in love the afternoon he met Stella."

Dixie slipped Jane's sneaker into the shopping bag. "I rest my case."

"I'm not sure I understand," Angela looked Tom in the eye. "You're telling me you think I'm British?" They were sitting on the sofa bed she and Jane shared. Ten minutes earlier, Tom had walked into the house insisting he speak to Angela. With Sam and Justin doing homework in the dining room, Stella busy making an Indian costume for Sam's Thanksgiving play next week, and Jane cleaning up after dinner, upstairs or the front porch were the only free spaces left in the house. Since it was bucketing rain, upstairs won.

"Not necessarily," Tom replied. "Let's say it seems extremely likely you've recently spent some time in the UK and a handmade coat from a shop in a small town in the West country is a whole lot easier to trace than your trainers or blue jeans which could have come from anywhere."

"What next then?"

"I'll investigate it the minute I get back to England."

"You'll investigate?"

That earned her a surprised look. "Of course, I can hardly hire a private detective to uncover a ghoul's identity, can I?"

"It's my identity we're talking about. How about I go find it?"

He looked amazed, puzzled, then delighted, all in the space of seconds. "You'd come over to the UK?"

She shrugged. "Why not? It would mean leaving Stella in the lurch a bit, but we both knew from the beginning it was only temporary."

He nodded. "Yes, but the trouble is . . ."

"Dammit! I'll need a passport! I just remembered."

Tom brushed that aside with a wave of his twisted fingers. "That's no problem. Takes a little longer than those driver's licenses but I can do a passport. I got one for Kit, Justin, me. I keep the whole colony in identities."

"How do you do it?"

"It's getting trickier. These days everything is computerized and people are born in hospital, but there are ways. Used to be easy enough fifty, even twenty-five years ago. You'd just register a birth and then twenty or so years later, apply for a passport. Once you had it, you were set for another twenty-five, thirty years . . . Photos were the problem back then."

"Vampires don't take photos, right?"

"We don't appear on photographic film. We got round that. Antonia, a member of our colony, is a skilled artist. She'd draw a black-and-white picture, color it in with shades of gray and we'd take a photo of the picture. Took a lot of touching up, that was Toby's forte and after all, passport photos are supposed to look awful. Now . . ." He grinned. ". . . it's easy. Just take a digital photo, crop it on the computer, and Bob's your uncle: instant photos."

"So you can get me a passport?"

"Yup. Will have to be a Brit one. I'm still working out how to do a US one. I'll need to for Dixie eventually."

"I'm not picky."

He reached for her hand. His skin was cool but his touch was utterly reassuring. "I'll do the best I can. The name won't be yours, you realize that?"

"The one I'm using now isn't mine. I stuck a pin in the phone book for it." She didn't mean to sound self-pitying.

His fingers tightened over her hand. "We'll find out who you are."

Angela looked down at his misshapen hand and took it between hers. "What happened to your fingers?"

"I got arrested. Years back, when I was still mortal. They put me on the rack and broke a few fingers for extras."

Her throat tightened in horror. "Why?"

He shrugged. "They wanted information and I wasn't forthcoming."

Now her heart tightened. "What information?"

"About Kit . . ." He spoke lightly, as if trying to minimize it, but his eyes told another story. She said nothing, waiting for him to continue. "We'd once shared lodgings. We were friends, two writers trying to make a living with our quills." He paused. "Kit had another means to pay his debts. He worked for Walsingham."

"Walsingham?"

"The head of Queen Elizabeth's Secret Service." At her gasp he met her eyes. "The first Elizabeth. They were hard times. Turbulent times. Kit worked for Walsingham for a while then tried to get out. They wouldn't let him. He moved to new lodgings when he was afraid I'd be caught in the net, but they came for me anyway. Kept me in Bridewell until long after Kit was dead." He gave her a lopsided smile. "Or long after the powers that be believed him dead. Gave me a right turn when he walked into my rooms a month or so after my release."

"And he made you a vampire, like him?"

"With Justin's guidance, yes. My health was broken when I left jail. It was only a matter of time until I died . . . and Kit gave me back life."

"I wish there was a way I could get my life back!"

"You will. I promise. I'll find it."

*   *   *

"Tom looked very pleased with himself," Stella said to Justin as she spread mayonnaise on two pieces of bread and slapped a slice of bologna in between. Justin handed her the box of lunch bags. "Thanks." She pulled one out. "What do you think?"

"That human taste buds must have evolved since my mortal days, judging by the stuff Sam enjoys."

She rolled her eyes at him. "Cute! I mean about Tom and Angela."

He gave her a slow, thoughtful look. "He was excited at finding what he calls a 'clue.' Funny, I never took him for the gumshoe sort. It might lead to something, but I'm not sure Angela can construct her lost life around it. They might be better off waiting for their memories to return. It's only a matter of time; new things keep coming back to them."

She slipped the sandwich in the bag and zipped it. "I don't know. I wouldn't sit around and wait for it to happen. I'm with Angela, I'd be out there trying to find out who I was."

"That's you all over, Stella. Follow your heart and not your head."

"Yup, that's how I ended up falling for a vampire." She stepped close and kissed him on the forehead.

He caught her upper arms with his hands. The glint in his eyes offered a passel of promises and she wasn't about to refuse a single one. "Want to feed first or afterwards?"

"First." Sex was even better after feeding. "I need to check on Sam first." She put the sandwich in the fridge for the morning. As she closed the door she saw Angela's note under the magnet. She pulled it off and read.

"Yes, it was your mother who called," Angela confirmed. "Calling from an airport perhaps? There was a lot of background noise." Stella bet there was. Prisons were noisy places.

"No, it's no problem," she replied to Angela's worried look. "I just wasn't expecting her to call just now."

"It is a problem, isn't it?" Justin asked as they drove north towards the zoo.

"No. Because I won't let it be. I made that clear to her when I visited and I'll repeat it next time I go. It may be Mom's house but my kid lives here and there is no way either of the Holt brothers is crossing the front door. And it doesn't make sense. Joe wasn't convicted with Jimmy and Mom, but I heard he got jail time for a housebreaking charge. They're both bad news."

"They were your mother's partners in transgression?"

She had to chuckle. "Justin, you have a lovely way of putting things! They were her accomplices, yes. Her lawyer tried to make out she was a gullible woman led astray by a lover." Stella let out a snort. "Mom leads herself astray and always has. She's not dragging Sam into her mess, that's all."

"You think you should go back this weekend? Sort it out with her."

Stella thought on that a few seconds. "No, we promised to take Sam to the children's theater on Saturday afternoon. I'm not breaking my word to him. It can darn well wait a week."

Chapter Eighteen

"What do you think?" Dixie asked as she counted out dollar bills for the till. She neatened the sides of a stack and slipped them into their slot in the tray. "About Tom, I mean."

Stella looked up from tidying a display of bat jewelry. "You want my opinion?" Dixie's face clearly showed she did. "I think he's got it bad, but has no idea of how hard he's fallen."

Dixie let out a whoop of self-satisfied glee. "I knew it! Christopher keeps insisting I'm imagining everyone is in love, but if you could have seen the look on Tom's face as he bolted out of the house to tell Angela that we had a clue . . ."

"I saw his face when he walked in *my* house." She had to grin back at Dixie. "You're right, he's in deep."

"Think Angela realizes?"

Stella held her reply until Dixie finished counting the stack of fives. "Angela is too occupied with finding out who she really is to notice much else."

"But she will." Dixie pushed the till drawer closed. "You know," she said, walking over to unlock the door. "It's really something else. These three, good-ole-boy Brits, if there is such a thing, falling for three . . ." She paused.

"Yanks?" Stella suggested.

Dixie gave a snort. "Watch who you're calling a Yankee! I've got ancestors turning in their graves at the suggestion!"

"Okay, New World women?"

She liked that a lot better. "Makes us sound like some modern day Amazons."

Now there was a thought . . . "Do you really think this coat of Angela's will lead anywhere?"

"Who knows? It's the best lead they have. If it's a small shop as the label and coat suggest, they may keep track of sales and it's unlikely someone paid cash for a coat like that. At least we'll know who bought it."

"I'd hate for it to turn out to be her husband or lover. That would hit Tom between the eyes."

That thought obviously hadn't occurred to Dixie. "Hell, it would! This digging out the past might be murky."

They broke off as the phone rang. Stella straightened the bookshelves while Dixie dealt with a customer, who, by the sound of things, wanted a whole list of mail order books. Good news, that, the more business the Emporium got, the more likely she was to stay employed.

Dixie finally hung up. "One more order. At this rate we'll end up doing more mail order and web sales than in-store. Want to give me a hand with this one?" She picked up the sheet of paper that eased out of the printer.

Stella found all but one of the books and carried the stack behind the counter. "Thought any more about going to England?" Dixie asked casually as she wrapped the first book in bubble wrap.

"I've thought about it," Stella replied. "I've got misgivings about yanking Sam out of school . . . and then there's Mom." Dixie nodded in understanding. "Mind you, I did say

I'd come over with Sam for Christmas, just to look. We've got to work something out, and Justin can't stay away from his clinic forever."

"And you want to be with him?"

"Dixie, I need to be with him." She paused. "I can't explain it, but when he's around I . . ."

Dixie reached across the carton and squeezed her hand. "You don't need to explain. Believe me, I understand. I needed Christopher so much I went haring the length of England looking for him." Stella knew, Justin had told her the whole story one night as they'd perched on the dome of the capitol. "But I warn you one thing," Dixie went on, "once you get over there, you won't want to come back. At least not for a couple of hundred years."

"Why on earth not?"

"Because when you connect with your native soil, your strength grows amazingly. Think what a difference there is between walking without your shoes and with them and multiply that by ten."

"Good heavens!"

"And the big plus, I only feed every week or two. Don't need to any more often."

And she had to feed at least every other night. It certainly made you think—and worry. Making life-altering decisions wasn't any easier as a vampire.

"Should I answer the door, Angela?" Sam asked, looking up from the math worksheet in front of him. Angela was stirring the promised hot chocolate. "Real hot chocolate," she'd insisted, made from milk and chocolate he'd help grate, and she was going to let him count out the marshmallows. Angela made a great baby-sitter. He sometimes missed the crowd of kids at Mrs. Carter's after school, but at home he could get his homework done early, he could pick what he wanted on

TV and he didn't have to jostle with Eddie and Mike for a seat on the sofa. "Want me to get it?"

Angela stopped stirring a minute, looking from him to the front door as if deciding. "No, I'll get it. The hot chocolate can wait." She took the pan off the heat and crossed the kitchen. The bell rang again, twice, as she walked towards the front door.

Sam followed, kneeling on the sofa to peer out the window as Angela hooked up the chain lock. Standing on the porch was a tall man with a coat over one arm and a large bag at his feet.

Angela had the door open the limit of the chain. "I'm here to see Stella Schwartz," the man said in rough voice.

"Mom wasn't expecting anyone," Sam said. "I know she wasn't. She'd have said."

"The name's Holt, Joey Holt. She's expecting me."

Angela looked around the edge of the door. He had days of stubble on his chin and his eyes were downright shifty, but she remembered the name from the phone call yesterday. "Stella's not here right now."

"Never mind. I can come in and wait." Angela hesitated. It was darn cold out for a mortal—Sam's hands had been frozen when he got off the bus—but she didn't like the piggy, dark eyes that peered through the gap.

"Mom would have said," Sam insisted as he slipped off the couch to stand by Angela.

He was right. "I'm sorry. You'll have to come back later. Ms. Schwartz will be home in a hour or so."

"That's all I need."

It was then Sam saw the dirty boot on the threshold and the knee braced against the door. "Angela," he said, pointing a toe at the foot planted inside the open door.

That made up her mind. "I'm sorry," she said and made to close the door. She couldn't, not against the weight of Bluto.

Sam landed a kick on the man's shins. When it didn't budge him, he tried again.

"Shit, kid, you'll be sorry!"

In the shocked silence, the only sound was old wood splintering. "Run out the back, Sam; get help!" Angela yelled.

He hesitated only seconds. He hated to run and leave her, but if he could get next door to Mrs. Zeibel he could dial 911. Sam turned and sped towards the back door, only to realize the wood splintering wasn't the front door. The back door hung crooked and a man stood in the kitchen. Sam tried to run past, but a great sweaty arm snatched him up. He kicked and managed to sink his teeth in the wrist that held him. All that got him was a curse and a hard slap upside his head.

"I got the kid, Joe," his captor yelled. "And you," he hissed at Sam, who was trying to bite a second time. "You keep still." Sam went still a few seconds and then bit down again. The man yelled and shifted. More wood splintered. Angela screamed. Sam heard a slap and a muttered curse and felt something cold pressed against his forehead. "Keep still, kid. You don't want your mom coming back and finding her little boy with a big nasty hole in his head, now do you?"

Sam froze. He didn't want his mom coming home where these men meant no good. They had guns and he was dead scared he'd pee himself like Johnny Day did on Halloween and that they'd hurt Angela.

The man set him on his feet but kept a tight hold; the cold metal never let up. "It's in here, Joe."

Joe came in dragging Angela. She had a red mark on her face and his hand was clamped over her mouth like on TV. But this wasn't TV. It was frightening and horribly real, even down to the greasy smell of the man's shirt and the scared look in Angela's eyes.

"Listen up good, bitch," Joe said to Angela, twisting her

so her terrified eyes met Sam's. "One peep out of you, one smart-ass move and he gets it. Understand?"

Angela mumbled something behind the hand on her mouth and nodded.

"Come on, Joe, quit feeling up the help and let's get what we came for."

"We gotta get them taken care of first. Get the tape outta my bag, Bud."

Sam's throat tightened and his stomach felt cold and heavy. He didn't feel any better when they stuck him and Angela on chairs and taped their arms and legs down with duct tape. They even stuck more over their mouths. What did these men want? To steal? He could have told them Mom didn't have much to take. They didn't even have a DVD player like Mrs. Zeibel and their TV was old.

It seemed the fridge was what they wanted. From his perch on the chair, Sam watched them huff and grunt as they pulled the fridge away from the wall. He hoped they would take it so they could get a new one that made ice in the door, but he wanted them gone before Mom got home. He didn't want them hitting Mom and dragging her around like they did Angela. There were tears in Angela's eyes. Sam tried to make her feel better, but he couldn't smile and he couldn't hold her hand and . . .

He heard a noise at the front door.

So did Joe and Bud.

Stella parked in front of Mrs. Zeibel's. A large black van was smack dab in front of her house. She envied Dixie her nice, functional garage with automatic doors. The battered cinder block structure at the end of the yard wasn't big enough, even if Stella could open the doors that had been rusted shut long before the Day boys started using them for target practice. She walked the few yards to her front gate, her mind still on what Dixie had told her about the pull of one's native earth. Would moving to England be best? She opened the latch on the iron gate. She'd just have to talk to Mom next visit and promise to find a careful tenant.

The front door was half-open. Every mother's instinct roared with worry as she leaped up the steps and through the door. For two seconds, all looked normal. She knew it wasn't. "Sam? Angela?" she called as she moved into the lit doorway of the kitchen.

In an instant, she took in Sam, Angela and the two men. She felt Sam's terror, and fury boiled inside her. "How dare you!" She raced to Sam's side and the nearest of the men looked. He blinked, obviously startled at the sudden move.

"Well, if it isn't little Stella!" She recognized Joe Holt, older, grayer and nastier. Time had not been good to him. "Didn't your momma say we were coming? We're here now and might just sit tight a coupla days. If you don't want nothing unfortunate to happen to that kid of yours . . ." He reached for the gun that lay on the countertop.

As his fingers closed over it, she leapt. There was a bang and a dull thud against her shoulder but she barely noticed it, or the smell of cordite, as she propelled his body backwards into the fridge. She half-expected to keep going but the fridge stopped them. She stepped back and watched Joe thud to the floor.

"Shit! You bitch!"

She turned to see number two glaring at her with a mixture of fury and fear. She liked the taste of the latter in the air. She stepped closer and watched him back up. "You scared my kid," she said in a whisper. "You'll suffer for that."

"Not before you, I won't!"

She smiled at the knife in his fist. She was between him and Sam. Let this mortal gloat for a second. She reached out, faster than his eyes could register, and grabbed his wrist with one hand and the knife with the other. "Thanks. I'll need that to let Sam free." She tossed the knife sideways and it embedded up to the hilt in the countertop.

At last, he realized something wasn't quite right, and by then she was on him, grasping him under the armpits and lifting him over her head. One flailing foot caught the light fixture, sending waves of light and shadow around the kitchen. What the hell did she do now? Knock him out like Joe? She caught sight of the duct tape in the middle of the table. She dumped thug-man on the floor, being careful not to be gentle, and reached for the tape. It took only seconds to secure his hands behind him, and then for good measure she hog-tied his feet to them. Since the language he used was unsuitable for anyone's ears, much less Sam's, she followed their example and taped his potty mouth shut.

Then she stood up.

She eased the tape off Sam's mouth. "Mom!" he sobbed, and she held him tight.

"It's okay, honey. It's okay. Mom's here. They scared you, but they won't hurt you anymore." Over Sam's head she met Angela's eyes. "I'm going to cut him loose first, okay?"

Stella pulled the knife out of the countertop and cut Sam free. Maybe one of those thugs had a smidgen of mercy, because Sam's tape was on his shirt and pant legs, not much on his skin—although he winced a few times as she pulled. He was clinging to her and sniffing. "I've got to get Angela loose now." She stepped back.

"You've got blood on you," Sam said. "They shot you."

They had. A great splodge of red spread over her shoulder and, come to think of it, it was sore and smarting.

"It's okay, Sam. Really. Let me get Angela free."

Angela had been less lucky, or maybe Joe and his buddy just felt nasty—the tape was all over her wrist and ankles. "Don't worry," she whispered as Stella pulled the tape off her mouth. "It won't hurt me like it would Sam."

Just like the bullet didn't harm her. But, heaven help her! She'd have to concoct some story to satisfy Sam.

It wasn't until Angela was free and apologizing for having let two men force their way into the house that Stella looked around at the broken back door, the fridge half-pulled out, unconscious Joe still out for the count on the floor, and his hog tied partner. What in the name of heaven was she to do now?

"Justin," she called, her arms tight around the still-shaking Sam. "Help me!"

Justin came, barely glancing at the mayhem and mess. "Stella!" She heard worry, pain and love and reached an arm to him, as the other still hugged Sam. Justin clasped both of them against his steady, strong body. "What in the name of Hades happened?"

"They had Sam and Angela tied up. I . . ." She gave up trying to explain.

"He shot Mom," Sam said, his voice still shaky. "But she took care of them." He gave a nervous giggle. "She didn't let the bad men . . ." The giggle became a sob. Stella held him close as his tears dampened her clothes.

"What happened?" Justin was in her mind and she welcomed him there.

"I came home and found them tied up and these two specimens wrecking my kitchen. We'll have to ask Sam and Angela what happened before."

"Don't worry. We'll take care of everything."

Kit and Tom had followed Justin. Tom had Angela tight in his arms and Kit was looking down at Joe. "You put him out, Stella?"

"Yeah. I hope I didn't kill him." In her heart, she honestly didn't care—the man had threatened her baby—but now was not good timing to tangle with the vampire code.

"Nah!" Kit shook his head. "He's still got bad breath." He leaned over Joe's limp body and placed a hand on his head.

"That'll take care of him for a couple of hours, until we sort things out, and as for chummy here . . ." He walked over to number two, still mumbling obscenities behind the duct tape. A touch of Kit's hand on his shoulder and he went limp and silent.

Sam hadn't missed a second of it. His eyes were wide with confused amazement; then he looked up at her face and the red stain ruining her new Vampire Emporium sweatshirt. "Mom," he said. "He did shoot you. I saw." He put his hand on her shoulder.

"Yes, honey."

Her eyes met Justin's. The others had all gone quiet. "You cannot hide it anymore," Justin said. Aloud.

He was right but . . .

Sam frowned. "What's going on?" His gray eyes met hers. "Mom?" His voice shook with worry.

She squatted down so they were eye to eye. "Sam, listen carefully, as this is hard to believe." He nodded. "You're right, that man did shoot me but he didn't hurt me. Look." She pulled her ruined sweatshirt over her head, taking her tee-shirt with it.

"Mom." Sam looked and sounded shocked. Disrobing in a crowded kitchen offended his sense of decency.

"It's okay, Sam," Justin said. "Your mom wants you to see where she was shot."

Blood had soaked into the top of her bra and the strap, but only a fading red mark remained of the bullet wound. Sam reached up and touched her shoulder. "Mom, I saw. I heard it."

"Yes, you did, honey."

"But . . ." He looked at her.

Now was the time. "Sam, remember a couple of weeks back when I was sick for a weekend and we stayed at Dixie and Kit's?"

"Sure. Kit and Justin took me to Cosi because you had the flu."

"I didn't have the flu. We told you that because I wasn't sure how to tell you the truth."

"You lied, Mom." His young eyes accused.

"Sam," Justin said, "you know part of the truth. Now listen to the rest."

Sam waited. Stella wished she could take a deep breath. Why? She was vampire; she didn't need a mortal's crutches. "That weekend, on the Friday night when Justin and I were out, someone shot me." Sam's forehead creased and his brows all but met in the middle. "They killed me." His eyebrows shot up. "Justin knew you need me to look after you, so he made me vampire. Like himself."

The only sound in the kitchen was the hum of the refrigerator.

"You're dead, Mom, and a vampire?"

"Yes."

The refrigerator got louder. "And Justin's a vampire too?"

"Yes."

He cocked his head on one side. "You said they were just make-believe."

"I was wrong."

"Mom." Sam glanced around at Kit and Tom and Angela, and Dixie, who'd just arrived and was staring at the mess. "You'd better put your shirt back on."

He was right. Displaying a bloodstained bra to the local colony wasn't her style. "Here." Justin handed her his cashmere sweater.

"I can't put this on, I'll ruin it."

"If you don't, you'll scandalize your son."

He was right there. It was far too large but wondrously soft. "Better?"

Sam nodded. "It's a big secret about you and Justin being vampires, right?"

Justin answered him. "Yes, Sam. A very, very big secret. No one is ever to know but us."

"I won't tell!" He took the insinuation as an insult. "I'm not a baby. And anyway, you think people would believe me? They'd laugh. I'll never share this with anyone." He grasped hands with her and Justin. "It's our secret. Cross my heart and hope to die."

The irony was entirely wasted on Sam.

Stella couldn't help smiling at Justin over Sam's head. She'd agonized over how to tell him and he'd accepted it so easily. The others all relaxed in the same instant. They'd been as tense as she but as they moved, Sam looked around them with a frown. "They know, Mom?"

"Yes."

"Are they in the secret, too?"

They'd better get used to Sam's inquisitiveness. "Yes."

Dixie stepped forward. "I'm a vampire, too, Sam."

It took him a few seconds to digest that. "Cool! What about the others?"

"I am," Kit said with a twisted smile.

"So am I," Tom said.

Sam looked at Angela. "I'm not." Sam's face fell. "I'm a ghoul."

He brightened again. "Neato. This is better than the *Addams Family.*"

Justin winced.

"Angie? Sam?" Jane called from beyond the front door. She was instantly reassured and shocked as the others called back and she walked into the kitchen. "Ohmigod! What happened?"

"I wouldn't mind knowing that myself," Tom said, his arms still around Angela's shoulders.

Sam had that honor, with a little help from Angela. Stella's heart went a little tighter and colder at each step of the story, but it was Kit who asked the question on everyone's minds. "Why would they try to steal an old refrigerator?" He gave Stella a lopsided smile. "All due respect and no intention to insult, but it's not exactly new or modern, is it?"

She couldn't be offended by the truth. "It's on its last legs. I was afraid I was going to have to pay someone to take it away." It had never looked good, and now with the dent in the front where she'd slammed Joe . . .

Dixie walked over to it. "Maybe it isn't the fridge they wanted."

"Why move it then?" Tom asked.

Jane picked up on Dixie's line of thought. "Because there's something behind it!"

Kit picked up the still-comatose Joe and dumped him, not particularly gently, on top of his partner in home invasion. Dixie reached around the sides of the fridge and lifted it a good yard and a half forward, as far as she had space to move it. She slipped in the gap. "Good heavens!"

"What?" Stella couldn't stand watching anymore. It was her darn kitchen.

Behind the fridge was a gaping hole in the wall. A gaping hole stuffed with brown grocery bags. As she stared, one fell and burst as it hit the floor, spilling out bundles of bills. Twenty, fifty, even hundred dollar bills scattered over the discolored floor. The others crowded around. Kit had even climbed on the top of the fridge to have a good view, and Justin held Sam so he could see over everyone's shoulders.

The sight of bundles of yellowed bills stirred up a wild anger inside Stella. This was the never-recovered money from the bank robbery. Her mother had sent these thugs to fetch it and intimidate and threaten Sam. She'd bet Joe had broken out of jail. Did Mom plan on the same? A cold fury gripped Stella's heart. Her mother had never been the room mother, brownie leader, cookie-baking sort. Stella had long accepted that. Mom had been in and out of jail too much to ever do much in the way of nurturing, but to send men who'd threaten her own grandson . . . She and Mom would have a very long conversation next time.

"Mom." Sam tapped her head from his perch on Justin's shoulders. "It's hidden treasure! We're rich."

This was an afternoon of hard truths. "No, Sam. It's not ours. Someone stole it and hid it here. Those two lowlifes came to take it. We should call the police."

"No," Justin said. "We'll take care of everything."

Sam disagreed. "I think they should go to jail!"

"They will," Justin promised. "But we don't want your mother bothered."

She was past being "bothered," but since she had no brilliant ideas for disposing of two crooks and a couple of million in loot, she'd, just this once, let him take over.

Kit disappeared and Justin invited Sam to help tape up Joe. Stella detected a mite of vindictiveness in the way Sam wrapped the tape around Joe's arms and legs, but considered it totally justified. For her part, she'd happily hang them from the ceiling fan by their balls.

She didn't need to. Justin had a better idea.

While Sam and Justin made patterns with duct tape, she helped the others empty the cache in the wall and stuffed Joe's leather carryall and a couple of shopping bags Jane brought from upstairs. Then Kit came back, through the back door. He'd moved the black van around the alley. At Justin's nod, Kit and Tom hoisted a robber apiece over their shoulders, and the rest of them followed with money-stuffed bags, Sam riding on Justin's shoulders.

For once, having poor lighting in the alley was a definite advantage. In minutes the van was loaded and Kit drove off.

"Where's he going?" Sam asked.

"To leave the van where the police are sure to find it."

That idea pleased Sam to no end. Just to be sure the police didn't miss this golden opportunity to tie up the loose ends of a five-year-old crime, Tom slipped out to a pay phone to pass on the information, taking Angela with him. Dixie went to fix the broken chain lock on the front door. Jane offered to help Justin fix the back door and was as impressed as Sam at seeing Justin put in screws with a twist of his thumb. Stella moved the fridge back with one hand. Now she'd never have an excuse for not cleaning behind it.

The house was reasonably straight. Kit returned with the news that the van was nicely crashed into a lamppost on Third Street. In a little over an hour, their lives had been tipped over and righted. All that remained was to get Sam's supper and see about his homework.

"You all right, Sam?" Justin asked.

Sam shook his head. "I don't want to stay here. I'm scared."

"Don't blame you." Justin scooped him up in his arms. "Want to spend the night at Kit and Dixie's?"

"Please."

"You've lost your room," Dixie said. "Tom's in it."

"So's Angela, I think," Jane added.

This conversation was getting a bit much for a nine-year-old to hear. "Hold it, you guys!"

Justin didn't seem to notice. "We'll manage. How about the settee? Don't you have that pull-out bed in the attic?"

Sam raced upstairs to grab his pajamas and toothbrush. "This is going to be better than a slumber party!"

"What's a slumber party?" Justin asked.

"It's when a bunch of kids stay overnight together and don't get any slumber." Stella told him.

"What's it called when two adults stay overnight and don't slumber?" She should punch him, but she kissed him instead and hoped the others weren't watching.

"Kissy, kissy," Sam said as he came downstairs, dragging his bag behind him. "Are you two ever going to get married?"

"Are we?" Justin asked. His dark eyes warming her heart with a hundred promises.

"It might be tricky, the blood tests and all that."

"What would I need blood tests for?"

"You do here," Dixie said, "to get married. It's the law."

"Silly, mortal law," Justin muttered. "We don't have such nonsense in the UK."

The reasons to go with him just kept mounting up.

"We'll take Sam and Jane and stop off on the way to pick up something for supper," Dixie said. "See you guys later."

They were alone, and somehow it was almost as scary as walking in and seeing her son taped up and two monster thugs invading her home.

"I want you," Justin said. His words bypassed her mind and hit right on her heart. "Not just for sex, although I've never had a woman like you. Not just for your mind and courage. Not just for your smile and your noble heart. Not just for a hundred wonderful things about you, but because I need you to be complete." He ran a hand through her hair. "Marry me, Stella. Come to England and marry me and give me what I've been missing for close to two millennia."

Her heart flipped as she looked up at the want in his face. She nodded.

"Tomorrow?"

This time she shook her head. "Sam can't miss the Thanksgiving play, not after I made that darn Indian costume."

"Don't try using that excuse for angel costumes."

She kissed him. "I won't. We don't have angels in holiday programs over here—just Santa and reindeer."

"You'll come when the school term is over?" You bet she would, after she said goodbye to Mom and told her how she felt about her siccing Joe Holt and his buddy on Sam and Angela. "How about now?"

"Now?" Hadn't they just discussed this?

"I don't know how long Dixie and Kit plan to spend in

the Giant Eagle. But I sure as hell want to get there in time to reclaim my bed. Tom and Angela can have the settee."

Stella didn't much care where she slept as long as Justin was beside her and Sam safe. Having the man she loved for eternity was just a bonus.

Try these other great titles in Rosemary's vampire series!

KISS ME FOREVER

He's Hot. He's Sexy. He's Romantic. He's Immortal . . .

If there is one thing Dixie LePage does not need in her life, it's complications. And the man sitting across the table from her in a crowded English pub, the one offering to buy the library of her inherited estate in a small English village, is a major complication. For starters, there's the broad shoulders. The slightly amused smirk. That smoldering look that makes it impossible to concentrate. And that infuriating, old-fashioned, and well, okay, incredibly appealing sense of chivalry. No doubt about it, the guy is hot and sexy. Of course, there is one wee little problem: He claims to be a vampire named Christopher Marlowe, as in THE Christopher Marlowe, famous playwright, contemporary of Will Shakespeare. Right. Amend that to hot, sexy, and totally insane. Please see "no more complications." So why can't Dixie seem to resist the warmth of Christopher's charm, the protective feel of his strong hands, or the tempting pull of his full mouth when the sun goes down?

BE MINE FOREVER

Just For The Thrall Of It . . .

Six months ago Angela Ryan woke up from a mysterious attack with no memory, no ID, and no idea why what had once been girlish about her suddenly seemed . . . ghoulish. Being rescued by a clan of vampires is strange enough, but nothing compared to the fact that one of them is the kind of man she's always fantasized about. Tom Kyd has smoldering eyes, a sculpted body, and supernatural staying power. True, Tom is sure he knows best about everything, including how to figure out who she was before her life turned into an episode of *Dark Shadows*. But when his kisses are so dark, so sinful, and so damn good, Angela is tempted to say yes to whatever he wants . . .

KEEP ME FOREVER

Some Guys Are Real Animals . . .

Antonia Stonewright isn't about to change her views on love. A sexy mortal companion is fine every now and then, but a soul mate? A partner for life? Please. She was burned once, and hundreds of years haven't healed the wounds. But reclusive potter Michael Langton is . . . different. His gorgeous wares are perfect for her new art gallery—and his gorgeous body is perfect for her. She can't get enough of his toned muscles or his amazing, dark eyes. Their nights together make them both purr with pleasure—except in Michael's case, purring comes naturally. So much for finding a regular boyfriend. Antonia has a truly sexy beast on her hands . . .

MIDNIGHT LOVER

There Are Beings Worse Than Vampires . . .

Vampire Toby Wise knows there is a spy in his organization. He thinks Laura Fox, the beautiful nurse who looks after the invalid founder of Connor Corp., is one. But Laura is no mere spy—she's a reporter out for a hot story. So when Toby receives a call for aid from a witch, Toby reluctantly involves Laura. There are sinister goings-on in Dark Falls, Oregon. A bloodthirsty beast of the night has been plaguing the town. As Toby struggles with his feelings for the irresistible Laura, she struggles to accept the alluring yet perilous world of the vampires. And as their attraction grows, so does the danger. For the prey they are hunting will prove to be a more deadly predator than either can imagine . . .

And if you're in the mood for a romantic snack,
try one of Rosemary's novellas
in these great Brava anthologies!

TEXAS BAD BOYS

These bad boys can deliver passion and pleasure with their boots on—and they're more than happy to let a woman mess with Texas . . .

"In Bad with Someone" by Rosemary Laurey

Rod Carter was supposed to end up running the Ragged Rooster. Instead, Old Man Maddox gave the bar to his granddaughter, some prissy Brit art gallery owner right off the boat from London. Miss Juliet Ffrench—yeah, two "f's"—knows jack-all about beer, winning friends, and running tabs, but she's got a killer smile. All the lady needs is someone to give her an education in Texas hospitality, up close and personal . . .

"Run of Bad Luck" by Karen Kelley

Nina Harris loves photographing naked, sexy men. But when she inherits her grandfather's ranch in Texas, and meets foreman Lance Colby, she thinks she may have met her match. Lance is pretty sure real cowboys don't drop trou for national magazines. Still, as a Texas gentleman, he'd be more than happy to give Nina a private showing . . .

"Come to a Bad End" by Dianne Castell

Silver Gulch Sheriff John Snow thinks women have their place—in his kitchen or his bed. He would certainly never go for some women's libber businesswoman like Lillie June. The men in town want him to close down her fancy new spa, and he's happy to oblige. But once he meets Lillie, soothing massages, personal pampering, and one-on-one body wraps don't seem like such a bad thing at all . . .

THE MORGUE THE MERRIER

Take one town devoted to Christmas. Add a mysterious morgue-turned-hotel, a wonderland snowstorm, star-crossed lovers, determined spirits, and three of today's hottest romance authors, and you've got a sizzling treasury of hot and haunted Christmas tales . . .

In Christmastown it's always a special time of year. Just ask Annette. While visiting for the holidays, she discovers her Big Mistake from high school is in town and hotter than ever. A few Christmas spirits later, she finds out what she's been missing all these years. Or Sydney, the songwriter on sabbatical—until a ghostly Elvis impersonator gives her a hunk, a hunk of Christmas cheer. And is it the weather or a meddling ghost that forces Holly's ex-husband to land his plane right down in the middle of a steamy, delicious reunion?

Romantic, sexy, funny, and spirited, time to unwrap your gifts from . . .

Rosemary Laurey
Karen Kelley
Dianne Castell

. . . includes special holiday bonus story!